She gazed up into his glittering dark eyes . . . speech didn't seem necessary.

She did not think then that they were strangers, or that he was an enemy whom she had never forgotten or forgiven. She thought only that he, for whatever reason, had come looking for her, and more, had saved her life when lightning could have struck her dead. In dazed gratefulness she felt the strength of his arm where it supported her back, and the heat of his firm thighs that cradled her in his lap. Slowly, his fingers curled along the slope of her neck, then rose as his thumb branched to bracket her chin in his hand.

She was surprised by the tremor of emotion that passed through her as his gentle touch skimmed her cheek, then smoothed her brow. She felt moisture on her cheeks. Was she crying or was it raining again? She couldn't tell. Her lips trembled as they tried to form words that would not come. . . .

For Love's Sake Only

LAURA PARKER

A DELL BOOK

Published by
Dell Publishing
a division of
Bantam Doubleday Dell Publishing Group, Inc.
666 Fifth Avenue
New York, New York 10103

If you purchased this book without a cover you should be aware
that this book is stolen property. It was reported as "unsold and
destroyed" to the publisher, and neither the author nor the publisher has received any payment for this "stripped book."

Copyright © 1991 by Laura Parker

All rights reserved. No part of this book may be reproduced or
transmitted in any form or by any means, electronic or mechanical, including photocopying, recording, or by any information
storage and retrieval system, without the written permission of
the Publisher, except where permitted by law.

The trademark Dell® is registered in the U.S. Patent and
Trademark Office.

ISBN: 0-440-20918-8

Printed in the United States of America

Published simultaneously in Canada

August 1991

10 9 8 7 6 5 4 3 2 1

RAD

Prologue

The half-risen mists of midmorning left behind a dew-drenched garden of incomparable beauty. It was a bewitched garden. Everyone said so. Where else on the moors of north Devonshire did wild pink-belled foxgloves and bell heather grow side by side with such imports as tulips and daffodils? Where else but in the garden of the Marquess of Ilfracombe's ancestral home, Blood Hall, did springtime rhododendron and Chinese peonies share space with summer blossoms of yellow gorse and tormentil? Only here did whortleberry and sweet-smelling heath bedstraw interlace their delicate scents with the indolent Oriental perfume of a dozen varieties of rose. Lush, green-ferned, and sheltered from the world by the high stone wall that surrounded it, the garden's mystical air of remoteness and solitude was broken only by the sound of a young lady's voice, soft with wistful pleasure.

"He loves me. He loves me not. He loves me. He loves me not. He loves me!"

"Cheat!" The booming voice broke the quiet with a loudness more fit for a battlefield than a garden. "You plucked two petals to make your game, madame!"

The young woman sprang to her feet, the full silk skirts of her gown rustling in a luscious manner just short of indecency. Yet she did not hurry as she turned to him. The harsh voice of the speaker was as familiar to her as her own. "You come at last, Captain."

He looked down at her from his superior height, hands on hips, shoulders stretching tight his leather jerkin, and his eyes narrowed on the petalless stem she held. "As usual, madame, I arrive just in time to keep you honest."

She gave him a melting glance from beneath cornsilk lashes and said in a lovely voice with husky undertones, "It's much too late for that, as well *you* know."

He took her in with a hot arrogant glance, the same he had used in intimidation the first time he had set eyes on her. As God was his witness, he thought, she'd changed not a whit. She was unbelievably pale, bringing to mind inanimate substances of beauty like pearls and alabaster and marble. Yet one had only to look at the deep blush of her lips and the startling intelligence in the wide blue of her eyes to know that she'd been fashioned from flesh and blood. And what flesh it was! Five feet of soft, shapely womanhood that a man would risk his neck to caress, as he had.

Hers was an incomparably pretty face, round-cheeked and petal soft, full of impudent glances, sweet smiles, and that essential femininity that men often speak of but seldom ever witness. A stranger might never have suspected that the courage and ferocity of a lioness lay quietly within her shapely breast. Yet he knew her gentleness came from a deep wellspring of certainty about herself and her place in the world. She'd been blessed with a rare temper too. The product of centuries of pampered gentry, she suffered no doubts, no reconsideration. She knew what should and should not be. When society defeated her, it was their loss, not hers.

She had quite astonished him the first night they shared a bed. Oh, she had been a maiden and flustered as only maidens can be, but she had not been afraid, nor without passion. She had matched him kiss for kiss, and later thrust for thrust, the maiden turned lusty wench without regard for either her position or his importance in the world. It was then that he knew he loved her, would lay down his life for her without regret or scruple or plea.

The lady in question was far too consumed with her own perusal to be daunted by the man standing before her. From the first, she had thought of him as inviolate, like an ancient oak that has endured centuries of wind and rain and storm and thrived proudly. He was remarkable of feature, handsome but not pretty. His was a soldier's face permanently weathered and scored. He bore two scars, a small one on the cheek and a longer one above the left brow. His flat gray stare gave little away, but when he smiled those eyes would suddenly brighten with a pirate's gleam that betrayed his true nature. With clipped brown hair just brushing his collar and a cutlass ever at his side, he seemed well suited for the life of highwayman, smuggler, or brigand.

Years earlier he had come as a conquering soldier into this brooding forbidden moorland of gray granite tors and rolling wild expanses. Yet what he'd captured was her heart, and though they were sworn enemies, in the end he'd surrendered in love to her.

His insolence no longer disturbed her. She knew his rages when directed at her were mere storms upon the wind. His fierce embrace was the sweetest of joys. She knew him, welcomed him, found in him the rare secret pleasure of loving a strong, uncompromising, difficult man.

"Have you no proper greeting for your lover, lady?" His eyes never left her face as he took a step toward her, wanting yet savoring the expectation of the kiss he knew she would offer. After all these years it still set him afire. She wore her hair in beribboned ringlets on either side of her face. Reaching out, he touched one. She was a pretty bit of fluff, all golden curls and fine lace. The devil's device was such a woman. And well it might be so, he mused, as the deep stirring that was as familiar as breathing surged up within him.

He seized hold of her as if she might flee. Yet the expression in her eyes as he drew her to him promised far different and more pleasant exertions. He was faintly surprised, as always, by her fervor, which sometimes forced him to the brink of desire in just moments. Lost, utterly and completely lost to reason, right, and sense, he surrendered to the miracle of her kiss.

Without warning a woman's shrill cry suddenly split the silence. An instant later breaking crockery was heard from above.

Jolted by the racket, he looked up to the window that overlooked the garden. "God's body! What is that infernal clatter?"

"Do not swear, love. It is only the maids. They're turning out the house. We're expecting guests."

"Guests? On whose authority?"

"As if you've forgotten." A look of annoyance crossed her perfect features, for he had released her quite before she was ready. "The notice came only yesterday. Our kinsman wishes to retire from London for a fortnight. He will arrive by the end of the week. He's bringing guests."

"Maxwell? Coming here? Why? It's been a half-score years since the young scoundrel deigned to show his face in Devonshire. I do not want him here. He will disrupt things."

"It is his home, after all, my love."

Unimpressed, he turned gray eyes unwarmed by humor on her. "It is first, last, and always *our* home. Disruption!

Consternation! Infernal fiddling with things!" His expression darkened with realization. "So that is why my favorite painting has again been removed from the dining hall."

She touched his sleeve, a touch so light it drew his eyes to verify its reality. "It was requested in the letter. Not all share your love of the hunt displayed in graphic detail while they dine on the results."

"Weak stomachs produce weak hearts," he answered curtly. "No wonder the lad never amounted to much."

She stroked her fingers down his arm to tease the fine hair on the back of his wrist. "I hear he's quite well thought of in London."

"London? That decadent cesspool of corruption. What would they know of character? They once crowned a poxed bitch Queen of England!"

She turned a delicate shoulder away from him, insulted that his ardor, so easily extinguished, was not yet revived. "Pray do announce when you've finished, Captain, for I shan't listen another moment to your priggish tones." She glanced at him, all coquettish smiles. "I know you too well."

He smiled back. "Very well. But the Maxwell lad shan't remain here above three days." A glint of mischief appeared as he said, "Perhaps I will arrange something special by way of welcome."

"Don't you dare! He is our kin, our last and only heir. He's to be welcomed as such." Stamping a small foot, she added, "I demand it!"

"A man's home is his—"

"Castle?" she suggested sweetly. "What would your Roundhead friends make of such a comparison, I wonder?"

"Lady, you press me too hard!"

She reached out to him. "Come with me into the shadows of the rose bower, my love, and you may press me as hard as you will."

"Shameless bitch," he said mildly, all too aware of the source of her distress. Pleased yet willing to make her beg just a little more, he folded his arms casually and lifted one brow. "Where are your blushes, madame? Have you no shame?"

"I am certain that it must be tucked away somewhere," she answered, lifting the edge of her skirts to display the tips of her white kid shoes. "You may seek it out, Captain, at your leisure."

His humor momentarily restored, the wintery look left his eyes. "Whoever was responsible for your upbringing, madame, did a remarkably poor job!"

"To your everlasting benefit," she tossed back, sensing that victory was, at last, in sight. "As I was saying—"

A flurry of hammering drowned out the rest of her speech.

"A pox on humanity!" he roared, startled into looking toward the house a second time. "Relatives be damned! I'll put an end to this!" So saying, he strode off toward the house.

"Now, John. John? No, I say! John!" She hurried after him but his soldierly stride easily outdistanced her graceful glide.

He was in a rare rage, so much so that he didn't even bother to use the gate. Instead, he strode right up to the west wall of the garden that buttressed the house and through the hard granite stones as if they were no more substantial than the morning mist.

And, because he gave her no choice, she followed him.

Chapter One

FALL, 1800

*T*he winds of an Atlantic gale roared into shore along the coast of north Devonshire, heaving up the in-rushing tide. Great angry plumes of whitened water shot past the cliffs and lashed the barren moors with salty spume. Even the local folk took shelter when the wind blew in from this direction, but there were strangers abroad in the afternoon gale, strangers with more will than sense.

Inside the small traveling coach racing along the lonely coastal lane of Exmoor, Lady Regina Willoby Lynsdale, widow of the recently deceased Earl of Amesbury, clasped her chamois-gloved hands tightly and closed her eyes. Anyone who saw her might have thought she was at prayer because she was in fear for her life. But the thoughts that occupied the young lady's mind were far from those of terror. Beneath the deep brim of her silk bonnet, her round brow was deeply furrowed by anger, and the thoughts that occupied her were as wild and dangerous as the wind and tide.

Cold, her in-laws had called her, altogether unnatural in sentiment and lacking in feminine sensibilities. Nor was that all. They'd labeled her a calculating chit who'd married Harry Lynsdale, Earl of Amesbury, for his money and, now that he was dead, hoped to reap the spoils of her ill-gotten gains. The fact that she would not cede her widow's inheritance to her mother-in-law, the Dowager Countess of Amesbury, was proof of her fortune-hunting ways.

"Ohhh!" The exclamation rushed hotly out of Regina as if the accusations were freshly laid instead of a week old. How dare the dowager judge her! How dare any of them threaten her. If she had become a cheat and a liar, it was because she had no other choice.

She hadn't wanted to marry. From the moment of its conception the marriage forced on her by her uncle had been a fraud, and she a mere pawn in a game in which she had no stake . . . until now. She cared nothing for money or titles, felt only a vague relief at the loss of her husband, a man she'd known less than two weeks before his demise. Yet with his death she had inherited the one thing she thought she'd never possess—power over her own life.

No one had been more surprised than she to learn that Lord Lynsdale had revised his will upon their marriage to make her the sole inheritor of all that was not entailed to his peerage. In the usual course of events, there would have been provisional clauses added to make it impossible for a young bride to inherit the fortune straight out, but this time there were none. The earl had died suddenly of heart failure, and now everything he owned belonged to her, his widow.

A shudder passed through Regina as she recalled her mother-in-law's rage when the will was read. The woman had demanded on the spot that Regina sign the will over to her, then pack her bags and leave London under the cover of dark like the trollop she suspected Regina to be. The venomous attack hadn't frightened Regina as much as it might have a month earlier. In fact, it had made her defiant.

The first smile in weeks curved up the ends of Regina's mouth, a mouth meant for laughter but rarely used for such recently. The Dowager Countess of Amesbury hadn't reckoned that a green girl of twenty-one, fresh from an Italian convent and denied even the experience of a London season, would fight for what was hers. Yet that was exactly what she had done.

She was grateful for her husband's largess yet she knew her claim to the Amesbury estate was tenuous, perhaps not entirely legal. In time her in-laws might wear her down, or prove their claims against her. It was this fear that had made her pack her belongings and leave London two days ago. The uplands of Exmoor with its wild and terrible beauty had been her childhood home. It was to this place that she now fled. If only she could be certain that she'd be left in peace. Yet accusations had been traded and threats leveled against her. Trouble might well be following her from London at this very moment.

Raucous winds buffeted the coach, setting it rocking on its hinges, but Regina scarcely heeded the discomfort. More penetrating than the storm winds were the memories of her last hours at the Amesbury residence in London. Only now, when she was within a few hours of reaching her goal, did she allow herself to remember the dowager countess's exact words, words that had set her fleeing for the wilds of north Devonshire and a home she hadn't seen in more than eight years.

Regina remembered every detail, would never forget: the dowager countess's ashen complexion, her eyes reptilian slits, her face contorted in such savagery as to make her almost unrecognizable. When she spoke, her words were hissed in a dreadful raspy voice. *"I will live to see the end of you! I will hunt you, break you! Do you hear me? You will live in fear of me until you lie groveling in the dust! And then, when you beg for mercy, I shall spit on you!"*

A clap of thunder broke her concentration and Regina

shivered as the last threads of memory ran out. She didn't quite believe in curses, and yet the effects of the evil venom the dowager had spewed that night had not left her. That was why she traveled to Exmoor in a rented coach when she might have ridden in the luxury of the Amesbury traveling barouche. That was why she had not stopped the night at any inn or idled an hour in public places where she might later be described and remembered.

She was sore and sick of heart, and every mile of the past five had seemed like an eternity. She would rest in Ilfracombe. She began to repeat the village name like a litany of prayer. Inland from Ilfracombe, where Sherrycombe Water rioted through the wild valley below, lay her family home, a half–tumbled-down cottage tucked away in the shelter of a wooded combe. Given to her father in payment for his services as a teacher to the children of the nearby fishing communities, it had never been much more than shelter from the unpredictable clime. But it was the only place of refuge she had. Soon she would be inside its dingy walls, safe and protected.

She was amazed by the abruptness with which the wind ceased keening as the coach moved off the coastline road and into a country lane that led away from the sea. The coach had traveled no more than a few hundred yards when she heard a hoarse cry from the driver and the sharp crack of his whip. The sudden lurch of the coach as the horses picked up their pace threw Regina forward. As she grabbed for the strap to steady herself, she heard the driver's curses answered by those of another man and then the loud report of a pistol.

For a moment longer the coach continued to roll forward and then abruptly, as the coachman sawed on the reins and then threw the brake, it jerked to a halt, tossing Regina onto the opposite seat. The edge of the seat caught her in the middle, knocking the breath from her in a painful grunt. Moments later, the coach door was flung open.

Gasping for breath, Regina lifted her head for what she very much feared was her first and last glimpse of one of Devonshire's legendary highwaymen.

Maxwell Tipton Kingsblood, Marquess of Ilfracombe, was by nature a patient man, a tolerant man, a considerate man. Among his peers he could always be counted on to be the voice of reason in any discussion or argument. In addition, there was an almost scholarly bent to the marquess's mind. Why, he might be found reading a book when he spent the odd evening at home. If not for his bruising reputation as a rider and sparring partner at Gentleman Jack's Gym, his friends might have looked askance at his preoccupation with such things as agriculture and literature.

A favorite to his staff, the marquess had never been known to raise his voice to a servant. Others could vouch that he never kicked a dog or beat his horse. In fact, it was sometimes remarked upon, when he was out of earshot, that the marquess was amazingly reserved for a gentleman of so robust a physique and obvious masculine tastes.

The ladies of the *ton* considered him to be the perfect, though often elusive, dinner guest. He could be counted upon to soothe and flatter the ego of the most recalcitrant partner. Thus, hostesses often seated him next to the elderly, the royal, or the difficult. Mothers of eligible daughters had sought since his majority to catch his eye. Yet, until very recently, he had been plainly uninterested in a permanent attachment. There was talk, of course, of numerous affairs, but it was to the marquess's credit that names of ladies of rank were never linked to his by word or look or breath of scandal.

Yet on this day, all of the marquess's admirable aplomb

had been severely tested, not by the incessant wind and rain lashing the north Devonshire coast, but by the one person in the world with whom he had thought he would have the most patience, Lady Eloise Lytton, his soon-to-be wife. As he sat in the great discomfort of his overturned carriage, supporting her frail weight against his shoulder, he wondered not for the first time since leaving London how he would ever adjust to married life.

The ride from London had been wretched. The frequent stops, interminable meals, and generally leisurely pace required when traveling with a feminine companion were all new to the marquess, and none of it was to his liking. By nature, he was an exacting man who traveled frequently and with economical grace. He was now enduring the fifth day of a journey that he was accustomed to completing in two, and they had yet to reach his ancestral home, Blood Hall.

Two hours ago, within ten miles of his home and in the midst of a driving rain, his coachman had misjudged the depth of a pothole. A broken axle was the result. Stranded on the isolated road, wet, and grievously in need of a brandy and a pair of dry Hessians, the marquess felt the set of circumstances bedeviling him would tempt the patience of the proverbial saint.

"How much longer, my lord, do you suppose that wretched man will be about rescuing us?" Lady Eloise questioned, plucking at a damp patch in the skirt of her gown.

"Not long," the marquess answered, his deep voice sounding more restrained than calm. He'd sent his footman —an apt title for his present journey—to find help while his coachman remained with the horses. Unfortunately, they had turned off the main road before the accident, and no vehicle had since traversed the lane on which they were stranded. Though he wouldn't say so, he'd lost hope of reaching his country residence before nightfall.

They were all thoroughly drenched, bearing splashes of mud on their persons, but thankfully, none had suffered serious injury. "We are sound of limb and as comfortable as possible, under the circumstances. We must be grateful that we've suffered no real harm," the marquess said, confirming his thoughts aloud.

"His lordship should be grateful that we're not all lying in the mud with our necks snapped!" Mrs. Dorrity Rogers, Lady Eloise's chaperon, responded crossly.

A sharp-nosed, self-important woman who'd been in the Lyttons' employ since before Lady Eloise's birth, Dorrity Rogers considered herself to have earned the rare privilege of being able to speak her mind, even to peers of the realm. " 'Twas a frightful spill we took. I'm certain I don't know why we weren't all killed."

"Oooh!" The whimper signaled a new onslaught of tears from the viscountess.

"Now, now, my lady, we mustn't do that again." Dorrity leaned forward to pet Lady Eloise's hand. "My dear little lamb, I'll be quite astonished if you don't come down with the ague after this." She pinned the marquess with a censuring stare. "I'm quite amazed, my lord, that you urged her ladyship to make such a journey at this time of the year. Horrid weather! Horrid land! Horrid—" She paused, feeling, as the considerable power of the marquess's black eyes came to rest on her, that perhaps her vaulted position was not quite high enough to chastise this lord after all.

"I believe there's nothing wrong with Lady Eloise that a hot bath, an early supper, and a good rest can't cure," the marquess said evenly, shifting his shoulder to allow the viscountess to lean more comfortably upon it. "My housekeeper is an excellent woman who'll have everything in readiness, and Cook will have you feeling fit as fiddle after a few spoonfuls of her cock-a-leekie soup."

"I'm just as certain I shall be out-of-reason cross for days," Lady Eloise said in her soft, perfectly formed upper-crust tones when she'd mastered her tears.

The marquess reached up and lightly patted her cheek. "You have been beyond good, Lady Eloise. I promise you will be amply rewarded for your patience by tomorrow's fine weather. Perhaps we shall try our luck at fishing."

As his broad muscular hand dropped from her face, Eloise was reminded again of the fact that he was an oddly reserved lover. Fishing, indeed. Why did he not promise her a necklace of pearls?

Unlike the half-dozen other seekers for her hand, the marquess hadn't penned poetry to her, extolling the virtue of her eyes, hair, and demeanor, nor had he sat gazing forlornly after her when she chose another partner for a waltz. The marquess had simply asked to dance with her twice at Almacks, gone to Sunday tea with her parents present, and then, after sharing with her a cold supper at Lord and Lady Ashmonts', asked for permission to speak to her father on a certain "delicate matter." Flattered to have drawn the attention of a marquess, and well aware that twenty-two was pressing the upper limits of the marriage market, she had accepted his offer of marriage when her father brought it to her.

And why not? His manners were flawless. He sent lovely, if quite ordinary, bouquets. He was a considerate and generous escort, and he never failed to compliment her dress. Yet she had the disquieting feeling that he moved and spoke and did the correct things because they were correct, not because he was moved by any great emotion.

It was all quite vexing, when she stopped to think about it. He was handsome, of course. She was partial to the rare chestnut brown of his hair, though she hoped their children would inherit her wide blue eyes instead of his obsidian glance. His strong features of jaw, cheekbones, and nose were fine enough to be carved in marble. All that was missing was a certain emotional depth that, she had been assured by her mother, she most definitely wouldn't want in a husband.

"Hot blood makes for poor husband material," her mother had said with a tiny regretful shake of her head. "Mark my words, dear, you are far better off with a man of even temperament and cool rational spirit. With such a man you'll never need wonder who or what has taken his fancy, be it cards, or liquor, or the vice of passion."

Eloise blushed at the thought of passion. She knew so little of it, and had experienced even less of it, beyond a few chaste kisses traded with other young men behind a shrub or in the moonlit corner of a balcony. The marquess had kissed her once, briefly, on the cheek when she had accepted his proposal. Even now his arm about her shoulders was impersonally supportive, his hand braced on the seat rather than at her waist. He was always correct. Always proper.

Lowering her lids, she gazed up through a golden tangle of lashes, a feature she had been constantly complimented on by her other admirers, at his mouth. It was a good mouth, wide with well-shaped lips. What would it feel like to be kissed, really kissed by him? Perhaps it would make up for the lack of—intensity of their courtship thus far. Not a deep thinker, she resolved quickly to discover the answer as soon as possible. But, certainly, she didn't wish to do so in some wretched manor house on the coast of Devonshire. Romance required the proper setting, and Blood Hall most assuredly did not sound the part.

"Don't you think, my lord, that it would be a splendid

idea to return to Bath for a few days? I was much cheered by the spa where we broke our journey earlier in the week."

"I think not, my dear." Maxwell Kingsblood closed his eyes briefly to keep her from seeing the annoyance her words provoked. God! Two days ago they had been as near to his home as Bath. What a circuitous, confounded, protracted journey this had been! He had done everything he knew how to provide for her comfort. Even now he sat in the spot where rain trickled in from a burst seam in the carriage's roof. On and off the cold drip had fallen upon his shoulder until it had soaked through the cloth of his great-coat and jacket. Now his shirt stuck in an icy sheet to his skin. He was at his wits' end, and still the journey was not over.

Suddenly the marquess sat forward and let drop the window of the carriage, which let in a burst of rain and cold wind. Sucking in a breath, he strained for the elusive sound. Finally a smile broke upon his lips and he jerked the handle, opening the door.

"What are you doing, my lord?" Eloise asked.

"I hear the sound of a coach, my lady. We are about to be rescued!" So saying, he leaped from the carriage into the drizzle and gust of the autumn afternoon.

"Help is coming!" he shouted to his coachman. "Get the horses off the road!"

Lifting a hand to his brow to keep off the rain, he stared until, out of the damp and mist, a traveling coach appeared on the road before him. In expectation that the oncoming driver would halt to offer assistance, he stepped fully in the road, arms splayed.

But the coachman didn't slow at the sight of a man waving his arms. A veteran of England's highways and byways, he'd been trained to recognize a trap, and the setup on the road before him bore all the signs of a highwayman's tricks.

After reaching for his whip, he cracked it sharply over the heads of his pair in harness, shouting at them to pick up their pace.

Stunned, the marquess realized that the coachman was not only not going to stop but was preparing to ride him down. At that moment something inside the Marquess of Ilfracombe snapped. Driven beyond patience and past consideration by the various difficulties, disappointments, and doubts of the last days, he pulled from his pocket a pistol and in blind fury fired a shot over the oncoming coachman's head.

As the coach swung wide to pass him, the driver sawing in the reins in a frantic attempt to stop, the marquess flung himself on the coach and wrenched open the door.

He didn't know what he expected to find inside when the coach came to a rocking halt on the road's edge, but it certainly wasn't a woman on her knees, her bonnet knocked askew, and her skirts in a tangle about her ankles. The picture only added to his rage at the vagaries of life and so his temper didn't improve, it shifted into a higher form of fury.

"Damn you, madame! I'm not so easily put off!"

Startled by his voice, she looked up. With a shock two parts pleasure and one part chagrin, the Marquess of Ilfracombe found himself gazing into what, he thought, must be the greenest eyes in Christendom.

Chapter Two

꧁

$\mathscr{R}$egina stared helplessly at the tall, broad-shouldered man in a garrick coat of many capes who filled the doorway of her coach. Wind whipped the dark-brown hair covering his head into wild tangles while the curly ends funneled the falling rain into his face and collar. Suddenly backlit by a flash of lightning, his features were thrown into sharp relief, and so hard and angry was his expression that a startled gasp escaped her. Surely he was the embodiment of all the nightmares she'd ever had as a child growing up on the moors, a dreaded highwayman.

The urge to fling herself against the opposite door was so strong Regina felt every muscle in her body tense in expectation of the action. Then she spied the pistol in his hand and the desire to flee died. She found her breath instead. "Who are you and what do you want?"

"Who I am is of no consequence. What I want will presently be made known. Move aside, madame!" he roared as if she were yards away instead of less than three feet.

Too surprised to do anything but obey him, Regina rose from her knees and slid onto the seat as far away as possible from him. He climbed into the coach beside her, bringing a generous splash of fresh cold rain with him, slammed the door behind himself, and sat down opposite her. He turned on Regina a stare so vivid she could not help but return it.

His eyes were dark and shiny as sloe plums, and trained on her as if by the power of looking alone they could keep her from bolting.

"Your coachman nearly ran me down!" he said with a volume that continued to be pitched for the out-of-doors.

"It's too bad he failed," she answered back, regaining a little of her composure with her breath. There was only so much fear she was willing to endure. After all, she had recently bested the Dowager Countess of Amesbury. She wasn't about to cower before a lowly highwayman.

"You should hire your servants with more discrimination!" His dark brows contracted together in a way that made her instantly wish to reconsider her opinion. Lowly of birth, perhaps, but there was nothing modest or unassuming about his manner—or his dress. He wore a greatcoat of the finest cloth, and a pair of expensive Hessians that gleamed with polish where the mud didn't mar the surface. She had expected a murderous scoundrel to be filthy and ill groomed.

He looked around the tiny space as if he expected to find someone lurking behind the bolsters. "You travel alone, madame?"

"Yes," she answered with more deference this time, for he had stretched out his long legs as if to emphasize that by size alone he was more than her match.

His brows knitted into a single dark slash. "That is extremely foolhardy. On the moors you might easily be set upon by brigands!"

Under the circumstances, she couldn't have agreed with him more. She began to unbutton the tiny row of pearls on her left glove. If robbery was his intention, she would make it easy for him. "I'm duly impressed by your demonstration. However, you've chosen poor prey. I have nothing of value but a plain gold band, unless you'd care to add a lady's wardrobe to your booty."

A look of surprise erased the scowl from his face. "Booty, madame? Do I look like a highwayman!"

"Most certainly you do!" she replied honestly, noting a sinister dark spot on the left topmost cape of his coat. She had the nasty suspicion that it was blood. A brief glance at his left temple seemed to confirmed it. There was something dark matting his hair just beyond the hairline. As her gaze darted to the pistol held loosely in his right hand, thoughts of all the terrible stories she'd heard as a child about highwaymen and their cruelties flitted through her mind. Had he been injured robbing someone else, perhaps the owner of the coat? Recalling his comment on the fact that she traveled alone caused her thoughts of murder to switch to those of ravishment. Hurriedly she tried to slip off her wedding band, but her fingers were trembling too much.

The man's voice cut across her concentration like the crack of thunder. "What the devil are you doing!"

Annoyed because he frightened her so, she snapped, "Are you hard of hearing or do you simply lack an indoor pitch?"

The Marquess of Ilfracombe, who hadn't been chastised for his manners since leaving the nursery, experienced the unaccustomed sensation of embarrassment. "I beg your pardon, madame," he said slowly, as if needing to measure the pace as well as the volume of his speech. "I have been somewhat put upon these last hours. I assure you, I do not as a rule accost coaches."

The moment he began to speak in a normal tone, Regina's attention was caught anew. By the time he finished, she was wide-eyed with wonder. "You ape a gentleman's tones to perfection!"

The frank surprise in her voice set the marquess's teeth

on edge. "If I sound the gentleman, madame, it is because I *am* a gentleman."

"That explains why you attack innocent ladies with pistol in hand," she replied in a tone of voice that had gotten her knuckles rapped by the mother superior at the convent.

The marquess looked down at the pistol in his right hand, surprised to realize that he still held it. Pocketing it quickly he said, "I seem to owe you a second apology, madame."

Regina's brow furrowed in surprise and confusion. What sort of a highwayman gave up his most effective threat at a lady's request, or did he believe that the weapon wouldn't be necessary against her? For the first time, she really looked at him and what she saw confused her even more.

Despite the streaks of mud and blood, his was a distinctly well-fashioned face, broad of jaw and brow, the nose straight and bold. He wasn't at all what she would have imagined a cutthroat might look like. Had she not known that he was a robber and potential threat to her life, she might have been impressed. However, she had been threatened enough to keep her admiration at bay. "I don't want your apologies," she said carefully. "If you wish to improve my impression of you, then climb down and allow me to go on my way."

To her disappointment, he didn't move. Yet he seemed to take her scolding to heart, for he kept his voice well below its previous bellow. "Where are you bound, madame?"

"That is none of your business," Regina replied, thinking how careful she had been until now not to leave any impression on people as she traveled. She had even rejected wearing mourning—which at any rate she loathed—for fear it would draw unwanted attention. Yet this man had had a good long look at her, several in fact. Pulling the brim of her bonnet forward and tilting her head at an angle that cast her features in shadow, she added, "If you aren't set on robbing me, then I beg you allow me to travel on. I wish to reach shelter before nightfall."

"So, madame, do I. And your assistance is required in the matter." He pointed at the window. "Look here, and see for yourself the reason why I stopped you."

Regina reluctantly moved forward on her seat, annoyed that he made no attempt to move his long, well-muscled legs out of her way. "I don't see anything."

"That is because you will not look!" Grasping her by the arm, he dragged her closer, ignoring her cry of alarm, until she was stretched across his lap with her face pressed to the window. "Now, do you see?"

Looking between the mud splatters on the glass Regina did, in fact, see a coach. It was in a ditch by the road. Pitched at a steep angle by broken wheels, its door was thrown open to the sky as if its inhabitants might want to step out and up into the clouds.

"We broke an axle hours ago," he said. "There's a gentlelady not unlike yourself traveling with me. We would like to travel with you some short distance."

Regina didn't know what alarmed her more, the man's request to travel with her or the fact that his left thigh was pressed so intimately against her right side that she could feel each minute shift of his muscles as he spoke. She'd never had much traffic with men, had been terrified of her husband's suggestion that they share a bed and grateful when he did not press her. This man, loud, rude, damp with rain and smelling faintly of not unpleasant but strange aromas, made her feel vulnerable in a way that the dowager countess's threats had not.

When he abruptly pulled her back into an upright position and released her, Regina was more relieved than grateful. She turned sharply toward him to refuse his request, only to find herself looking once again into those plum-dark eyes. Quite without reason she wondered what she must look like, reflected in those indeterminable depths.

The marquess did a little staring of his own. Something about her was strangely familiar though, feature for feature, he couldn't say that he'd ever seen her before. It was her eyes, he decided, that made her at once a stranger and yet seem more open to him than any other person he'd ever gazed upon. Those deep-green pools were like mirrors into her soul. In them he saw anger, spirit, bewilderment, and a touching vulnerability. She was so young. Why had he not realized at once, despite her admirable pluck at fending him off, that he must be frightening her half out of her wits?

At once he felt contrition for his horrid behavior toward her. Yet even as his mind formed an apology he sensed that the hurt he saw lurking like fern shadows beneath the serene lake-green of her gaze came from a deep abiding hurt whose cause was much older than the moments of their chance meeting. The frank openness surprised him, touched him in a way that made him wish to recoil a little in need of self-protection. He'd never experienced such intimacy in a single glance.

Yet when her pretty face suddenly blushed and she looked away, he felt as if she'd snatched away a proferred gift he'd been too slow to accept. He swallowed his apology, annoyed at feeling unaccountably cheated of something that he wasn't at all certain he wanted.

Reaching for the coach door handle, he said curtly, "I'll be back in a moment with my traveling companion. Then, madame, we may all be on our way."

He left as quickly as he had come, with a splash of wind and rain accompanying him. With distaste Regina saw that the place he had occupied on the seat was dark with rainwater and the floor of her coach was slick with mud from his boots.

"Barbarian," she murmured as she gathered her mantelet closely about her and leaned forward to look out of the window again.

There was little enough to see. Besides the back of the man who'd just left her, she saw the coach whose outline was blurred by mizzling rain. Though it was early afternoon, the sky gave the impression of impending dark. The countryside beyond the road was lost to view because of the mists. A gust of wind suddenly shook the coach. Steadying herself, Regina heard a man call sharply to the horses as they stamped and lurched forward, making the vehicle sway erratically. The man's voice sounded again, his curses as familiar to Regina as those used by her coachman. The horses settled and the coach ceased swaying.

A few seconds afterward the door on the opposite side of the coach was opened, and Regina's coachman appeared in the doorway, accompanied by a second man who was a stranger. Both men pulled their forelocks in respect but Regina didn't miss the firm grip the stranger had on the shoulder of her coachman, and guessed that her coachman, bleeding from a cut lip, was under some duress.

"You be all right then, ma'am?" he asked, water streaming down his face as if he stood under a tap.

"What's going on here?" she demanded in a tone she'd heard the dowager countess use to good effect. Still, it was hard to maintain her dignity with a shower of droplets raining in on her.

"I asked them to let me see that you was unhurt, ma'am. Sorry, I am, for this," her coachman answered. "Only I own as how I did try to ride the bas—man down. How was I to tell he was a gentleman?"

"There's been no proof of it thus far," Regina returned.

"I don't blame you for your actions. Only please, let's be off. It will soon be nightfall."

The coachman ducked his head. "That I can't, ma'am. They say as how they don't trust me to take them to where it is they're going. This one here"—he jerked his head toward the man beside him—"will be handling the reins."

"But that's preposterous!" Gathering her mantelet about her, Regina moved to the open door, prepared to step down. Just then the other door opened and, without a word, a young lady was handed up into the carriage and the door shut behind her.

In spite of her readiness to dislike this new intruder, sympathy was the first thing Regina felt upon seeing the unwanted visitor. No doubt the lady had been elegantly attired before the accident. Now she most resembled a half-drowned kitten. Her white ankle-length lingerie gown, embroidered in sprigs of pale-blue flowers, was splattered with mud and clung to her in clammy wet folds. Her dark-blue velvet spencer was torn at the shoulder seam and the buckram stuffing showed through. Her soft heelless slippers were soaked and the ribbons broken. She was the perfect picture of misery and distress, at least that's what Regina thought until the young woman looked around at her.

The face beneath the broken brim of the silk bonnet was exquisite, heart-shaped with huge blue eyes that put one in mind of clear summer skies. Allowing for the faint tinge of pink in the whites of the eyes and a flawless complexion fretted by the temper of recently spilled tears, she was a beauty of the first water. Her small pink mouth trembled, but the feminine weakness only added to the confection of perfection Regina was certain she would present under other circumstances.

As the lady subsided elegantly onto the damp seat, two things struck Regina. First, this was a lady born and bred.

The other, never in her life, no matter how many titles and monies she inherited, would Regina ever be her equal.

"You must be our savior!" the lady said in a soft musical voice. She thrust two soiled-gloved hands toward Regina. "How good you are to receive us! Lord Kingsblood said that you were as kind as you are pretty."

Lord Kingsblood. Regina heard nothing beyond those words. They came as swiftly and stunningly as a bolt of lightning upon her. The hair lifted on her neck and the tingling of her skin made her shiver. Lord Kingsblood. It was he! He was the right age. Only he had been Master Maxwell, son and presumed heir to the title marquess, when she'd known him. They'd been children, she twelve and he nineteen, the last time she had been in his company —but she'd not forgotten a single moment of that last meeting—nor shed a single drop of the acute dislike she had harbored for him ever since.

"Are you ill?" Lady Eloise asked, releasing Regina's hands with a slight recoil for fear that what the stranger had might be catching.

"No," Regina said softly, "Just—just a bit fatigued. Traveling places a strain upon my nerves."

"Faith! I hate even the idea of it," the lady declared freely. "I can't think why I allowed the marquess to talk me into so hazardous a journey." She glanced at the window and shook her head. "Everything about this country is wretched. If he expects me to remain long at Blood Hall—a despicable name, don't you think?—he will have to rethink it."

Both ladies turned as the coach door opened yet again, admitting Lord Kingsblood. "There you are, my lord. I was just telling our dearest savior what a thoroughly despicable time I expect to have at your horrid manor on the moors," Lady Eloise said peremptorily. "Blood Hall, indeed. It sounds the very thing to bring on nightmares and vapors. I refuse to consider it as our permanent home."

Frowning, Maxwell seated himself opposite the two ladies. "It's of little importance at present, and I'm certain that our hostess doesn't wish to be regaled with our domestic differences."

"You are married?" Regina asked, unable to stop herself from voicing the question though it drew his black stare her way.

"We are affianced," he answered shortly, and began wiping the rain and mud from his face with a handkerchief.

"And we're chaperoned," the young lady added with a sweet smile at Regina. "Where, my lord, is Mrs. Rogers?"

"She is staying behind. There's barely room enough for three here. Four would be impossible." He shifted his drawn-up legs as evidence of the discomfort they already shared. "As soon as we arrive, I'll send a carriage from the house to fetch her and our belongings."

"I'm surprised that you didn't ask me to step down," Regina interjected into their conversation as the coach began to roll.

Looking across at her, Maxwell decided that he quite liked the way her eyes blazed green when she was provoked. "I found it sufficient to leave your coachman behind instead."

"Maxwell!" his fiancée cried, startled by the rudeness of his words. She smiled encouragingly at Regina. "Please forgive his intemperate speech. It's been a most trying day for all."

She turned a pleading glance on him. "Tell her, my lord, that you're only jesting. She has been so kind to us." When he didn't respond, she swung her head once more toward Regina. "Please do say you forgive us."

Regina knew she should apologize for her own remark,

but she was too shocked and tired and wretched to do that. The last man, the very last man on all God's green earth she had ever wanted to meet again sat within inches, insulting her by his silence. "I accept your apology, my lady, because it is freely offered. As for the other . . ." She allowed her gaze to rest brazenly for a moment on the man opposite her. "I will count myself lucky to be high and dry at this very moment."

"There!" Eloise declared, clapping her small hands like a pleased child. "We shall all be friends now."

His fiancée's placating manner seemed to be lost on Lord Kingsblood, Regina noted, for he continued in silence to offer her stare for stare. With the mud wiped away, his face was even more handsome, but she searched in vain for any real clue that should have made her recognize him before his name was pronounced. While he had no reason to do so, Regina suspected that, for his own purposes, he was evaluating her.

Her heart gave a nervous start as she looked away. Would *he* recognize *her*? No, of course he wouldn't. He'd scarcely given heed to her when they were both children. He would have forgotten her existence years ago. But she had never forgotten, nor forgiven him for his needless cruelty to her.

"But we haven't introduced ourselves," Eloise said finally to break the strained, not-quite-polite silence that prevailed. "It's rather awkward, I suppose, so I shall begin with me. I am Lady Eloise Lytton." Once again she offered Regina her hand.

Regina shook it but her gaze went to the marquess as she said, "I am Miss Willoby." To her great relief the marquess made no sign of recognition of the name.

Pleased to have brought formalities this far, Eloise continued. "And this is Lord Maxwell Kingsblood, the Marquess of Ilfracombe. But you will have heard of him if you are from the area."

Startled again, Regina asked, "What makes you think I am from Devonshire?"

"Your accent, surely. I'm no expert on country dialects but I know yours isn't London-bred. There's something almost foreign about it, don't you agree, my lord?"

"It isn't the Devonshire burr," Maxwell announced flatly. He'd been too preoccupied earlier to give the lady's speech any thought, but now he realized that she did speak with a certain softening of vowels that bespoke a foreign influence. Still, it wasn't his business to quiz their unwilling hostess. He'd foisted far too many indignities upon her already. That uncomfortable realization made him reluctant to speak at all.

Nothing held Eloise back. "Are you visiting in Devonshire then, Miss Willoby?"

"Yes."

The rude syllable didn't affect the lady's enthusiasm. "Then, perhaps, we shall see one another again, if you are staying close by." She darted a coquettish look at her fiancé. "I know no ladies in Devonshire. The truth is, I know no one at all. Please consider that you have a formal invitation to Blood Hall at any time during the next sennight."

"Fortnight," Maxwell corrected, "And I believe that we have imposed upon Miss Willoby's good nature quite enough."

Having said that, he turned to the window without another glance at the lady of whom he spoke. He didn't want an invitation extended to anyone. He'd persuaded Eloise to leave London in the hope that he and his bride-to-be might learn to know one another better, away from the usual distractions of balls, routs, and visitations that made up one's social life when in London. To his mind, marriage was no

small step. It was his intention to take the measure of the
woman who would be mother to his children, not because
of any scheme of his own, but because he hoped to achieve
what he had observed that most men of his acquaintance
lacked, a tranquil and loving domestic life. He liked harmony, sought serenity in his life, and thought the best way
to achieve it would be if they could begin marriage of one
mind about their future.

Regina took the marquess's silence for disapproval of his
fiancée's invitation, and old feelings shifted inside her. Even
though he didn't know who she was, he didn't deem her
worthy to share an hour or a meal under his roof. Ugly
emotions slithered and thrashed about. Had he caught the
word *Miss* in her introduction of herself and felt that she
was beneath Lady Eloise's regard? Anger worked fiercely
on the restraints of the childhood rage that struggled to be
free. If only she could pay him back in kind for snubbing
her.

"You will consider a visit, won't you?" Eloise pressed, for
she'd never seen Lord Kingsblood behave in so boorish a
manner to anyone and thought she must be mistaken in his
intent.

"Thank you, Lady Eloise, for your generous invitation,"
Regina replied formally. "However, I believe I must de-
mur."

"You must?" A tiny frown formed perfect ripples on the
lady's brow. "The marquess seconds my invitation, I assure
you."

"It isn't that, it's . . ." Regina paused, considering what
she should say. She glanced at the marquess who was stu-
diously watching the nonexistent sights of interest go by,
and a seldom-heeded devilish little voice whispered an ugly
thought into her ear. She turned and smiled at Lady Eloise.
"I don't mean to be difficult or evasive, Lady Eloise, only—

well, has the marquess not told you why it is Blood Hall bears its name?"

Eloise smiled back a little uncertainly. "Why, what can you mean? It is named after the Kingsbloods, of course."

"Of course." Regina's tone held just enough false agreement to make Eloise glance again at her husband-to-be. As he continued to stare out of the window for reasons she couldn't divine, she bit her lower lip in indecision. It would be poor manners to discuss his family with a stranger, especially in his presence. Yet he hadn't even deigned to inquire about her comfort since he had entered the coach. She was wet and cold and hungry and tired and, most of all, thoroughly put out with him for dragging her into this hostile, wild, and quite unrelievedly ugly countryside.

"If there is another reason," Eloise said to no one in particular, "there must be a story, a legend to explain it."

Regina waited five heartbeats before saying "Unlike those of many parts, the legends of Devonshire aren't for the nursery or the faint-hearted, Lady Eloise."

"Faint—" Eloise's heart began to beat a little rapidly. "You mean to imply that there's a dark tale to go with the naming of Blood Hall?"

"Stuff and nonsense!" Maxwell turned away from the window, a smile on his fine wide mouth. "It's local gossip, nothing more."

"What local gossip?" Eloise pressed, the thrill of discovery making her quiver. Tales of dark deeds were so much more entertaining than riding in silence.

The marquess didn't reply to her directly. Instead he said to Regina, "I'm amazed, Miss Willoby, that you would have heard the tale, being a stranger to Devonshire."

"Stories of the evils of Cromwell's Commonwealth have no boundaries to a loyal subject of the crown, my lord."

"Cromwell lived two centuries past," Eloise said in disappointment. "I thought we were speaking of the present."

"After one is dead, what is time?" Regina mused aloud. "A hundred and fifty years may be but a blink of an eye in spirit reckoning."

"Spirit reckoning?" Eloise repeated softly. "What do you mean?" Suddenly her lovely blue eyes stared in a quite unladylike manner. "You can't mean ghosts?"

"She does not!" Maxwell answered in a cutting voice. "I'll thank you, Miss Willoby, not to frighten Lady Eloise with your wild foolishness," he added with a bitter look at Regina.

"I've said nothing. I'm determined to say no more," Regina maintained, but it was hard to keep amusement from showing in her expression. She would like nothing better than to frighten the wits out of Lady Eloise, not to do the lady any harm, but because it would vex and confound his lordship.

Torn by revelations not altogether to her liking, Eloise swayed back and forth between wanting to know more and feeling that preservation of her peace of mind lay in remaining ignorant. Curiosity won out. "Are you saying that some people believe that Blood Hall is haunted by a ghost?"

"There is believed to be a pair of ghosts, is there not, my lord?" Regina's tones were so sweet she nearly licked her fingers in relish.

"Star-crossed lovers, I believe," Maxwell said between gritted teeth. "Some say it was a foolish young woman who overstepped the bounds of society and paid a dear price."

If looks could do violence, Regina thought, she'd be in severe jeopardy at the moment. The marquess's dark eyes were amazingly powerful, and it took every ounce of her will to reply to him. "Do not forget her intrepid lover, my lord. A Roundhead, Cromwell's man sent to lay waste to

the Kingsblood lands. Instead, it's said he fell in love with a
Royalist Kingsblood, the lady of the manor. I wonder at
the nature of her fascination that it would make a seasoned
soldier turn sword against his own. Do you not wonder, my
lord, what power of feminine persuasion so enthralled such
a valiant man?"

Gazing across at her, Maxwell felt a quickening in his
pulse that he knew should not be occurring. In the presence
of his intended wife, no woman should attract him so
shamelessly. What was she doing to him, this stranger with
green eyes? "History shows us that men have often enough
made fools of themselves over an unsuitable woman."

Regina had the feeling that he was no longer talking
about some distant dead relative. Her cheeks began to flame
as his dark eyes held her green gaze trapped. She knew she
should look away from him. Staring at a man was more
than rude, it was unforgivably bold. Yet she wasn't ready to
give up the heady sensation of matching wits with an old if
unacknowledged enemy. "I rather admire a man of independent spirit, my lord. Rare is the man who can look past
the obvious barriers to see what is real and honest and true.
Most men see only what society tells them to. In their
shortsightedness they are often petty, small-minded, and
needlessly cruel to those who can least defend themselves."

The anger in her quiet speech moved Maxwell. In her
eyes he saw that those words were meant in a particular
sense for him. Had he so offended her earlier that she
should summon such heat against him? Or was it something else, something his innate sense of self-preservation
told him he should remember? "Have we met before, Miss
Willoby?"

"We were speaking of ghosts," Regina replied.

"So we were." At this moment nothing had ever seemed

more real to him than the black-haired young woman seated opposite.

The coach lurched in a rut, and they swayed. For a fraction of a second their limbs met, her knee pressing against his lower thigh, and he inhaled sharply. He released the breath in embarrassment. He was not a green schoolboy, so perplexed by the lure of the female sex that he could not trust his own body to behave from one moment to the next. He understood quite well where feelings of this kind led and knew, with some accomplished skill, the pleasures to be had in the right circumstances. But these were not the right circumstances and she, most definitely, was not the right woman. He must make that clear at once.

"Allow me to disabuse you, Miss Willoby, of the notion that stepping out from behind society's strictures exacts no cost. The 'ghosts' to whom you alluded were my distant ancestors. He was a Cromwellian soldier, and she the lady of the manor. Against all reason, they fell in love. Both her family and his men renounced them. They were branded outlaws, and finally beheaded in the main entrance of the Kingsblood manor house."

" 'And hot ran the blood from the lovers' severed necks until it made crimson the very flagstones of the hall!' " Regina repeated just as she'd first heard the lurid story told to her as a child. "And ever after, the place has been known as Blood Hall."

The little gasp came so softly it was almost unheard, but neither Regina nor the marquess could ignore Eloise when she swayed forward and collapsed in a swoon between them.

"Now look what you've done!" Maxwell said roughly as he gathered Eloise's limp body from Regina's knees and pulled her into his lap. "Devil of a woman!" he muttered, leaving Regina in doubt as to whether his anger was directed at Lady Eloise or herself.

Maxwell tapped his fiancée's pale face lightly with his fingertips. Her eyes fluttered but did not open. "Lady Eloise . . . Eloise . . . darling," he added with a quelling glance at Regina.

Regina opened her purse and pulled from it a small vial. "Smelling salts. I never need them myself," she said stiffly as she bent forward to hold the concoction under the lady's nose.

Eloise choked, coughed, and then sputtered as the offending odor entered her nostrils. "Oh! Oh! I think I'm going to be ill!"

"Not in here!" Maxwell replied with more force than was required. "There's no room." With that thoughtless bit of masculine logic to cue her, Eloise burst into tears.

"Now, now, darling, you mustn't cry. I am sorry. You have every right to be cross with me. I am a villain. Here, rest your head against me." He lifted off her bonnet and then pressed her head down to lay against his shoulder as he awkwardly patted her cool cheek. "There, isn't that better? You'll be fine in a moment. I'm sorry if we upset you."

A little appalled to be subjected to the man's treacly—and to her mind—wholly inept lovemaking, Regina snapped the cap back on her salts and stuffed them angrily into her bag. How, she thought inconsequentially, could so handsomely formed a man be so totally ignorant of how to treat a woman? Had she been Lady Eloise, she'd have slapped his face.

"It's a horrid tale! Horrid," Eloise wailed.

Maxwell glanced over the top of Lady Eloise's head at Regina. "I promise, my dear, that neither of us will say another word on the subject. Not . . . one . . . word."

Abashed that in her reckless desire to discomfort the

marquess she'd hurt an innocent bystander, Regina shrank
back into her place and hugged her arms tightly about herself. It had been a complete and utter mistake to bring up
the subject. She wished now that, from the beginning, she'd
pretended to be deaf and mute.

"It's a ghastly name for a home," Eloise said when her
sobs lessened. "You will change it immediately, before we
are married. I demand it."

"Yes, dear," Maxwell answered, feeling a certain resignation in those two words.

With an expelled breath, he turned to look out. The rain
had momentarily stopped, the scudding clouds showing
rose where the afternoon sun shot through them. In the
distance he saw the familiar stone outline of his family's
ancient home silhouetted against the slate-gray sky. Made
of granite from the surrounding hills, Blood Hall's porch,
oriels, and many chimneys stood out in medieval splendor.
The manor house appeared to be quite near, but he knew
the road swung down past it before turning back to climb
the cliff on which it was anchored. It would be nearly an
hour before they arrived.

Gazing at the home to which he hadn't returned in
nearly ten years, Maxwell suddenly felt a lightening of his
soul. Though he'd always detested the name Blood Hall,
suddenly he knew that, no matter what his bride-to-be's
protests, he'd never change it.

He glanced back at Miss Willoby. She'd deliberately
frightened Lady Eloise with the harrowing legend. Now she
sat as contrite as a child who'd not realized her harm until
it was done. Did she know that she'd given away her own
interest in the house by the emotional intensity in her
voice? She was attached to Blood Hall, he could feel it
when she spoke of it. What was the mystery? Who was she?

* * *

Regina started awake when the coach came to a halt, only then realizing that she had been dozing. Reaching to right her bonnet, she saw that Lady Eloise and the marquess were conversing, their heads close together and their voices low. Pretending to arrange her mantelet, she strained to catch their words.

". . . to worry about, I assure you, my lady. Mrs. Rogers will be with you before dinner. Come now. We must stand down."

"I prefer to go back," Eloise said in a peevish tone.

"You must see, my dear, that that is impossible." The marquess's tone was gentle and reasonable. "In any case, I'm here to protect you. Does that not make you even a little brave?"

He must really care for her, Regina thought, a little shocked. From what she had experienced at his hands today, and years before, she knew that he was neither nice nor gentle by nature. This tender display must be the result of passion. She wished the lady well but she doubted of her continued success with the marquess. It was common knowledge that husbands were never as attentive as suitors.

Regina looked up as Lady Eloise reached out and touched her arm. "Thank you so much, you've been more than kind. Please say that you will come to see me. Promise that you will."

Avoiding the marquess's eye, Regina said, "I doubt that I shall be able, Lady Eloise. I have some distance yet to travel. But," she added, seeing that a new protest was about to be put forth, "I'll consider it, that I promise."

Maxwell didn't reach out to her but said in a strangely quiet tone, "I feel, Miss Willoby, that we aren't yet done. Do consider my fiancée's invitation as one with mine." After a pause he added, "So that you may suffer no more delay, my coachman will drive you on to wherever it is you are traveling. Your hired man will be well preserved by my staff until his coach can be returned to him. Good evening, Miss Willoby, and thank you."

"A pretty speech, my lord," Eloise said with a smile. "Let us go and face the ghosts." Her laughter was a little too sharp for musicality but she stepped bravely down with the marquess's help.

Regina had one last glimpse of the pair. As they reached the bottom step the door to the house was thrown open, spilling golden light into the gray dusk of day's end.

As the coach began to roll Regina let the window down, uncaring that the cold rushed in. The rain had stopped, the winds dying with the onset of evening. It would be dark within the hour. As the coach swung wide on the drive, she spied a half-open gate in the walled garden at the west side of the house. To her amazement she saw candlelight streaming across the flagstones, and a couple dancing.

The couple was dressed most peculiarly. The woman wore a gown with tight-fitted bodice and wide skirts that had been the fashion a century and a half earlier. As for the man, he wore heavy boots with wide bucket tops, full breeches, and a Cavalier's coat. There must be a masked ball being held in the marquess's honor, Regina thought, and then, before she gained a second look, the coach rolled on and the sight was lost.

Only when she had shut the window and sat back did Regina realize that what she'd seen was impossible. No one lighted candles in a garden, and certainly no one would hold a ball out-of-doors after an autumn storm. She must have been mistaken.

Chapter Three

"A tumbling-down cottage fit only for field mice and a scholar's family!" That is how Regina's mother had often described their very modest home. "We're as poor as church mice," Regina would agree with a grin at her adored mother. Her mother would smile back, ruffle her black curls, and say, "Church mice would be a touch above our aspirations, dear."

Regina remembered those words now as she stared in blank surprise at the remains of what had once been her home. Backlit by a dying sun that bled red through the swift-racing purple clouds, the cottage had seemed intact as the coach came to a halt before it. Yet when she had stepped down for a closer inspection, she saw that only shadows filled in the huge gaps in the thatching. Once-trim lines delineated the three-foot-thick walls. Now bulges had formed where the cob had become damp and begun to disintegrate. The neat flower garden that had once flanked a cobblestone path to the door presented a tangled, nearly impenetrable barrier of snaking vines, untrimmed privet hedges, and treacherous wild rose runners. During the years of neglect, the "tumbling-down" cottage of her childhood had actually tumbled down.

Regina stood rooted to the spot in a combination of bitter disillusionment, stark disappointment, and a bone-crushing weariness she hadn't realized until this instant. Nothing. There was nothing left. All her fine plans were in ruin at her feet. How the dowager countess would laugh if she could see her now.

I will live to see the end of you! I will hunt you, break you! . . . You will live in fear of me until you lie groveling in the dust! And then, when you beg for mercy, I shall spit on you!

The damning words seemed to echo in the sound of the wind soughing through the nearby trees. Regina shivered at the sound, and black ripples of despair followed. The first tears in weeks brimmed in her eyes. Nothing. Not one thing to call her own, after all.

"Forgive me meddling, ma'am, but this can't be the place you want," the coachman called down doubtfully when the young lady continued to stare at her dream-in-rubble. "You'll be wanting another place, perhaps," he offered helpfully. "There'll be other cottages a little farther down the lane."

Regina looked up at him, having forgotten his existence. "Oh, no, this is the place, the very one. You may hand down my things."

"You can't be thinking of stopping here, ma'am?" His incredulous tone acted like a lash upon her strung nerves.

"But of course!" she answered crisply, because there was no place else to go. The nearby village, she remembered, was too small to have an inn. Nor did she want to be put up in a neighbor's home where she would be submitted to a dozen difficult questions she had yet to form answers for.

"But, ma'am," he began in protest as he climbed down to her level. "You can't stay here." He glanced briefly at the ruins to confirm his opinion. " 'Tis no fit place for the meanest sort of ruffian, let alone a lady."

Regina offered him an indulgent smile. "I assure you that I'll be fine."

The coachman regarded her curiously, wondering what a pretty young matron—for according to her former coachman she was married—was doing traveling the moors alone. "Don't mean to offend, ma'am. Only his lordship wouldn't like it above half if I was to leave you here like this."

The reminder that he was Lord Kingsblood's servant doused the tentative flicker of friendliness she'd begun to feel. "It's not his lordship's affair, and I'll thank you not to mention it to him!"

The rebuff scotched the coachman's friendly expression. Refusing to apologize, Regina did soften her next words. "In any case, I shall remain. You may set my bags down inside the door so that they won't be ruined if it begins to rain again."

The coachman turned away, grumbling. "Inside, outside, 'twill all be the same if it rains. Not half a roof of thatch remains!"

"All cob wants is a good hat and a good pair of shoes," she replied. It was one of father's favorite expressions and, remembering it now, Regina suddenly felt a little of her courage come back.

The cottage was badly in need of repair. That wasn't unusual, she reminded herself. When she had lived here with her parents there had seldom been money enough for either shoes for her or a new hat for her mother. When there were a few extra coins, the cottage's "hat" of thatch had always had priority. Many was the Saturday, weather permitting, when one of her father's sturdier school lads could be found patching their roof with a combination of reed, straw, and heather.

As she cautiously picked a path toward the doorway, Regina heard the clucking sound of chickens coming from inside. Spying a broken pane of glass, she guessed that several had taken up roost in the rafters. The muffled clank of a brass bell brought her head up sharply from the path. Squinting into the distance, she detected the silhouette of a cow standing in what had once been the vegetable patch.

Once inside the doorway, Regina found herself halted by a malodorous combination of dung, mildew, and rotting vegetable matter. Quickly she whipped out a handkerchief and pressed its scented folds to her nose.

"Something wants to have crawled up in here and died," the coachman grumbled as he walked up and set her small trunk and one leather bag not too gently on the filthy floor.

"There have been many changes in nine years," Regina agreed aloud. One of them, at least, was for the better. She could afford to mend the roof. She could even purchase a new one. In fact, she could afford to do anything she chose. She was the Countess of Amesbury, and a very wealthy woman.

She turned to the small but burly man beside her. "All the cottage needs is a good airing out. I shall walk into the village tomorrow and hire laborers to do the heavier work. I'll bring back supplies, food, a broom, new glass and curtains for the windows, perhaps even a new rug for the floor." The thought of being able to beautify her home made Regina smile. She could now afford the smallest luxuries that would have made her mother's life a delight.

"There be no bed or bath, no water or fire," the coachman pointed out. Glancing about in the damp gloom, he snorted his impression of her plans. "Wouldn't be surprised but what wild dogs don't know it as home."

Because he was pointing out with logical consideration all the problems she didn't wish to face, Regina whirled about and vented the impotent fury of her disappointments on his head. "Do be silent! I'll have none of your impudence in my home. You've done your duty. Now depart."

The man braced his hands on his hips and planted his feet firmly. "I don't know but what I should. You won't see reason, then, ma'am?"

"I'm quite capable of building a fire," she answered by way of mollifying him, for she could see that his concern was genuine as any stranger's might be. "That should keep away the creatures. As for loneliness, I'm accustomed to being by myself for long intervals."

The coachman's sour expression did not alter. "I never said nothing about loneliness being a bother. 'Tisn't a proper place for a gentlelady. What would your husband be thinking were he to see you now?"

The mention of her husband startled Regina for she had not even become accustomed to the idea of him before he was gone. "I—I don't have a husband."

The coachman's eyes narrowed in sly assessment. So, that was the way of it. She was running away. He'd had some experience with ladies and their running away. All his life he had worked for the nobility and knew firsthand the kinds of nonsense of which they were capable. No doubt, she was as foolish as that Lady Lytton his lordship was about to take to wife. Full of fits and vapors was Lady Lytton.

As a man of reasonable intelligence, he'd never understood why a sensible nobleman of breeding and wealth invariably took to wife a lady of such refined sensibilities and fanciful notions that it required a man's full attention just to keep her contained. Still, it wasn't his business. But if this young lady standing before him had been one of his own five daughters, he'd have taken her across his knee then sent her packing back to the man who, no doubt, was tearing his hair with worry for the pretty wife who'd gotten away from him. It was enough to make a man spit!

He remembered then how the marquess had alighted

from the carriage they had accosted, swearing fit to make a saint blush. It had come as something of a shock for him to discover that a lady, not some hell-for-leather old soldier, occupied the coach. Lord Kingsblood kept a curb on his speech most times, and anger wasn't an emotion he'd ever seen the nobleman display in a lady's presence. Now he understood his lordship's temper and his frustration. The lady was as stubborn as an old mill horse. It was just as well that she was as beautiful as a lark's song, or someone would probably have strangled her before this.

"Well, coachman!" Regina said impatiently, for his staring was making her most uncomfortable. "Will you dawdle about all evening? I've things to do. Be off with you!"

Stung once more, the coachman doffed his cap. "Evening to you, ma'am." With every line of his stocky body rigid in affront, he turned on his heel and strode out.

Regina followed him to the end of the path then stood watching as he climbed with surprising agility into his seat, lifted the reins, and shouted at his horses. The coach jumped to life and began to roll. Within moments horses, coachman, and coach had moved beyond her view, eclipsed by the surrounding woods and a sudden dip in the road.

It wasn't until the sound of carriage wheels and horses' hooves died away, and Regina experienced the almost unearthly silence of twilight in the combe, that she realized how very much alone she really was.

Maxwell regarded the remains of his dinner with some satisfaction. The joint of beef, boiled potatoes, new peas, and generous supply of wine had gone a long way toward restoring his temper. A hot bath and fresh clothes had done the rest. If only those simple pleasures had worked their magic on Lady Eloise.

He looked toward the far end of his table where she sat

and offered her an amiable smile. She offered him a less than warm return and picked up her fork. Her plate was almost empty. Had he not seen the minuscule portions she'd accepted only after the most strenuous prompting by Mrs. Rogers, he would have thought she'd completed a satisfying meal. As it was, she looked quite wretched, if beautiful.

"Aren't you feeling well, my dear?" he inquired for the third time since the meal began.

"She should have been put straightaway to bed with warm milk and a dose of cod liver oil," Dorrity Rogers said stiffly. She sat to one side before the fire, knitting. "Can't think why she insisted on coming down after the perfectly horrid day we've had."

"Nana, please," Eloise said in her melodious voice. "Lord Kingsblood is to be commended for his enterprising method of salvaging our unfortunate journey."

"Thank you, Lady Eloise. Now that we have arrived, I assure you that nothing else will go wrong that is within my power to oversee." Ignoring Mrs. Rogers's frown, he continued, "I shall very much enjoy showing you around Bloo —my home. It will be our first order of business after breakfast."

"As you wish," Eloise answered, hoping that the rest of his home was more up-to-date than the great chamber in which they dined. Gazing about with some trepidation, she noted again the medieval design of the open-timbered roof from which hung gothic banners and several shields. The chimneypiece, richly decorated with paneled stonework, tracery, and carving, was much too heavy and ornate to suit her modern mind, as were the wood-paneled walls that the occasional tapestry overlay. As for the painted battle scene that hung above the hearth, the less said the better, she decided with an elegant shiver.

Upon arriving at the manor house, she had noticed a pair of oriels. The long, dark shadows reaching out from the corners of the poorly lighted hall prevented her from observing if they were part of this room. The stone manor house was dark, oppressive, and too gothic for her taste. Once they married she would have a major renovation project on her hands. She had no intention of crossing the threshold of Blood Hall again until both its name and interior had been completely altered.

She looked back down the length of the table and realized that Lord Kingsblood was observing her perusal of his home. The hopeful expression on his face reminded her that she should say something. "Your home is obviously a place of ancient design, my lord, yet there have been changes made, I'm certain."

"Little enough," Maxwell replied happily, thinking that she'd be pleased to know that his residence had been authentically preserved. "Unlike many, I don't believe in tearing down and rebuilding for the sake of fashion. Beyond creature comforts added to the chambers and, of course, new privies, you'll find little that was not present in 1471 when the house was built."

He paused as servants entered to clear away the main course and place dessert bowls before them. "Apple dumplings and cream, my favorite!" he declared, knowing that one of the footmen would carry his pleasure back to the kitchen and Cook's ear.

As he tucked in, he noted a relapse of the deafening silence that had enveloped them during most of the meal. He wasn't indifferent to the weariness of the ladies dining with him, but he had hoped for a more cordial first evening. It was to be devoutly wished that they had arrived earlier, so that they might have napped before dining. But that was water under the bridge, Maxwell decided, and finished his favorite dessert with the same relish with which he had attacked the rest of his meal.

When they were all done and the table cleared, Dorrity Rogers turned to him. "I beg you to excuse me, my lord, but Lady Eloise is pale with exhaustion. I fear she will become ill if she isn't put right to bed."

As if on cue, Eloise rose to her feet, drawing him to his. "Oh, yes, please do excuse me, my lord."

Maxwell swallowed his annoyance, for he had looked forward to a long quiet evening before the fire, perhaps with her head resting on his knee while he indulged himself in the rare pleasure of smoking a pipe indoors. "Won't you stay even a moment longer, Lady Eloise?"

He sounded so disappointed that Eloise couldn't bring herself to refuse him. After all, he was soon to be her husband. She must become accustomed to accommodating his moods and pleasures. "As you wish, my lord." She turned to her duenna. "Perhaps you will be good enough to warm my sheets. I will be along shortly."

"Very well, my lady." Dorrity dropped a curtsey to her mistress and a briefer one to Lord Kingsblood before retiring.

Pleased to have won so easily, Maxwell strode the length of the table with hands outstretched. "I'm so glad you remained."

She wore a deep-blue tunic banded in gold cord at the low neckline and sleeves. Gold tassels fringed the edges that overlaid a white muslin gown. Her short blond curls had been dressed in the classic fashion with short ringlets about her face and a gold cording Strophos headdress about her head. The coif made the most of her delicate features and huge blue eyes. She was a beauty.

Unaccountably, a vision of compelling green eyes wreathed in coal-black waves swam before his mind's eye.

The recall annoyed Maxwell; the lady in the coach hadn't been Lady Eloise's equal in beauty nor had she left a pleasant impression upon his mind. She was willful, stubborn, and quite thoroughly disobliging. Yet her vision encroached upon his thoughts in a way that he couldn't dismiss even as he reached out to his fiancée.

He caught her small hands in his. "You look so lovely that I can scarcely credit the difficulties you've been through this day."

Encouraged by the smile she bestowed on him, he drew her closer to banish the annoying persistence of his thoughts and bent his head to hers.

Taken aback by his sudden ardor, Eloise averted her face just in time to keep his lips from touching her own. Instead, she felt his warm lips brush the apex of her cheek and then travel to her ear, which, to her astonishment, he kissed with a distinct smack. "Please, my lord!"

Maxwell lifted his head, one black brow arching. "What is it, Eloise? Am I not pleasing to you?"

She looked up at him, at the eager shine in his dark eyes, and a flush burned her cheeks. "It isn't that, my lord."

"Then what, my sweet? You needn't fear your husband's kiss." He smiled warmly as he took her gently by her upper arms. "You'll find it a most pleasant exercise, and one in which I intend you to become most accomplished."

Eloise caught her breath though her own thoughts had run precisely along those lines earlier in the day. Her gaze strayed to his mouth. His lips were firm and nicely shaped but as his smile widened, revealing strong white teeth, she had a sudden image of being swallowed up by that broad masculine mouth. Instinctively she took a startled backward step.

"Eloise!" Maxwell said encouragingly, not releasing her

arms. "Please, a single kiss only, and then we'll shake hands as friends and say good night."

The formality of his speech plus his assurance that she would be released to bed afterward made Eloise a little braver. She wasn't at all certain that he deserved a kiss after the events of the day. Nor was she encouraged by the gothic surroundings of the hall, which were, to her mind, anything but romantic. Still, he was her fiancé and, as such, should receive some token of her affection. Resolutely she clasped her hands before her breast and, lifting her chin, closed her eyes.

Amusement struck Maxwell as she assumed the attitude of a postulant at prayer. Amusement turned rapidly into vexation as her soft mouth became a tight pucker. He hadn't considered that she would be so innocent that even a kiss would tax her courage. But then, so be it and all the more reason for them to have these days together. Two weeks was but a short time to settle her not only into accepting his kiss but to encourage her to accept, after marriage, his more intimate embraces in bed.

Bending forward, he very carefully laid his lips upon hers. The contact disappointed him. The smooth mouth under his might as well have been a child's. She moved him not at all.

Reluctant to accept this, he drew her closer, deepening just a fraction the pressure of his mouth upon hers. She tasted of baked apple and sweetened cream—not unpleasant but hardly the stuff to stir strong emotion. Seeking some sense of the possibilities that might be between them, he opened his mouth and very gently applied the tip of his tongue to her lips.

Eloise immediately balked at this unexpected intrusion into what she had thought was a passably pleasant experience.

Her eyes snapped open as the marquess instantly lifted his head, and what she saw didn't encourage her. He was frowning as if she'd done something wrong. The thought infuriated her. What did he expect? This wasn't the proper setting for romance and he, with his rude behavior, wasn't her idea of an ardent suitor. As disappointed in her own way as he, she said in frosty tones, "My lord, it is most— unseemly for you to tease me so."

"Tease?" His voice was incredulous. "But surely, Eloise, you've been kissed before?"

"Perhaps I have," she hedged, and lowered her eyes before his gaze. "Once or twice, when I was taken off guard by some overly forward suitor." Her head snapped up. "That doesn't, my lord, give you right to insult me for my indiscretions!"

Her reply irritated him for he recognized it as a ploy to make him apologize. "You consider my kisses an insult?"

"I consider your indecent conduct with a certain indelicate portion of your—" She blushed furiously. "It's wholly unacceptable. I ask that you never repeat it." She splayed her hands before him as he appeared about to move toward her. "No, my lord, let us say no more of the matter. I assure you that by morning the incident will be gone from my mind. Good night to you, my lord. God keep you."

He let her go, feeling not only chagrin but a certain amount of animosity toward his bride-to-be. She hadn't wanted his kiss, at least not the most enjoyable portion of it. The thought came as a distinct surprise, so much so that in his inattention he poured himself a larger portion of brandy than was his usual wont.

"She dislikes kissing," he said to the room, as if he expected an answer.

He knew that the rearing of gently bred ladies was a most curious combination of intentional ignorance and inconsequential accomplishments. But for her to believe that his kiss was an insult, that was carrying delicacy too far! He had kissed dozens of women, and more than a few ladies. The ladies were married and were familiar with carnal matters. They didn't reject his ardor or his embraces as lewd. A goodly number of them had initiated the moments, especially in his younger years.

He smiled and swallowed a sip of brandy, savoring the tingle on his lips in place of the tender caress of another's kiss. Pleased, he took another sip and his eyes glazed as he spent some moments in quiet reflection with sweet memories of more pleasant and willing partners.

Quite without his calling it forth, his reminiscences turned to a pair of soft fern-green eyes ringed in a black fringe of lashes. He frowned absently, thinking that none of his lovers had ever had such eyes. And then the memory resolved itself into the proud features of the lady from the coach.

He was only mildly surprised to find himself thinking of her again. This time he didn't resist the insistent images floating through his mind. In bemusement, he recalled the exact shape of her full rosy lips and how pleasant he had found it to watch them form the words of her speech. The desire that had lain inert despite the prompting of Eloise's very real touch came springing to life within him.

With a half smile, Maxwell let himself imagine what it would have been like to kiss the green-eyed stranger. Somehow he knew that she wouldn't have started away from her lover. She would have offered her mouth willingly, even passionately, and met him kiss for kiss. Certainly she had met his ire with a self-possession that most men of his acquaintance would have been hard-pressed to match.

The thought gave him pause. Why on earth had he fastened on this woman to pique his desire? He hadn't even liked her, had found her rude, disobliging, even vindictive. Why else had she spun out that ghastly tale about beheaded ghosts, if not because she'd enjoyed baiting Lady Eloise and had wanted to make her cry? Later, when she'd witnessed the results of her enmity, she'd been abashed. But that didn't excuse her conduct or make her any less to blame. She was a termagant, a harridan to whom no sane man would ever willingly leg-shackle himself. The devil of it was, he couldn't release the vision of her glorious gaze. The green-eyed chit had found a way into his senses that precluded thought or calculation!

He drank the last of his brandy in a generous gulp as he went to stand before the fireplace because, as often happened inexplicably at Blood Hall, the room had become quite chilled. She had introduced herself as *Miss* Willoby yet he'd seen her wedding band. Why, she'd even tried to twist the gold ring off her finger to give to him when she still thought him a highwayman.

His lips lifted at the corners. Had he looked as desperate and villainous as that? The notion gave him a rare thrill of self-satisfaction. He knew what others thought of him, that he was unflappable, deliberate, and perhaps even a bit stodgy. It was a cultivated image that had taken him years of self-will to establish. No one knew the deep ugly side of his nature and, God willing, none would ever again suffer from it. What had once erupted from him in a moment when circumstance and companions, and an overindulgence in liquor, had sapped his good sense would remain forever as an indelible black mark upon his soul.

He shifted uncomfortably as his memory ranged on, in spite of his wishes, and it brought a bleak look to his expression. Nearly ten years after the fact, he couldn't quite forget it, or forgive himself for his part in it. A hundred, no, a thousand times he had gone over it in his mind, wondered what had happened to the poor little wretch, and then battered himself with recriminations for ever having allowed it to begin.

The *snap* of the crystal snifter quite surprised him. He looked down to find he had pushed his thumb through the delicate glass and that he was bleeding. With a muttered curse he set the glass down and gingerly extracted his thumb from the break. After dabbing at it with his handkerchief, he discovered the cut wasn't deep and would heal without stitch or physicking. He glanced longingly at the brandy but stopped himself from reaching for it.

"That's quite enough of that!" he murmured, and, wrapping the handkerchief tight to stop the bleeding, he strode rapidly out of the great hall.

The draft created by the closing door flickered the candles and fanned the flames in the hearth. For an instant the room dimmed then the firelight brightened, revealing two figures seated on the window seat set in the oriel at the far end of the room.

"Well, what do you think, my dear?" the captain said as he stood up.

"I detest her!" the lady answered, smoothing the wrinkles from her wide skirts.

"And our great-great-great-great-grandson, what of him?"

"Oh," she said with a womanly softening in her tone. "Has he not grown into a most handsome specimen?"

"No, he has not!" her partner said roundly. "God's death! He's naught but a suckling in a man's form. Did you witness the manner in which he allowed that skinny wench to elude him? What sort of kiss was that he gave her?"

"A tentative one," the lady replied, for it was, to be honest, a quite insipid and uninspiring kiss. "Still, she gave him little encouragement."

"Since when does a man need lessons from a maid on how to proceed? Shamed, that's what I feel, shamed by my own flesh and blood! No wonder the bloodline's dying out. I should have dozens, nay, scores of male heirs from which to take my choice. But here I sit with a bashful violet. They should have named him Maxine!"

"You are too hard, Captain. Maxwell simply lacks—experience."

"London sluts must have come down in the world since my day! He'd have done better to stay in the West Country and bedded farmers' daughters. Then he'd know how to go on with a woman."

"With which, pray tell, pretty farmers' daughters did you hone your skills before you came acourting?"

With a roguish twinkle, he replied, "Some men are born for the sport, my love. And some women," he said significantly as he reached out and pinched her cheek gently, "are born to spread themselves most charmingly for such men."

Pleased by his answer but refusing to show it, she brushed his hand away. "We were speaking of Maxwell."

"Then we were speaking of incompetence, inferiority, and impotence!"

"I disagree. There's a fine manly passion in Maxwell. Didn't you sense in his thoughts that some other woman holds his interest?"

He grinned. "I saw the placket of his breeches stir, if that's what you mean."

"I mean, Captain," she said, "that he is capable of strong emotion. By the by, they call them trousers these days, my dear."

"As long as the lad learns how to use what's inside of them, I don't give a damn what he calls the covering!"

"The same blood that flowed in your veins flows in his," she reminded him.

"Don't be insulting. I cannot be held accountable for every drop of blood your line has thinned to oblivion. He's a Kingsblood, after all." He frowned. "Because of them I was never able to openly claim our child as mine!"

She reached out and gently touched his sleeve. "For that I carry an eternal sorrow, my love. Yet you must credit my kin for hiding our child and, after Cromwell's fall, naming him the legitimate heir."

"That is because none of your kinsmen possessed the balls to produce their own! They claimed 'Satan's spawn' to insure that a Kingsblood would retain the title of marquess. 'Tis *my* surname that should carry the title!"

"All the same," she said soothingly, "In Maxwell there is promise." Once the captain's hatred of the Kingsbloods seemed to include one and all. Now, for the first time in more than one hundred and fifty years, he was taking an unaccountable interest in the life of one Kingsblood, possibly because Maxwell was the direct heir of their love child. "I see something of you in Maxwell. Oh, you are of different shape and coloring, but don't you see the likeness? Like the secret currents of a deep river, there are things about him that he hides even from himself."

The man beside her reached out to wrap a long arm about her tiny waist and bring her tightly against his side. "Secrets, is it? Then I suggest we uncork a few of them!"

"First we must make certain that he doesn't marry that straw-headed wench!" the lady amended.

"Jealous, my love?"

She smiled up at him and touched her fingers to his lips. "I am most jealous, my love. Our many-times-great-grandson deserves a woman worthy of him, as you were fortunate enough to find me. Then we will allow her to uncork his secrets as, my love, I am about to uncork yours!"

So intent was the captain upon the tantalizing play of her

fingers upon his lips that it came as a complete astonishment to feel her other hand brush the placket of his breeches. "We mustn't run the straw-headed wench off too soon," he continued to muse through gritted teeth as she slipped the last button of his breeches free. "The lad must needs practice upon something female."

"Buy him a London slut!" she suggested as she slipped her arm about his broad neck and brought his head down to meet hers. "Or, perchance, Providence will provide," she added against his lips.

"Didn't like calling so late, your lordship." The coachman glanced nervously about the marquess's elegant bedroom into which he'd been admitted. "Especially as you gave me leave to stop in the village. But I couldn't rest, you see, not with the lady staying on alone in a place like that."

"You'd better start at the beginning," Maxwell said, as he retied the sash of his Turkish dressing gown.

The coachman did, repeating in exact detail what he'd seen and said, and what the lady in question had said and done. He omitted nothing, not her rejection of his concern for her or the apparent mulishness in her refusing to see reason. The only thing he did omit was the fact that he'd had a second pint at the Stag and Boar before his conscience got the better of his thirst.

"So you see, my lord, I didn't have choice but to leave her. Only, I couldn't leave off thinking about her, alone, in that desperate place. Then, with the weather whipping up again, I thought I'd best seek your advice. I'll go back after her, my lord, if you think it best." The reluctance in his tone didn't belie his sincerity.

"Daft woman!" Maxwell finished in one gulp the brandy he had poured for himself while the coachman talked. "Damnation! Why did I ever stop that coach?"

"Begging your lordship's pardon, but her man did try to ride you down."

"Because, like a dolt, I was in the road," Maxwell finished tightly. Nothing about the day had gone well and now it was ending badly. "I'll go after her." He said it without pleasure or even anger, just a weary resignation that his warm dry bed would be without his grateful body for a few hours longer.

He looked up. "Thank you. You may go to bed."

The coachman hesitated though bed with his wife, Sarah, was where he longed to be. "Won't you need me to show the way?"

Maxwell shook his head. "Your story was quite detailed. I think I even remember the place. The cottage belonged to my tutor when I was young. I will find it."

The coachman pulled his forelock. "Very good, your lordship. If there's anything I can do in the morning . . ."

"I'll send for you, you may be certain."

When the man had gone, Maxwell went to put his glass down and found, to his surprise, that the stopper was out of the bottle. Frowning, he picked it up. He had never before forgotten to replace it. He started to put it back but the warm color of the liquor caught his eye and he paused. It was his habit never to drink more than one brandy when he was alone. He had no desire to become a drunkard for lack of company. Tonight, because of the intrusion as he was preparing for bed, he'd had a second. Still, the thought of dressing again and going out into the cold bluster of the night made him decide once more to amend his habit. To protect against the cold, he would have a third.

He picked up the crystal decanter and poured himself a short one. He was about to lift the neck when something seemed to bump his hand and another, generous, serving splashed into his glass.

As he replaced the stopper the wind gushed down the chimney, spewing sparks across the hearth, and the sound it made was very much like the faint huskiness of a man's laughter.

Chapter Four

"God save me from a devil in woman's guise!" Maxwell roared against the gale, but the words were whipped from his mouth and lost in the moaning of the wind. The hem of his greatcoat flapped about his horse's flanks like the wings of a giant bird. On the dark road, lord and horse appeared more like Pegasus in flight than mortal beings.

Maxwell cursed again as he came to the abrupt end of the dirt lane he'd been following. He had thought he knew exactly where he was headed but had forgotten until well into his journey that his memories of the moors were ten years old. The roads had changed some in the intervening years, or else his sense of direction had become slack in a country unforgiving in its demand of journeyers. If not for the occasional spill of moonlight through the scudding drapery of rain clouds he would not have made it thus far. Yet even that was about to desert him. Vivid flashes of lightning were running on the horizon, harkening the arrival of the new storm that would soon reach them.

Maxwell stood in his stirrups. The bleak sea of the moorlands rolled away from him in all directions. He had come as knight errant to rescue a lady but, he thought grimly as he eased back into his saddle, if he didn't soon find her, *he* would be the one in need of rescue. As much as he hated to admit it, he stood very nearly in a state of utter confusion.

"Can't be lost!" he muttered. His horse, unfamiliar with his master, shied at the angry tone. Maxwell bent and patted his nervous mount's neck. He deserved better than to become hopelessly befuddled after his chivalrous nature had sent him out on a night fit only for goblins and wild, mad things. Being a man, he refused to consider that he should have taken up the coachman's offer of aid. It was the damned brandy's fault. While it had kept him warm for a time, it had also lulled him into straying far afield. He took a deep breath and expelled it, waiting for his anger to calm in the hope that reason and direction would return.

Spume borne on the stiff breeze had formed a thin crust of salt on his lips. Absently he licked at it, reminded of how long he'd been away from his childhood home, and of the fact that the saltiness meant the wind blew in from the sea to the northwest. *Northwest winds.*

Maxwell lifted his head and touched a finger to his tongue before holding it high. The wind blew before him. The cottage, if he remembered aright, stood a little east and south of Blood Hall. He scanned the horizon behind him. Over his left shoulder he made out a dim glow that could be naught but lights from Blood Hall. With a reassuring pat on his horse's neck, he turned and began a canter back down the lane. He would keep the wind at his back for a mile or two and see where that brought him.

He was wet, cold, and ached in every joint. "If I do not find her this time, may the devil take her and be welcome!"

Regina murmured softly in her sleep and hugged her knees tighter to her chest. Afraid of spiders and other crawly creatures, she had made a bed of her trunk and a pillow of her smaller case. In the beginning, the silence of the night had pricked at her nerves until every shift of a hen in the rafters, each scratch of mouse claws and chirp of insect seemed designed wholly for her torment. More than once she had sat upright, certain that someone was skulking about just outside the cottage door. Finally, out of sheer exhaustion, she had succumbed to sleep, but it was no more comforting than the supposed specters of the night.

Dream spun out upon dark restless dream, each one bringing her closer to reliving the final moments of her stay in London. Half conscious, half delirious with anxiety, and shivering with cold, she fought the inevitable backslide into a memory threaded with apprehension and dark foreshadowing. It was the wind when it came up, roaring one instant then moaning and wailing like lost spirits the next, that finally tipped the scale of her dreams.

Once more she was in the Amesbury London town house. As the doors swung open of their own volition, a burst of stifling heat rushed on her, making her gasp and her head spin. Resisting the giddiness, she stepped into the room.

Despite the dimly lighted interior, she recognized with a prick of alarm two men. One was her husband's cousin, Percy Buckram, who had inherited the title of Earl of Amesbury at her husband's death. The other, Sir Nigel Foxworth, was the dowager's crony. She'd known both men a month, and disliked each for different reasons.

Buckram was what her father would have called a rutting sot. His youthful face already showed the effects of the dissolute life. Yet his thick blond hair with its willful wave dipping low over one brow gave him a faintly rakish air that, she'd been told, many young ladies found nearly irresistible. She, on the other hand, had come to think of him only as detestable. From the first day of her arrival in London, he had made it known in no uncertain terms that he hoped to seduce her. She could not step alone into a room when he was about without finding him close behind her, ever ready with some excuse to touch her. On no less than the evening of her husband's burial, he'd so pressed her with his drunken, indecent suggestions about becoming the mistress of the new Earl of Amesbury that she'd finally been driven to slap his face right in the midst of the crowded salon. Since then he had kept his distance. Yet now, in the room's oppressive atmosphere, he appeared more predatory and distasteful than usual.

Beside him stood Foxworth, his scalp shining beneath the few oiled strands that branched his dome. Notorious for his venomous wit, his waspish tongue gave voice to all that was selfish, pitiless, intolerant, self-centered, and arrogant within the aristocracy. The London *ton* walked softly in fear of him.

Regina stiffened as Buckram came forth to salute her hand. "Cousin Regina. A delight, as always." The warmth of his breath touched her skin and then the damp pressure of his lips lingered too long for what was polite. When he lifted his head he was smirking. Apprehensively she lowered her gaze and saw that he had left a thread of saliva on her skin.

Revulsion shivered through her. It was a deliberate act meant to disconcert her. It did. In only thirty desperate days she had learned not to underestimate the cruelty and crudity of those who lived and visited beneath this roof.

With a tremble of trepidation, she extended her offended hand to the second man.

Foxworth merely stared at her with faint contempt. "You'll forgive me, madame, if I resist the temptation. I've a fastidious constitution, and find no appetite in sharing another man's meal."

As Buckram's bark of laughter sounded in her ears, Regina felt her perspiration turn to ice. Her gaze shifted through the room to rest on the dowager countess.

Instantly she felt the old woman's hatred reach out to her. Like steel claws gripping her, the woman's indomitable will sought to crush her, to reduce her to a cowering, quivering broken spirit. Instinct urged her to run as far and as fast as her trim legs could carry her, yet she was too shocked to move.

"Come here, gel!" the dowager demanded gruffly in a voice that had been darkened over the decades by the habit of a daily cigar.

She sat on a wing chair drawn up before a roaring fire. The dowager's attire had startled Regina the first time she saw it. Forty years out of fashion, the older woman still wore the powdered wigs, rouge, and robes à la française made fashionable during her youth. Like its wearer, the costume was outrageous, faintly offensive, and evocative of an *ancien régime* with all its autocratic excesses.

As Regina neared the dowager's gaze traveled over her. "You look like death! Faith, I hope you're not sickening. I won't have you idling about beneath my roof with the excuse of illness. Now tell me, gel, have you come to your senses?"

"Yes, ma'am," Regina responded, wishing she could back away from the fire but afraid to show any sign of weakness before so formidable an enemy. "I'm of quite sound mind."

The dowager's lips unfolded from their pinched pleats into a genuine smile. "That's what I wished to hear. Nigel, get the gel a pen. She's ready to sign."

Regina pressed her nails more tightly into her palms but her voice was firm. "I'm sorry to disappoint you, Countess, but I won't sign anything that curtails my position as beneficiary of my husband's will."

The dowager's eyes narrowed until there were only glints of light reflecting through the slits that looked like the eyes of a lizard. "How much?" she said in an unexpectedly mild voice.

"How much?" Regina repeated, stiffening her spine for the onslaught.

"To buy you off. Ha! You didn't expect me to be generous, did you?" Her smile revealed half a dozen teeth and shrunken gums. "I've bought off better-pedigreed sluts than you. Name your price, damn you, and let's have done with this charade!"

The lady's speech astonished Regina. "Aren't you afraid that rumor will follow on the heels of such a transaction?"

"Who would dare cross me?" The dowager turned to Foxworth, and though Regina couldn't see the woman's expression, he took a hurried backward step. When she turned back to Regina, the dowager's expression was as mild as milk. "Come then, pretty, for I'll give you that. You're as pretty as a summer's night with that inky black hair. No doubt some gypsy tumbled one or the other of your grandmothers. 'Tis plain to see why my son went against my wishes to spurn you outright. Still, you might have reached higher, into a marquess's or even a duke's pockets. But marriage, surely, was not your desire."

"You know it wasn't my desire to marry your son. If not for my uncle—"

"Damn him!" the dowager cried, the fury of those two words adding flame to the already smothering atmosphere of the room. "That schemer! That Shylock who would barter his own flesh for gain!" She pounded her chair arm with a gouty fist. "How did he persuade my son to agree to marriage with a convent orphan, that's what I'd like to know! Confound you, answer me!"

As the dowager's anger gained momentum, Regina's

anxieties subsided a fraction. "You would be in a position to know more about that than I, my lady. When my uncle arrived in Italy, the papers of the marriage agreement were already signed by your son. I frankly admit my reason for accepting his proposal. I sought freedom from the cloister to which my uncle had banished me." She met and held the older woman's silvered gaze. "You might ask yourself what your son gained by marrying me."

"Gain? There was no gain!" She leaned forward, the reptilian look coming back into her heavy-lidded eyes. "And there'll be no gain for you, unless you name a reasonable figure. Five hundred pounds would seem to be ample payment for a week's worth of domesticity. Don't you agree?"

A rapping on the door sounded sharply in the room.

"Come in!" the dowager roared impatiently. "You were told we were not to be disturbed," she added as the butler appeared.

"Begging your pardon, my lady, but a Mr. Joshua Gilbert has arrived. He said I was to say that he is here at the request of the Countess of Amesbury."

"He lies! Show him the door!"

Too daunted to correct her, the harassed butler merely glanced resentfully at Regina, who said, "I believe, ma'am, that the gentleman is here to see me."

The dowager pinned Regina with a baleful stare. "Is he? And asking for you by the title of countess!"

Because there seemed nothing to be lost, Regina replied, "It is my lawful title." Quickly she turned to the butler to avoid whatever new terrors might appear on the dowager's face. "Please show Mr. Gilbert in."

"If he sets a foot inside this door, you're fired!" the dowager shrieked at the butler.

Regina slowly turned back to her mother-in-law. She wanted to rail at her, to fall on her knees and ask, "What have I done to you? Why do you hate me so? I don't want your name or money or titles. Keep them! Keep them! Just let me go!" But she knew she mustn't do that. All her life she'd been poor and scorned for her family's poverty by titled people of wealth like the Amesburys. Yet the same capricious fate that had trapped her in a sham of a marriage now dangled before her the possibility of possessing that of which she'd never dared dream. She wouldn't relinquish it to this room of aristocrats who despised and disdained her.

"This is my house," she began, tasting the seldom-sampled, honeyed brew called power. "I may have in it whom I please."

The words filled the room like strokes upon an Oriental gong: brash, full of timbre, and resounding long after their utterance.

The dowager stared at her and, to Regina's utter surprise, a smile played about her sunken mouth. "Who would have believed it? The chit has teeth. You've a deceptive manner, gel. You look for all the world like something too good for the rest of us, more refined, unearthly, and—damn you!—pious. But that green gaze is a traitor to you. That's where your temper shows through, and a certain amount of wit and cunning."

She leaned forward in her chair, her voice coming more softly but with a sinister hiss in its wake. "You're sharp when you would have others believe you a simpleton with meek manners and no spirit. Yet your eyes promise more than you intend. In the end, no doubt, that will be your undoing."

The dowager beckoned to a darkened corner of the room and a man, heretofore unnoticed by Regina, stepped into the light. "The girl ain't breeding," the dowager said to the man, "I've looked on enough to know. But I want proof, physician, and you're here to get it." Her attention swung back to Regina. "Still, if I'm wrong, I've other methods of thwarting you. Haven't I, nephew?"

Buckram stepped forward, confident once more. "I'm at your disposal, as always, Aunt." He smiled smugly at Regina. "'Tis well known how fond I am of my cousin's bride. If she should be found to be breeding, I wouldn't blush to claim the bastard as my indiscretion."

Regina, more wretched than shocked, saw now how a trap was being laid for her. The fact that she wasn't carrying the Amesbury heir wasn't enough to cancel the will, yet her pulse began to quicken. There was something else, something only she knew but that a physician could discover. *She was a virgin.*

According to both church and civil law, an unconsummated marriage was grounds for an annulment. If the dowager learned the truth, she would lose everything.

Regina felt again the treachery of the ever-shifting sands of fortune. It wasn't fair! She deserved something. She would not, could not, concede the dowager countess a shilling!

She turned on Buckram an expression of loathing. "You'd look the fool, cousin, were I to deny your suit in favor of another, less socially acceptable lover. But if you're determined to go against me, then understand that I'm fully capable of any outrage that will make you the laughing-stock of London."

He stared at her as if she had suddenly grown horns, fangs, and a forked tail. His eyes darted to the dowager for direction but she said nothing, only sneered at his predicament. Caught between Scylla and Charybdis, he began to gnaw a corner of his beautifully modeled mouth.

Had she not been quivering inside like so much quince jelly, Regina thought she might have felt a little sorry for him. Even so, she turned her attention to the dowager. She was a foe who wouldn't be so easily vanquished.

"Mr. Gilbert is my personal solicitor whom I have retained to see to my interests. If I cannot receive him in what is legally my own home, then I'll seek residence elsewhere, ma'am, for I'm not yet too far past shame as to put an elderly lady on the street."

There was stunned silence.

Instantly Regina wished she could take back the words, but it was much too late. Buckram's hiss of amazement grated on her lacerated nerves like nails on a slate board yet her gaze remained riveted on the countess.

The dowager countess's complexion turned ashen, the rouge becoming two brilliant coins of color in a gray field. Her eyes became slits, her face contorted into such savagery as to make her almost unrecognizable. The force of her rage drove her to her feet. "You dare threaten to put *me* out of my ancestral home?"

Pointing a gnarled finger at Regina, she said in a dreadful raspy voice, "I will live to see the end of you! I will hunt you, break you! Do you hear me? You will live in fear of me until you lie groveling in the dust! And then, when you beg for mercy, I shall spit on you!"

The dream ended but the words spun on, circling, rising in pitch and volume until they were wild shrieks in Regina's ears.

I will live to see the end of you! I will hunt you, break you! . . . You will live in fear of me until you lie groveling in the dust! And then, when you beg for mercy, I shall spit on you!

With a whimper of fright, Regina jerked awake. She forced her eyes wide to prove to herself that she no longer dreamed, but the night was too black to reveal anything of substance to her sleep-blurred vision.

I will live to see the end of you!

The quote keened in the wind, driving Regina to her feet. Flinging her arms wide, she felt wildly about for the concrete reality of the cottage doorframe, but it was not there. Her desperate fingers clutched empty air. Wind whipped at her skirts, shoving her into the darkness, pushing her into the night. A single thick droplet of rain stung her cheek. Suddenly the wind dropped, as if hushed by an omnipotent hand.

Then she heard it, the distant but discernible sounds of muffled hooves. Something, someone—was it real or nightmare?—was coming across the moor.

I will hunt you, break you!

The nightmare of moments before remained too strongly with Regina for her to resist its mood. She had suspected that she might be followed. The dowager had threatened as much. Perhaps the dowager's man had already discovered her trail. Here, alone in this isolated place, was the perfect scene for murder.

Giving way to fear, she broke into a run, her arms thrust out before her. Wildly, with only one thought in mind, that she must reach the lane and follow it to another cottage and safety, she scrambled blindly across the yard in search of the white road that had seemed nearby in the last hour of evening. Brambles and brush snagged and tore at her gown while the toes of her slippers caught repeatedly in the vines snaking treacherously across her path. The bitter taste of fear lay like iron filings on her tongue, weighing it down so that it was impossible to utter the prayers that came to her mind.

You will live in fear of me until you lie groveling in the dust!

The ground sagged suddenly beneath her feet and Regina screamed as she turned her ankle and fell forward into an icy slick puddle of mud.

Inexplicably, she thought her cry was echoed from a distance in a deeper, gruffer voice. A man's voice!

In a frenzy she scrambled for footing in the weed and slime. Her mother's reminders of the dangers of the moors came back. The lands were pocked with bogs that could suck down a cow or a man in only minutes. Sobbing, the words broke from her despite her fear. "Help me! Please! Help me!"

Miraculously, she found the solid impression of earth beneath her hands. Digging her fingers into the tough mat of grass, she pulled herself free from the ditch. Once she gained her feet she felt the hard-trampled surface of the road beneath her slippers.

Above the moaning wind she heard hoofbeats driving toward her. The horse was on the road, its pace quicker than before. Any moment it would be upon her. Devil or mortal, she believed the rider meant her great harm.

She tried to take a step but pain stabbed down through her ankle, making flight impossible. And then they were upon her so quickly she had no chance to act.

A brilliant blue-white flash cracked open the night at the same moment they came apace. Rider and steed were a great looming black shape against the sky. A cry broke from Regina at the same moment the man reined in his mount with a curse and the horse whinnied in fright. Before the light died, iron-shod hooves pawed the air before her and Regina saw, for the second time that day, what she thought was the last moment of her life.

And then, when you beg for mercy, I shall spit on you!

As the air shook from the violence of the thunderclap, the hooves were eclipsed by the return of night. A moment later she heard a smothered oath as rider and horse stumbled and tumbled.

The horse screamed in pain and its master swore a long

string of oaths in a voice that caught Regina's attention despite her horror of the moment. That roar was familiar to her. Its shout had been directed at her only a few hours before. Yet it seemed impossible. For an instant she stood in abject terror that the nightmare still gripped her.

A second flash of lightning rendered midnight as noon, and in that suspended instant revealed to Regina the sight on the road. The man had gained his footing, the horse struggling to do so as his master pulled on the reins. He was enveloped in a greatcoat, his face obscured by uplifted collar, but the commanding voice urging the horse to its feet was unforgettable.

As midnight descended again, followed by a cannon-shot of sound, Regina took an instinctive step toward him. Pain gripped her ankle, sending a scalding-hot burst of agony upward to her knee, and she cried aloud.

Maxwell swung around at the sound of a woman's cry, squinting in the darkness to find the shape of the lady whom he knew stood nearby. To his utter astonishment, she'd been on the lane the moment before his tumble. "Madame! Madame! Attend me!"

But, not trusting her senses, Regina made no answer. What if she was mistaken, what if a trick of her imagination had lured her into the clutches of her assailant? The Marquess of Ilfracombe would be the very last man to be on the moors on a night like this. Thunder rumbled overhead as she took a step backward, biting down hard on her lower lip to still a cry.

"Who is there, damn you?"

The voice was so insistent that she nearly shouted back childishly "No one!" Instead she turned and fled down the path. But though she was above consideration of it, her ankle was not to be mastered, even by fear. It gave way beneath her after the first step and with a moan of pain she lurched forward, certain that she would fall headfirst onto the lane.

Yet hard hands grasped her from behind, preventing her sprawl, and turned her about.

"No! No! Don't touch me!" Using all that remained of her strength, she kicked out at him, twisting and pulling to break free.

"Be still, you little fool!"

Strong arms enclosed about her, bringing her up against the hard firm warmth of another body. She didn't cease struggling at once, and so he tightened his embrace until she could scarcely breathe. "Miss Willoby," he said more gently.

"I—I . . . Lord Kingsblood?" Regina could scarcely credit her own voice for it sounded so strange in her ears.

His voice was harsh. "Had I known how you would receive me, I've have kept to my bed!"

"Lord Kingsblood," Regina repeated stupidly, staring uselessly into the darkness above her head. And then she reached out to seek proof with her own hands. She felt first the blunt tip of his nose press into the middle of her palm and then her fingers closed over the sculptured line of a cheekbone. His arms tightened about her waist, surprising her with their power, as her fingers slid into the thick hair at his temple.

Suddenly there was a tingling inside her. The hair lifted on her arms, and the top of her head itched as if a thousand ants were swarming over it.

With a roar of surprise, Maxwell shoved her down onto the lane, covering her with his own body.

A shaft of lightning streaked down, its vivid branches digging deeply into the moor in a jagged pattern around them. A shattering crack of thunder rolled with the physical force of a tidal wave over them, shaking the ground and deafened them both.

Terrified, his horse whinnied and jerked the reins from Maxwell's hand. He leaped up in angry surprise but it was too late. His mount had danced away from him and, in the darkness, he could not find him. The sound and fury of the last moments seemed to have rent the sky, for the next instant a deluge of rain poured down upon them. With it, the wind came swooping low and fierce.

"God—dammit!" He bit out the last word with an exclamation of disgust as the clatter of hooves rang on the lane. "Come back, you accursed creature!" He whistled sharply, but to no avail, as the hoofbeats retreated.

Defeated in this, Maxwell turned and bent down over Regina, who lay in the mud. He inhaled a quick breath as a new flash revealed how still she lay. Gently he touched her, smoothing back the black tangle of hair from her face. She was staring up at him, her eyes wide though the rain fell into them, and his heart lurched. Then she blinked.

Fright and fatigue had robbed Regina of full consciousness. Her heart beat with a dull ache. She was aware of pain, more so in her leg. She knew that cold rain pelted her, and that the ground beneath her was hard and slick with mud. But all these things were distant, vague impressions of a reality she no longer felt connected with. The only reasoning left to her told her that Maxwell Kingsblood bent over her and the only emotion stirring within her was anguish. There were things she should say, words that were needed, but she couldn't think of any of them. Darkness came upon her like a silent shadow, and a favor.

Maxwell received the closing of her eyes as a blessing. She had begun to moan and he knew that she was hurt. How badly she was injured he couldn't tell, but he knew he had to move her out of the storm and that the movement would cause her pain.

As carefully as he could, he slid an arm under her shoulders and another under her knees, and lifted her high to cradle her weight against his chest. He waited for the next flash of lightning to show him the way to the cottage, then began to slowly pick his way along the overgrown garden path.

Once he reached the doorway, lightning revealed the interior to his disbelieving eyes. He had listened to the coachman's description but knew enough of the man's state of mind to temper those impressions with reason. Yet in this instance, to Maxwell's consternation, he would say the coachman hadn't been vivid enough in his portrayal of the squalor. A good portion of the roofing was missing and where it ended, rain poured in like a waterfall, flooding the back half of the cottage.

In disgust, he realized that there wasn't a single stick of furniture on which to lay her. There wasn't even a clean spot on the floor. The damp odors of dung and mildew and fetid matter clung in his nostrils. His anger revived as he wondered what had possessed the young woman to come here, let alone remain. Because of her foolish whim they were now both stuck in the ruins of a cottage without fire or comfort and damn little shelter.

Turning away from the sight, his temper was such that, had his horse remained, he would have put her senseless body up before him and ridden through the storm back to Blood Hall. Yet that choice was denied him. He was marooned with an unconscious woman in his arms, a stranger about whom he knew nothing and cared—well, confound it, he would have cared for the comfort of a stray on a night like this one!

The injustice of his predicament fed his anger until his

heart drummed out the measure of his rage. Why had he allowed himself to be dragged into the matter? No doubt she would rail at him in the morning and he would feel every bit as much a jackass as he felt now. She'd tried to run from him on the road. She was mad, and he was just as mad to have meddled in her affairs. For all he knew, she might be dying in his arms at this very moment. What then would he have to show for his good works?

He looked down at her, waiting for a flash to reveal her face, and when it did, what he saw didn't ease his mind. Her eyes, which were closed, appeared as bruises in her alarmingly pale face. A trickle of something dark ran from the corner of her mouth down over the curve of her chin. Whether it was mud or blood he couldn't tell. But she was alive, and the heartbeat where his left hand clasped her tightly over her left breast was steady.

She moaned then and turned her face into his chest, and something quite profound stirred in him as he stood in the darkness holding her.

Once before in his life he'd held a helpless young girl, a child really, in his arms. She had begged for his help, pleaded for mercy, and he had turned his back because her stark vulnerability had frightened him, had made him feel as helpless as she, and that had angered him. He'd been not quite a man himself and afraid to expose any weakness to his friends. Yet there was no one to see him now. And if there had been, none would have dared to criticize the Marquess of Ilfracombe. With that realization, the bright anger in him died.

Very carefully he lowered himself to the floor, uncaring for the mud and muck, about which he decided the less thought given the better, and settled the unconscious woman in his arms onto his lap. He was no longer resentful that he'd come to rescue her. Given the choice he wouldn't

have altered his actions. nor would he desert her now. He
thought again, as he had upon ɪeaving her company in the
coach, that they were somehow connected and that the consequence of that connection would have repercussions in
his life that he could not yet imagine. But, whatever they
were, they would have to wait until morning.

Bracing his shoulder against the wall beside the door, he
prepared himself for the long wait for rescue, or first light.
Beyond the doorway, the autumn storm wore itself out
upon the ancient unyielding expanse of the moors.

Behind closed lids Regina awakened to silence. The night
was as still as a pent-up breath. She lay motionless at first,
fearing that she was dreaming again and that the least
movement would bring new terror. Gradually she became
aware of another heartbeat, just under her ear, and the
warm light stirring of another's breath on her face. Senseless to where she was and what had happened, she stiffened.
The slight movement sent pain ricocheting through her and
she groaned, her eyes flying open.

The first thing she saw in the gray light of dawn was
Maxwell Kingsblood's face just above her. More amazed by
his presence than any phantom from her dreams, she simply stared at him.

Maxwell awakened the moment he felt the lady in his
arms tense. Looking down into her wide green eyes, made
dusky by the dim light, he forgot everything he had thought
he would say to her when she at last awoke. Instead, he
reached inside the collar of her coat for her pulse. The
tender skin of her neck was appealingly warm and, against
all reason, the inviting throb of her pulse persuaded him to
let his fingers linger there.

Regina felt no compunction to speak either. Gazing up
into the glittering dark eyes just inches above hers, it didn't

seem necessary. She didn't think then that they were strangers, or that he was an enemy whom she had never forgotten or forgiven. She thought only that he, for whatever reason, had come looking for her and, more, had saved her life when lightning would have struck her dead. In dazed gratefulness she felt the strength of his arm where it supported her back and the heat of his firm thighs that cradled her hips in his lap. Slowly his fingers curled along the slope of her neck then rose as his thumb branched to bracket her chin in his hand.

The intimacy should have dismayed her. She was aware that propriety was being forsaken but she couldn't resist and saw no reason to try. She was surprised by the tremor of emotion that passed through her as his gentle touch skimmed her cheek then smoothed her brow. A second followed in its wake. By the third she felt moisture on her cheeks. Was she crying or was it raining again? She couldn't tell. Her lips trembled as they tried to form words that would not come.

Looking down into those eyes that revealed every nuance of feeling, Maxwell felt as he had the first time: that he'd never really looked at another human being until he met her leaf-green, too-compelling gaze. Discomfited once again, he looked away but his gaze moved no farther than her trembling lips. Frowning, he moved his fingers to cover this pitiful vulnerability. Her soft lips parted at his touch, her breath shivering over the tip of his thumb. The action sent a quiver of pleasure through him.

He thought of Eloise's kiss, how unsatisfactory it had been, and how in the very act he had wondered what it would be like to kiss this woman. And here she was in his arms, as quiescent as any miracle was ever likely to make her. With his thumb he removed the dark streak at the corner of her mouth, relieved to find that it was mud.

Then he, who was never reckless or impulsive, felt the impelling force of both improper motives as he slowly bent his head and lightly laid his lips upon hers.

The touch of his mouth was not so much a shock as a simple surprise to Regina. His hesitant exploration of her lips lasted but a moment and was gone. Yet in that moment, reason had lost all sway with her. All she could think of was that he had stopped too soon, much too soon. Reaching up, she touched his cheek.

Maxwell needed no further encouragement. There was an urgent flood in his blood quite unlike anything he'd ever experienced. This time, there was no hesitation as his lips slid over hers.

Sighing under the weight of his mouth, Regina instinctively offered back an equal measure of effort. She had never before felt a man's mouth on hers like this. As his lips moved on hers, sweet sensation swept from her tingling mouth to her middle.

The instant Maxwell felt her response, he sought the advantage by parting his lips on hers. Her sigh filled his mouth and then he filled hers with the slow sweep of his tongue.

A dozen new sensations scored through Regina as his tongue moved sinuously in and out between her damp, parted lips. Then he began a delicate licking that made her softly gasp. As his arms tightened about her she felt a hunger in him, tasted tension in the primal rhythm of his stroking tongue, and suddenly, without understanding fully the cause, she was very much afraid of him.

"Please!" She whispered the word urgently when his lips moved to press a kiss in the corner of her mouth.

Maxwell came to reason slowly, regretfully, like a man who was drowning and craved the final ecstasy of unconsciousness. And yet, as he dragged oxygen into his lungs, he had never before felt so alive. He captured her hand where it had risen to his chest. When she tried to pull away, he held it tight. He wanted her to touch him, for her caress to grow bolder. Still holding her hand, he parted the front of his coat and, with two free fingers, gave the fabric of his shirt a vicious tug that tore it open. Then he pressed her palm to the flushed skin over his heart.

"Touch me," he said in a hoarse whisper.

Regina stared up into his dark gaze, black as pitch in the dawn's faint light, and didn't snatch her hand away.

How to tell her his need, he thought a little desperately, in words that wouldn't frighten her? She was unaccustomed to a man's kisses, that much was clear, but it didn't matter. He wanted the feel of her fingers gliding over the planes of his chest. He wanted those slim cool fingers on his back, his belly, his swelling manhood. He knew his thoughts would shock her, send her fleeing from his arms, and so he hid them by lowering his lids so that she wouldn't see the hot surge of passion brought on as her fingers brushed his skin.

The raw aching consumed him. He had received pleasure through a dozen different mistresses' tricks, but at this moment, above all else, he wanted simply to be inside this woman, to fill her with himself until neither knew where she ended and he began. Ignoring the confusion and hesitation in her expression when he once more looked down, he whispered, "Just touch me, lady, and I will only touch you."

Without needing a reply, he sought the curve of her breast beneath the covering of her gown. Even with many layers of clothing, he discovered a womanly full softness and then the hard swelling of a tender nipple under his fingers, and exulted in the proof that she was not indifferent to him.

Regina held her breath as his hand caressed her. She

knew that she should stop him, say no, deny his touch. But the heat of his kneading fingers spread through her clothing, making her breast ache with bliss and shame. What was this glorious, frightening thrall in which this stranger held her? Without conscious thought she began to lightly stroke the hard warmth of his bare chest in answer to his bolder caresses. It came almost as a relief when he kissed her again, distracting her from the stroking of his hand.

Finally, when even he could no longer hold back reason, Maxwell raised his head and removed his hand from her breast, not allowing himself to think of the possibilities he held within his embrace.

He'd been ready for her even before the second kiss was complete. Understanding dawned of what he'd felt in the coach but could not credit: to look at her was to be in rut. He longed to plunge into her, ached to be inside her, to experience her feminine caress, to be shattered by her hands and mouth, to feel, only feel, and then give into that feeling in a long, hot, shooting burst of desire. Yet it was all impossible, every aching moment of it was impossible.

The floor was filthy. He had yet to learn the exact extent of her injuries. They were cold, exhausted, crusted with mud and who knew what else. He couldn't take her there, in the muck and the mire. It would have to wait. But, dear Lord, how was he to wait? And, if he waited, would the moment ever come again?

When he could breathe evenly his gaze dropped to her face. She lay quiescent and trustingly within his embrace, a world of astonished senses in her eyes. An accomplished mistress could not have been more provocative.

With a disagreeable shock, he recalled that she wore a wedding band. She was a married woman! How could he have forgotten? Deep disappointment swept him. No wonder she understood so well how to rouse a man. How easily she had drawn his passion. Where was her spouse—or should he say unfortunate cuckold? Did the poor devil know what sort of tricks his wife got up to when he allowed her to ride about the countryside alone?

He thought again about the possibilities of ignoring the squalor about them but his lust was not sufficient to overcome his distaste. There would be another time.

"I'm certain men have often told you that you are beautiful," he said with rueful allowance for his own vulnerability. "You look especially beautiful at this moment. But I will forget this moment . . . at least, I hope to God I do!" he added darkly as he bent his head to kiss her a last time.

When he lifted his head, Regina said nothing. She had watched in bewilderment the myriad expressions that had glided over his features as he stared down at her, but didn't understand the cause of most of them.

Confusion and shame and a glorious tension in her body were all she had left when he shut his eyes and rested his head back against the wall. After a few long moments, she heard his even breathing deepen and knew that he had fallen asleep.

Chapter Five

❧

In a crushing silence superseded only by the intensity of her discomfort, Regina sat on her trunk, watching as the Marquess of Ilfracombe bandaged her throbbing ankle. He knelt on the ground before her, one knee in the mud that swamped the cottage, the other a prop for her foot. Because his dark head bent over his work, she couldn't see his face. Which was just as well, she supposed, for she was still at a loss to reconstruct the events of the night. Nor was she at all certain she wanted to remember in exact detail the actions that had left every inch of her body aching.

She had never been more shocked in her life than when she had awakened in the marquess's arms a quarter of an hour earlier. She had been dreaming of a handsome man, a lover, who had embraced and kissed her until she was dizzy with joy and strange new sensations as troubling as they were pleasant. To actually find herself in a man's arms had quite appalled her.

Indignation and embarrassment followed quickly upon the first shock and she had started up and out of his arms, only to cry out in pain as her ankle refused to hold her weight. He'd awakened instantly and, realizing her distress, hadn't stopped to explain his presence but had made her sit while he stripped the ruined silk stocking from her leg to examine her ankle. Finding it bruised and swollen, he had opened her trunk and withdrawn one of her favorite petticoats. Without seeking her permission, but with great efficiency, he had torn it up to make strips for a bandage.

"I don't think it's broken, do you?" she asked to take her mind off the very odd feelings that accompanied his familiar handling of her naked ankle. Though he used the gentlest of touches, every movement pained her.

"Not being a physician, I couldn't say with absolute certainty," he answered curtly. "However, I don't think your toe would be twitching quite as freely if it were."

"My . . ." Sure enough, she realized, she'd been nervously tapping her big toe in time to the drip of rainwater from a rafter. She stopped immediately. "It's very good of you to come to my aid, my lord," she said, trying to sound unruffled. "I suppose you must have been caught out in the storm."

He looked up then and this time she noted all those things she had been too rattled to notice before. He was dirtier and more disheveled than he had been the day before after his carriage had overturned. She had thought then that he didn't look exactly like a highwayman. If he had come upon her now, she would have never doubted it. His boldly handsome features were streaked with mud, his dark hair wild and matted, his chin smoky with a new-grown crop of whiskers. Even his dark eyes held secret shadows. With growing trepidation, she searched his expression for some hint of his mood, but what she saw wasn't heartening. Square-chinned and unsmiling, he looked like a man who was keeping a very tight rein on his emotions.

Disappointed that her bemused perusal of his face had not spurred her memory, he said, "Don't you remember my arrival, *Miss* Willoby?"

She shook her head. "I'm afraid not. I remember that there was a storm with quite a bit of light and noise."

One dark brow rose, whether in skepticism or surprise, she could not guess. "What else do you remember, *Miss Willoby?*"

Feeling less and less sure of what she should remember, she said, "Only that a man came here during the night. I now realize it must have been you."

For reasons that she couldn't imagine, his dark eyes blazed suddenly. For a moment he seem to strain against an invisible leash. The effort made his chest rise and fall a little rapidly, then opaque aloofness shuddered down over his gaze like a cat's inner eyelids. "You now know that man was I. Were you expecting someone else?"

"No, of course not." Regina found, in excessive embarrassment, that she could no longer meet his stare. Something was circling at the back of her mind, just out of reach. She frowned as a new thought came to her and looked up out of the gaping doorway. "How did you come here? I don't see your horse."

"That's because he bolted in the storm, damn him!" Looking down once more, he made a simple knot to the ends of his bandage. "There, madame. That's as neat a job as you'll find outside a doctor's care." So saying, he removed her foot from his knee and rose. Looking out toward the lane, he said to himself, "My horse would have gone back to Blood Hall. Why the devil hasn't a servant come looking for me?"

Regina followed his gaze and his thoughts. "It may be difficult to cross that low bridge where the stream runs. After last night's storm, it could well be flooded."

His head swiveled toward her. "Your memory is accurate on some accounts, I see." He towered over her, broad shoulders emphasized by his stance with hands on hips.

Such a pose drew Regina's eyes immediately to the fact that his shirt had been torn open. Her gaze lingered a curious moment on the wide, shallow-rippled planes of his chest. Convent life had ill prepared her for the company of men and, certainly, she had never been near a man without his shirt. In amazement, she noted the threads of dark hair that sprouted from the broad expanse of his chest. Belatedly she snatched her gaze away as some errant thought struggled more insistently in her memory to be recalled.

Sensing that she was, indeed, as muddled-minded as she claimed, Maxwell turned again to the doorway. His gaze ranged over the empty countryside before him as he absently massaged his brow. He, too, had his troubles. His head ached abominably. He thought wistfully of a glass of brandy that might have dulled the edge of his hangover and warmed his sore, aching muscles. Instead, he was stranded in a hovel without even a cup of coffee to dispel the discomforts of a night spent on the damp ground. At least she had had the ease of his body's protection against the cold and mud. While he had had nothing to keep him warm . . . but a few kisses.

Reluctantly he glanced back at her. She sat on her trunk, her hands folded primly in her lap, looking for all the world like a schoolgirl. Her face was smudged with mud and there were lavender crescents beneath her sea-green eyes. Her hair had come down, revealing a long cascade of black silk that any young lady of the *ton* would have clipped into fashionably short ringlets. Yet he was suddenly glad that her luscious black mane had been spared the scissors. It shimmered darkly in the early-morning light, seeming to possess a life of its own.

How innocent she looked, how guileless her pose. Was it possible that she didn't remember what had passed between them in that unreal hour between night and dawn? Well, *he* certainly wasn't going to throw it up to her, not when the memory of holding her in his arms, kissing her until he ached and she whimpered, was still so fresh that even now he felt a pang in his loins just thinking about it.

I'm as randy as a stallion downwind of a mare, he thought in displeasure with himself. When she looked up and caught him looking at her, chagrin made him seek a plausible excuse for his ungentlemanly stare. More experienced than she at hiding his thoughts, he deliberately chose a topic certain to put her at a disadvantage. "I see you've ruined your mantelet and your slippers are in shreds. The devil take it! Women dress foolishly!"

Regina put a self-conscious hand to her hair and then looked down at her mud-slicked clothes. They looked as if she'd sprawled facedown in a ditch. A ditch! Her head snapped up. "We met in the lane last night!"

He nodded curtly, his expression bland but his body alert.

"Oh!" Memory returned swiftly, the nightmare and the foolish fear that had sent her rushing out into the storm. "I remember now. I heard a horseman coming and went out to see who it was, but I twisted my ankle in a ditch." She glanced up at him in pained realization. "I'm sorry, my lord, that I spooked your horse."

She saw that her apology didn't please him. His expression was as remote as the granite tors of the Devonshire moors. Yet there was a tenseness in his superb physique that made her aware that he was as ill at ease as she with their situation. "Is there something else I should remember?"

"No." Maxwell turned abruptly away and took a few steps away from her. A change of subject was in order, he decided. "I'm surprised by your choice of accommodations, madame. It would seem you've chosen a hovel for your sojourn in Devon."

Regina's uncertainty vanished in defense of her home. "The cottage is sound enough. It wants only a little repair."

He turned to her an expression of complete incredulity. "It wants razing! Afterward a new beginning may be made."

"I should never allow that."

"Whyever not? Are you partial to rot and mud?"

The sarcasm found its mark in a way he couldn't possibly have expected. The ugly memory, nearly ten years old, came back to her of a handful of mud the instant before it had been flung in her face. Just as quickly, she shut out the recollection.

Maxwell glanced up again at the empty lane, his face tightening with impatience. "You haven't said what you're doing in this place."

Resenting his high-handed tone, she said briskly, "I don't know that that's any of your business, my lord."

The challenging look he turned on her was nothing compared to the force of his speech. "It is, when I've risked my neck to save your life!"

"I didn't ask to be rescued," she shot back, hoping to match his effortless hauteur though she knew she was being ungracious.

Astonishment replaced rancor in his expression. "What do you intend to do when help arrives?"

Regina lifted her chin. "I shall remain here."

His answering silence was deafening, and insulting, yet when he did finally reply he spoke in an impassive tone. "I doubt, *Miss* Willoby, that you'll find that a comfortable experience."

"Why do you keep referring to me in that odious tone?"

"Odious?"

"Yes. You say 'Miss' as if it were an insult."

A smile appeared on his face but Regina wasn't fooled

into believing that it was meant to be pleasant. "Forgive me, madame, but hard upon the first moments of our acquaintance you led me to believe that you were married. Later you corrected that impression by introducing yourself as *Miss* Willoby. Yet there are things that continue to puzzle me."

She followed the pointed line of his vision to where the gold band on the third finger of her left hand gleamed in the early-morning light. "I see," she said slowly, casting about in her mind for an appropriate explanation. Perhaps the truth was in order. "I am—was married."

"Am—was? Which is it, madame?"

The scorn in his voice underscored the disdain on his face. Shaken, Regina reminded herself that though he might be the Marquess of Ilfracombe, she was the Countess of Amesbury. That made her his equal. Wrapping the title about her flayed pride, she met his skeptical stare. "I am a widow."

"How very convenient for you."

"I beg your pardon?"

But he merely turned away from her. "Keep your secrets, madame. I wash my hands of the matter!"

His last words fell like hailstones on the bell of her temper, setting it pealing with resentment. How could she have forgotten even for a moment just how much she'd always disliked this man? "I don't need nor did I ask for your interference in my life. In my opinion, you accomplished exactly nothing by riding out into the night to rescue me— except, perhaps, to make me lame!"

Maxwell surveyed her with an icy glare. "Madame, you may be certain that I'll never again act on my finer feelings where you are concerned." Turning away, he strode rapidly out of the cottage and into the yard.

The fresh scents of green earth and sea breeze enveloped

him while the wind tugged playfully at his coat and ruffled his hair like an impudent hand. On the horizon the sun shown orange red. A good omen for a day without rain. Overhead a pair of gulls chased one another across the sky. In the nearby brush the last blackcap of the season piped out a lovely song. Any man less stirred by internal strife would have welcomed so pleasant a beginning of a day. But the Marquess of Ilfracombe was not in the frame of mind to more than register with fleeting relief the clear weather as he paced the yard. If one of his men didn't soon arrive, he was determined to set off on foot for Blood Hall rather than spend another minute under that roof with Miss, or rather, Widow Willoby.

He paused at the edge of the road, ostensibly to look toward the northwest, but in his mind's eye he saw nothing but a pair of taunting jade-green eyes. There was something vaguely familiar about her and her name, but his head ached too intensely for him to pursue the matter. Why shouldn't he simply ask her?

Glad to have him out of her sight for the moment, Regina had turned her attention to tidying herself. After all, when rescue came, she didn't want to be found with mud on her face and her hair looking like a bird's nest. Though she felt perfectly awful and was sore in too many places to name, she knew country people and their ways. They would remember their first impression of her ever after, and nothing, not even the title of countess, would erase it from their memories. Yet she couldn't fetch water from the nearby stream to wash properly, nor could she change her gown with the marquess so nearby. The best she could do was change the bertha of her gown, replace her stockings and slippers, and brush her hair.

Looking about, she spied a drip from the rafters that trickled down within inches of where she sat. After removing the soiled bertha that filled in the low neckline of her navy-blue gown, she held it under the drip. When the material was soaked, she scrubbed her cheeks and forehead until all the mud was gone. Next she slipped her mantelet off her shoulders and spread it on the ground to use as a mat. Then, slipping to her knees beside the trunk, she lifted the lid and began to search for clean stockings and slippers.

The sight that met Maxwell's gaze as he reentered the cottage brought him up sharply. Turned away from him, she was bending over her open trunk. He swallowed the question he had been about to ask as his gaze remained on the magnificent curves of her flared hips presented to him by the tight pull of her slim skirt.

As Regina rooted among her belongings she became aware of an expectant silence and looked back over her shoulder to find the marquess standing once more inside the doorway. His gaze raked her from head to toe with such alarming intensity that she felt for the first time how very vulnerable and quite alone she was. Instinctively she reached up to cover her near-naked bosom with both hands, using the mirror she held as added protection.

She saw his gaze move to the mirror and away, and then swerve back to it. "Where did you get that?" He marched over and summarily took the mirror from her. Staring at the ornate design molded into the mirror's back, his dark brows contracted to form a straight line. "Where did you get this, I say?"

"My husband gave it to me," Regina answered, only to realize too late why he had asked. The sterling silver vanity set had been a wedding present, and, as with all the linens, towels, and bed hangings they received, they bore the crest of the Earl of Amesbury.

"Your . . . husband?" Feeling that he'd suddenly become slow-witted, Maxwell traced the crest with his free hand. The heraldry was familiar to him, as were all those of the noble houses in Britain. "This is the Earl of Amesbury's crest. *He* was your husband?"

Reluctantly Regina nodded. The kitten was free of the sack. What else could she do? "Are—were you acquainted with him?"

Acquainted with the most notorious profligate in all of England? Tearing his gaze away from the mirror, Maxwell turned a strange look on her. "Yes, madame, I knew him." He added after a moment's reflection, "But I didn't like him."

"Was his reputation so very black, then?"

Her ingenuously phrased question caught him unprepared, and he'd had enough starts in recent days not to take it politely. "I should say, madame, that his reputation exceeded that of the Prince Regent. Unless, of course, you would wish to make more definitive comparisons with the likes of Don Juan, Casanova, or Bluebeard."

"I wouldn't know, having never heard of such people," she replied innocently. "However, whatever his faults may have been, he was kind to me."

Kind! Maxwell felt the urge to laugh. Harry Lynsdale might have been many things—a drunkard, a seducer of women, a gambler, and inveterate reprobate—but "kind" wasn't an appellation that even Lynsdale would have applied to himself.

Once again his expressive brows dipped low over his dark eyes. He had been in Lynsdale's company only rarely. Not surprisingly, their taste in companionship ran along different lines. He'd scarcely given heed to what London rumor had said about Lynsdale's marriage. There had been a breath of scandal about it, which was nothing new. The name Lynsdale had been synonymous with scandal since the days of George the First. Now he wished he'd paid closer attention.

Snatches of half-forgotten rumor came slowly to mind. The bride was said to be something of a mystery. No one knew exactly who she was. Some said she was of foreign nobility, which came as no great surprise. Not even the title of earl could whiten the blackened Lynsdale name enough for most families to welcome him as a son-in-law. Other rumor claimed the bride was a convent foundling from Italy. The fillip that ran the gossip over the top was the preposterous notion that Lynsdale had married the girl by proxy, without benefit of ever having laid eyes on her. Being a man of some sense, Maxwell had discounted this last as tripe. What man in this day and age would marry a complete stranger?

He bent a hard look on the young woman still on her knees before him. So, this was the Earl of Amesbury's widow. It was difficult to believe that she had married the reprobate, had lived beneath his roof, had shared his bed! Gazing up at him, she seemed the epitome of young innocence, all youth and tender cheeks, all lovely soft mouth and incredibly ingenuous gaze.

Regina rose slowly and gracefully to her feet, and balanced her weight on her good ankle, well aware that the knowledge he now possessed could jeopardize her plans. Yet she chose to ignore that fact. It wasn't yet common knowledge that she had run away. He might not have even heard the rumors sweeping London. "You have every right to be vexed, my lord. Still, we must try to make the best of things. Someone from Blood Hall will be along presently. You will then go home to a hot bath and a good breakfast, and a well-deserved sleep."

Her little speech amused Maxwell. "You sound like a nanny appealing to a child in the hope of eliciting good behavior. I'm surprised that you didn't promise me cookies and cocoa, my lady. It is *lady*, isn't it? The Countess of Amesbury, to be exact?"

He was looking at her as if he expected her to deny it. "Yes, I am the Countess of Amesbury."

He suddenly smiled, and the attractiveness of it struck her as quite exceptional. "Even if you are a countess, that doesn't necessarily signify that you are a lady, does it?" He took a step toward her, the dark light in his eyes kindling as his gaze lowered meaningfully to the generous expanse of young bosom exposed by her gown. "Your manner a few hours past wasn't at all what I would consider ladylike. Don't mistake me, I rather liked it." His smile widened. "If you wish to divert me until rescue arrives, I suggest we continue where we left off. I assure you, you'll have my full attention."

Startled by his new tone, Regina tried to sidestep away from him but a sharp pain scotched the action. "I don't know what you mean," she said quickly, and fanned slender fingers across her bosom. "If you are referring to the fact that we passed the night beneath the same roof—"

"I'm referring to the embraces we shared," he cut in, and stepped closer.

Regina flushed, remembering with trepidation that she had, after all, awakened in his arms. "I don't know what to say in my defense, my lord, except that I was senseless to our—situation until I awoke." But there had been dreams, dreams of being embraced passionately by a man like the marquess. Of course, he couldn't know about her dreams. All the same, as if the day had abruptly warmed, she suddenly felt flushed from head to toe. "I beg your pardon for the liberty of sleeping in your arms."

"That is not all."

"What else?" she asked a little wildly, for he was now within a foot of her.

He reached out and took her by the shoulders. "You've strange manners for a gentlelady. Will you now apologize for the liberty of pressing your kisses on me?"

"I didn't! I couldn't!" she whispered in shock as his hot hands slid up over the slope of her shoulders to the bare skin of her neck.

"Oh, but you did." His voice had deepened, becoming more insistent with every word as his hands rose up to frame her face. She was a married woman, a widow, he reminded himself. There wouldn't be missish airs or maidenly confusion once he'd made his point. "You did that and more, my lady."

His kiss caught her utterly by surprise. The stories the nuns had told of the evils of lust had taught her to expect only violence, humiliation, and defilement at the hands of men. Yet there was nothing repugnant in the warm smooth lips pressed over hers. Too astonished to struggle, she stood perfectly still.

Abruptly his kiss deepened. The heat of his breath came through parted lips, moist and hot against her mouth. The gentle flick of his tongue against her lips made her gasp and then his tongue boldly entered her mouth. The action was shocking and unexpected but, for reasons she couldn't fathom, not altogether unfamiliar. Spurred by a natural curiosity more powerful than any artificial rules of modesty, she allowed him to stroke her lips with his tongue, surprised that his intimate caress pleased her in a way she hadn't known possible until this instant.

Reaching out, she found the strong column of his neck and encircled it with her arms. The nuns had said nothing of this, nothing of the pleasure a kiss could impart. As she gave up to the beguiling sensation of his kisses, she wondered in bemused humor who had been the source of their misinformed tales.

Then it came back, in a wave of realization so strong she did not need to question it. She had been in the marquess's arms before, during the night, and had kissed him as he accused! She had not only welcomed his embraces, she had actively aided them. Shame stung her with a blush from head to toe. How could she have done such a mad thing? Why, she was encouraging him even now. "No, no, Marquess, let me go!"

Maxwell lifted his head but he didn't release her. "Now do you remember?" he said in a heavy voice that betrayed the fact that she was not the only one affected by their embrace.

Regina drew a quick breath. What could she have been thinking of to allow the Marquess of Ilfracombe to kiss her? Snatching her arms from his neck, she turned her head away from his mocking expression. "You're hurting me, my lord."

He looked down at where his hands gripped her. The fabric of her sleeves was puckered where his fingers pressed deeply into her flesh. He released her so quickly she stumbled, forcing her full weight on her sprained ankle. Even as she cried out in pain, he instinctively reached out to steady her, catching her about the waist with one arm.

"Lord Kingsblood! My lord! Where are you, my lord?"

Maxwell turned with relief toward the voice and footsteps approaching the cottage. "In here, coachman!"

"So here you are, my lord. We've been searching these—"

The coachman stopped short and snatched his cap from his head when, peering into the gloomy cottage, he saw that the marquess was not alone but held a woman within his embrace. He took in her tumbled-down hair and soiled gown and then the marquess's disheveled state, and the conclusion he came to was nothing less than shocking. With widening eyes he suddenly recognized her. She was the lady he had sent the marquess to rescue.

"Where the devil have you been!" Maxwell demanded, well aware of the picture they presented but unwilling to react like a schoolboy caught in some mischief.

The coachman's shrewd gaze met the marquess's stare. "I was worried about you, my lord. When your horse returned last night we sent out a search, but the lane was swamped by rain and the bridge was flooded by the stream. We come as soon as we could." He darted a second, worried glance at the limping young lady whom the marquess began helping cross the floor. "Morning, ma'am. I trust you've kept well?"

Regina's cheeks flamed with indignation because the marquess had refused to release her until they reached the trunk and she sat down. "As well as a turned ankle will allow." Suspicion made her add, "I suppose I have you, coachman, to thank for the marquess's presence in my home?"

The servant reddened to his ears. "Well, ma'am, 'twas hard to leave you behind, what with the state of things." He let his eyes roam the cottage, which looked even more wretched than he remembered. "When the storm came on, I felt bound to tell his lordship how things stood with you."

"Perhaps I should be grateful for your interest in my welfare, Mr.—"

"Bassat, ma'am."

"Mr. Bassat, but I'm not. And I'll thank you to refrain from interfering on my behalf in future." She gave the marquess a cursory glance. "Good-bye, my lord. Your gallantry is no longer required."

Maxwell's jaw tightened. He wouldn't be so easily dismissed by her, not when she had just kissed him as if making a promise for the future. "If you could stand, madame, and walk about, perhaps I would be convinced that what you say is true. Otherwise, I must insist that you come with me."

Damn him, she thought, and set her teeth into her lower lip. She would show him. "Very well," she said tightly. With every ounce of strength left in her, she rose to her good foot.

The first step sent pain streaking up her calf from her ankle, but she bit down hard and quickly shifted her weight to her good leg. One step. Two. Three.

"My lord?" the coachman appealed, for plainly the lady was in great distress, but the marquess silenced him with a glare.

Refusing to give up, Regina continued to limp toward the doorway though with every movement the white-hot pain increased until it screamed along her nerves. A wave of nausea swept her and she thought she would be sick. Though she didn't realize it, tears scored down both cheeks.

"Enough!" Maxwell reached forward to catch her weight against his body. "Madame, you needn't torture yourself simply to prove that you are as great a fool as I!"

Regina had no strength left with which to defend herself. Instead, she leaned her head against his shoulder and gave up to bitter tears of pain and mortification.

Maxwell hadn't expected her acquiescence so easily. Frowning suspiciously, he looked down at her. As he did, she exhaled up a weepy sigh and released her lower lip. Immediately blood welled up and streaked in a scarlet rivulet over the fullness of her lip. He knew then how much her defiance had cost her. Disgusted with her, with the situation, but mostly with himself, he turned angrily to his coachman. "You brought my horse?"

"Aye, my lord," the coachman responded respectfully though there was reproach in his gaze. "It's on the lane."

Maxwell lifted Regina into his arms. "Lead on, then."

Tugging on his cap, the coachman stepped out into the yard ahead of the marquess as once more a fatherly concern for the lady overtook him. He didn't like the idea that the lady had come to harm at his master's hands, not when he'd sent his lordship out to rescue her. Still, he supposed that it was none of his business. The marquess was an honorable man. If he had seduced the lady, he would be counted on to look after her.

"Clem, bring his lordship's horse off the lane," he called to the young groomsman who had accompanied him.

Within a few moments, Maxwell had mounted his horse and, with the coachman's help, had lifted Regina up to ride before him. Through all the maneuvering, she was surprisingly silent, but he supposed that she was as worn out as he, and in a good deal more discomfort.

"I'll try to make the journey easy for you," he said in a neutral voice as he secured her to him with a hand about her waist.

"I don't want to leave my cottage."

Maxwell smiled grimly at her words. "I know, madame, but since I have the upper hand for a change, we'll do things my way."

Regina looked up at him, resentment, acute embarrassment, and smoky pain expressed in the green currents of her gaze. "You're a bully," she said so softly only he heard her.

"I know." The vulnerability in her expression made him feel every inch a bully. He fished a wrinkled but clean handkerchief from his pocket and gently wiped away the blood from the corner of her mouth. The rush of protective tenderness sweeping over him was new in his experience.

"What will you tell Lady Eloise?" Regina asked, thinking as women are wont to do about appearances.

Eloise! He'd nearly forgotten about her. What would he say to her? "Why, the truth, of course."

After all, he told himself as he nudged his horse into a walk, Eloise would not have expected any gentleman to act other than he had done under the circumstances.

After a moment's more thought, during which he recalled the stinging sweetness of a kiss, he amended that conclusion. Perhaps he might have done one or two things differently, but Eloise was not likely to learn about that.

Chapter Six

Lady Eloise awoke sluggishly with the impression that she had never fallen fully asleep. But, of course, she had. Several times, as a matter of fact. And each time something had awakened her. For a supposedly quiet country place, north Devon seemed prone to disagreeable experiences and annoying occurrences. As if the sudden onslaught of a middle-of-the-night storm was not enough, with its deafening crashes of thunder and wailing winds, she'd been subjected to other disconcerting interruptions during the night.

Just before midnight, the yowl of cats had brought her fully awake. She detested cats. They made her sneeze and her eyes water. In full pique, she had rung the bell only to have it answered, after an interminable time, by a sleepy servant who claimed there were no cats at Blood Hall. She didn't believe the maid, who appeared to be all of fifteen. She'd heard cats! Why the marquess would allow them beneath his roof she could not fathom, and she mentally added the elimination of all cats to the growing list of changes she planned for this medieval monstrosity her fiancé called home. Satisfied to have found a solution to the matter, she had gone back to bed.

Eloise patted her cheeks, certain that her complexion must have suffered from the night's ordeal. But at least she hadn't begun to sneeze. If the cats had been the last interruption of her rest, she might not now be so vexed. But a little later, just when sleep had claimed her a second time, a new storm announced its arrival with blasts of winds, brilliant spears of lightning, and cannons of thunder. A London-bred girl unaccustomed to the elemental forces of an Atlantic gale, she had lain awake for more than an hour, half expecting the house and everyone in it to be blown into the sea. Over and over she had reminded herself that she was soon to be a marchioness and that marchionesses were never blown into the sea by storms, nor allowed to give in to childish fears. Eventually, when the worst of the storm had spent itself, she had succumbed to sleep once more, only to be awakened a third time by the most disturbing event of all.

In the eerie quiet of the storm's aftermath, she had been startled from sleep by the faint but unmistakable sounds of spurred boots dragging across her bedroom floor. Even as she reached for her candle, her lips pursed in disapproval, she felt no great alarm. Her mother had warned her that the marquess might take the opportunity during their sojourn to press his ardor on her and that she was, under no circumstances, to succumb to his blandishments.

But when the candle's thin flame flickered to light, she had not seen the marquess. A man in the armored breastplate, wide-topped boots, and heavy gauntlets of a soldier stood by her bedside. Weathered and scarred, with gleaming silver eyes and a leering grin, his brutally handsome face had been within inches of hers when she had given up all attempts to preserve her dignity and dissolved into shrieks of fright.

Those screams had brought Dorrity running, minus her slippers and robe, from the adjourning chamber. But when the woman arrived, there was no man to be seen. Still, Eloise had pressed Dorrity to light every candle and search every shadowy corner to make certain of the fact. A servant had been summoned a second time—this time the butler—to aid in the search. Eloise's description of the man who she said had entered her room had brought a strange look to the butler's eyes, yet he'd insisted that such a thing was not possible. No man of that description resided at Blood Hall. He suggested very gently that she must have had a nightmare. Eloise's indignant demand that the marquess be summoned at once had met with the news that the marquess was out for the evening.

Eloise sat up in bed. Out? Where on earth could the marquess have gone on a stormy night? She frowned, something she had been taught never to do because it might spoil her perfect complexion with lines, but the events of the night had provoked her beyond caution. Peering down at the foot of her bed, she saw Dorrity, her ruffled bed cap the only part of her not covered by a patterned quilt. For her own peace of mind, Eloise had demanded that her duenna share her bed for the rest of the night. The foot of it, that is.

Eloise arched her slender spine and caught an outsized yawn in the palm of her right hand. Then, because she was not about to start her morning without her usual cocoa and toast, she playfully prodded Dorrity with her foot. "Wake up, Nana. I'm hungry."

With a groan of protest, the older woman groggily poked her head up from the covers, her nightcap askew. "My—my lady?" She closed her eyes briefly and then widened them deliberately. "Are you all right, my dear?"

"Yes. No! I'm positively miserable!" Eloise flung herself back against the pile of pillows in a show of temper. "This is a beastly house with all manner of rude shocks. I want to return to London immediately. As soon as I've had my cocoa and toast, I shall inform the marquess of the fact!"

Grumbling against the indignities of life, Dorrity Rogers

heaved her stiff and aching body off the foot of her mistress's bed. A poor traveler at the best of times, she had prepared herself before retiring for a deep uninterrupted sleep by taking several generous swigs from the brandy flask she carried for medicinal purposes. However, she had been rudely awakened by Lady Eloise's screams at 3:00 A.M. and then been forced to spend the remainder of the night on the narrow end of her mistress's bed. Not only had she lost a good night's sleep, she felt as if her nightcap were stuffed between her ears. Still, she was not one to complain. She had her duty to perform.

She came to her mistress's side and eyed her in a shrewd and appraising manner, taking in every detail of Lady Eloise's beautiful but unhappy face. With twenty-two years of experience, she knew the lavender crescents beneath the lady's eyes and the ever-so-slightly drawn appearance of her skin were signs of fatigue that would express themselves in peevishness.

Dorrity pursed her lips in consideration. Her ladyship's father had agreed to this journey in the hope that it would induce the marquess to name the wedding date. In doing so, he'd given Dorrity strict instructions to see to it that his daughter behaved in a manner that would allow the marquess to enjoy all her adorable charm and none of her peahen wit. "A delectable dunce" is what Lady Eloise's older brother Charles called his pretty sister. It was Dorrity's duty to make certain that the marquess didn't make a like observation before the wedding day. Things had gotten off to a bad start; it was now up to her to put them to right.

"You best remain abed this morning, my lady," Dorrity began as she smoothed the wrinkles from the bed sheet. "The marquess will forgive your absence at breakfast, considering yesterday's events."

"Oh, no, I must go down eventually," Eloise answered

wistfully. "The marquess mustn't think me a lay-abed. Besides, we've things to discuss. Father says I can't hope to do better than the Marquess of Ilfracombe, and I suppose he's right. After all, the marquess possesses two characteristics I prize most: He is both young and handsome and rich."

"That would make three," Dorrity amended with a mental shake of her head. Lady Eloise had never been very clever with numbers. Yet Dorrity resisted the notion that her mistress was stupid. It was rather that her ladyship possessed a careless mind, which was more than compensated for by her beauty.

Eloise sat up again. "Father says that if I marry the marquess, I need never concern myself with household budgets and dunning creditors."

"There's worse things than bills," Mrs. Rogers answered as she went to drawn back the draperies on the morning sunshine.

She held her own opinion of the marquess. Being an old and valued member of the Lytton household, she felt entirely within her right to judge him. Yet, being a servant, she kept that judgment to herself. For instance, she'd seen the lustful look the marquess had bent on her ladyship after dinner and, later, her ladyship's flushed cheeks as she came to bed. Tall, handsome, and strapping, the marquess was a most imposing specimen. Far too healthy and robust for her ladyship, in Dorrity's opinion. No doubt, her little Eloise would come to the birthing bed within a year of her marriage. It worried Dorrity that in bearing the marquess's sons, certain to be large like their father, Lady Eloise might suffer unduly. How much better was the Earl of Dartmoor suited to her mistress. Tall but slender, handsome but not so bruising as elegant, the earl was by far the better match. If only the earl had been more forward in pressing his suit, they might now be enjoying the warm southern clime of

Torbay, the earl's home, rather than the chilly breath of the north Devonshire coast.

Dorrity glanced back at her mistress, thinking that it might not yet be too late to plant in her ladyship's mind a few objections to the marquess. "Drafty halls, creaking floors . . . 'tis a queer place the marquess calls home. I pray that after the wedding, you'll be able to coax him to spend a bit of his wealth on improvements."

Reminded of the discomforts of the night, Eloise sighed. "The marquess's hospitality leaves a great deal to be desired. I mean to tell him so though I don't know when, for I believe I feel a headache coming on."

"Poor dear," Dorrity said soothingly as she moved to the next set of windows. "I don't doubt you do. Now you just lie quiet while I go and prepare a draught for it."

"That won't be necessary," Eloise replied in a stronger voice as she subsided against the pillows. Dorrity had many sterling accomplishments, but her potions were not among them. "I do so wish to return to London. Why, if we left tomorrow, we'd be back in time for the duke's ball on the twenty-fourth." She sat upright and clapped her hands. "But of course! That is how the marquess may make it up to me for his poor hospitality. If he escorts me to the duke's ball I shall be persuaded to forgive him. Isn't that a wonderful plan, Nana?"

But Dorrity didn't reply. As she opened the drapery of the windows that overlooked the front of the house, the sight that met her sharp gaze had quite reduced her to speechlessness.

Riding up the drive with a pair of servants flanking him was the Marquess of Ilfracombe. But that was not what struck Dorrity dumb. It was the sight of a young female person riding up before the marquess. Though she was swathed from shoulder to ankles in what appeared to be the marquess's greatcoat, there was no mistaking the yard-long inky flood of a woman's hair spilling over the marquess's arm. As the marquess neared the house, she saw that he was quite disheveled. In fact, Dorrity thought, her lips thinning in disapproval, he looked as if he had spent the night carousing!

"Nana, did you hear me? What are you staring at?"

"Nothing, my lady." Dorrity snatched the drapery closed and turned abruptly back to the bed, her plain features perfectly composed but for the brilliant surprise still gleaming in her eyes. "Now, Lady Eloise, you'll be wanting something to warm you. Your toast and cocoa, perhaps? I'll go below and get it. Tsk tsk!" she added quickly when she saw that Eloise was about to climb out of bed. "Now you rest while I do for you, just like when you were still in the nursery."

She hurried toward the door, saying over her shoulder "Not a toe out of bed until you're properly fed. If you don't do as I say, I won't be responsible for your looks or your digestion."

Eloise made a moue. "Very well. I don't suppose the marquess will be in a very good temper himself, having braved the night's storm."

Dorrity paused at the door, her face blank. "How would you know how the marquess spent the night, my dear?"

Eloise smiled. "Don't you remember? The servant we summoned to search for the booted intruder told us that the marquess was absent. I can't think what persuaded him to go out on such a night. Perhaps he was greatly in need of something."

"Looks to me as if he found it!" Dorrity muttered under her breath and hurried into the hall.

Lady Eloise lay for a moment in indecision. She wanted the marquess to know at the soonest possible moment that she intended for him to return her to London. Yet she was reluctant to rise until she had determined exactly which morning gown she should appear in when putting forth her desires. In her experience, there was nothing like the right gown to attract a gentleman's attention and yet distract him enough so that he would agree to anything the wearer might propose. There was the pretty satin with long sleeves that seemed appropriate for the chilly weather. Then there was the green velvet . . .

Eloise's reverie was disturbed by a rustling sound. Suspicious, she sat up and stared at the draperies that Dorrity had opened and then closed. Even as she stared, the bottom of one of the velvet curtains danced out a bit, as if a small creature was behind it.

"A cat!" Eloise cried in a combination of glee and dread. The servants had said there were no cats in Blood Hall, but now she had proof in her very own room. She would capture the animal and present it to the marquess as evidence of his servants' perfidy. Even as she scrambled from the bed, she heard the distinct sound of purring. After donning her wrapper and slippers, she hurried over to the window and snatched open the drape.

More quickly than she could follow, a blur leaped from the floor to the windowsill and, to her astonishment, bounded right through the windowpane! Unable to believe her own eyes, Eloise snatched open the window and leaned out.

Below on the drive she half expected to see the smashed remains of a furry beast. Instead she saw the marquess dismounting from his horse. He was in his shirtsleeves and his greatcoat was about the shoulders of the person who rode before him. Before she could call to him she saw him reach up for his companion, who slid into his arms, and long black hair swung forward to veil the marquess's shoulders.

A spurt of very female jealousy sprung full-blown within Eloise. The marquess's companion was a woman.

Recklessly she leaned out of the window and called down in a carrying voice, "Good morrow, my lord!"

Startled by the unexpected greeting, Maxwell looked up to find his fiancée framed in a window above his head. Several thoughts registered in his tired brain at once: that she was awake earlier than he had expected, that she was the very picture of well-rested contentment while he felt as if he had been dragged backward through brambles, and that the very last person he wanted to explain the last hours to was staring down at him in expectation of just such a recitation.

Thinking quickly, he decided to make the best of the awkward moment. "Good morning, Lady Eloise. I hope you've slept well, for I've brought you company. Miss Willoby has agreed to accept your invitation to visit Blood Hall for a short time."

Regina's delicate black brows flew upward at this great lie. She, too, had looked up at the sound of the voice, and if she could, she would have shrunk instantly to the size of a pea. She needed no mirror but the lady's expression to realize how things must look. "You may put me down, my lord," she said in a carrying voice.

"Why, Miss Willoby? It *is* you!" Lady Eloise's lovely face registered all the surprise of which she was capable as she heard the lady's distinctive accent. "Whatever are you doing in the marquess's arms?"

Stewing, Regina thought in full pique, but the marquess spoke first. "Miss Willoby has turned her ankle. Allow me to bring her inside so that she can be looked after. Later you may question her at your leisure."

To Regina's surprise, the marquess made no attempt to set her on her feet. Instead, his mouth bowed into a smile, the warmth of which was directed at the lady in the window. "Put me down!" she muttered in a tone that made her suggestion more an order than a request. How dare he smile and simper at his fiancée while he held her like a sack of meal!

As if he'd not heard her, Maxwell turned to his coachman. "Bring Miss Willoby's belongings into the hall." So saying, he started toward the entrance to Blood Hall.

"Devil of a situation!" he muttered to himself, thinking that his explanation to Eloise would need to be more thorough now.

"It is no more to my liking than yours," Regina assured him. Hoping to regain a little dignity, she held herself stiffly in his embrace, refusing to lower her aching head to the very tempting comfort of his shoulder.

Throughout the ride to Blood Hall she had repeatedly found herself leaning against him. For a man who she felt deserved nothing but her dislike, distrust, and enmity, he possessed a surprisingly comfortable shoulder. If not for the enduring scrutiny of the coachman and stableboy, she might have made a complete ninny of herself by succumbing totally to the pleasure. Now she had Lady Eloise's presence at Blood Hall to remind her that she should not trust the marquess's largess. He was practically a married man, yet it hadn't prevented him from pressing fervent kisses on her.

Regina suddenly wondered what vivid tales the marquess's stablemen would weave for the rest of the staff about the night she and the marquess had spent alone. No doubt her reputation was about to be shredded beyond repair. It was all the marquess's fault. She hadn't asked him to come to her aid, would not have accepted it had he offered, yet his arrogance had placed her in an intolerable and compromised situation.

As they reached the main entrance Regina suddenly forgot her enmity. It had been more than nine years since she'd last crossed this threshold, but the sight of the vaulted entrance with its crest emblazoned above brought instantly to her mind the last time she'd set foot inside the hall.

Carved in deep relief in the pediment above the door was the legendary dragon and a likeness of Saint George himself, the patron saint of England, riding hard upon the hapless creature. Each year her family, along with half the village of Ilfracombe, had been invited to Blood Hall to participate in the annual Kingsblood celebration of Saint George's feast day. Contrary to popular sentiment, Regina's sympathy had always been for the scaly beast. It was the seemingly unbeatable combination of armored rider and flinty-hooved charger that had prompted her allegiance to the serpent.

Regina found herself smiling as she remembered her own derring-do in which she had transformed the much put-upon creature into a full-color, fire-breathing mythological being worthy of the title dragon. She had been ten years old the last time her family took part in the Kingsblood festival. Using a long-handled broom and a few oils stolen from her nursery easel, she had rouged the stone tongue and gilded the dragon's ashlar back. The task was accomplished so quickly that none of the holiday guests had caught her in the act.

Maxwell glanced down at her, startled to see the stunning smile upon her lips. The smile was vivid, brimming with life, and far too provocative for his peace of mind. "What, madame, so amuses you?"

"Why, nothing, my lord," she answered in a voice he found rich with unuttered laughter.

It was on the tip of Regina's tongue to ask him if Blood Hall still celebrated St. George's feast day, but she knew that to do so would give a little more of herself away. He already knew a great deal too much about her for her peace of mind. An indiscreet word from him might make her flight from London futile.

Keenly aware of the spectacle she made by entering the house in the marquess's arms, Regina glanced about the entry hall and saw servants standing in every doorway. Their avid interest only added fresh reasons for Regina to wish she had insisted upon remaining in her cottage. "It really isn't necessary for you to carry me," she protested more from embarrassment than any real desire to be set down.

"I've seen enough of your attempts to walk for one day," Maxwell said under his breath as he came to a halt in the middle of the entry hall. "Do me the kindness of not creating a scene beneath my roof. There's only so much that can be explained by a sprained ankle."

Regina blushed, remembering her conduct before his coachman and stableboy. "I'm sorry if I've made things difficult for you."

"I've made fool enough of myself without your help," Maxwell temporized. "In any event, we must both contrive to make it appear that nothing untoward has occurred."

Regina didn't ask him what untoward thing he thought had occurred. His kiss was still too easily recalled for her to dare to press the matter between them.

To the accompaniment of starchy rustling, a middle-aged woman with white cap and apron accenting her black gown entered the hall, looking as all housekeepers should: crisp, neat, a little stout, and bustling with efficiency. Two sharp claps of her hand dismissed the gawking servants, and then she came forward.

"My lord." As she dropped a brief curtsey, her eyes slid sidelong to the person in his lordship's arms. She cataloged the young woman's miserable state without comment then said, "You'll be wanting a room for the young lady. Regrettably, my lord, the Chinese Bedroom is the only one in readiness."

"That won't do," Maxwell said flatly. "Ready another."

"Yes, my lord," the housekeeper answered but there was resistance in her tone. "Only there's much in disrepair."

Maxwell frowned but held his temper, knowing that the intemperate expression of his feelings had been the major, if not entire, cause of his present situation. "What of the Blue Room?"

"It's full of mildew, my lord, owing to a leak in the roof that we only just discovered."

"I seem to recall a green bedroom on the third floor."

"The bedsprings have gone. Will, the blacksmith's son, took them into the town to be mended just yesterday."

Maxwell took a deep breath, calling on all his reserves of gentlemanly conduct. "I give up. Perhaps you will be kind enough to tell me the answer to the puzzle."

The housekeeper's expression became long-suffering as she began twisting her fingers in her apron, making whirly-gig pleats in its smooth expanse. "Begging your pardon, my lord, but we weren't expecting another guest. What with the house standing all but empty these last years, well . . ." She spread her hands in a helpless gesture. "I was only after following your orders."

"I'm certain you've done your best," Maxwell answered, fully aware that his orders concerning Blood Hall had been explicit in order to curb expenses for a place he hadn't visited in years.

"What's wrong with the Chinese Room?" Regina asked as a short silence fell.

She saw the marquess and housekeeper exchange looks before he said, "The Chinese Room is uncomfortable."

"It cannot be more uncomfortable than the place where I just spent the night."

Maxwell shot her a warning look from beneath his heavy brows. "Other guests have found it drafty, the heat unreliable, and certain noises discomfiting."

Regina smiled. "The way I feel, I doubt a chorus from Hell itself could awaken me once I fell asleep."

The housekeeper's gasp was clearly audible in the silent hall, further displeasing Maxwell. "Your ill-chosen words are, of course, a coincidence, Miss Willoby, but you should know that more impressionable minds believe that the room is haunted."

"It's true, my lady," the housekeeper interjected. "Begging your pardon, my lord, but even your lady mother, God rest her soul, believed it." She looked again at Regina. "The Chinese Room is a particular favorite of the spirits. That's why we keep it up." Realizing she should show her loyalty to the marquess, she added, "And a very nice room it is, for those who don't mind keeping company with ghosts."

"Well, now you have it on the best authority, Miss Willoby," Maxwell said in a guarded tone. "Blood Hall is haunted."

"In that case, I'll be happy to take the room, if you don't object, my lord," Regina said with challenge bright in her gaze.

Maxwell looked at her, remembering how she had taunted Eloise with the legend of ghosts, and how he'd wanted to both kiss and shake her for the impertinence. Suddenly he was aware that she was in his arms, her face only inches from his, and he found himself wondering how her eyes could be so clear and untroubled a green after all that she had been through.

Distracted, he turned to the housekeeper. "You may pre-

pare the Chinese Room. In the meantime, send up a maid
with hot water and fresh bandages to the library. Miss Willoby has wrenched her ankle, and it needs to be soaked to
relieve the swelling."

"Very well, my lord." After a last speculative glance at
the bedraggled young woman wrapped in his lordship's
greatcoat, the housekeeper dipped a curtsey and left.

As Lord Kingsblood headed for the grand staircase that
led to the first floor, Regina refrained from speaking again.
Instead, she surveyed the beauty of the Jacobean staircase
they mounted, listening to the pleasant creaking of the an-
tique oak treads and observing the fancifully carved statues
on each newel post. Once she'd known the statues by heart:
the soldier, the pirate, the damsel, the courtier, the hunter;
but their familiarity had dimmed with the passage of time.

When they reached the first landing, Maxwell turned
down a long gallery with tall windows and then entered the
room at the end of the hall. It was a Tudor room of dark-
paneled walls yet tall, strategically placed heraldic-glass
and diamond-pane windows enlivened the walls to make
the room seem as airy as a birdcage. The lines of bookshelves and long tables with leather-bound chairs pro-
claimed this to be a library.

Placing her on the nearest leather chair, he said, "I apologize for the delay but so far you've shown yourself to be
more than equal to a little inconvenience."

"I'm equal to any delay that will gain for me a bath and a
clean bed," she assured him.

She expected him to scowl at her but a sardonic smile
lighted his face. The handsomeness of his smile was so unexpected that she nearly smiled back. "You think you're up
to doing battle with my spectral ancestors, do you?"

"Not precisely," she answered, unwrapping herself from
the thick folds of his coat. "I don't know that I believe in

ghosts. I've never seen any, or witnessed evidence of them."
She paused to pluck at the dry crust of mud that coated the
back of one hand. "However, because I'm not averse to the
idea of them, I don't believe they'd begrudge me a peaceful
night's sleep."

"Your fearlessness is to be admired," he answered evenly.
"I only hope you don't frighten easily. Having rescued you
once, I don't relish another stint as knight errant."

She heard the irony in his voice but chose to ignore it.
"My lord, there is a small favor I would ask of you."

Maxwell's features reformed themselves into austere
lines. "Madame, I believe I have served you sufficiently for
one day."

Regina's delicate black brows lifted in question. "As I
recall, I have yet to ask anything of you, Marquess."

The gentle set-down brought a look of amusement to his
features. "Very well, madame. Make your request."

She chose her words carefully. "My request makes no
demands on your time or energies." She looked up at him
in appeal. "I would consider it a kindness if you were not to
correct Lady Eloise's impression that I am Miss Willoby."

"Why?" he demanded, unwilling to make it easy for her
because he was more curious about her than he wanted to
admit.

Regina saw the narrowing of his eyes and wondered how
much she might safely tell him that wouldn't set him deliberately on the path to her ruin. "You're aware of my husband's recent death. I came to Devon in search of solitude.
I would prefer that the world remain in ignorance of my
identity."

His face registered surprise. "Are you in hiding, Countess Lynsdale? Perchance you've run off with the Amesbury
jewels."

"Odious man!" she shot back before she could stop herself. Then, because she couldn't possibly gain his agreement to do as she asked if she antagonized him, she stifled her anger and said in measured tones, "It won't harm anyone if you omit my married name in conversation. Surely you wouldn't deliberately seek to hurt a lady?"

The plea in her voice amazed him until he saw that somber shades had entered the clear green of her eyes. Like cloud shadows on the surface of a stream, he saw anxiety, wariness, and yes, fear enter her gaze. The deeply felt recognition shocked him into nearly reaching out a hand to her. She was afraid, very much afraid. Of what, or whom? He had done nothing to terrorize her. Had the Amesburys threatened her? From what little he knew of them, he wouldn't be surprised to hear it. Or was this just more of her seemingly boundless guile to catch him off guard? The thought jerked him back to reality. How could any woman be so appealingly winsome and yet so enigmatic?

"I never meddle in another's affairs," he began a trifle stiffly, jamming his hands into his pockets to keep from touching her. "I assure you I'm as fond of privacy as you. If it will relieve your mind, I promise not to mention your name or your circumstances to anyone."

"Not even Lady Eloise?"

Maxwell frowned, not liking the idea of keeping secrets from the one person in the world with whom he hoped to share everything. Yet Eloise was bred in a society for which gossip was the cream of life concocted for delight and mild titillation. She would consider the widow the perfect *on dit* for future gossip. She was too naive to realize the implications of having this lady beneath her roof. To be linked with the widowed Countess of Amesbury might well jeopardize Eloise's social status. He didn't like the idea of shielding a lady whom rumor had made a tidy meal of these last weeks, yet silence on his part seemed the only answer. "The matter of your marriage and the subsequent scandal are beyond the bounds of suitable topics for an unmarried lady," he said grimly.

In stunned affront, Regina realized that he'd just labeled her unfit company for his fiancée, as if his own behavior in the past hours had been spotless. "You, sir, are a prude!"

"I am not!" Maxwell said hotly, more angry than if she had accused him of being a seducer and a roué. "However, I suppose I'm unlike the company you usually keep, madame." He let his gaze rake insolently over her low-cut bodice, attracted by the full swelling of her lovely breasts in spite of himself. "Your husband's taste in women always was more . . . careless than mine."

Regina dug her nails into the smooth leather of the chair arms. So, he thought her an unsuitable woman, fit only as grist for the London rumor mill. Well, she wouldn't give him the satisfaction of denying it.

From out of nowhere it seemed a tiny feminine voice whispered the most outrageous set-down in her ear and, without a thought for the consequence, she hurled it at him. "Don't flatter yourself, my lord. If I'd set out to seduce you, you'd not now be boasting of your lucky escape!"

The bold declaration, worthy of the most accomplished courtesan, startled Maxwell out of his usual calm. A sudden overpowering urge to sweep her up in his arms and kiss away her self-possession made him take a step forward. "You try me at your own risk, madame!"

"I intend not to try you at all!" Regina answered, and then, as a hot flush flared up suddenly in his cheeks, she realized that she'd made yet another outrageous statement.

The ebb and flow of emotions in her face kept Maxwell from replying at once. She had insulted him with the brash self-confidence of a king's mistress, yet now she looked as abashed as a schoolgirl. Absurdly, he wanted her as he had never before wanted a woman in his life. Watching the subtle and bold expressions of feeling animate her expression, he doubted if he saw her every day for the rest of his life that he would ever understand her.

As he continued to stare at her, Regina sat in perfect amazement with herself. Never before in her life had she behaved so shockingly. She felt flushed, as if she had run a race. Her hands were clammy and her breath was slightly labored. Mortified and yet defiant, she had never been more exhilarated in her life. Finally, she realized that he was waiting for her to speak. Gathering what remained of her manners she said, "I beg your pardon, Marquess. I spoke in anger. I'll not try your patience again, and you may rest assured that I won't spend more than a single night under your roof."

Only because he didn't want her to have the final word, he said, "If we're to be successful in this farce then I suggest you remove your wedding ring while I see what's keeping the maid." He turned away and headed toward the door.

He thought it was to his credit that he didn't look back as he heard the soft whisper of feminine laughter behind him. Yet he did pause as he felt something brush past him. When he looked over his shoulder he saw only Regina, silent and still, sitting in the chair where he'd left her. From the corner of his eye he thought he caught sight of the hem of a lady's skirts just beyond the library door, but when he stepped into the hall, there was no one there.

Chapter Seven

❧

The captain and his lady stood bending over their unexpected guest who occupied the canopied bed of the Chinese Room. She was sleeping soundly, one arm thrown above her head where a flood of blue-black hair spilled over the edge of her pillow. Her black lashes lay in silky fringes against her cheeks, but a tiny frown of pain contracted her winged brows. The red bruise about the size of a coin on her chin did not obscure the beauty of her face. Beneath the sheet, the supple, curvaceous silhouette of a young woman's body was provocatively outlined.

"What do you think?" the lady asked.

"She's got courage, wit, and as fine a pairs of tits as ever I clamped eyes on!" As if to confirm his assessment, he reached out to lift back the sheet.

"Tsk! Tsk!" His companion hastily snatched the sheet from his hand and rearranged it over the girl. "Lust addles your brain, Captain. That's not what I meant."

"She won't do!" he said decisively. "Damn shame too. Finest pair of limbs I've seen this century!" Much to his delight, he'd been present to view every charming inch of the young woman's slim calves, shapely thighs and hips, surprisingly slender waist, and generous thrust of young breasts on display as the housekeeper helped her bathe before putting her to bed. Being a man of the world, he had dropped in to view Lady Eloise's ablutions the night before, and the comparison had been educational. One was delicate and fragile, the other bursting like ripened fruit with the juices of her femininity. "Maxwell's got taste, after all, but she won't do as marriage goods."

"I disagree." The lady peered into the vulnerable face on the pillow. "She's perfect for him. Perfect!"

The captain shook his head, as if his regret were a personal denial. "She's a widow. Maxwell must have a virgin bride."

"Whyever must he?" she asked in amazement.

"Because a wife who's sampled the fare elsewhere might stray if she finds the second man's meat no equal to the first."

"Vulgar man!" she cried as he chuckled over his joke. When his rowdy laughter subsided, she said, "Was not your second wife a widow?"

"Aye, but she had nothing to complain about, as you well know!"

"Maxwell's your kin. 'Twould not surprise me to learn that he's like you in more ways than not," she said sweetly, never one to shove when a gentle push would do.

"Aye, well, we'll discover the truth of that soon enough. But I'm not so serious a man as young Maxwell. I've a doubt a widow would sit well with him. She might give him great pleasure in the beginning, but he'd soon find himself preoccupied with the business of how to keep her. Jealousy's a serious affliction. Like a worm in an apple, it riddles a man's mind. Where Maxwell loves, he will do so more passionately than wisely."

She turned to look at her captain, quite amazed that such depth of characterization had come from him. By nature he was a man of quick and blunt judgment. Maxwell must have greatly taken his fancy for him to have strung so many words together on his behalf. Even so, she wasn't at all persuaded that he had taken the true measure of the situation. When she had prompted the girl to outrageous speech, she had seen the effect it had had on Maxwell. "If you would deign to appear before midmorning, you'd have seen and heard for yourself how they were together in the library. Maxwell's half in love with her already."

"He's in high rut for her, that's what he is," the captain countered. "I don't need to see the lad tingling with desire to guess his need for her. Can't say that I blame him." His gaze kindled as he looked upon the young lady lying so innocently beneath his regard. "She reminds me of my first mistress. Young she was, though not so young as this. With hair of flame. And sweet pleasing thighs a man—"

"You continue your reverie at your own hazard!" she cut in, having heard quite enough of the women who had preceded her into his life. "Lord, but are all men so randy?"

He grinned at her, that old wicked gleam in his eye. "Aye, the best of us are."

"Pray, don't preen, Captain. It ill becomes a man of your years. Still, what's to be done about her?"

"Nothing. Maxwell could scarcely do better than to exercise his lust on so fetching a piece. Of course, the lad runs the risk of scandal by bringing his mistress under the same roof with his fiancée. But, God, I like a man who's not afraid to hazard everything on a gamble!"

"Just yesterday you said you didn't like Maxwell at all."

"Well, he grows on a body," he answered defensively. "Give the lad a chance, that's what I always say."

"You never say that."

"Well then, I say it now!"

Satisfied to have drawn enough out of the captain for her own purposes, she turned and walked away, the whispering rustle of her wide silk skirts the only sound in the room. As she knew he would, the captain followed her.

When she reached the window, she turned back to him. "As you have pointed out, Maxwell is a serious lad. Though he desires the widow, I won't think he will do anything about that need while Lady Eloise resides beneath this roof."

"There are ways of removing her!"

"There are ways of doing everything," she temporized, for she had much more in mind than simply sending the lady packing for Londontown. "The method must be such that it removes not only the lady but the betrothal."

He lifted a brow. " 'Mischief, thou art afoot!' "

"Don't quote that scribbler to me. My grandmother always said Will was highly overrated, even in his day. Now, to the matter. Maxwell should be suitably wed by the end of the year."

" 'A young man married is a man that's marred.' "

"Enact one more Shakespearean verse, and you will play to a audience of none!"

He bent a flat-iron stare on her as he roared. "The man who's not been properly bedded should never be wedded!" He winked at her. "Quotation, courtesy of yours truly."

"You were ever a horror at verse," she replied saucily, offering him a smile she knew made his loins thicken.

"Aye, But I've other skills, madame." He made her a courtly bow with surprisingly grace. "Ask of me what you will, for I am ever at your service."

She tilted her head back to look full into his storm-gray eyes, her heart beating a little faster as it always did when he looked at her in that way. She'd gotten his compliance on the matter that mattered most, ridding Blood Hall of Lady Eloise. As for the rest, time and human nature would take care of it, perhaps with a gentle nudge or two from her. "Do tell me, Captain, how you propose to end a betrothal."

The captain grinned at her. "A good swift swiving would do the trick, but Maxwell would have hell to pay behind it. So, I'm thinking of how much the lady doth dislike the beasties. And Devon being so full of natural creatures, it should come as no surprise to find one or two of them roaming about Blood Hall."

"Aye," she agreed with a melting glance that fell from his face to his groin. "The hall is fair to bursting with wild things."

His mind instantly erased of thoughts of Maxwell and Lady Eloise, the captain squeezed her hand. "Ah, madame, allow me to show you my favorite."

Yet as they slid easily through the stone walls of the chamber he added in afterthought, "But understand me. The widow's for the lad to bed, not to wed. You're not to tinker with their finer feelings." With a gust of temper that rattled the panes in the windows he finished. *I forbid it!*

"Forbid what?" Regina murmured groggily from the bed, startled out of her sleep.

For a moment she lay dazed and listening, certain a man had spoken to her. Yet when her eyes focused, and she lifted her head to glance about the room, she saw no one. A small but lovely bedroom imaginatively decorated with all manner of Oriental commodes, porcelains, lanterns, rugs, and silk bed hangings met her gaze. The hand-painted Chinese wallpaper depicted delicately branching bamboo with jewel-toned birds perched in its limbs. The faint exotic fragrances of sandalwood and cinnabar wafted in the air. On the tiny black lacquer table beside the bed a cloisonné clock chimed four o'clock. Four o'clock! She had slept for hours.

Regina sat up and glanced to where the windows were heavily shrouded in drapery to keep out the light. Drawing

the drapes had been the housekeeper's last task after she
had put Regina to bed. Regina smiled, remembering how
the older woman had clucked over her, too polite to express
her shock that Regina had no personal maid, but promising
her a scullery maid until a "proper lady's maid" could be
found. Not that it mattered, Regina thought, for she had
better things to do than to lay abed like a lady of luxury.
There was the matter of the cottage to be seen to. Throwing
back the cover, she put her feet on the floor.

But as soon as she stepped down, the sharp reminder of
pain recalled her injured ankle. With a muffled "drat!" she
lay back against the pillows, wondering what she should
do. She looked up at the silk-embroidered bell pull hanging
within easy reach but resisted the urge to use it. A day ago
she'd been alone in the world and perfectly content with
that condition. She might as well get used to looking after
herself again, sore ankle or not.

She glanced at the tray the housekeeper had left for her.
At the time she had been too tired and sore to eat. Now,
when she was hungry, the porridge was a cold gelatinous
lump and the tea was no better than dishwater. As for the
toast, its only useful purpose would be as crumbs for the
birds. Still, if she rang for a servant, she was afraid that
Lord Kingsblood would answer the summons, and that she
most certainly did not want.

The light knock on her door came an instant before the
great oak door swung open and Lady Eloise's golden head
of curls peeked through. "You're awake!" she cried in delight, and slipped inside, closing the door carefully behind
her. She came forward in small swift steps, giving Regina
plenty of time to admire her white muslin gown overlaid
with a knee-length tunic of pale pink velvet. The high-
waisted gown with deep rounded neckline made the most of
the young lady's slender, swanlike neck and flawless straw-

berries-and-cream complexion. Regina was a little daunted to realize that the lady was even more beautiful than she remembered. Beside her, I must appear as dark and ugly as a raven, she thought, and pulled her sheet higher to cover her nakedness.

Unaware of the discomfort her appearance caused, Lady Eloise's delft-blue eyes sparkled with joy and mischief as she neared the bed. "Lord Kingsblood said I shouldn't disturb you until dinnertime but I couldn't resist. Since you're awake, you won't mind if we visit?"

"No, of course not," Regina replied with less graciousness than she should, for with the exception of Lord Kingsblood, Eloise was the last person she wanted to converse with. There were too many things that couldn't easily be explained about her night on the moors with the marquess.

Eyeing Regina speculatively, Eloise said, "You look remarkably well, considering all you've been through."

"All I've been through?" Regina repeated, made even more uneasy by the curious tone in the lady's voice.

"Lord Kingsblood told me all!" Her eyes rounded as she said each word with emphasis. "I can just imagine how you must feel."

"Can you?" Regina responded in a neutral tone.

"Yes! I'd be unbelievably vexed were I to have arrived at our country estate in Somerset and discovered that everything was in disrepair. Though, I must own, after only a night in Devon, I'm not as surprised as I might have been. Having seen Devonshire folk at work at Blood Hall, I can imagine how your servants have allowed your country house to go to rack and ruin."

Amusement thawed a little of Regina's reluctance to speak. What sort of Banbury tale had the marquess foisted off on the lady? The tiny cottage she hoped to call home had never known the administration of a single servant. Feeling that the safest way to continue the conversation was to return the lead of it to Lady Eloise, Regina said, "My country place is only a cottage."

"Lord Kingsblood said it is a charming cottage."

"Did he?" she remarked, a little amazed at this generous description of a place he'd labeled to her face as good only for razing. Why had he deliberately given the impression that she owned a country manor house with servants to act as chaperons . . . unless it was to protect his own good name?

But of course! Indignation pounded through her bruised body, making every tender spot throb. He'd lied to his fiancée because telling her the truth—that they had spent the night alone—would have made him seem unfit for the lady, as he most certainly was!

She rejected on the instant the fleeting notion that his tale had also saved her a great deal of embarrassment and possible public censure. She doubted he'd given her situation a thought as he wove his supple lies. How she'd like to set the lady straight and watch him stew in his own juices. For a farthing she'd do it, if it wouldn't cause the innocent Lady Eloise more hurt than it ever could the hypocritical marquess!

Unaware of Regina's thoughts, Eloise continued in the vein in which she had begun. "I do so like country cottages. Perhaps you'll invite me to visit once you've set things to right." Her face suddenly suffused with the loveliest shade of pink Regina had ever seen. "What rudeness! I shouldn't be inviting myself. Please forgive me. As a matter of fact . . ." She came closer to the head of the bed and leaned near to whisper conspiratorially "I don't expect that I shall remain here long enough to accept your kind invitation, were you to extend it."

"Why not?"

"Well." Eloise glanced back at the door as if she expected someone to be standing there, then turned on Regina an ingenuous smile full of sweet mischief and pretty design. No doubt this coquettish ploy had gotten her her way since she was a child, Regina decided with not a little envy. "After all that's been said, I won't be carrying tales to say that Lord Kingsblood's staff is the most undisciplined and undeferential that I've ever dealt with. He's been away too long, I suppose. Still, he's a marquess and his staff should act in accordance with the consequence of his rank."

She perched lightly on the edge of the bed. "Would you believe it? There were cats scrapping in the hallway last night. Cats! Imagine! And I am allergic to the beasts. I rang for a servant and what do you suppose happened?"

"I can't imagine," Regina answered, beginning to smile.

"The maid said there were no cats in Blood Hall! Can you believe it? She said I must have dreamed them." Her lovely face suddenly transformed itself in the regal hauteur common to all of royal birth. "She might as well have called me a liar!"

"What has Lord Kingsblood to say in the matter?"

Eloise shook her head quickly as though to dislodge a disagreeable thought, making golden curls bob at her brow. Lord Kingsblood had been openly skeptical of her claim, and had laughed outright at her tale of a man in her bedroom. He'd taken her hands and assured her that these figments of her imagination had been stirred up by the taxing events of their journey, and that they wouldn't repeat themselves now that she was settled.

Too proud to admit this gentle set-down, Eloise decided to continue with her story of the cats. "The marquess also said there are no cats in Blood Hall, and that I must have been mistaken. Of course, I told him that he was in no

position to question my judgment when it's been nine years
since he set foot in this medieval pile of stones. Why, I saw
a cat in my room this very morning, just before you arrived!"

Ignoring the last of her speech Regina said, "Are you
sure Lord Kingsblood hasn't visited Blood Hall in nine
years?"

Eloise nodded but there was a faintly puzzled look in her
eyes, for she wasn't sure why this point was important
when cats were the subject of their conversation. "He made
a point of saying so when trying to persuade me to come
with him. He said his last memories of the place had been
disagreeable ones and that he wished to replace them with
those of our first journey together."

"I see." Regina saw a great deal more than she ever intended to tell Lady Eloise. "Did he say what his disagreeable memories consisted of?"

"Oh, no. He wouldn't by so much as a word speak of it."
Eloise leaned close. "The very mention of it seemed to
throw such a melancholy mood over him that I was loath
to mention it again. I suppose it had something to do with a
loss."

"Perhaps it's something less sentimental," Regina offered. "Perhaps it's something he did, something of which
he is ashamed."

Eloise's golden brows soared up her smooth brow. "Oh,
but I can't believe that. Lord Kingsblood is the most honorable, upright, even-handed, even-tempered man I've ever
met."

"Is that so?" Regina looked away, pretending to smooth
a wrinkle. How little the poor lady knew of the man she
meant to marry. "His lordship strikes me as a man of sudden moods and temper."

Eloise's laughter charmed as did the rest of her. "Oh,

Miss Willoby. He's not at all like that. In fact . . ." Her lovely voice dropped to a near whisper. "You will think me a little fast, but sometimes I wish he were more romantic." Her gaze faltered as Regina looked up at her. "He's ever the gentleman. Hardly ever given to, well, romantic professions of love. For instance, he's never ever written me even one line of poetry. Not one line!"

"How ungallant," Regina replied, wondering if the man reserved his romantic excesses for women who couldn't defend themselves.

"He's kissed me twice," Eloise blurted out, then again turned berry-red from chin to brow. "Now you will think me noodle-headed, or morally corrupt, or both!"

"Hardly, Lady Eloise. After all, you are engaged."

"True. I suppose that makes his kisses unexceptional. Yet I do wish that he would avail himself of the more romantic parts of courtship, like sending me flowers every day, or writing love letters full of fine feeling and deep sentiment. I so like love songs where the poor gentleman is near dying for love of his lady fair, don't you? Then, too, I wish he were more fond of dancing and balls."

"He has kissed you," Regina said, wanting to offer some comfort.

Eloise pinkened a third time. "Have you ever been kissed? But of course you haven't," she added hurriedly. "It's not done before one is engaged, I think. I'll share a secret with you." She moistened her pink lips, feeling as if she were about to reveal the deepest secret of her soul. "I don't know that I like kissing. Not as much as I thought I would." Her brows drew together in a puzzled frown as she remembered Lord Kingsblood's lips on hers and the shocking surprise of his tongue touching hers. "I don't know when I'll allow him the liberty again. There was an—oh, excess of feeling in his last."

Regina didn't trust herself to reply without giving in to her own "excess of feeling" where Lord Kingsblood and his kisses were concerned, so she merely nodded.

"Oh, I'm so glad that you came!" Eloise burst out, and impulsively hugged Regina. "I can't talk to Nana about such things, and my friends are all in London. Just a few hours ago I was feeling so lonely. But now, sitting here, exchanging confidences with you, I feel more myself. Say you'll stay, at least until your servants have set your cottage in order."

"I don't know," Regina began, thinking that though it would take masons and thatchers and a gardener more than a week to set things to right, she had vowed not to spend more than one night at Blood Hall. "I wouldn't wish to wear out my welcome, and I should think Lord Kingsblood's tolerance for houseguests is limited. But we shall see," she added hastily as she saw an argument forming on Lady Eloise's lips.

The knock at the door sent both young ladies' startled glances toward it. "Come in," Regina said as Eloise slipped off her bed.

The housekeeper's white mop cap appeared. "You're up then, miss." She pushed open the door with a foot and came forward, carrying a silver tray laden with teapot, sugar and creamer, a dish of finger sandwiches, and another of cakes. "His lordship says we're to keep city hours while he's here." The housekeeper glanced at Regina's untouched breakfast tray. "Being that dinner won't be served until nine of the clock, I surmised you might want a hearty tea."

"Yes, thank you," Regina said enthusiastically as the woman placed the tray on the bed beside her. "Is that Devonshire cream I see?"

The housekeeper nodded proudly. "The very thing. Along with strawberry preserves I put up myself. There's wildflower honey too, if you like. The aviary's produced well this year."

Lady Eloise gazed longingly at the sandwiches but backed up a step, determined not to make a nuisance of herself. "Lord Kingsblood shouldn't take his tea alone."

The housekeeper looked at her with an approving expression. "His lordship said he'd be most pleased if you would join him for tea, Lady Eloise. He's in the great hall."

Eloise sighed. "Good-bye for now, Miss Willoby. I look forward to seeing you at dinner."

Regina merely smiled; she had no intention of sitting through a meal in which she would be placed between Lord Kingsblood and his bride-to-be. She detested the first and quite liked the latter, and couldn't think of anything worse than being a party to their courtship.

When Lady Eloise had gone, Regina tucked into the meal set before her with unladylike relish.

"Will there be anything else, miss?" the housekeeper asked when she had opened the drapery to reveal the autumn beauty of the later afternoon.

"As a matter of fact, there is," Regina answered. "I'm especially fond of this room. In light of what you said this morning, I'm curious to know why ghosts who predate this style of decorating by more than a hundred years would be so fond of it."

The housekeeper looked abashed, the marquess's scolding still fresh in her ears. "I spoke out of turn this morning, miss. I'll be asking you to forgive me, on account of my foolishness."

"That's a fine apology. I will accept it, if you will answer my question."

Her round face stiffened. "His lordship wouldn't like it."

Regina added a generous dollop of Devonshire cream to a portion of scone as she said, "Then we won't tell him!"

The housekeeper smiled, liking the young woman his lordship had rescued from, according to the coachman, the terrors of the previous night's storm. "Very well, miss. Only I'll be after losing my position if his lordship hears of it."

She came closer to the bed. "It was like this, miss. The present marquess's grandfather had a liking for the East Indies. Traveled right around the Horn himself in his younger years and brought back all manner of foreign objects. These porcelain vases, those carpets of heathen design, the fine silk bed hangings, even this little table here, and that one"—she pointed to various pieces in the room—"were part of the great wealth of things he brought back."

"So it was he who furnished this room," Regina said a little disappointedly. She had expected something better.

"Oh, no, miss. The old marquess collected these things to be part of a grand display he planned for the upper salon." Her round face grew more animated. "Only the day the laborers came to hang the wallpaper in the salon, they were met by a man who told them to hang it instead in this room. When the old marquess saw what they'd done, he was furious. Threatened to turn them off without a penny. Still, the men maintained that they'd been given instructions by one of Lord Kingsblood's own relatives. When the old marquess asked them to name the culprit, one of them pointed to the painting hanging in the front hall." Her voice dropped to a bare whisper. "It was that of Captain John Monleigh, the Cromwellian soldier who'd been executed in this very house a hundred years earlier!"

Though she tried to hide it in the folds of her skirts, Regina saw the woman make a hex sign with her fingers to warn off the evil eye. "How do you know so much about the episode?"

" 'Twas my very own father pointed out the picture to the marquess," she answered proudly. "Course his lordship called them cowards and liars to be backing such a tale. Only the very next day, all the furnishings and bric-a-brac the old marquess had collected from the Orient was found in this very room, moved during the night by unseen hands. His lordship had it all removed, but the very next morning it was all back. 'Tis said the business of carting and carrying went on for nearly a week, the servants moving it during the day, ghosts returning it during the night. Finally, unconvinced that he wasn't the butt of a joke, he decided to spend the night in the room to keep watch."

Spellbound by the tale, Regina hung a moment in suspense before saying "What happened?"

The housekeeper smiled. "No one knows for certain because his lordship wouldn't ever say. But the very next morning he set his servants to furnishing the room just as it is now. And no person has seen fit to remove so much as an ivory fan from its place ever since." The housekeeper shrugged but a smile played about her lips. 'Tis said by some that his lordship had the honor of meeting his deceased relative in this room that night and that the captain told him in no uncertain terms what he wanted and how he wanted it done."

"That's quite a tale," Regina said, expelling her pent-up breath. "Yet I don't suppose the present marquess gives it any credence."

"We think well of him here, miss," the housekeeper said warmly, "even if he has been absent these last years."

"I'm certain that you do," Regina answered, annoyed by the housekeeper's defense of her odious master. "Yet he doesn't strike me as the kind to encourage romantic notions."

"I won't be knowing about that, miss, but he's a good and fair master, and a great man. Did you not hear about his most recent speech in the House of Lords?"

"Why, no," Regina answered, surprised to learn that Lord Kingsblood took an interest in such things.

"A fine speech it was, by all accounting, miss. The London gazettes called him a 'man of reason' and 'an intellectual oasis of rationality in a desert of hysteria.' We're that proud of him, miss. Now that he's seen fit to return to us, and him with his fiancée, 'twill only be a matter of time before the house is once again fair to bursting with the laughter and tramping feet of children. And that's as it should be."

Suddenly the scone Regina had been thoughtfully chewing tasted like sawdust. The marquess's children. His and Lady Eloise's. Would they be like he had been as a child, haughty, arrogant, cruel, and merciless? Of course they would be. They'd be peers of the realm, privileged, spoiled, unassailable. Though Lady Eloise and his housekeeper might be full of praise for the man, they didn't know him as she did. She knew the truth about him, and the truth was he was violent, dangerous, and unscrupulous.

"Will there be anything more, miss?"

Regina looked up, her tongue heavy with a mouthful of scone. "Yes." She swallowed, barely able to make the biscuit go down. "Yes. I would like to see the coachman."

"The coachman? Here, miss?"

"Yes!" Regina demanded a little angrily. She wasn't familiar with dealing with servants, but surely a guest could send for whomever she pleased. "I want to see him today, before the sun sets. Isn't that possible?"

"Oh, yes, miss, it's possible, but I don't know what his lordship will say about having the coachman abovestairs."

"It doesn't concern Lord Kingsblood," Regina answered in a peremptory tone.

"Very well, miss." Stung by the young woman's suddenly curt tone, the housekeeper quickly left.

* * *

The coachman had had his wife brush down his best tweed coat, then he'd stopped by the kitchen for a bit of lard with which to polish up his heavy workman's boots. His hair had been parted in the middle and slicked back with water. As he stood before the young lady seated in a chair who had sent for him, he looked as presentable as he had on his wedding day and felt just as nervous. "You sent for me, ma'am?"

"I did." Regina's inclination was to smile at him for she quite liked his easy country manner and speech, but she was very angry with him at the moment. "I believe that I have you to thank for my present circumstance."

A smile of relief broke over the man's weathered face. " 'Twas nothing, ma'am. I own as any man would've done the same."

"I doubt he'd have had the temerity!" Regina snapped, allowing him to see her displeasure. The result was the drooping of his smile into a comical expression of bewilderment. "You overstepped your bounds, Mr. Bassat. You had no right to interfere, particularly after I told you I didn't wish Lord Kingsblood to be informed of my circumstances. If you serve him as poorly as you have me, it's a wonder he keeps you in his employ!"

"Now, ma'am," the coachman began, feeling as if his collar had suddenly constricted about his throat. " 'Twas only your welfare I was thinking of. You're a stranger in these parts. You found yourself without welcome or shelter. How could any sane man have walked away from you without so much as a backward glance?"

He made sense but Regina didn't intend to let him wriggle out of this. "You might have comforted yourself with the thought that you were obeying a lady's wishes. Instead, your meddling has inconvenienced me, the staff at Blood

Hall, and, not the least, your master. Didn't you notice the
state your master was in when you came to our rescue this
morning? His horse threw him in the storm." She saw the
man's face pale but she was not finished with her scolding.
"That is to be laid at your door also. But, be that as it may,
I have found a method by which you may make up to me,
at least, for your meddling."

"How would that be?" the coachman asked, abashed yet
suspicious. When a noble wanted something special it usually meant that he would be put to a great deal of disagreeable labor and inconvenience.

"As I'm in no condition to walk to town myself . . ."
She looked down at her bandaged foot, which had been
propped up on an ottoman before her chair, "and because
you are indirectly responsible for my injury, I charge you
with the task of finding laborers to repair my cottage. I
need masons, thatchers, and a gardener."

"Now, ma'am," the coachman hedged, " 'tis still har-
vesting season. What with the weather taking a nasty turn
yesterday, every able-bodied man will be in the fields these
next days to reap the last of the grain before another
nor'wester blows in. In a week or two, perhaps, I can find
you all the men you'll be wanting. But now, ma'am, well,
there just ain't any to be had."

"That's not my problem," Regina returned smoothly. "It
might have been my problem, had I been left to my own
devices. But you, Mr. Bassat, removed the responsibility
from my hands when you sent Lord Kingsblood out to
rescue me. So, yielding to your opinion at last, I place myself in your care. I must remind you that, because of your
disobedience, I'm an uninvited guest at Blood Hall. I suspect your master will soon begin to wonder when he may be
relieved of my company. I shall tell him that he should

consult with you, that you, for the present, are in charge of the restoration of my home. It's only fair, don't you think?"

What he thought wasn't fit to be said before a lady, the coachman mused sourly. He already knew she was stubborn and contrary and difficult. He hadn't known she possessed a devious mind as well. So, it was to be his fault, was it, if she taxed his lordship's patience beyond all reasonable bounds? He had no reason to hope that she wouldn't do so, not after he'd seen how the marquess behaved after only a brief time in her company. She made a man ache to swat or swive her, and neither choice was one Lord Kingsblood could act on in good conscience.

The coachman turned his cap round and round between his hands, thinking quickly. No matter how great a stew quality folk made of their lives, somehow they always managed to turn the responsibility of it onto someone else, usually someone of lower station. Only Lord Kingsblood was different. He was a man who took responsibility for his actions and treated all parties even-handedly, no matter their status. As such, he owed Lord Kingsblood his best effort. If his lordship wanted the lady out from under his roof, then he would try to achieve that.

Regina had given him a moment to think over her challenge, but now she was anxious that he agree. "Do I have your word that you will help me, Mr. Bassat?"

"Very well, ma'am." He bobbed his head, dislodging a slicked-back lock of hair that sprang forward onto his brow. "I'll do my best but I can't promise the time 'twill take. As for the cost . . ." He let the delicate matter hang.

Regina reached for her reticule, which lay in her lap, and opened it. "Here are ten crowns. That should get things started."

"Oh yes, ma'am, that'll help," he answered as the coins

were dropped into his heavily calloused palm. "I'll seek the marquess's advice about how best to spend them."

"You will do no such thing!" she burst out, startling the man. "What is it about Lord Kingsblood that frightens his staff into groveling at his feet on any and all occasions?"

"We don't grovel, ma'am," the coachman answered stoutly. "The marquess is a wise and knowledgeable man. I've worked for him all his life, and a better manager of property you'd need go far to find."

"How interesting, considering that he hasn't set foot in Devon in nine years," Regina retorted, annoyed beyond reason to have to listen to the man being defended yet again.

"There're reasons why he's absent," the coachman countered, not liking above half that she seemed determined to slight the marquess. "He's a great man, makes speeches of worth in Parliament, and still he keeps abreast of his own. Why, he sent Blood Hall's estate man a new plan for irrigation two years ago that doubled the harvest yield. Was written up in the *Times*."

"He sounds a regular paragon," Regina said tightly. Did every Kingsblood servant read the news? she wondered inconsequentially. "You may go, Mr. Bassat, but I'll expect to hear news of your progress very soon."

"Yes, ma'am." With a nod of his head, he turned, grumbling too low for her to hear how he wished his lordship had left her to drown.

Regina knew she had thrust him into a terrible spot, but at least now he knew how she felt. Softening a little toward him, she said as he reached the door, "I know you did what you thought was right." When he turned to her she added with a smile, "Under other circumstances, I might have done the same. But I'm now a hostage to Lord Kingsblood's hospitality and I don't like being beholden to anyone. Surely you understand that?"

"Yes, ma'am." The coachman did understand pride, and beauty. The lady was a rare one; just her smile made him consider forgiving her her hard words of moments earlier. But before he did that, he knew he should discover just how difficult a task she had set for him. "Evening, ma'am."

When the housekeeper came in a few minutes later, Regina said firmly, "I've decided not to go down for dinner."

"Very well, miss, only I don't know what his lordship will say."

"Tell him my ankle pains me and I'm fatigued by interviews."

"Very well, miss."

When the housekeeper was gone, Regina mused over what she had learned this day. Every person she had talked to had defended Lord Kingsblood, even against his own best interests. It seemed that everyone but she was taken in by his manner. Blind allegiance such as the housekeeper, coachman, and Lady Eloise had for the marquess was a dangerous thing, but she had no desire to embroil herself further in the life of the marquess and his household.

"You've troubles enough of your own," she murmured to herself.

Chapter Eight

The first thing Maxwell noticed when he entered the breakfast room was that his newspaper had arrived. Baked to dry out the ink and pressed to iron out the wrinkles, it lay like a loyal pet beside his plate just as it did every morning in London. The second thing he noticed was even better. He was alone. It was a good omen, an ordinary beginning to an ordinary day. Regularity and predictability were comforts to an orderly mind. If disgruntled feelings still nagged him, he felt certain that a few days of normalcy would rout them.

As he added cream and sugar to the steaming bowl of porridge a silent footman had set before him, he considered his day. In London he always went riding after breakfast. Still a bit stiff from his recent misadventures, he had none-theless decided to have his horse saddled. It would do him and his skittish mount good to travel the moors together in the daylight hours and reestablish their bond.

As coffee, so strong and hot it made clouds before his face in the nippy morning air, was poured for him by a footman, Maxwell felt himself relaxing further. Considering all, the evening before had gone very well. When the house-keeper had announced that Miss Willoby wouldn't be join-ing them for dinner, he had been so relieved that he had scarcely been able to contain expressing it. It seemed she had tired herself out with interviews with both Lady Eloise and his coachman.

Maxwell frowned. He hadn't wanted to seem anxious about the details of either conversation, but when Eloise brought up the subject during dinner, he'd encouraged her to talk. Her assessment of Miss Willoby was that she was thoughtful, tactful, and discerning. In point of fact, she possessed all the traits of a titled lady.

Maxwell's coffee cup paused in midair as a bemused expression came over his handsome face. How clever of Eloise to see through the countess's disguise. It pleased him to think of Eloise as clever. Though he had been reluctant to admit it even to himself, he'd begun to question her wits on more than one occasion.

Amusement lifted the corners of his firm mouth. She had been most charming in her confusion when he'd mentioned at dinner, to impress her, his part in the recent formation of the Second Coalition among Britain, Austria, Russia, and the Ottoman Empire. Thinking that coalitions had something to do with miners, she'd asked why Britain should depend on another country for fuel when there was said to be enough coal in Newcastle to furnish the world.

Maxwell chuckled and sipped his coffee. The more fool he for trying to impress her with things about which she knew nothing. She had defended herself by saying that she never, ever read the news—if one discounted the fashion gazettes. He had agreed that wars and alliances weren't fit conversation for ladies. He would make it up to her by taking her on a tour of his estate in a day or two, especially if the weather held.

Glancing out the window, he looked upon a clear day enveloped in rising mists shot through with golden sunshine. In the distance, the moors were growing brown with the encroaching autumn. He knew from childhood that the wind would be sweet and the apples in the orchard blush and ripe. There would be plenty of chestnuts and walnuts. Shooting would be exceptionally fine now as wild fowl came to sanctuary on the man-made ponds of Blood Hall estate. In a few weeks there would be a great rustic, half-pagan celebration on All Hallows Eve. Perhaps Eloise could be convinced to remain in Devon to attend. She seemed to prize parties above all else.

He sighed, remembering their last, strained words before retiring. She had wanted to return to London for a ball. He had refused. Yet he tried to understand her feelings. As a child, the rhythms and patterns of country life had chafed him too. His London cousins, when they came to visit, had further shamed him into despising all that was good and simple and pleasant about Devon. As a youth, he had wanted nothing so much as to get away. And he had, first to Harrow then to Cambridge. His mother had died when he was nineteen, his father a year later. By then he had an education that made him more than capable of looking after himself and providing for his estate. With the help of wise managers and able workers, his had been one of the few West Country estates to turn a profit while he toiled away in Parliament.

Yet lately he found himself wishing to retire from the noise, clutter, stench, and breakneck pace of London, perhaps permanently. Was it reasonable to hope that Lady Eloise would come to like Devon as well as he realized he did? How could she, if he didn't encourage her to stay and experience it for herself?

"Oh, I didn't think anyone would be about at this hour."

The extraordinarily rich voice broke pleasantly into Maxwell's thoughts. Even before he turned to find the Countess of Amesbury standing in the doorway, he felt an unaccustomed tug in his loins.

Leaning slightly on a cane, she wore a pale-lavender, high-waisted morning gown with puffed sleeves and under-sleeves of white. In the crooks of her elbows she carried a long, narrow cashmere shawl embroidered in a paisley pattern. Her long, shiny black tresses had been caught back and tucked under a simple mop. Feathery wisps of curls, light as smoke, framed her brow. Though her features were a little too pronounced for popular standards of beauty, he couldn't remember ever gazing into a more compelling face.

He had expected her to be less than his memory would make her, but she was far more. Now he realized that she had always been at a disadvantage. The first time they met, she had been frightened out of her wits because he had attacked her coach. At her cottage she had been wet and mud-daubed and in pain. Now after a day and night of rest, she radiated health and a natural beauty made all the more vivid by the light of day.

Masculine admiration, pure and undeniable, quickened his movements as he stood in automatic greeting. "Good morning, *Miss* Willoby."

Regina allowed him the jibe because she was too pleased by her quick recovery to allow him to spoil the pleasure. She had negotiated the stairs with only the aid of an ivory-handled cane that she'd found in her room. Still, she was the intruder, not he. "I didn't expect to find anyone about so early, my lord." She took a backward step. "I'll come back when you've finished your meal."

Maxwell bit back the inclination to say what he truly felt, that he did prefer solitude in the morning and that he detested chatty women at his breakfast table. He had behaved churlishly enough to her on previous occasions to want to make a good impression this time. "Your company is welcomed," he said, and rounded the table to escort her to a chair.

As he came toward her, Regina had a moment to study him. Her first thought, like his, was that she'd never before seen him well groomed. And groomed he was, from his freshly shaved cheeks to the mirrored-surface polish of his Hessians. He was dressed for riding, in fawn breeches, a superbly tailored coat, and flawless linen. Properly dressed, he was a superb example of male nobility. No wonder his household went about in awe of him. Clothes might make most men, but the marquess's fine physique made him fit for adulation.

He was quite extraordinarily handsome she noted, with the dispassionate judgment one woman might reserve for another. Not in any romantic way, of course. There was nothing elegant about his blunt chin, bold broad nose, and high wide forehead. Rather than invoking thoughts of shining knights of perfection, he reminded her of the depictions of Olympian athletes she'd seen on ancient Greek vases in Italy. Girded in loincloths or sometimes naked, their uncompromisingly masculine profiles were boldly rendered, as were their limbs, as they grappled in wrestling holds or sprinted through races.

On impulse, her gaze lowered to his breeches where the outline of long, powerful muscles stretched the fabric. Even as her gaze slipped away from him, imagination formed a scandalous image of what he would look like in a loincloth. The picture, though as scanty as her knowledge of men, was enough to make her cheeks burn.

"I trust you rested well," Maxwell said politely, and offered his arm, "and that your ankle is healing rapidly."

"Yes," she murmured, suddenly shy. The thought struck her that if he were another man, she might have considered seeking his protection from the dowager countess. She felt certain that if he so chose, he'd be her enemy's match. "Do you box, my lord?"

Preoccupied in a search of his own for a topic of conversation, the question took Maxwell by surprise. "Yes, actually. I've been known to spar a few rounds. Why do you ask?"

"No particular reason," she answered.

The scent of sandalwood teased his nostrils as he walked beside her, and Maxwell realized in bemusement that she had absorbed the fragrance of the room in which she had slept. The exotic scent became her, he thought distractedly, and then remembered his manners and pulled out a chair out for her. As she moved to sit down, he noticed the cane she used. "May I ask from where you obtained that cane?"

The sudden change in his voice alerted Regina to the fact that she had done something wrong, but she sat before replying. "It was in a porcelain umbrella stand by the door in the Chinese Room." Looking up into his stricken face, she added, "Is it too valuable for use?"

"No, no, of course not," Maxwell answered, but he couldn't take his eyes off the gilded dragon's head with inlaid eyes of semiprecious stones. As a child, he'd been fascinated by the dragon that reminded him of the one above Blood Hall's lintel, but he'd never dared touch it. Yet after the contempt with which he treated the housekeeper's superstitions, how could he explain that he'd always honored the stipulation that nothing was ever to be removed from the Chinese Room?

"I hope that my use of the cane won't disgruntle your ancestors."

Maxwell smiled ruefully. She had read his very thoughts. "Don't disappoint me, Miss Willoby," he said in his most ironic tone as he took his seat beside her. "After only one night beneath my roof, you can't have been won over by superstition?"

"But of course I have," she returned with an ingenuous smile. "Blood Hall wouldn't be half so charming had legends not sprung up about its history. Such stories are like decorative vines that entwine themselves about the old stones to lend them grace."

"The poetic bent of your mind is to be applauded, Miss Willoby," he replied, impressed despite himself. "Henceforth I shall contrive to consider my ghostly ancestors as decorations."

His smile deepened and Regina felt the warmth of it spread pleasantly through her. No wonder no one else resisted his charm. He made her feel—

At that moment, a footman appeared, bearing on a silver tray a steaming bowl of porridge, which he placed before Regina. She stared at it a moment and then looked up at him. "I would rather have scones and jam, if it's convenient."

"Of course, ma'am." He scooped up the bowl and hurried out.

Regina turned to her host. "I detest porridge above all things."

"So do I," he answered even as he lifted a spoonful of it toward his mouth. Then, realizing what he'd said, he let the spoon drop with a chuckle. "I've hated it for as long as I can remember, but I learned long ago that self-discipline is not usually pleasant."

Regina regarded him skeptically. "If a man of your rank denies himself a breakfast of those things he craves, where does he exercise his appetites?"

Before he could stop himself, Maxwell's gaze shifted from her face to her bosom. His breath caught midway between lungs and nose, and he choked. Raising a hand, he pretended to cough. "Bread crumb," he sputtered after a moment.

The footman reappeared, with a silver coffeepot this time, and as he poured the lady's cup before refilling his master's, Maxwell had a chance to recompose himself.

He wasn't the sort of man to rise in his breeches at the sight of any and every pretty face. His passion, like the rest of his life, had always been directed by propriety. Impatient with his own weakness, he told himself that once she was gone this aching for her would vanish as if it had never been. Yes! The sooner Lady Regina Lynsdale, Countess of Amesbury, was out of his life the better!

The main doors to the breakfast room opened, just as the footman retired, and Lady Eloise entered dressed in a morning gown of red velvet and matching silk turban with an ostrich feather plume. "Oh, there you are," she said as her gaze came to rest on Regina. "I couldn't quite believe it when a servant told me you had come down. I'd hoped you'd breakfast with me in my room." Her eyes shifted to the marquess, who had risen. "Good morning, Marquess."

"Good morning, Lady Eloise. Come and join us. Miss Willoby and I were just having"—his gaze lowered to his bowl—"porridge."

"Yes, do join us," Regina said enthusiastically, for she didn't want to be alone with Lord Kingsblood a moment longer. She reached for the paper beside his plate. "I just came down for the gazette. You may keep the marquess company while I read the news."

Maxwell barely resisted the desire to snatch the gazette from her hands. No one in his household ever read his paper before him. "Yes, why don't you read it before your scones arrive?" he said tightly. "I prefer not to read a paper stuck together with jam spots."

"You appear very well rested, my lord." Eloise tossed a

perfect smile in his direction as she sat down. Almost at once, she popped up with a horrified "Dear Lord!"

Regina and Maxwell said together, "What's wrong!"

Eloise pointed at the picture above the mantel. "That, that painting. But it's horrible! Disgraceful!"

Maxwell glanced up, annoyed to find hanging on the wall the hunting scene that he'd specifically asked the staff to remove before his return. "I'll take care of it," he muttered, reaching for the bell by his place.

Subsiding into her seat, Eloise murmured, "What a horrid thing to place before guests when you expect them to eat!"

Regina gave her a bracing smile. "I agree that it's a poor choice of subject for a dining room but, overall, it is a well-executed painting. Flemish, is it not, Marquess?"

"I believe so," Maxwell answered, his scowl deepening with every moment. "You," he said sharply as a footman appeared with Regina's plate of scones. "Take that picture down. At once!"

The footman's eyes widened as he saw the picture to which the marquess pointed. "I—I took it do-down three d-d-days ago," he stuttered in amazement, and set the tray of scones down so suddenly the little pitcher of cream overturned.

"Don't be a fool, man!" Maxwell rapped out. "Someone's playing a trick on us. Take it down and tell the butler to make firewood of it."

"I wouldn't do that," Regina said quickly, causing three pairs of eyes to light on her. "The painting's too fine to be destroyed. If you wish to be rid of it, Marquess, I'll purchase it from you."

"Why?" he asked ungraciously.

"Because you don't like it, while I, well, I think it deserves a better fate than the kitchen stove."

"That won't be necessary." He looked at the footman. "Remove it to the attic. Tie it to the rafters, if you must, but see to it that the confounded painting remains above-stairs as long as I'm in residence."

"Yes, m'lord." The put-upon footman hurried over to the mantel and lifted the painting from its hook, but the frame was so heavy that he almost toppled over backward when it came free. Struggling under the mighty weight, he just managed to carry it out of the room.

"There now," Maxwell said in a conciliatory voice as he smiled at his fiancée. "The matter is taken care of. Will you have a scone?" He picked up what was to have been Regina's breakfast and placed it before Eloise.

Eloise knew she had behaved childishly and wished to show him that she wasn't all vapors and hysterics, but scones didn't look very appetizing at the moment. Looking up, she spied the newspaper that Regina was just beginning to unfold. "I should like to read the paper first."

"I beg your pardon?" Maxwell replied.

Eloise's pink lips thinned to a narrow line as her blue eyes snapped with displeasure. "I said I would like to read the paper. You aren't the only one, my lord, who wishes to know what is occurring in London in our absence."

Maxwell looked across at Regina who, deliberately, chose that moment to raise the paper to a level that prevented him from catching her eye. "I'm certain Miss Willoby will be happy to share the paper with you," he said with more force than was polite.

Regina lowered the paper and smiled at the lady seated opposite her. "Do you keep abreast of the wars, Lady Eloise? I fear I'm too hen-witted to keep the generals' names straight. If it weren't for Boney—such a dreadful name, don't you think?—I should be rooting for the wrong side half the time."

Eloise smiled, grateful for this alliance. "Oh, yes. I hardly ever keep current with events." She might not know about wars and such but she knew when a gentleman was amused at her expense, as the marquess had been at dinner the night before. She cast a sidelong glance at him through golden lashes. "I think it's most unfeminine to do so, don't you agree, Miss Willoby?"

"Certainly, unless, of course, one has a brother or father or husband engaged in the conflict," Regina suggested.

The thought alarmed Eloise. "You don't think it will come to that, do you? I shouldn't like it above half if London were emptied of all its young gentlemen because of a petty war."

Maxwell had held his tongue long enough. "Petty is hardly the word to describe what may soon become a full-fledged European conflict, Lady Eloise. Bonaparte is determined to fashion an empire for himself and, I assure you, England shan't sit idly by while he attempts to do so. But what do you think, Miss Willoby? You're full of opinion this morning. Surely you have something to say on the matter?"

Having returned to her reading, Regina didn't hear him address her, but finally she realized that all conversation had stopped. Lifting her eyes from the newsprint that had blurred before her vision, she said, "I beg your pardon?"

The pallor of her face startled Maxwell. "What's wrong, Miss Willoby?"

"I—I was reading of a mine cave-in in Scotland." She folded the paper and set it beside her knife.

Maxwell didn't believe her but as he reached for the paper to try to guess the reason for her upset, Lady Eloise said, "May I have the paper, my lord?"

Hiding his annoyance, he passed it to her.

Determined not to be caught out in ignorance of the

world's events twice, Eloise unfolded the paper and began to read.

Maxwell stared at Regina, wondering what had frightened her. She was gazing into her coffee cup and nibbling the inside of her lip, clearly more distressed than he'd ever seen her. He felt again the strange sense that there was much more to know about her than the obvious. She'd said that the scandal following Amesbury's death spurred her penchant for privacy, yet he suspected that there was more to it than that.

Engrossed in the novelty of actually reading a news gazette, Eloise was unaware of the silent drama going on around her. With a tiny frown of disappointment, she realized that the front page contained nothing but columns about Parliament, wars, royal decrees, stocks, revenue reports, agricultural predictions of the current harvest, and shipping discharges. Finally, just as she was about to give up in defeat, she found a bit of gossip on the second page, and she began to read.

"Oh, my!" she said after ingesting the first two sentences, and lowered the paper. "My lord, do you remember the discussion at Lord and Lady Everett's supper the evening before we left London? It centered on the Amesbury scandal."

"I don't," Maxwell lied. His gaze never left Regina so he saw her head lift suddenly.

"You won't credit it but the Amesbury widow has vanished!"

"Has she?" Maxwell murmured, his dark gaze reaching out to snare Regina's wary green one. So, that was what had upset her. "I wonder why that should be news?"

"Don't you remember what Lady Everett said at supper? The rumor had just been verified that the widow had retained legal advisors to help her dispute the dowager countess's claim to the Amesbury estate." Eloise's blue eyes danced merrily as she now had the attention of both her companions. "Lady Everett was of the opinion that the marriage contract between the deceased earl and his bride was fra-fra—"

"Fraudulent?" Maxwell suggested, only to receive the full thrust of Regina's enraged stare.

"Yes," Eloise said, and pinkened because she wasn't very good with long words. "What is frau-fraudulent?"

"It means dishonest," Regina supplied softly. Matching the marquess stare for stare, she held her breath and waited for him to reveal her identity. But though his gaze was questioning and skeptical, he remained silent.

"You'll never guess the rest," Eloise continued in happy ignorance of the turmoil she was causing. "It says here that, fearing that her son's widow has been kidnapped, the Dowager Countess of Amesbury has offered a reward for information leading to her discovery and safe return!"

"That can't be!" Regina murmured, shaken out of her silence by this piece of news, which she hadn't had time to read.

"Oh, yes. There's even a description of her. Let's see . . ."

Maxwell reached out and snatched the paper, tearing it in the process. "Really, Eloise! This isn't a fit subject for the breakfast table!"

The action so surprised both ladies that, to Maxwell's astonishment, Eloise burst into tears while Regina rose to her feet and, in her attempt to flee, overset her chair and dropped her cane.

Maxwell rose, torn as to which lady he should attend to first. He whisked a clean linen handkerchief from his pocket and pressed it on Eloise, saying "I didn't mean to frighten you, dear. Take this. Please don't cry."

Turning away, he moved quickly to scoop up the cane and hand it to Regina. Even as he touched it, the hair lifted on his neck, and he quickly passed it to her.

"Thank you," Regina said stiffly, but her gaze went past him to the torn paper lying on the breakfast table.

Understanding her concern, Maxwell picked up it up and wadded it between his hands. "Nasty business, scandal," he said to no one in particular, and tossed the paper into the unlit fireplace.

Almost at once the paper burst into flame, extracting a cry of surprise from Eloise and a murmured prayer of thanksgiving from Regina. Maxwell simply stared. There must have been live embers there from the night before, he decided, yet the suddenness of the blaze was unusual, to say the least.

Though she was ravenously hungry, Regina turned to her host. "If you will excuse me, my lord, I shall return to my room."

"Are you all right, Miss Willoby?"

The intensity of his scrutiny gave deeper meaning to his polite inquiry, and the genuine concern in his expression disconcerted her. He had acted to protect her. It was the very last thing she'd expected. The realization both elated and disturbed her. Why had he done it?

"I'm fine, my lord," she said, leaving her questions unasked. "If you will get the door for me, I will retire."

Maxwell moved to do as she asked, holding it open to allow her to pass through. As she did, he again caught the faint whiff of sandalwood rising from her skin. The exotic perfume stirred in him the sweet aching that had become a part of being in her company. Unwilling to just let her go, he followed her into the hall, closing the door behind himself.

"A moment, please." He reached out to snare her by the elbow.

Regina turned to him so quickly they nearly touched. His grip on her elbow tightened, steadying her, and the reassurance of his touch made it impossible for her to leave him. Looking up into his handsome face, she suddenly wanted very much to know the reason behind his actions. "Why did you do that?"

He didn't pretend to misunderstand her. "I don't know." While her beseeching gaze demanded nothing less than absolute honesty, he shied away from the real answer. "Perhaps to protect my own privacy."

The gratitude died in her eyes. "Of course."

Regretting his cowardly words, he reached out to her again but she shrank back. "Don't touch me!" she choked out. Her expression became one of such intense dislike that he took a step back. "You may think as little of me as you like," she said tightly, as if each word cost her great effort. "But I won't be fondled by you as if I were a strumpet!"

Her words stung but he refused to withdraw another step. "I meant no disrespect. Forgive me."

She stared at him a moment longer, at what seemed to be a genuine desire to be forgiven reflected in his open expression, but she didn't trust him. "No, Marquess, I don't and won't forgive you."

As she turned away, impulse impelled him forward like a hand shoved against the small of his back, and he trod on the hem of her gown. The action made Regina stumble and she stepped down too hard on her injured ankle. With a gasp of pain, she lurched forward. To keep her from sprawling, he caught her about the waist and pulled her back against his chest to brace her.

"Let go of me!" Regina whispered furiously even though she knew that if he had not saved her, she would have stretched full upon the carpet. She didn't want his comfort, didn't want the warmth of his touch that made her feel that safety lay within his power to give her. This simply could not be. She wouldn't accept it! "Please," she begged without heat, "let me go."

But Maxwell wasn't nearly ready to let her go. He turned her in his arms and then tightened his grip on her waist. "What is this mystery between us?" She thought he sounded almost as desperate as she. "There is something between us, don't deny it." His eyes were nearly black with intensity. "What is it?"

"If you don't know, Marquess, I cannot tell you."

"Cannot, or will not?"

Regina's chin rounded in silent stubbornness.

"Then I shall have to discover it for myself."

She saw his intention reflected in his eyes a scant instant before his lips descended upon hers. Yet his mouth did not engulf hers as it had in past kisses. His lips met hers softly, lingered a moment, and lifted. The action so surprised her that she didn't turn away. And so his lips descended again as his arms slid more firmly about her. This time he caressed only her lower lip, drawing the tender fullness between his to gently suckle it.

Contrary to the gentleness of his touch, her body reacted with a violent response that astonished her. Heat, sweet and liquid, burst forth within her, setting her heart slamming against the walls of her chest. The flick of his tongue against the moist inside of her lip made her gasp as if he had suddenly sucked all the air from the room. With tantalizing languor, he dragged his lips back and forth across hers until she heard him groan softly.

When he lifted his head, his eyes were wide with passion and wonder and challenge. He stared at her, daring her to deny what she had felt and what she knew he felt. With a lowering sense of defeat Regina knew that she could do neither. Instead, she drew together the shreds of her pride to keep from weeping.

"Are you finished with your inquiry?" she asked coolly though the thundering of her heart in her ears nearly drowned out the sound of her own words.

"Not nearly finished, madame!" he answered forcefully, yet released her and stepped back. "But you'd better go up to your room and bolt the door before we both regret where our feelings could so easily lead us."

Regina felt his embrace still enveloping her. It took only a kiss to make her feel things she should not feel for this man, above all others. Afraid to remain in his company, she gathered the folds of her slim skirt in one hand and, turning, hurried away as quickly as her sore ankle would allow.

With every step she took Maxwell wondered where the strength to let her walk away came from. It wasn't as if she were a virgin, timid and shy. She was a married woman, accustomed to a man's embrace. She wouldn't have been frightened witless had he followed her up the stairs and turned the lock on the world. She would have fought him, denied him, but then, he knew from her kiss, she would have surrendered to a pleasure they both might have shared.

"Damnation!" He swung away to face the dining-room door, belatedly reminded of Eloise's presence within. He was trapped in his own household by two very different but temperamental females: one he would marry and one he ached to bed. Why couldn't they be one and the same? "So much for peace and quiet!" he muttered, and thrust open the door.

In the shadow of the stairwell, two figures had watched the entire altercation.

"Cloth-headed fool!"

For Love's Sake Only   157

"You shouldn't have shoved him so hard."

"He would have allowed her to escape!"

"I don't think so," the lady answered consideringly. "I think Maxwell is very much smitten."

"For all the good it does him. I detest hesitation that loses the moment!"

"He's a gentleman," she said in a tone that made it clear that she prized the attribute. "He did protect her from that peahen, Eloise."

"Just so." There was a smile in his grim tone. "Did you not like the manner in which I made a cinder of the gazette?"

"Very impressive, Captain, if a trifle excessive."

"Oh, I am excessive! And what do you call your game of Puss n' Boots with Eloise yesterday morning?"

"How do you know about that?"

He grinned. "I heard the peahen telling Maxwell about it. Since we have no cats, I surmised the rest."

She shrugged. "I thought she would behave as a jealous woman but she actually likes Lady Amesbury. There can't be a female bone in her body!"

The force of the captain's laughter echoed like far away thunder up the stairwell. "You'd have made a strong ally. Intrigue suits you. As for *your* candidate for Maxwell's heart, you must see that she's entirely unsuitable. A bold adventuress. God's body, but there are times when I wish I were flesh and blood again!"

He didn't see it coming but he felt the pain of a hard little fist against his ear. "Ouch! There's no call for violence!"

She didn't answer him but slipped away so quickly that he missed seeing which direction she took. A maid appeared in the back of the hall, her arms piled with dusty furniture covers. As she crossed the corridor, a brisk breeze blew past her, sending a cloud of dust and cobwebs spinning into the air. The maid yelped in alarm and then lost her burden as a fit of sneezing overtook her.

The captain smiled and took off in pursuit. He passed the maid just as she bent to reclaim her laundry, and gave her a swift smack on the behind. As she yelped in surprise a second time, he slipped through the west wall, headed for the rose garden.

Chapter Nine

R egina paced the Chinese Room in a rare state of agitation. She was no nearer reaching a decision about her future than she had been three days ago when she left Lord Kingsblood and his lady at the breakfast table. Feigning a greater degree of discomfort that she actually felt, she had since kept to her bedroom, even for meals. Except for Lady Eloise's daily visits, she'd been isolated from the rest of the household. Now her patience was at an end. Boredom had rubbed her nerves raw. She couldn't hide forever, but what was she to do?

One thing was certain, she had to leave Blood Hall where even the housekeeper and coachman kept up with the news. Surely it was only a matter of time before the ransom notice appeared in the papers again, and when it did, someone in this household might read it. If only she hadn't lost her composure upon spying the article, she might have read the description herself and known how likely it was she would be recognized.

"Damn!" she swore as her ankle twinged in response to a swift turn. She had suspected that the dowager countess wouldn't simply allow her to leave London, but not that the lady would make headline news of her search for her daughter-in-law. Such a thing had never been done before. Ladies' names were never, ever mentioned in gazettes. But her name had been printed, with her description, and a ransom offered for her return.

Regina's laugh was mirthless. The dowager was more fiendish than she had ever imagined. The ransom was nothing more than a bounty set upon her head as if she were a common thief!

I will hound you! I will find and break you! And when you lie groveling at my feet, begging for mercy, I will spit on you!

The old terror came swooping back on her. The dowager hoped to run her to ground. Indeed, she felt like a fox with the distant sound of baying hounds in her ears. She could almost feel the teeth of scandal and disaster at her throat.

The churning in her stomach became so painful she balled her hands into fists and pressed them to her middle. She had never intended to keep the entire Amesbury estate, until the dowager threatened and insulted her. She regretted the momentary but very natural anger that had driven her to make counterthreats. She had hoped when she left London that time and distance would cool both the dowager's temper and hers. Now she knew she had made a dangerous and unforgiving enemy.

That thought brought her up sharply before a window and she paused to look out. Suddenly she knew she had to get out of the confines of Blood Hall or she would go mad.

She quickly exchanged her slippers for a pair of heavy walking shoes, tied her bonnet securely under her chin, and picked up the walking cane. With no clear direction in mind, she took the servants' stairs to the first floor and then went out through the back entrance. With surprising ease, she slipped out of the gate at the back of the kitchen garden and onto the path that led to the moors.

The day was sunny but a stiff breeze from the sea reminded her that autumn held sway in the countryside. As she hurried on, clutching her paisley shawl closely about

her, she breathed in deeply the clean, refreshing scents of
grass, gorse, and bramble.

She didn't know how long she'd walked or how far but,
finally, she topped a rise of humpbacked cliffs and caught
her first glimpse of the sea. Inspired by the sight, she
quickly gained the summit and then hurried down to the
edge of the cliff to look out over the bay.

Far below her, long breakers, gray green and white-
foamed, rolled toward the shore with a mesmerizing
rhythm more ancient than life itself. Curlews circled in the
mists rising up from the jagged shoreline. From the crags
towering behind her, she heard the occasional bleat of a
canny-footed goat. Each crash of wave upon the shore
pounded at the chains of fear and indecision that held her
shackled until, after several minutes, she felt an easing and
quieting of her spirit. As the breeze roared in her ears and
tugged at her skirts, it blew away the gnawing indecision
that had plagued her for days.

This is where she belonged. This was her home. No matter what happened, no one could take this away from her.
Air and sea and sky, they all belonged to any creature lucky
enough to reside here. Not the Dowager Countess of Amesbury nor King George himself could deny her the simple
pleasure of spending the rest of her days on this wild north
Devon shore.

She didn't hear the horse and rider until they were nearly
upon her. And when she did, she turned reluctantly from
the sight of the foaming surf below. The horseman was
following the shoreline lane at a cantor. Though she wasn't
a horsewoman she knew at once that he was a superb rider.
Man and animal moved together in perfect synchronization. They didn't seem out of place in this wild setting, nor
an interruption to her solitude.

She recognized him before he recognized her. When he

did, he pulled his mount up short and then came riding
toward her.

"Countess!" Maxwell called as he reached her, too surprised by her presence on the cliffs to realize that he used
her married title. "You're the last person I expected to encounter."

"Good day, Marquess," Regina returned evenly, relieved
that he had not been looking for her. The wind whipped his
chestnut hair into his eyes and a slight sheen of perspiration
slicked his tanned cheeks. "I trust you've had a good ride?"

"I have," Maxwell answered from the saddle. Exercise
always did wonders for his spirit. No doubt, she had sought
the same form of release. He looked about the empty
moors. "Where is your pony cart?"

"I don't have one."

The look of incredulity on his face made her smile. She
lifted her elegant cane and pointed at her toe to show off
her heavy-soled shoes. "I'm an excellent walker."

"But your ankle?"

Enjoying his amazement hugely, she smiled. "Since I am
not a horse, and cannot be shot for an injury, I thought I'd
better exercise the soreness out of it. As you can see, I've
come a long way on my own."

"I do see." He saw a great many other things, too, like
the fact that her cheeks were pink from the wind and that
beneath her bonnet her black hair had come undone and
streamed in long, silky pennants behind her. The brisk
wind molded her slim-skirted gown to her figure, revealing
the full curves of her breasts and accenting the shapely
silhouette of her slim legs.

Once again he was acutely aware of the emotional turmoil that had sent him pounding across the moors at a full
gallop. Another frustrating encounter with Eloise the night
before had left him restless and troubled when he awak-

ened. She didn't like his embraces. The thought still amazed him. His bride-to-be, the would-be mother of his children, had all but admitted she didn't like his kisses. He had hoped to learn many things about Eloise, but *that* was certainly not one of them! Nor did he appreciate her unsupported claims that, for three nights running, she had been plagued by the yowling of cats. No one else heard them, not even Mrs. Rogers. Reluctantly he had come to the conclusion that she was making up tales in an effort to force him to take her back to London.

Belatedly he realized that the countess was watching him with a clear interest in his thoughts. She appeared to have forgotten their turbulent encounter of three days ago, and for that he was grateful. "I'd forgotten until my return what a pleasure it is to ride for miles with only the wind and moors for company. Do you ride, Countess?"

The use of her title made Regina uneasy, but she didn't see any mockery in his expression as he continued to gaze down at her from his saddle. "No, my lord."

"Then I should be honored to teach you," he answered as if his offer were the most natural thing in the world.

But Regina, all too aware of how strained their relationship had been, could not refrain from saying "There's no need for false civility, Lord Kingsblood. You don't even like me."

"Don't I?" His expression was mildly quizzical. "Whyever would you say that?" His dark eyes suddenly warmed with good humor. "Could it be because I've held you at gunpoint, commandeered your vehicle, and more than once abused your delicate ears with my immoderate voice? Have you not heard that I make the acquaintance of all beautiful ladies in such a manner?"

The absurdity of his speech made her chuckle. "You are the most singular individual I've ever met, Marquess."

Maxwell grinned down at her, pleased to have provoked something from her besides anger, insult, or wariness. She had a most beautiful smile. He wanted it to remain. "Diplomacy is my *métier*, Countess. I'm a fair hand with a rod and reel as well. When the spring comes, I intend to catch my breakfast every morning for a week."

"You fish?" Now it was her turn for incredulity. With the broad shoulders of his riding coat dusted with dirt and his long-muscled legs flexed in the stirrups, he seemed too vigorous a man to find pleasure in the quiet, thoughtful patience required to be a successful fisherman.

"Contrary to appearances, I appreciate the virtues of tranquility," he said as if he had read her thoughts.

He dismounted to stand beside her then turned to stare out over the sea as she had been doing when he first saw her in the distance. He didn't have to ask her why she had come here. The beauty of the day was answer enough. Finally he turned to her and saw that she hadn't been looking out as he had but was watching him with eyes more changeable than the ocean below them. Unlike Eloise, there was a directness in her that defied a man's calculation.

"Do you realize, Countess, that this is our first encounter where one of us is not in desperate straits?"

"I am aware that this is our first encounter out-of-doors when neither of us is wet, furious, or bedraggled," she returned smoothly. "You scrub up well, my lord."

The words came out without thinking, and the sudden gleam of his dark eyes made her cheek sting. But he only said, "Thank you, Countess. You, on the other hand, look well in everything, even mud."

We're flirting, she thought in faint alarm that brought a deeper shade of rose to her cheeks.

Maxwell watched the play of emotions give vivid animation to her expression, and found himself thinking that she was more fascinating than even the sea. Refreshing, that was the word that came to mind when he looked at her. The same day her name had appeared in the gazette, he had sent inquiry to London to learn all he could about her. As yet there was no reply. Rumor painted her character with the vilest of colors. Yet nothing of the hard schemer, the practiced seductress, or the shrewd woman of the world marred her expression. How could she be all that gossip claimed and look as innocent as she did in moments like this?

His lips began to tingle with the remembered passion of her kiss. He was attracted to her and, despite everything she said, he knew she returned the interest. He couldn't blame her for being wary. Only the most jaded of women would not be daunted by the fact that she and his fiancée shared the same roof. Yet a quiet conviction came over him that what he had told her three days earlier, in the heat of the moment, still held true amid the serenity of their surroundings. An unspoken bond lay between them. He felt its tug even now. Yet he too was wary. The question that had been circling at the back of his mind for three days soared to the fore. Did he really want to discover what drew him to her? And if he did, at what price?

Regina bore the scrutiny of his intelligent dark gaze without turning away but, hidden in the folds of her skirt, she flexed her fingers repeatedly. For all the good it did her, she might read a thousand things into his enigmatic expression, or nothing at all. The last time he had looked at her in this way, which made her heart pound irregularly, he had kissed her. Would he do so again?

Unaware of her expectations, Maxwell turned from her, his voice made husky by his reflections as he said, "I've been by your cottage this morning, Countess, and was amazed to find a team of workmen on the job. More surprising, I discovered that my coachman is in charge of the brigade." He turned his head to slant a look down at her. "You seem capable of contriving every sort of miracle when you put your mind to it. I'm only grateful that there are still men left in my fields to see to the last of the harvest."

His words struck in Regina a pang of conscience. "I didn't mean for men to desert your fields in order to work for me."

"Unlike my coachman, whom you commissioned without my knowledge?"

She was plainly in the wrong and she knew it. "I didn't think he would neglect his duties to you to do so. I will speak to him."

"I already have," he answered with such gravity that Regina's eyes widened.

"You didn't discharge him?"

Unable to maintain his severity against such appealing distress, Maxwell smiled at her. "I did not. I gave him the rest of the week to find another foreman for the project. And, so you will stop looking at me with such alarm, I'll tell you that your men are fishermen from Ilfracombe who are grateful for the employment. We lost our fishing fleet three years ago when the damned French sailed into our harbor and sank everything in sight. Recovery has been slow, with Barnstaple and Bideford hard on our heels to win our sea trade."

The genuine concern in his tone surprised her. He sounded like the soberest of peers, concerned for his people as well as his estates. "I'm amazed that you keep abreast of country matters."

He nodded pleasantly despite the skepticism in her voice. "A starving family makes a man discontent. There've been rumors of renewed smuggling along the coast. As God is my witness, I don't blame the men above half, yet I can't condone lawlessness. My plan is to introduce new industry into the area. Sheep do well on the moors but they don't require the manpower that fishing does, and men must have jobs. Since ancient times there's been some mining in these parts. I've a man checking my land, and I intend to reopen the Kingsblood mines if his report supports my design."

"So many plans," Regina said, impressed. "Yet how do you intend to carry out your projects here with a new wife and your commitments in Parliament?"

"You seem amazingly well informed about my activities, Countess," he said blandly.

"Your staff is very loyal, and amazingly well informed. They read the gazettes with more relish than . . ." Regina snapped her mouth shut because Lady Eloise was the last person she wanted to criticize to him.

He smiled at her, secretly pleased that she had cared enough to learn so much about him. "Lady Eloise does seem to have an—um, allergy to news, doesn't she?"

"She is young and very beautiful, my lord," she answered in stout defense. "You cannot blame her for aspiring to be no more than she needs to be."

"It's a good thing my former tutor isn't here to hear you say such a thing. He would rap your knuckles."

Regina started. "Your tutor?" He was speaking of her father!

"Yes. His name was John Willoby." Maxwell's expression suddenly altered as a thought struck him. *Willoby was her name as well.* "Tell me, Countess, how is it you claim not only my tutor's name but title to the cottage in which he once lived?"

She had had three days to think of a lie and now only hoped she could speak it with convincing ease. "When Lady Eloise insisted upon introductions I didn't wish to reveal my identity, for reasons of which you are now aware.

The name Willoby came to mind because I'd recently seen it on the deed to the cottage I'd purchased."

Maxwell's instincts told him that something more than her reluctance to be known as the Countess of Amesbury had prompted her action, but he didn't have a clue as yet to what it was. As for the source of the name, he believed her. Why should he not?

Satisfied that he accepted her story, she set about to satisfy her own curiosity. "Tell me more about your tutor."

Maxwell picked up a small pebble and hurled it over the side of the cliff. It arced high and wide before curving toward the sea. "When I was about thirteen I refused, as all boys are wont when the trout streams are running with fish, to attend to my lessons. I'd sneak off just before my tutor arrived and stay away until the appointed hour had ended. To my surprise, he said nothing to the marquess, my father. So, I thought, I'd gotten off scot-free."

A crooked smile lifted one corner of his mouth as he glanced at Regina to see if his story was entertaining her. Her solemn, leafy-green gaze encouraged him. "After a few days I felt guilty and came back early. There in the classroom were the ostler's two boys and the cook's son doing my algebra lessons! Mr. Willoby said not a word, only waved me into my seat and handed me a practice slate. When the lesson was done I had learned that education wasn't above the heads of commoners. In fact, every boy there had scored considerably higher than I." His dark eyes sparkled. "Lord, but I was lowered in my own estimation of myself. I never missed another lesson!"

"You sound as if you admired him," she said softly.

His grin widened to show strong white teeth. "How could I help but admire a man who showed me the worth of an education by using my own puffed-up sense of self-importance against me?"

Keeping her tone neutral, she said, "Were you puffed up with self-importance, as a boy?"

He didn't miss the hesitation before she added that final phrase. Her wit was one of her most pleasant attributes, he realized. "Had you known me then, you'd have thought I was reared with all the privileged excesses of a feudal lord. Instead, I had good parents who simply couldn't control me. My father despaired of making a useful peer of me. My mother could only wonder that she'd produced such a boisterous, arrogant male child."

Regina looked away as she deliberately shifted their conversation onto more dangerous ground. She was playing a risky game, but at this moment she relished the sport. "Was your tutor a bachelor?"

"No. He had a wife and daughter." An odd expression came into his face as he bent to pick up another stone. "The girl was years younger than I." With that, he sent another missile soaring over the edge into the sea.

His action seemed a dismissal of something unimportant, but before Regina could prompt him again, he plunged on in his rich baritone. "I remember a stunning sense of loss when he and his wife drowned one summer afternoon. Their boat capsized in a sudden squall."

Unaware of the anguish that entered his companion's expression, he focused once more on the silver-backed expanse of the ocean below that gave both life and death to the people who lived along its shores. "It was inconceivable to me at the time that life was so fragile. I had just been by their cottage . . ." His voice trailed off as his thoughts carried him far beyond his words.

Regina looked up. There was a bleak expression on his face, a deep abiding sense of personal loss that she would never have credited him as capable of had she not seen it for herself. The sight angered her. How dare he display anything like sorrow over the loss of her parents after what he had done to her! "Whatever happened to the child?"

Her sharp words jerked him from his reverie. "The daughter?" He looked suddenly uncomfortable. "I don't know. I was down on holiday with friends from Cambridge when the accident occurred." He drew a long, harsh breath and said, "I remained only until after the funeral and then had to go back to school."

"You stayed for the funeral?" Regina couldn't believe that he had been there, that she wouldn't have remembered him at the graveside. After what had occurred between them just before her parents' death, how could she have been oblivious to his presence? Had she known, she might have blurted out his crime, or run away in shame.

Maxwell was too lost in his own reflection to hear the astonishment in her voice. "He was dear to me. He was Merlin to my Arthur. Kind, wise, sage enough to give a young man his head when he needed it most, he was my saving grace. When he died, it was a moment of reckoning for me. I knew then what he had tried to tell me for years, that I was responsible for my life and my actions, and that if I didn't take control of both, I would be destroyed."

Regina listened in utter amazement. She had never known what her father was to the nobles of Blood Hall besides an underpaid tutor to their insufferable son. "Of course, if you felt that way, you must have paid him well and settled a considerable sum on the orphan," she said bitterly.

Maxwell shook his head. "You won't credit it, but being a child, I never thought to inquire. I only learned how destitute my tutor must have been when I inherited Blood Hall after my own father's death. In checking past years' accounts I found we had paid the poor man almost nothing! I was so stunned when I saw the old entries that I made inquiries after the daughter. But several years had passed and I learned only that she had been taken in by relatives at her parents' death. No one knew who she was with or where they had gone."

I could tell you, Regina thought as she clenched her jaw and looked away, remembering a loneliness so deep and complete that for more than a year after her parents' death, she'd rarely spoken. He said he had looked for her. Had he? Or was he lying to impress a "countess" with his kind heart? One thing was certain, he hadn't recognized her as his beloved tutor's child.

Maxwell looked out again at the vista before them. "So there, Countess. You know a great deal about me while I know little or nothing about you." He smiled as he gazed into the distance. "Shall I make a few guesses? Your accent is slight but telling. I suspect that you've lived many years abroad. Did you live by the sea before, perhaps, in Italy?"

"You are a student of rumor, my lord."

Chagrined to have been caught in so obvious a ploy, he simply said, *"Touché.* Yet I'm a man who makes his own conclusions." He looked toward her with a direct appeal for honesty in the velvety brown depths of his eyes. "I will listen to whatever you have to say with fairness."

"How kind of you to so assure me," she said frostily, insulted that he worded his invitation to confidence in such a condescending way. "I'm afraid the truth would pale by comparison to the gossip circulating about me."

Too late, Maxwell saw that his offer of a fair hearing was not worded in the most encouraging manner, and that he was prying into her privacy without any assurance that he could be trusted. Yet none of that kept him from feeling that his kindness had been thrown back into his face. His expression stiffened. "Very well, Countess, I'll leave you to your solitude."

He turned and set a boot in the stirrup. "Luncheon will be served shortly. We always begin promptly at one."

"In that case, enjoy your meal," Regina answered, driving home the point that she couldn't walk back to Blood Hall in less than twice the time it would take him to ride the distance.

Maxwell glanced back over his shoulder in consternation, for she had once again made him feel churlish. "Would you care to ride up before me?"

Pretending that she had not heard him, Regina turned away from the sea and began to walk across the uneven ground made rougher still by bracken and tufts of dying heather.

Given no other gentlemanly choice, he lifted his foot from the stirrup and set it back on the ground. "It seems," he murmured to himself, "we will both walk."

By deliberately avoiding the lane, Regina hoped that he would ride away in disgust, but, to her acute embarrassment, he fell in step beside her, trailing his horse along behind them by the length of its reins.

Picking up her pace so that he wouldn't blame her for being responsible for his late lunch, she began covering the rocky ground with more speed than agility. After no more than five yards, she misstepped. Hampered by her long skirts and sore ankle, she teetered for a moment as a rock rolled under the ball of her foot and then her ankle began to give way. Thankfully, the marquess was beside her, and, grasping her by the upper arm, he kept her from sprawling at his feet.

"How wise of you to choose the most direct route," she heard him say mockingly as his hand gentled on her arm and his fingers began to caress the inside of her upper arm. "The salt air has given me a rare appetite."

The words were simple but there was nothing simple

about her reaction to them, or his touch. A blush hot as fire swept over her when she turned to him. He took a step closer and she intuitively lifted her face, half expecting that he would kiss her. For, in spite of common sense, that secret hope had been at the back of her mind from the moment she'd first seen him on horseback. His back was to the glare and in the shadow his eyes were dark as night.

When she had looked up at him, her lips parted in invitation, Maxwell had recognized the feminine gesture of surrender, but thought he must be mistaken. She had only just forgiven him for his last indiscretion, and he didn't want to do anything that would spoil their truce. Difficult as it was, he backed up a step and released her arm.

Regina turned quickly away, pursing her lips together in a refusal to acknowledge either her desire or his polite rejection. She had been mistaken in his intention, that's all. And she should be glad—she was glad!—that she had been wrong.

Yet, not five yards farther along, she was again forced to accept his hand in support because her ankle had stiffened as she stood on the cliff, making climbing difficult.

Grateful that he had matched his steps to her slightly halting gait, she waited for him to release her hand again, but he seemed to have no such intention. "Keep the pace, Countess," he said without looking at her. "You've stood too long on the cliffs and your clothes are damp. A brisk walk will keep your blood warm until you can change."

A contrary streak prevented her from thanking him for his concern, but she welcomed the continued firm clasp of his large, strong hand as they walked on.

Her mind a flurry of new information, Regina tried to sort out a pattern in the patchwork quilt that seemed to make up Lord Kingsblood's character. She remembered how her father had often brought home tales of his titled

pupil's misadventures. Because her mother had always
clucked her tongue in disapproval, she'd assumed that both
parents disapproved of the young lord's behavior. Yet he
had just told her of her father's indulgence in response to
his boyish antics. If he could be believed, her father had
been quite fond of him, had labored to show him the right
path without breaking his spirit.

She glanced at the strong profile of the man walking beside her. He frowned slightly, as if deep in thought. Was he
still remembering her father? She valued his gift of a
glimpse of her father as a tutor as more valuable than
pearls. She might have told him so if in doing so she
wouldn't have given herself away. Then again, perhaps not.
For, while he had greatly admired her father, he hadn't
been above humiliating her in a fashion she wasn't likely
ever to forget.

Maxwell was equally preoccupied with his own thoughts.
He had told the woman beside him things about himself
than he had not told his Eloise, nor was ever likely to tell
her. There were few true scholars among the *ton*. One was
supposed to despise one's tutor, play nasty tricks on him,
and resist as heartily as possible all efforts by the man to
impart a bit of knowledge to his unwilling pupil. His first
year at university, friends had nearly convinced him of his
stupidity in taking his lessons seriously. If not for his
tutor's death the next summer, he might have sailed
through without having learned anything more important
than how to tie his cravat in the latest fashion and how to
drink like a fish.

He wasn't certain why he thought of John Willoby this
day. Perhaps it was because he was in need of sound advice,
and there was no one else to give it. How did an honorable
man act when he realized he had made a mistake that affected the life of another? If Eloise was disappointed in him,

so was he with her. Would she agree if he suggested they call off their engagement? Her father certainly wouldn't welcome the news. A broken engagement held the potential for scandal that, though he would weather it, she might not. No, there seemed nothing he could do. He'd asked for her, now he was bound by duty to her. What a miserable state of affairs for them both!

They arrived within sight of Blood Hall more quickly than Regina remembered leaving it. When they rounded the side of the house in step, they found a splendid carriage in the drive.

Halting suddenly, Maxwell muttered, "Damnation!"

Regina saw lines of consternation mark his expression. "It would seem you have company, Marquess."

"Infernal unwelcome company!" he rapped out. "How the devil did Stanford know where to find me?"

Without an apology for his language or an explanation, he strode quickly forward, leaving her behind. He crossed the drive and tossed the reins of his horse to a young boy who rushed from the stable to meet him, and then entered the house without so much as a backward glance.

Peeved that he should dismiss her so easily at the news of other guests, Regina took her time in arriving at the door herself. Her leisurely pace allowed her to take a good long look at the elegant vehicle she passed on the drive. It was painted a deep blue with fine brass lanterns and an impressive crest, which she did not recognize, mounted on the door panel. The wheel rims were gilded, and through the etched glass window she glimpsed white velvet upholstered seats trimmed in gold tassels and deep-blue velvet cushions.

By the time she reached the entry hall, she fully expected Lord Kingsblood to have disappeared from view. Instead she found him standing in the entry in deep discussion with two other gentlemen. A young lady her own age stood beside them holding hands with Lady Eloise.

"Don't be a wet blanket, Max," the taller of the two young men was saying. "Eloise thought it would be capital fun to beard the lion in his den." The young man glanced about the great dark hall hung with coats of arms, boars' heads, and imposing examples of the Kingsblood peerage. "Gad! You call a dungeon home, Max. Is there nothing in the place that's not dead, stuffed, or mounted?"

Just then the other young man noticed Regina's arrival. "Now there's something not dead and mounted," he offered in an appreciative tone. "As for stuffed," he added under his breath, "I wouldn't mind questing out the truth of that for myself."

Maxwell bit off the retort that sprang to his lips and said only, "Shut up, Giles." After all, none of the ladies had heard the remark. If he made a point of defending her, Leslie and Giles would likely take note.

He stepped forward as he saw Regina glance toward the back hall as if she would make an escape. "Miss Willoby, you're just in time," he said in a carrying voice. "I would like for you to meet my unexpected guests." By force of will he caught Regina's gaze and drew her reluctantly toward him.

When he was satisfied that she would, however unwillingly, allow herself to be introduced, he turned to the young lady in a garnet traveling gown who stood beside Eloise. "Delia, I'd like to present you to Miss Regina Willoby, also a guest at Blood Hall. Miss Willoby, this is my favorite and prettiest female cousin, Miss Cordelia Reavis."

The petite lady blushed and said, "The marquess says that I'm his favorite female cousin because I'm his *only* female cousin."

"I notice you don't say anything against my labeling you

pretty, puss," he answered, and tugged the russet curl turning by her ear. He beckoned next to the young man with bright reddish-blond hair that waved softly across his head like drifts of strawberry mousse. Dressed in the latest London fashion of skintight coat and alarmingly high collar, he looked as stiff and uncomfortable as a trussed goose. "The dandy is her brother, Giles Reavis."

"Delighted," Giles murmured, and bowed over Regina's hand as best he could without choking himself on his neckcloth.

The second man did not wait to be introduced. Tall, with gilded hair and eyes so blue they appeared to be lighted from within, he stepped forward before Giles had completely released her hand and said, "Miss Willoby, though you don't know me, I'm certain we are meant to be fast friends." He clasped Regina's hand warmly. "Lord Leslie Stanford, at your service."

"The Earl of Dartmoor," Maxwell supplied in a dry voice, "and a more insincere flatterer you're never likely to meet."

The Earl of Dartmoor glanced at his best friend in open surprise. "Thank you, Max. I'll remember to return the favor. If I recall, now that you've taken Lady Eloise, the rest of us are being given the field." He looked at Regina who was trying unsuccessfully to extract her hand from his. "Am I being rude, Miss Willoby? It must be the clime." He smiled into her eyes. "Do you not feel the wild nature of the West Country in the air? There's nowhere else in England like it. I myself am half Cornish, half a Devonshire man, and—"

"All ham," Maxwell finished flatly. "Do leave off over making love in my hallway, Leslie, before you spoil my appetite for luncheon."

"Very well, for the present," Leslie said, releasing her.

Not waiting for another topic to introduce itself, Maxwell said tightly, "You were about to tell me what brought you to Devon this time of year, Leslie . . . besides Lady Eloise's invitation." He sent a cutting glance at his fiancée, which made her pinken.

"Don't blame Lady Eloise," Leslie answered with a tender smile for the lady who matched him perfectly in coloring and beauty. "I pried your destination out of her before you left London. As for the rest, I don't know that I should tell you, after the way you've just abused my reputation. But I will." His voice rose in timber as he said, "The most spectacular game's afoot, Max! It began as a wager at White's but now half the *ton* has joined in. Society hostesses are in despair because their invitations are being turned down as people pursue the sport."

"What sort of wager could possibly interfere with the Season?" Lady Eloise asked in a breathless voice of excitement.

Leslie's eyes lighted up. "It's a scavenger hunt! The winner will be the first man who can ferret out the hiding place of the missing Countess of Amesbury!"

Chapter Ten

❧⚜❧

$\mathcal{R}$egina felt as if the room had suddenly been given a vigorous shake by a giant hand. She was being hunted! Not only by the dowager, but by the *ton*! Like some varmint or notorious criminal, she'd been slapped with a price on her head!

"I can't believe—" Maxwell began angrily.

"Ain't that a pip?" Leslie cut in.

"No, really?" Lady Eloise breathed excitedly.

"Whoever—" Giles began.

As the excited voices of the young aristocrats rose in an attempt to outtalk one another, Regina took a step back from them. In their finery and youthful handsomeness, they seemed like a flock of well-bred peacocks. Yet she now knew better. They were elegantly feathered vultures whose breeding and manners were mere camouflage to hide the sharp talons and merciless instincts of hunters. To feed their rapacious appetite for scandal and mischief, they were capable of any cruelty in order to capture their prey. And she was it!

The room took another sickening lurch. Ice replaced the warmth of her blood as Regina felt her knees unlock.

Then, amazingly, Lord Kingsblood was beside her, his firm fingers gripping her arm. Steadying her, he said in his deep voice, "I assume you've been out walking, Miss Willoby?"

Regina looked up dazedly into his dark eyes and saw caution in their depths. "Yes, I have."

Maxwell had been watching her from the corner of his eye when he saw her sway. He had risked drawing attention to her by moving to her side, but he knew that if she fainted it would have attracted even more. Her complexion was dull as ash but her voice was stronger than he had expected. "You shouldn't have gone so far," he admonished in a voice that could be plainly overheard. "The moors can be fatiguing. Allow me to escort you to your room." By exerting pressure on her arm, he coaxed her past the others and up the first steps.

As he reached the third stair Maxwell turned to look down. "Lady Eloise, would you kindly act as hostess for our guests? Luncheon should be ready in the great hall. Ask the housekeeper to have extra places set. I'll join you as soon as I see Miss Willoby to her room."

"Very well," Eloise answered, torn between what she thought should be her duty to her new friend and her eagerness to hear more of the latest gossip from London. "I hope you'll join us too, Miss Willoby," she called after Regina. "You'll want to hear Lord Stanford's other news."

"Not if it's in no better taste than the last!" Maxwell answered for Regina, and urged her farther up the stairs.

Neither Regina nor the marquess spoke as they climbed the stairs and traversed the hall, but the moment she stepped inside her room, he came in swiftly behind her and closed the door.

Astonished by his actions, Regina whirled on him only to have him say with distaste, "What exactly have you done?"

"Done?" Regina echoed bitterly. "Just what *exactly* do you mean?"

Maxwell took a step toward her, his face a study of exasperation and annoyance. "I'm inquiring into your activities,

madame, those that have led London into a frenzy of anticipation over your discovery."

Regina felt what was left of her pride shrivel under his
disapproving stare. "I've done nothing but marry a man I
did not know or love!" she retorted, advancing on him a
step. "Since then, through no fault of my own, I've become
a wealthy widow. It's a stroke of ill luck that the Dowager
Countess of Amesbury is my mother-in-law! Those are my
crimes!" she cried, punctuating her words with taps of her
cane upon the carpet. "Heinous, are they not? Grounds for
scandal and censure and ridicule, surely!"

"You are becoming hysterical," Maxwell said shortly,
and grabbing her by the arm, pulled her away from the
door, fearing that they might be overheard.

"Oh, by all means, I should not become hysterical!" Regina shouted at him and tried to draw away. "How un-
thinking of me! How unladylike! How common I must
seem to you!"

Maxwell drew her to himself, catching both her arms,
and shook her slightly. "Now listen to me, Miss Willoby, or
Countess, or whatever the devil it is you wish to be known
as. You're beneath my roof! No one and nothing shall harm
you as long as you are my guest!"

"Yes. Thank you. I should have remembered that," she
answered, the ragged edge of her self-control fraying still
more. "The Marquess of Ilfracombe is a Tartar beneath his
own roof, a medieval lord, a feudal master of all he surveys.
No one must cross you, must she, my lord? Certainly not a
helpless widow whom the world despises and for whom her
last haven is about to become a hunting ground!"

"Don't be a fool," he replied, freeing her. "No one sus-
pects you."

"But they will!" she said despairingly, backing away
from him until she reached the barrier of her bed. "There

was a description in the gazette. Your friends will have read it."

Maxwell made a gesture of denial though the very thought had been in his mind as he mounted the stairs. "I can handle them. You mustn't give yourself away."

Her green eyes as brilliant as emerald flames, Regina felt the last thread of her sanity come unknit in a tirade of words. "I wouldn't be surprised if you turned me in yourself! The deed would make you the most popular man in London for a season. Why, you could tell the *ton* all about me, couldn't you? How you commandeered my carriage before you knew who I was. Think of the tale your midnight rescue would make when I—how was it you put it?— I so wantonly tried to seduce you. That tale alone should keep you dining out for months!"

"Don't be a fool!" he repeated. "I wouldn't!"

"You will! You will!" Her cries came as short jerky gasps, rising to a crescendo of fear and self-pity as she eluded his hands as they once more reached out for her. "You're just like the rest! You'll use me! Cast me away! Care nothing for—"

He stopped her cries with a kiss. It was a hard kiss, an angry kiss, but in it was a desperation to match her own. She was very much afraid of being betrayed by others, while he was very much afraid of betraying himself. As her soft mouth trembled under his, he knew it didn't matter any longer who fought whom, only that neither of them lose the moment.

As his mouth opened on hers in hungry urgency, Regina experienced a sensation of unreality so strong that she didn't fight the urges suddenly rising up in her. Fear, anger, despair melded under the white-hot persuasion of his kiss into a moment of desire so strong she raised her arms to encircle his neck. She had to keep him from snatching the pleasure away. He was strong and solid beneath her hands, his shoulders a secure place upon which, for a moment, she was willing to rest her world.

At her touch, Maxwell felt desire stroke down through him like a saber. And then her fingers were tangling in his hair to hold his mouth to hers. With a groan, his lips opened on hers and he thrust his tongue into her mouth. She stiffened at his invasion but his hands came up to hold her close as he murmured encouragement. "Please," he said against her mouth as he hastily untied the strings of her bonnet and tossed it aside. "Please. Don't deny me. Please."

His voice, deep and dark, sounded as needy as her own love-starved soul. Nonsensically, irrationally, and with the recognition that what she was doing was as dangerous as skating on spring ice, Regina pressed herself to his longer, harder frame and opened her mouth to his seeking tongue. His groan of satisfaction drowned out her sigh of surrender as their mouths blended in kiss after long, searing kiss. His tongue plunged repeatedly into her mouth and then retreated in a primitive rhythm that her body if not her mind understood all too well. Finally, when he paused, instinct overrode modesty and she pressed forth her own tongue. He immediately drew it into his mouth where he urgently sucked the pink tip.

The shock of his act sent warning bells jangling along her nerve endings. What was she doing? She was encouraging him in this madness. Even now her hands were kneading the heavy muscles of his back in an unconscious need to bring him even closer than he was. But she could not, did not want to stop.

She felt his arms go around her, lifting her high off the ground and crushing her to his chest. The buttons of his coat chafed her suddenly sensitive breasts and then he was laying her on her back on the bed, following her body down onto the coverlet. Bracing himself on an elbow, he half lay over her, his lips hovering a scant inch above hers as he sought the expression in her eyes. What he saw both encouraged and daunted him. Her eyes were as wide and mist-laden as the restless sea they had been looking upon together so short a time ago. In their depths was hesitation, confusion, and the smoky beginnings of a desire he longed to bring fully to life.

He touched his mouth briefly to hers in the gentlest of kisses, and the meeting sent a shiver through her that was answered by a quiver in his belly. The second kiss embraced her lower lip and he set his teeth in the plush fullness, exacting a womanly moan of desire from her. She was made for love, he thought as lust hammered in his veins, and she must be his. It no longer mattered what she had done or not done. She was young, beautiful, and in his arms.

Even as he struggled out of his coat, he kept part of himself in contact with her, his mouth, a hand, his leg pressed heavily across her hips. He luxuriated in the insistent throb of his manhood pressed against her thigh. The buttons of her gown came free easily as he reached under her, lifting her against his mouth for more lingering kisses. When her hand came up to prevent him from lowering her bodice, he bent his head and kissed each knuckle before sliding his wet tongue between her ring and her middle fingers and licking the sensitive skin. Instinctively she drew her hand away and he tugged the fabric free.

Though he would have liked to avail himself of a long, leisurely perusal of all that he had touched and caressed in the darkness of the cottage ruin, she quickly shielded herself with her hands. Smiling tenderly, he lowered his head and nuzzled one hand aside to suck one rosy peak.

Raw lust streaked through him as he heard her artless

gasp of pleasure and felt her arch up under him. As her hands fell away from her breasts, his hand came up to gentle and caress the one his mouth did not embrace. His thumb and forefinger kneaded the hard peak until she moaned repeatedly, lost in the sensual world of his creation.

Finally a nagging sense of right dragged Maxwell reluctantly back to himself. He lifted his lips from her breast only to lower his cheek to the perfect mound as he fought for control of his ragged breathing. He hadn't meant to go so far. This was scarcely the time and place.

There never is a right time or place, he thought wryly, remembering their other encounters. But this time he wasn't about to rip up at her for her shortcomings, not when he felt the difference between self-restraint and rape to be no more than the intake of a few shallow breaths. If she was lost to propriety then so was he. If she was a wanton then, God help him, so was he! In all honesty, he wanted her, had wanted her from the first, and he wouldn't chide her for offering him what he so badly desired.

He lifted his head to look at her and found unshed tears summing in her eyes. "We must stop," he said thickly. "I'm sorry. I didn't . . ."

Regina couldn't look at him but neither could she deny the truth. If his conscience hadn't gotten the better of him, she doubted hers would have stopped them. She turned her head away as a tear escaped and slipped silently down the curve of her cheek.

He reached for her hand and cradled it against his cheek, then pressed a kiss into the center and very slowly licked it away. As his tongue curled into her palm, she gasped softly and heard him sigh. "You are so responsive, love. So sensitive. I have only to touch you and you burn for me."

His velvet voice was like the heated stroke of his tongue, tantalizing, persuasive, faintly embarrassing, yet because of it she didn't want to deny him anything. His tongue trailed up her palm to her wrist, which he lathed until his breath came coolly upon her damp skin. "I must see you again." Regina's head moved restlessly on the coverlet. "I'll come to you tonight," he said in a rough chuckle. "Then I'll be able to lick every smooth tender inch of you and kiss places you have never even thought of. Say that I may do that. Promise me the pleasure of you," he murmured, and licked a path up to her elbow where he sucked at the soft skin on the inside of her upper arm.

"Please," she whispered, too overcome by the onslaught of differing emotions to know whether she wanted him to stop or continue.

"Don't be afraid of me," he whispered encouragingly. He drew her bodice together over her nakedness without looking at her because he was certain he wouldn't have been able to leave her otherwise. "I'll protect you from harm. Only you must trust me."

"Trust you?" For an instant he saw such suffering in her eyes that he nearly bent to lift her into his arms, but he hesitated. Then the misery was gone, shut down by the more familiar sight of righteous indignation. "Why should I?"

The question was one Maxwell had been trying to find an answer for himself, and failed. He had been anything but a gentleman in his conduct with her. He had bullied and roared at her, and taken her kisses even when she would have denied him. Even now he still lay on her, his swollen desire blatantly caressing her hip.

He lifted his leg off of her and in one graceful movement came to his feet beside the bed. Looking down at her he said, "I know you have no reason to, but believe me when I say I would be your friend, if you'd allow it. I can protect you. I will protect you." His eyes slipped from hers to where her open bodice did not completely cover her blushing breasts. "And not for what is between us."

"Because you are a gentleman and a gentleman can always be counted on to protect a lady's honor?" Regina asked softly.

Maxwell shook his head impatiently then ran both hands through the thick hair at his temples. "It has nothing to do with that, and you know it! You've had a series of rude shocks that would have collapsed a lesser being or sent her screaming into Bedlam. I don't know all that you are or what you've done. But I do know that no one less contemptible than a Tyburn-bound murderer deserves the kind of hounding humiliation the Dowager Countess of Amesbury has set upon you. The woman must be mad!"

His anger had never really frightened her, nor his scorn, nor his lust, but the look of fierce protectiveness that came into his expression as he spoke of defending her against the dowager was Regina's undoing. To have him offer himself as her champion when she hadn't even dared hope that he would not side with her enemies left her no defense against the sudden rush of gratitude that overwhelmed her. Tears welled up and spilled through the thicket of black lashes she had closed to keep them at bay. "I wish you wouldn't be kind to me, my lord," she whispered brokenly, and turned on the bed away from him. "You may live to regret it."

Surprise shot through Maxwell. But even as he bent toward her to ask her what she meant, he heard footsteps in the hall and then voices.

He straightened, looking around until he located his coat. Even as he moved away from the bed and scooped it up, he heard Dorrity Rogers's voice. He stood a moment in consternation. His exit was blocked. Even though his reasons for being in this room were legitimate, the closed door negated them. If only there was another way out.

The distinct sound of a cat's meow made the hair rise on his neck. Eloise's cats! He turned, expecting to see a kitten by the fireplace, but there was nothing there. With a puzzled frown, he stepped over to the fireplace as the mewling grew stronger. When he reached the mantel he realized that the feline noises came from the other side of the wall. All at once he smiled.

Reaching up, he felt along the paneling beside the fireplace, sliding his fingers along the gilded molding. "Regina," he whispered urgently, "you must bathe your eyes, change your gown, and come below for luncheon."

Mired in self-pity, Regina didn't even look at him. "I can't. Don't ask that of me."

"You must come below," he whispered as he felt the latch he'd been searching for. "What better place for the fox to hide than in disguise among the pack of hounds?"

Regina sat up as a knock sounded on her door and whispered back, "No! What they do is disgusting. I'd never harm anyone in the manner they so intend."

Smiling, Maxwell turned back to her as the latch gave and a hidden door swung open. "Come below for luncheon and let me prove myself. You'll find that I'm a rather formidable champion when the need arises. Now answer the door."

Regina saw him disappear but the moment the secret passage closed behind him, she doubted that it had ever been there. Even as she scooted off her bed, prompted by a second louder knock, she couldn't resist going first to the fireplace to try to discern the location of the passage. But it deceived her eyes.

"Coming!" she called as she hastily stepped out of her sea-damp gown and flung it over a chairback. After a quick dash of her hands over her eyes to dislodge shed tears, she opened the door. "Yes?"

"I'm Dorrity Rogers." Dorrity's practiced gaze went past the young woman to the room beyond. "Lady Eloise sent me. She said you'd taken ill and that the marquess had brought you upstairs."

"I—I thought I was fatigued, but actually I think I'm famished," Regina lied as she moved from the door toward her wardrobe. "I just need to change my gown and then I intend to join the others for luncheon."

"Very well, miss." Dorrity stepped deliberately inside the room. "I'll stay and help you. Or do you already have company? I thought I heard voices."

Regina's lips thinned but she kept her face turned away from the woman and her probing questions. Lord Kingsblood had been wise to slip from her room rather than brave out a meeting. "Quite alone. Perhaps you heard a servant in another room."

"Perhaps," Dorrity answered, but she'd seen the telltale flush of the young lady's skin, her softly blurred mouth, and shining eyes that tears had glazed. Something had taken place here. If she hadn't seen the entire room at a glance, she would have suspected that Lord Kingsblood was lurking just out of sight. Even so, she didn't trust the young woman or the marquess. Though Lady Eloise didn't suspect a thing, Dorrity had seen enough to convince her that the marquess could not be trusted . . . and that this young woman was the reason.

Shrewd by nature, Dorrity kept a sharp eye on those who interested her, and usually it paid off. For instance, she'd seen the marquess and Miss Willoby, walking hand in hand, arrive back at the hall, not separately as they had made it appear to the others. No doubt they'd spent the morning on the moors together. Should she tell Lady Eloise that, or wait until she had better proof of the marquess's perfidy with what, she suspected, was his new mistress? Experience told her to wait, and watch, until she had irrefutable proof.

Going over to the vanity, she picked up the silver-backed brush lying there. "Shall I help you with your hair, miss?"

"Yes, that would be lovely," Regina answered as she stepped into a gown of pale yellow. "Will you button me first?" Regina turned to the woman and went pale when she saw that Mrs. Rogers was staring at her brush back.

"That's a pretty piece," Dorrity said when she lifted her eyes to the young woman. "It's a royal crest, isn't it? A gift, by chance?"

"It's a family heirloom," Regina said, and began trying to button herself up the back to cover her shock. First the marquess and now a maid questioned her about the crest. She would have to hide that brush! "We're what you might call poor distant relations with only a few trinkets to remind us of the connection."

"How fortunate for you," Dorrity said as she gave the crest a thorough perusal. "What is the family name? Lady Eloise may know a number of your kin."

"I doubt that, but I'll ask her myself," Regina replied, turning her back to the woman. "Would you mind?"

"Of course not." Dorrity set the brush aside to fasten the young woman's gown. Yet, like a terrier on the scent, she wasn't ready to give up. "You've a nice figure, miss. You must have half a dozen beaus. Anyone special, is there?"

Regina bit her lip. Really, the woman's meddling was more than she could endure after all that had gone before and what yet waited for her at the luncheon table. "I'm sorry to disappoint you but there's no one, absolutely no one. I prefer it that way. Now, if you would kindly inform Lady Eloise that I am on my way, I would appreciate it."

Dorrity glanced at the brush but Regina moved past her to pick it up first. "What about your hair, miss?"

"I've changed my mind, I'll see to it myself." Regina pulled nervously at a long curl lying across her shoulder.

Seeing that she'd been maneuvered to a standstill, Dorrity retreated. "Very well."

But as she left the room, Dorrity mentally tucked away the scraps of knowledge she'd gathered. A young woman who traveled alone without maid or relative, who owned expensive things, and who accepted invitations to stay in a gentleman's home needed watching. There was no other conclusion to be made, Miss Willoby was the marquess's mistress!

When Regina had arranged her hair, still damp from the sea breeze, she made her way to the great hall only to find that the gentlemen were no longer present.

"Come in, Miss Willoby," Lady Eloise greeted. "As you can see, we've been deserted by our gallants who wish to view Lord Stanford's new coach before the stableboys unharness it."

Regina pinned her best smile on her face, more relieved than she dared express, and took a chair. "Gentlemen will have their pleasures," she said.

"I think Cousin Maxwell's suggestion to view the coach was a pretext," Lady Cordelia said with a mischievous smile. "Did you see the thunderous look he gave Lord Stanford when he balked at the idea of missing his kidney and steak pie?"

"I did, actually," Eloise answered, a thoughtful expression on her face. "Why do you suppose Lord Kingsblood would drag them away from their meal?"

"So that he can give them a royal dressing-down out of earshot of us ladies," Cordelia answered. "You know what a stickler Cousin Maxwell is for proper conduct. I dare hazard Giles's ears will be red for a week!"

"What do you suppose annoyed Lord Kingsblood?" Regina asked as she picked up her fork and broke the crust on her pie. If she was to hide among the hounds, as he phrased it, she'd better join the game.

"Why, the wager at White's, of course. I knew nothing about it until Lord Stanford spoke up in the hall. I thought my brother and he were simply out to cause mischief between Cousin Maxwell and Eloise." She cast a speculative glance at Eloise and then turned to Regina. "Did Eloise tell you that the Earl of Dartmoor once entertained hopes in her direction?"

"Delia!" Eloise burst out as her flawless complexion dissolved into furious blushes. "Lord Stanford never made any overtures to me."

Lady Cordelia's mouth made a perfect "O" of surprise. "What a Banbury tale, Eloise! You yourself told me how he wrote the most perfect poetry to you—" Too late, she realized what she was saying and turned a shade darker than her red hair. "Oh, please forgive me! I didn't mean—"

Eloise's mouth trembled like a child's. "Had I known that you weren't to be trusted—" She broke off to swallow a lump of emotion. "Well, just so I now know!" She rose to her feet. "I feel quite full. I believe that I'll retire to finish the correspondence I began after breakfast. Miss Willoby. Cordelia."

When she was gone Cordelia turned to Regina and said contritely, "You must think us the most uncivilized pack of scoundrels you've ever encountered."

"To the contrary," Regina answered smoothly. "I find your conduct in keeping with the *ton,* indeed with all of the aristocracy. Don't give it another thought."

But, of course, Cordelia did because the lady's words

were so condemning. Nor was she as easily rattled as Eloise. "You are very like Cousin Maxwell, Miss Willoby. Your set-downs cut so smoothly that one might bleed to death before she knew she'd been dealt a mortal wound."

Regina paused in her eating and looked up at the pretty young lady seated across from her. "Do forgive my rudeness, Lady Cordelia. Your personal interests are none of my concern, and I should be the last to judge them."

"But you do," Cordelia persisted. "I know something of you." When Regina's startled gaze met hers, Cordelia felt a shiver pass through her body, for those green eyes seemed to see into her soul. "Eloise has done nothing but talk about you since I arrived. She thinks you are quite remarkable."

Attention was the last thing Regina wanted drawn to herself, and she hoped Lady Eloise hadn't included the gentlemen in her conversation. "I think Lady Eloise is the kindest creature on God's earth. If she has a fault, it's that she is too generous in her praise."

"That, and the fact that she won't stand up for herself," Cordelia answered. "She says that you encourage her, that you understand her."

"I scarcely know her," Regina answered in modesty.

"Yet she confided in you. She told me so."

Regina set her fork aside, her meal forgotten. "Just what is the point of this conversation, Lady Cordelia?"

Cordelia blushed, but the courage of the Kingsbloods didn't run in her veins for naught. Leaning forward she whispered, "That you may now judge for yourself how much Eloise loves Lord Stanford."

It was Regina's turn to form a perfect "O" with her lips. "You must be mistaken," she said when her voice returned. "Lady Eloise holds the marquess in the greatest respect and awe."

"So do we all," Cordelia replied. "Max—you'll notice

that I don't address him thus to his face—is a veritable
institution of respect and awe. But who would want to
marry an institution?"

"I don't understand," Regina answered cautiously,
aware that the servants who lurked just out of hearing
might be privy to this conversation.

"Max is a brilliant man. He's a great orator. I simply
adore his voice! So commanding, so firm and masculine.
Don't you agree?" At Regina's nod, she continued. "The
House of Lords fills to capacity whenever he's to speak.
Giles says that it's a miracle that he's considered both a
Corinthian and a respectable institution at one and the
same time. Usually men of Max's form and face are more
interested in the petticoat line than in Bills of Parliament.
Oh, I see that I've shocked you by my blunt speech."

"Oh, no," Regina assured her though the phrase "petticoat line" coming from the lips of a young lady of the *ton*
should have been shocking. "I am only amazed that Lord
Kingsblood invokes such respect wherever he goes. Still,
that's all the more reason for Lady Eloise to treasure her
impending marriage to him."

Cordelia smiled. "Perhaps, if her heart weren't given
elsewhere."

Regina knew that Cordelia was again referring to Lord
Stanford. "But, surely, if the gentleman in question had
returned her feelings, he would have asked for her hand."

"No, he wouldn't have, and now it is too late!" Cordelia
said in what soundly suspiciously like disgust. "I'm perfectly put out with him, and I told him so that day he came
to commiserate with Giles about the news of Eloise's engagement. He was so certain of his feelings and hers that he
thought she would wait until the end of the Season to receive his pledge. Only he didn't tell her what was on his
mind. Men can be so distressingly dense at times. When I

find the man I want, I shan't wait for him to screw up his courage. I shall simply grasp him by the lapels and demand that he ask Papa for my hand!"

Regina didn't answer except by a smile. The Kingsblood family seemed to have no difficulty in taking what they wanted, but did Maxwell Kingsblood really want Lady Eloise? "Lady Eloise is fortunate to have had two such estimable suitors, though I'm certain the marquess's love is a match for any man's."

"Do you think so?" Cordelia's expression grew thoughtful. "He seems a trifle high in the instep for my liking. Though I love him dearly, I wouldn't relish the idea of being married to a man of so many virtues. How very tiresome it would be to always know he was in the right. Besides, I can't imagine him pining away for love, or truly— Well, you know."

Regina did. Cordelia meant truly passionate. And that meant it was time to put an end to this extraordinary conversation. "I think, Lady Cordelia, we'd better finish our meal before it cools."

Regina picked up her fork but, though she resisted it, she found herself staring into her plate as she recalled the surge of desire Lord Kingsblood had drawn so easily from her. Lady Cordelia was wrong about him, and so was Lady Eloise. He was no cold statue or unassailable institution. He was a flesh-and-blood man, as she knew only too well for her peace of mind.

"I think you're being high-handed about what is just a spot of fun," Leslie Stanford said as he checked his fowling piece in the library after luncheon.

"I forbid you to speak of it again in my fiancée's presence, that is all," Maxwell answered as he turned his own gun over to test its balance. He had set himself a task that he had just begun to fulfill. "I don't recall the Earl of Amesbury being a particular favorite of yours, in any case."

"That rotter! He cheated at cards," Giles offered from his lounging position in a chair before the roaring fire. "I lost a hundred and fifty guineas to him a week before he died. Didn't have the decency to wait until I'd had a chance to win it back."

"I warned you," Maxwell answered.

"You warn me against every vice," Giles replied amicably. "Thank God I'm too sensible most times to give you any heed."

The three men laughed easily together. Though Maxwell was their senior by only a few years, both Giles and the Earl of Dartmoor considered him something of a mentor.

"I apologize for bringing the subject up in the presence of the ladies," Leslie Stanford said, and shook his blond head. "Certainly I had no intention of embroiling them in the business." He winked at Giles. "It's strictly a matter for the unvirtuous."

Using a chamois cloth to buff away an imaginary spot on the mahogany butt of his weapon, Maxwell gave the conversation an appropriate pause before saying "By the way, who set the wager?"

"The late earl's cousin, Sir Percy Buckram."

Maxwell's eyebrows shot up. "Buckram? I might have guessed. He always was Lynsdale's lackey." He added in an amused tone, "Didn't he recently take for his mistress that warbler from Dresden?"

"You mean the one with the bad teeth and wandering eye?" Leslie questioned with the beginning of a chuckle.

"Yes, but she has tits the size of summer melons!" Giles added, not a little impressed by the memory.

"Schoolboy!" Maxwell chided, and propped his gun carefully against the desk. "Have you thought of the irrevocable harm Buckram's little jest may cause?"

"We don't intend any harm," Giles maintained as he flicked a finger against his watch fob to watch it swing. "I hear the widow's quite beautiful. And, if Buckram is to be believed, she's quite accommodating to men who take her fancy."

Maxwell ground his teeth for he knew a great deal about how accommodating the Amesbury widow could be. He had scarcely been able to think of anything else since he left her arms. How much did Buckram know of her passionate nature? Affecting a nonchalance he didn't feel, he asked the question aloud. "And what would you know about that?"

"He's rumored to have been one of the widow's lovers," Leslie announced cheerfully, unaware of the black look that came into his friend's eyes.

"Have there been so many?" the marquess said softly.

"Rumor would have it so."

Maxwell turned abruptly away from the two men and reached for the brandy decanter. With his back to them he missed the surprised looks they exchanged as he poured himself three fingers. "Strange," he said in a measured tone as he lifted the glass. "When the marriage was announced rumor said the bride was an orphan who'd been reared in a convent. That hardly sounds like the breeding ground for an accomplished courtesan."

"I say!" Giles sat forward in his chair so quickly his collar points pricked him in the chin. "Now that you mention it, I recall hearing something of the same. Yet since the earl's death, the gossip mill has been full of nothing but her scandalous behavior."

"Perhaps the circumstances of the earl's death gave grounds for besmirching his widow's reputation." Maxwell took a long sip of brandy. "Doesn't it strike you as odd that a man wed scarcely a week would be found expired in his mistress's arms when he could have been sampling the charms of his supposedly salacious bride?"

"It does give one pause," Leslie mused aloud, "in light of the reputation that has since attached itself to the widow."

Maxwell nearly smiled. He had them thinking at last. Now to give them a few more cuds to ruminate over. "Haven't Buckram's offers of marriage been rejected by nearly every well-dowered debutante for the past two seasons?"

"True. His money ain't sufficient to cover up the stink of his reputation," Giles said with a chuckle. "Mama told Delia she'd ban her from Almacks if she so much as stood for a country dance with him."

"One wonders why a lady, a countess in particular, would dare risk her position over a minor knight like Buckram," Maxwell murmured. "He must be an excellent lover."

"Arabella says he was as rude and rough as a green schoolboy," Leslie said, and drained his glass.

"*Your* Arabella?" Maxwell inquired in amusement.

Leslie shrugged. "She was, till she caught the Duke of North Cumberland's eye. She met Buckram her first winter in London but quickly realized that he couldn't advance her reputation. One can't blame a girl for trying to get on in the world. Titles have their uses." He flashed the marquess a glance that gave away more than he intended.

The admission struck Maxwell with a jolt of realization. Stanford had lost his mistress to a man of higher rank. No wonder he seemed preoccupied, almost pensive, when he thought no one was watching. He had noticed Leslie's distracted state before he and Eloise left London but hadn't commented on it. Still, this wasn't the time to pry into his private woes.

"If Buckram is no Casanova, and we now have it on good authority that he isn't," Maxwell said casually, "then isn't it possible that the Countess of Amesbury rebuffed him and, because of it, Buckram decided to exact his revenge by setting in motion this little game of hide and seek?"

Giles's strawberry-blond head rose above the chairback. "By Jove! I'd never have thought of that! Yet it makes sense!"

Disappointment replaced revelation on his face for he'd very much wanted to meet the salacious countess, though he knew he wouldn't have known how to behave with her if he'd had the opportunity. He'd never cut much of a figure with the muslin set. He didn't have his cousin's formidable masculine presence or the earl's elegant beauty. Still, he had his ballerina Josie to cuddle and remind him that he was a man.

"You think Lady Lynsdale rejected him so Buckram wants revenge?" Giles asked, already accepting conjecture as fact.

"It seems possible," Maxwell murmured, content now to let that matter lie. "As for the earlier gossip, the Dowager Countess of Amesbury stands to lose a great deal if she can't discredit her daughter-in-law. The Amesburys always were a greedy family."

"Nothing short of thieves, my father always said," Leslie answered, and reached for the brandy decanter. It was at least two hours earlier than his usual time to imbibe, yet, if the marquess chose the moment as correct, he decided he could do no wrong in following his lead.

"You can count me out, Stanford," Giles said as he dusted a nonexistent particle from his coat sleeve. "I won't be a party to helping Buckram salve his pride with a lady's reputation. As soon as I return to London, I shall make that fact widely known."

Leslie Stanford, a man of much charm and more wit, saw reason in the results of their conversation, but some nagging suspicion led him to follow it to its natural end. "Why do you suppose the widow has disappeared, if she's nothing to hide?"

Maxwell turned to him with a bland expression. "Perhaps her husband's death and the resulting scandal drove her to seek a little solitude."

Sensing that there was no better answer, Leslie merely nodded.

"Let's plan our morning expedition, gentlemen," Maxwell suggested. "Shooting should be splendid."

As they began to discuss the merits of various types of shot, part of Maxwell's mind ranged back over the last minutes. He had been successful in diverting two minds from thoughts of pursuing the Countess of Amesbury. Yet it didn't follow that all minds would be so easily dissuaded. He knew enough of men to know that many of them would choose to believe the worst because they wanted it to be true. But for the moment, he had succeeded and Regina could rest easy.

A smile kindled in his dark eyes. He looked forward to the moment when he could tell her so, in private. Just as quickly he recalled how her fathomless green eyes had been wide with palpable fear, and his smile died. He had promised to protect her. He sensed then and now that in doing so, he was risking more than inconvenience and difficulty. He was risking the possibility of falling in love . . . with the wrong woman.

Chapter Eleven

"Oh, yes! Tell us a ghost story, Giles," Cordelia prodded.

"Not I!" Giles's rueful smile revealed a small dimple in his left cheek as he patted the beginnings of a slight paunch beneath his waistcoat. Ever one to see to his own comfort, Giles had chosen the chair closest to the fireplace of the great hall. "Dinner still occupies my thoughts. My regards to your cook, Cousin Maxwell. As for the other, sis, I'm really not very good at that sort of thing."

"I know who is!" All eyes turned to Eloise who sat in another of the wing-backed chairs drawn before the fireplace. "Miss Willoby!" A delicate shiver twitched her bare shoulders above the deep neckline of her silk evening gown. "She frightened me half out of my wits the day we met with the tale of how Blood Hall got its name."

She turned in genuine appeal to Regina, who sat a little distance away from the rest of the group. With surprise she saw that Regina's head was canted toward a leather-bound volume she held up to a candle's light. "Tell it again, Miss Willoby."

Regina looked up, pretending to be startled that the conversation she had been secretly monitoring should have turned to her. "Oh, no, Lady Eloise. Lord Kingsblood was perfectly right to scold me in the matter. I wouldn't dare abuse his hospitality by another such recitation."

"Well, I'm not afraid of our cousin's temper," Cordelia pronounced. "The only trouble is, we all know the tale of the beheading. I'd rather hear something new and grisly, wouldn't you, Lord Stanford?"

Upon hearing his name, Leslie Stanford looked up from his brooding contemplation of the fire where he lounged with an elbow against the mantel. "Whatever pleases Lady Eloise." His gaze went briefly to the lady in question, softened perceptively as she smiled shyly at him, and then moved back to the golden-red tongues of flame.

Regina glanced from the earl to Lord Kingsblood to see if he had noted the exchange, but his bland expression gave nothing away of his thoughts or feelings. He stood behind Lady Eloise's chair with one foot slightly extended to balance his weight, his hands folded behind his back. Not for the first time this night Regina thought he looked especially handsome in his dark-blue frock coat, white piqué waistcoat, and tight-fitted formal breeches of stockinet.

He had been oddly reserved during dinner, allowing his guests to hold forth on a variety of subjects while he merely nodded and smiled absently. If anything, he seemed preoccupied. Not even Lady Eloise had been able to hold his attention for long. It was only when Lord Stanford expressed his views on a matter that the marquess gave the speaker his full regard.

Yet more than once since dinner she'd looked up from her reading, sensing that his eyes were on her. It didn't matter that his gaze flicked away the moment hers met it. She knew what he was thinking because her own thoughts were equally occupied. He was remembering those forbidden moments in her bedroom when they had been locked away from the world and its concerns. It was an incredibly silly waste of time for both of them, she repeatedly told herself. She had no intention of allowing him into her bedroom on this night, or any other. What they had done was reckless in the extreme. The last thing on earth she desired was to come between the marquess and his fiancée.

As for her own feelings, she hadn't had time to sort them out, but when she did, she told herself, she was certain she'd find that her interest in Lord Kingsblood had more to do with romantic notions than a personal attachment to the man himself.

Regina returned her gaze to her volume but her mind continued to tease the matter. Was he aware that Lady Eloise held, if Lady Cordelia was to be believed, a fondness for Lord Stanford that exceeded her feelings for him? A pang of sorrow struck her. She hoped Lady Cordelia was wrong for she could think of nothing worse than to be trapped in a loveless marriage, as she had so briefly been. Lady Eloise deserved better, as did Lord Kingsblood if he loved her. Did he?

The question had come to her mind the day they met but then it hadn't seemed important. Now it did. If he loved Eloise, how could he have held another woman in his arms just this morning and kissed her with a desperate passion that made them both senseless to all other considerations? If he didn't, would he let Eloise go if he learned of her feelings for Stanford? And if he did, what would that mean to her?

Regina's hands began to tremble so badly she could no longer see the words on the page. She snapped the book shut. It was a ridiculous thought, and her reaction to it was even more ridiculous. The answer could not matter to her . . . but she longed for it just the same. And that thought made her more uneasy than any other she had had in connection with the marquess.

After a moment of silence Maxwell looked at his young cousin with an indulgent smile. "If you will have a tale of mayhem, Cordelia, perhaps I can supply it for you." He stepped forward from behind Eloise's chair and turned his back on the fireplace so that the flames threw his form in multiple serpentine shadows upon the opposing walls and ceiling. "Who knows the story of how Great Hangman Bluff got its name?"

"I don't!" Eloise said quickly followed by giddy laughter that betrayed her nervousness. "Do tell it!"

"Are you certain, Lady Eloise?" A frown of concern lined Leslie Stanford's handsome face. " 'Tis late, and harrowing tales can make for a restless night."

"Bosh!" Eloise answered in what, for her, was a daringly unladylike voice. "I'm no ninny, my lord." Her blue eyes shone brightly in the firelight. "Unlike some, I'm not afraid to face my fears or voice my desires."

Regina wondered if she was the only one to find another meaning in the lady's words of rebuke to a former suitor.

Cordelia sat forward in her chair and touched Maxwell's sleeve. "Do be quick, cousin, before the cold drives us to bed." She thrust her hands toward the radiant heat of the flames. "The fire seems strangely unable to warm the room."

"Very well," Maxwell replied in the deep resonant tones that made his parliamentary orations famous. "For those of you who are unfamiliar with this part of Devon, the craggy headland of which I speak lies some five miles to the east where the Sherrycombe Water tumbles into the small wild valley below.

" 'Tis said that long ago these hills were home to pagan gods. The bleak moors were their playground, the huge boulders their toys. When they laughed, the hillsides resounded with the thunder of it. When they fought, furious gales swept the coast and the sparks from their weapons fell as lightning from the sky. The village people, simple shepherds, went in fear of these gods who both protected and punished them. But for all the trials they endured at the hands of these gods, the worst calamity that befell them was the appearance one spring of a wily sheep-stealer. A bold and irreverent fellow, he carried out his thefts on moonless nights when good people stayed inside, for that was when the gods went abroad. For months darkness hid the thief while the thunder of the sea drowned out his steps and the dying bleats of the sheep whose necks he slit with the sharp edge of his knife!" He paused as Eloise gasped. "Would you like me to discontinue?"

"No, no, my lord," she answered. "I—I was only thinking of the poor dead sheep."

"Save your tears, Lady Eloise," Giles answered. "I rather enjoyed the roasted mutton we had for dinner, didn't you?"

"Oh, my!" Eloise answered, and swallowed convulsively.

"You're incorrigible, Giles!" his sister chided. "Please continue, cousin."

Maxwell turned to Eloise who added her nod of approval. "Very well. As I was saying, when the sheep-stealer had accomplished his bloody deed, he would sling the carcass onto his back, secure it with a rope about his chest, and bear it away.

"Now, one night his raiding had carried him far from home and deep into the homeland of the pagan deities. As he began the steep climb up the craggy hillside he began to tire, for the sheep he had caught was a particularly heavy one. By the time he reached the top, he was exhausted. Finding a boulder, he slung his sheep up on top and slumped down beside it. With only the sounds of the sea as company he soon fell asleep. But as he slept a strange thing happened."

Maxwell's deep resonant voice lowered, making his listeners unconsciously lean forward. "The sheep he thought was dead began to stir! It twitched once, then again. With each twitch the rope attached to it moved, gradually slipping from the thief's chest up to his chin. As the dying sheep gave one last great heave of its stricken body, it slipped off the rock over the other side, pulling the cord tight about the thief's neck!"

The collective gasp from his audience made Maxwell smile. "The thief awoke, thrashing and clawing at the cord, but the sheep was heavy and the rope too tightly drawn across his throat. The next morning shepherds found him dead, hanged by his own evil deed. Some said it was bad luck but more said it was the work of the ancient gods. And that is why the hills are called Great Hangman Bluff!"

Lady Eloise let out a pent-up breath and fell back against her chair. "Ooohh, but that is a horrid tale!"

You call that a ghost story?

The woman's scoffing voice sent all heads swiveling toward Regina. "I—I didn't say anything," she answered, and turned to see who had come up to stand beside her while she had sat mesmerized by the marquess's fine voice. Yet there was no one there. When she turned back to the others, she saw in their expressions that they plainly didn't believe her.

"If you think you can do better, Miss Willoby, then by all means let us hear it," Maxwell invited.

"But I didn't—" Regina broke off in embarrassment. An argument would only make her the center of attention. "Very well. I apologize."

"You will do more than that," Maxwell replied in challenge. "As penance, you must come forward and take your place among us."

She couldn't every well refuse her host. She stood up and, in the hope that her heartbeat would steady, took her time in closing her volume and placing it on her seat before joining them.

Lord Kingsblood's gaze, above all others, seemed to linger on her as she came forward. If not for her desire to know how the others planned to proceed in their search for the widowed Countess of Amesbury, she would have retired immediately following dinner. Yet so far not a word had been mentioned on that subject. She didn't know whether to be grateful or suspicious.

When she had come to stand beside him, she saw that his dark eyes were ashine with mischief. "What ghostly tale will you tell, Miss Willoby?"

"Make it a tale of a gentlemanly highwayman," Eloise urged.

"Yes! How romantic!" Cordelia breathed.

"It seems we will be subjected to a bedtime story," Maxwell murmured in a bored voice to Leslie.

"Not necessarily," Regina replied. " 'To beg is base, as base as pick a purse; To cheat, more base of all theft—this is worse. Nor beg nor cheat will I—I scorn the same; But while I live, maintain a soldier's name. I'll purse it, I, the highway is my hope; his heart's not great that fears a little rope!' "

"How clever, Miss Willoby. Is the verse yours?"

"No, Lord Stanford. The lines are attributed to a Royalist soldier who had been cashiered when Cromwell came to power."

"Cromwell again, Miss Willoby? I begin to suspect you have a particular liking for the period," Maxwell said lightly, but his brow was furrowed in thought, for the poem was strangely familiar.

"Perhaps it's because men of that age seemed to be greater of heart, braver of spirit, and higher of ideal than now."

"Bravo, Miss Willoby!" Leslie applauded. "Now, the tale."

Searching for a way to turn attention from herself, she suddenly remembered a scene from one of the dreadful novels Lady Eloise had loaned her. "If you are all interested in the spirit world, why not call upon the ghosts who are said to inhabit this house to entertain you?"

"Do you mean like at a séance?" Giles asked, and sat up, his interest in the proceedings captured at last.

"Yes, I suppose a séance is what I am suggesting," Regina replied, and cast a hasty glance at the marquess who was staring now at the flames as if he had never seen them before. What were his thoughts? He seemed not in the least interested in what she had to say after having coaxed her forward.

"Are you familiar with séances, Miss Willoby?" Leslie asked.

"No, my lord."

"I am!" Cordelia volunteered, and blushed prettily. "To be more precise, I saw one once as a child, at Grandmama's. She often called in a local gypsy woman to tell her fortune. On one occasion the gypsy offered to contact Grandfather for her."

"I would think our venerable grandsire was the least likely man in the kingdom to be interested in being called from the grave," Maxwell said in mild amusement as he slanted a glance as his female cousin.

"I can't say," Cordelia admitted. "My hiding spot behind the draperies was discovered before the spirits had been contacted, but from what I did see, the circumstances seem simple enough to re-create."

"Oh, yes, let's!" Eloise cried suddenly. It was the exact opposite of what she really wanted, but she found it too easy to be overlooked in this company when she spoke and acted as she had been taught a lady should. The only thing that made her bold now was the fact that Dorrity was abovestairs preparing her bed. "What do we do, Cordelia?"

"We need a table and six chairs," Cordelia said. "Then we must douse all the candles. And, of course, we need a medium."

"A what?"

"Someone who is familiar with the spirit world."

"I vote for you, sis," Giles said as he stood up and smoothed the points of his collar up along his throat. "You've had more experience with this sort of thing than the rest of us."

"Oh, very well," Cordelia said, pleased beyond words to be asked. "Which table shall we use?"

"I'll have a gaming table brought in from the card room," Maxwell offered. He pulled the bell rope and gave directions to the servant who came in answer. Within minutes, a table and six chairs had been brought in and placed near the fireplace. As the three footmen who accomplished the task were about to leave, Maxwell said to them, "Shut the doors and under no circumstances are we to be disturbed." His solemn pronouncement had a sobering effect on the gathering.

"Perhaps we should play cards instead," Regina suggested when the servants had departed.

"Are you now afraid of Blood Hall's spirits, Miss Willoby?" he asked. "You seemed fond of them when you moved into their room."

"Miss Willoby sleeps in the Chinese Bedroom?" Giles

asked, and whistled at Maxwell's nod. "You have my admiration, ma'am. I've never ventured inside it, even during waking hours."

"Shall we begin?" Cordelia intoned in a voice sharpened by anticipation. When every candle was extinguished, she lifted her shawl so that it covered her bright hair like a hood, then took her place in the chair facing the fireplace. "Giles, you and Lord Stanford sit beside me. Cousin Maxwell, you should sit opposite me."

Regina noted with a fluttering pulse that both remaining seats placed her next to Lord Kingsblood. Lady Eloise hurriedly chose the chair between Lord Stanford and Lord Kingsblood. Regina wondered if it was an omen that she was left to occupy the unlucky, or "sinister," place on the marquess's left whereas his fiancée sat on his advantageous, or "dexterous," righthand side.

Cordelia smiled. "We must place our hands on the tabletop." She did so and nodded in satisfaction as the others reluctantly did the same. "No speaking, now," she admonished as Maxwell bent to whisper into Eloise's ear. "Grandmama's gypsy woman was most adamant about the need for silence. Now, join hands but we must remain in contact with the tabletop."

Regina was so preoccupied with watching Lady Eloise's slight hand being enfolded in Lord Kingsblood's that when his firm fingers closed possessively over her own slim hand it startled her. His touch was much warmer than Giles's, who lightly grasped her left hand.

A sudden pang zipped through her as she wondered if Lord Kingsblood held Lady Eloise's hand as confidently. She glanced at him but he wasn't looking at either of them. Instead, he seemed to be preoccupied with a point at the center of the parqueted tabletop. With his back to the firelight, his expression was lost in the deep shadows and sharp angles of his profile.

"We are ready now," Cordelia said. "First we must close our eyes and empty our minds."

"That will be easier for some than others," Giles quipped.

"This is no time for jest, brother! Sincerity is a must if we are to be successful." She looked at the others and saw five ghostly pale ovals with shimmering dark pools for eyes staring back at her. "Close your eyes, everyone, and breathe deeply. You too, Lord Stanford. Breathe deeply. Slowly. Again." Her voice softened, the words taking on a chanting quality. "In. Out. Slowly. Allow your thoughts to drift . . . to dream . . . to become so relaxed . . . you feel you may . . . simply float away."

"Are we still in the hands of Grandmama's gypsy, Delia?"

"Yes," she whispered angrily to her brother. Then, in a more soothing tone, she went on. "Now, whom do we wish to contact in the spirit world?"

"Blood Hall's ghosts," Eloise said in a breathless whisper.

"Very well," Cordelia answered. She took a deep breath and said in a ringing voice, "We wish to speak to the spirits of the dead who inhabit this house. Come you forth and present yourselves to us!"

"You should be treading the boards, sis. Such fire! Such heat! Such overacting!"

Stung to the quick by Giles's humor, Cordelia snatched her hand from his and struck him in the shin with the toe of her satin slipper. "If you don't desist this minute you will be put out of the room. You're quite spoiling everything!"

Unimpressed, Giles leaned close to Regina and murmured, "I must own, I think this is too silly for words."

"Manners, Giles. One would think you fear that we might really be able to commune with the spirits," Leslie responded in good humor. "The ladies' entertainment is all we seek."

"Another disbeliever!" Cordelia cried indignantly. "I can see that we shall fail!"

"Of course we shall fail," Giles rejoined, his grin a white gleam in the darkness. "The only pleasure to be had, in my view, is the excuse it affords a man to hold a lovely lady's hand."

"Thank you for that astute observation, cousin. Now we may all feel like the very ass you are."

The dry-voiced comment from Maxwell provoked nervous laughter from Eloise. Chagrined as well, Regina tried to slip her hand from his but his fingers tightened, the tips curling into the center of her palm. Rather than make a tug of war of it, she relaxed her fingers so that it was obvious to anyone who cared to look that he held her hand and not she his.

To her acute embarrassment, he began stroking her palm with his thumb and the tickling made her want to giggle. Looking up, she shot him a withering glance but he wasn't looking at her. In fact, from the tension of his profile, she knew he was frowning at his cousin.

"Cousin Giles," she heard him say, "if you will kindly refrain from speaking again, I'll consider it a personal favor." The set-down given, he said to Cordelia, "Get on with your séance, sweet cousin, or I shall declare the evening at an end."

"Very well," Cordelia said primly, and grasped her brother's hand once again. "We must close our eyes and concentrate on that which we would most like to learn from the spirits."

Once again the room became quiet, the hiss and crackle

of the logs in the hearth the only sound. The seconds stretched out into a full minute before Giles whispered, "What happens now?"

"I'm not certain," Cordelia admitted softly. "Grandmama discovered me at this point."

"Oh, that's—" Giles's mouth snapped shut with a distinct sound for he had recalled, if belatedly, his cousin's command.

As the silence fell again, Regina felt the sudden inexplicable desire to laugh. She bit her lip, struggling with the urge, only to feel a burst of warmth flare up deep within her. Faintly embarrassed by the sensation, she opened her eyes in the hope that the urge would pass. The shadowed profiles revealed by the firelight showed that their eyes were shut. Looking up, she saw that dancing shadows circled the high ceiling and animated the wall hangings.

Suddenly a chilly breath brushed her face. Like cool fingers, the errant breeze lifted the tendrils of hair from her forehead and ever so lightly caressed her brow as a mother might a child's.

Irrational tears pushed behind her eyes where moments before laughter had provoked her. Yet neither emotion seemed connected directly to her. It felt as if they crowded in on her from another source. Her skin began to tingle. The warm firm pressure of the marquess's hand remained on hers, yet she could no longer see his shadow-hidden face for the unshed tears standing in her eyes. More faintly she knew that Sir Giles held her left hand. But the world was receding, drawing slowly backward from her as a gathering dense darkness crowded out the softer shadows of the night.

And then she saw it.

From the velvet-soft blackness at the far end of the room a figure emerged from the oriel. With it came a soft ef-

fluence of light. In stunned amazement Regina saw a young
lady dressed in the height of Royalist fashion emerge from
the shadows with a candle in her hand. No, Regina realized
with a frightened shudder that made her fingers flex tightly
on the marquess's hand. The apparition carried a flame but
there was no wax. The flame rose right out of her palm!

Her throat filled with a cry as the lady approached, but
she couldn't push the sound forth, nor could she look away
or make any motion that would draw the attention of the
others to the sight that filled her eyes. Paralyzed by fright,
she could only stare helplessly at the ghostly shape as it
came to stand between Lady Eloise and Lord Kingsblood.

The lady's beautiful pale face appeared to float above the
gentle golden halo of light shining in her outstretched hand.

What is your heart's desire?

Regina heard the words deep inside her mind and,
though the spirit's lips did not move, she knew that it was
source of the question. Fleetingly she wondered why those
at the table with her remained silent. Couldn't they see and
hear the spirit as she did?

What is your heart's desire?

The words came again, compelling by their very existence an answer.

Regina shook her head and tried to pull free of the hands
clasped with hers, but they would not release her. "Please,"
she whispered in choked anguish.

"What is it?" she heard Lord Kingsblood say, his deep
voice echoing through the cavernous depth of the great
hall. Yet when she turned her head, she could not see him
or any of the others. They had disappeared. There was only
the light and the womanly apparition searing the darkness.

Regina licked her dry lips to speak but still no sound
would leave her throat. She didn't realize when her hands
were freed or when she gained her feet but, suddenly, she

was following the lady with the flame across the cold slate floor of the great hall. The chill of the stones seeped through her slippers and up her ankles and into her calves. Finally, when she reached the oriel, she was trembling from an all-encompassing bone-deep chill and some other unnameable emotion that seemed too big for her body to hold.

The lady turned to her then, her magical light reflected a thousand times in the multifaceted lead glass windowpanes.

What is your heart's desire?

Regina shook her head, feeling tears break over her lashes and spill like drops of hot oil on her near-frozen cheeks. "Safety," she whispered brokenly.

Is that all?

The words were gentle yet reproachful, like the expression in the magnificent blue eyes staring into hers.

"Love!"

The word broke from her in a torrent of desperate longing that left her gasping for breath. She wanted to be loved, wholly and unconditionally. Forever.

The lady smiled at her and then curled her fingers over her palm, eclipsing the light.

For an instant the room was in utter darkness. Then like ripples on a pool that catch the sun's rays and reflect it into the eyes of the beholder, reality came purling back to Regina in eddies of light. She was once again seated at the table with the marquess on her right and his cousin Giles on her left.

"Is something the matter, Miss Willoby?"

Lord Kingsblood's voice sounded curiously worried. She turned to look at him, to reassure him that she was fine, but the words slipped right out of her mind as she met his gaze.

In his dark eyes were tiny flames more vivid than those behind the grate, warming her as no real fire ever had. She had seen him angry, had witnessed his impatience, his compassion, his pity, and his lust. But never before had she seen the depth of feeling that met her gaze. Suddenly she knew why the apparition had spoken to her. She was falling in love with the Marquess of Ilfracombe!

Her heart contracted as tremor after tremor shook her slender frame. With little or no encouragement, she could so easily love him with all her heart and soul, love him so much that she would willingly deny her pride, her virtue, and her sense of right for a chance to be in his arms!

Several things happened at once. The fire blazed up behind the grate, its flames thrusting out past the andirons. The flare-up sent all those seated around the table reeling back in fear of being burned. There was a great roar and then ashes rained down into the fire a scant second before a huge stone fell upon the logs. The accompanying crash that sent flame and smoke and a brilliant shower of golden cinders spewing out in all directions.

Regina heard the marquess cry, "Get back!" as a woman screamed. One moment she felt as if she were at the edge of an inferno, the next she was caught by strong arms. She knew at once that it was Lord Kingsblood's arms that held her in a hard embrace, one hand cradling her head protectively to his chest as he half carried her away from the blaze. For a moment she heard nothing but the thundering of his heart, and the wild tattoo of her own in answer, and then the darkness reached out for her again, and she welcomed it.

Lifting her easily, Maxwell carried her to the far corner of the room where the others had gathered and gently lowered her unto a chair, then knelt beside her.

"Good heavens, Miss Willoby's fainted," Lord Stanford said in a shocked voice as he held a sobbing Lady Eloise in his arms.

"Light a candle, Giles," Maxwell ordered as he chafed

Regina's cheeks then lightly slapped her face. "You'll find a Promethean Matchbox on the table behind you. Bring the device to me."

When Giles had done as he was asked, the little group huddled around Regina's still form.

"Is she all right?" Giles asked.

"Give her space to breathe," Maxwell answered tersely, wanting only to get her away from prying eyes. "She's just had a fright." He took the match from the bottle and held it under the unconscious lady's nose.

Regina gasped and jerked away from the sulfuric acid fumes, her eyes fluttering open. "Wh-what happened?"

"I'm not certain," Maxwell replied, his gaze locked on her pale face. "My guess is one of the chimney stones fell."

"No, no, it's all my fault!" Cordelia cried through the tears she'd been shedding. "I've released all the demons of Hell upon Blood Hall!"

At her words, the other three eyed one another warily.

"Really, Delia. There's only so much tripe even I'm willing to allow you," Giles said heartily in an effort to break the spell. "A stone fell, just as Cousin Maxwell said."

"Someone better call the servants," Maxwell said, though a quick survey of the room showed that nothing had caught fire.

"I'll do it," Leslie volunteered.

"No," Maxwell answered, looking up. "The ladies should be escorted up to their rooms. If you would oblige."

"My pleasure," Leslie answered, and offered Eloise his arm, which she quickly clasped in both of her own.

"Delia and I'll go along with you," Giles volunteered, looking over his shoulder into the dark corners despite himself. "Don't know as I believe in ghosts, but the goings-on at Blood Hall do give a man food for thought."

When they had gone, Maxwell rose to ring for a servant only to hear in surprise Regina say, "A moment, my lord."

Heartened by the strength of her voice, he knelt down before her again and covered her hand where it lay limply on the chair arm. "Very well, Countess. What happened to you?"

Inching her fingers out from under his, she looked away. "Nothing."

"Before the stone fell, you saw something, didn't you?"

Regina looked back at him. "Then you saw it too?"

"No," he said regretfully. "I didn't. What was it you saw?"

Regina turned her head away again, unable to look upon him with the new knowledge of herself so fresh in her mind. "Figments of my imagination. Nothing more."

"Are you certain?"

Regina sighed, too exhausted by emotion and nerves to play games with him. "Do you believe in ghosts, Marquess?"

A moment passed, and then another. Shaken, Regina turned again to look at him. His handsome face, made more dramatic by the play of candlelight, made her heart ache with newly discovered emotions. There was a quiet abiding strength in the composition of high cheekbones, strong jaw, and glittering dark eyes turned on her. She knew that even if he did believe in spirits, there was no mortal fear in him, only a certain wariness in the knowledge that he trod the earth with forces beyond his ken.

"I don't know what I believe," he said at last. "What do you believe?"

"Like you, I maintain a healthy skepticism," she answered with more bravado than conviction. "I'm not so foolish as to believe that shadows and daydreams are proof of spirits abiding." With her last ounce of strength, she rose from the chair, drawing him to his feet too. "Good night, my lord."

"No. Wait." As she turned away Maxwell reached out and took her hand.

Turning, Regina knew that all that was in her heart was written on her face, if he but knew how to read it. "Good night."

She said the words with such finality that he had no alternative. "Good night, Miss Willoby. Pleasant dreams."

The irony in his words remained in the air even after she turned and walked away. Something had happened to her, something that had changed the way she looked at him. A determined smile curved his handsome mouth. She would not get away that easily, not when he had read so clearly in those green eyes a fondness for him that went beyond gratitude and friendship.

"We'll finish this, madame. Tonight," he said softly to himself, and went to pull the bell cord.

When the last of the ash had been cleaned away by the servants and the doors shut on the great hall, a flame suddenly flickered at the far end of the room in one of the oriels. As ethereal as a bog fire, it shimmered icy green in the darkness, illuminating the quarreling pair.

"I heaved that stone into the fire to prevent you from continuing the séance, madame, for I knew very well that the Maxwell lad was to be your next victim!"

"You might have set the entire place afire!" she responded.

"Nonsense! That chimney stone has been loose these last three winters. 'Twas only a matter of time before it fell. I gave it a wee push. Just what did you think you were about?"

She glanced coquettishly at him. "Why, Captain, I was

moved by the assumption that all young ladies wish to be asked their heart's desire."

"You swore you'd not encourage her *tendresse* for the lad!" She merely shrugged, which momentarily distracted his attention to her lusciously formed shoulders.

Frowning hard upon her, he continued. "I don't mind rousing a healthy portion of lust in the pair, but matters of heart are best left in the hands of mortals."

"So you say."

"So I do say! I won't have her pixie-led by you, you unrepentant Royalist Devonshire witch!"

"Witch!" she cried, having no quarrel with the rest of his epithet. "You pompous hypocritical Roundhead, you dare preach to me? 'Twas not I who stroked her brow, you horny spawn of Satan!"

"Such speech, madame. 'Tis unbecoming a lady."

He was grinning at her in that devilish way she loved, but she was not about to be swayed. "Get thee gone from my sight, Roundhead! I've business elsewhere!"

Her image began to waver like a banner in a stiff breeze, then suddenly she was gone without so much as a whisper of sound.

"Impressive, madame!" he called after her. "But I will have final authority in the matter!"

The lady reappeared beside him as noiselessly as a ripple on the surface of a placid pond. "Do not depend upon it, Roundhead!"

His grin took on a wolfish gleam. "Do I hear a challenge?"

"You do!" she snapped, and winked out again.

Chapter Twelve
❧

Sleep eluded Regina. From deep in the center of the house a grandfather clock chimed the hour, precisely 2:00 A.M. She had heard it chime midnight and one as well.

With a mutter against things mechanical, she grabbed an extra pillow, pulled it about her ears, and rolled over onto a new area of the bed. The sheets had been warmed by a bed warmer before she retired, but the heat had long since dissipated where her body had not kept them warmed. The cold crept through the sheer fabric of her cambric night rail, making her gasp. Feeling as if she lay between two pieces of chilled watercress, she quickly drew herself into a ball.

For the dozenth time she began her prayers, an activity that the nuns of her orphanage had insisted was the cure for all ills. But, as before, the words would not form in her mind. Nothing remained permanently fixed in her thoughts for long but the image of Maxwell Kingsblood's face.

In that final moment in the great hall, she had seen a tenderness reflected in his dark eyes that superseded every other emotion he had ever revealed to her. Too late she realized that, contrary to her wishes, he *could* and *had* read the look of love so blatantly displayed in her own spirit-haunted gaze.

"Perfectly impossible!" Regina whispered angrily to herself, and flipped onto her back. Why in heaven's name had she suggested a séance? Now that she'd had time to mull it over, she understood what had happened to her. No spirits had been summoned. Circumstance had provided her over-active imagination with an excuse to indulge in flights of fancy that she wouldn't have permitted herself in the sensible light of day. She couldn't be in love with the Marquess of Ilfracombe!

Instead of counting sheep, she began to list aloud the many reasons why that statement was correct. "First, I am not of his world. I am a commoner, of common parentage. Second, Lord Kingsblood is formally affianced to a lady of his class. Lady Eloise is more beautiful than Sevres porcelain while I . . ."

The thought trailed off as she pictured herself: tall, raven-haired, and much too healthy to be called delicate or exquisite. Trying to be absolutely objective, she would say that while she was not as common as pottery, she certainly wasn't a beauty. While Lady Eloise, well, it wasn't difficult to see why any man would admire and adore her.

"Thirdly," she said crisply, forcing herself to say the words aloud, "I don't even like him." With that pronouncement she firmly closed her eyes, prepared to resist all thought to the contrary.

After a long moment, during which the absolute silence seemed to hum, she relaxed and turned her head into the pillow. After a few moments more, she felt her fingers release their tight grip on the covers and her knees ceased trembling from the cold. She didn't realize she'd fallen asleep until a whisper of sound awakened her again. Heart beating anxiously, she sat up. The fire in the grate had long since died. Contrary to custom, she had left the drapes drawn on the moonless night and the darkness was all but complete.

The sound came again, a mere whisper, like the train of a

lady's gown being swept over a carpet. For one horrified moment she wondered if the phantom from the séance had come to seek her out a second time. She was perfectly certain the soft tread upon her floor could only be made by a woman. Then the sounds of muffled boot steps and the faint squeak of an oiled door replaced the whispering.

Two thoughts rose together in Regina's mind: that Lady Eloise had told her about hearing a man's footsteps in her bedroom the night she arrived and, irrationally, that this couldn't be Lady Eloise's intruder because she heard no spurs jingling.

"Who's there?" she inquired in a voice that sounded so timid, she repeated it more forcefully. "Who's there, I say?"

Only silence answered. An unnerving urge to giggle, something that had never afflicted her before this night, made her put a hand to her mouth. She was dreaming, she must be. "If you're one of Blood Hall's ghosts," she suddenly called out, "then go haunt elsewhere. I need my sleep!"

The next instant a hand reached out to touch her bare arm. Even as she formed a scream a second hand stopped it by engulfing her mouth. "I don't mean to frighten you," a familiar deep voice said in amusement, "but you must be quiet." She was released.

"You!" Regina accused when she had recovered enough breath to speak. Though it was too dark to see him, she reached out and touched the marquess's smooth warm cheek, proof enough that he was no apparition. "How dare you!"

Once again her mouth was caught in a muzzling embrace as he bent a knee on her mattress. The bed sagged under his heavier weight as he followed her scuddling retreat across the mattress. She had nearly reached the other side when he hooked an arm about her waist and dragged her back to the middle of the bed. His hand touched her mouth then slid caressingly down her throat. "Softly, lady," he said, the strong undercurrent of laughter still in his tone.

Regina turned in his embrace, her thigh brushing the heavy corded muscles of his breeched leg and her bare arm raking his shirtfront. The heat of his skin came so strongly through the lawn of his shirt that she shied away. His white shirtfront seemed to gather whatever meager starlight there was into it, for it glowed faintly. Perhaps, she thought as his fingers continued their mesmerizing assault on the vulnerable column of her neck, she was dreaming after all. For, astonishingly, he smelled of spice and violets!

Satisfied that she wouldn't flee, he said, "We must talk."

"You shouldn't be here. If we are found—"

"We'll only be found out, Countess, if you don't lower your voice," he cut in. His deep baritone sounded more effective for being hushed. He reached behind her and propped up her pillows then pressed her back to lean against them. His hands seemed indecently warm where they touched her, yet when he removed them the cold invaded her skin once more and she regretted the loss. Automatically she reached for the covers, pulling them up to her armpits.

To her surprise he helped her, tucking them around her hips as he said, "I've come to tell you that you need no longer concern yourself about that accursed bet." He sounded quite pleased with himself. "They've abandoned the scheme."

"Why?" she questioned, quite aware that his hands lingered on the curves of her hips once he tucked the covers beneath her.

Amazed, she felt the warmth of his smile. "I told you I am a formidable ally, madame."

"You forbade them to mention it again?"

"Hardly!" Maxwell said, disappointed that she didn't sound more pleased. "The best way to change an opponent's mind is to convince him that he changed it himself. To that end, I pointed out various reasons why such an onerous bet might have been placed."

"And they were?"

"What does it matter as long as they are now convinced that the Countess of Amesbury is the injured party?"

Something in his tone was at odds with his words. "What else did they say about me?"

The bedsprings creaked as he shifted his weight. Though she could scarcely see him, his voice was suddenly much closer. He reached out and touched her hair then brushed her cheek with the tip of a finger. "I saved you. Isn't that enough?"

Regina sat absolutely motionless, wondering why she cared more about the fact that his every breath stirred the baby-fine hair at her brow than that he had saved her from humiliation. Yet he was waiting for a word of gratitude, perhaps several of them, and she ought to say something. "I didn't know what to think when the subject didn't come up during dinner. I began to imagine they suspected me and were keeping silent. Thank you for coming to tell me the truth."

His fingers curled over the back of her jaw as he began to stroke the summit of her cheekbone with the side of his thumb. "I promised I would come. Had you given up hope?"

"If you think I was—"

A finger across her mouth stopped her. "Softly," he reminded her. He pressed the pad of his thumb against the fullness of her lips as if delivering a kiss.

Not for the first time this night Regina felt the hapless,

helpless vulnerability of her love for this man. It was a full swelling of feeling that made her want to throw her arms about him and hold on for dear life. Realizing that she was on the verge of behaving like a hysterical child instead of a mature once-married woman, she forced herself to say something proper. "You are a peer of the realm. You must leave. Consider your vaulted position."

The bed vibrated with his deep chuckle. "I assure you, I'm not the first nobleman to enter a lady's bedroom after dark."

"You're the first to enter mine!" she whispered, and hugged the covers tighter. "Leave me at once."

"No." There was a strange energy in his tone, an unsettling burst of emotion that made Regina even more aware of how closely he sat beside her in the concealing dark. As she shifted restlessly, her arm touched his. Unconsciously she let it linger a moment because his heat was becoming more and more a temptation in the chill of the night. In fact, since he had entered it, the room had changed from cold to frigid. Or was it simply the contrast between his body's radiating warmth and the night air? A gust of chilly air, like an expelled breath, skimmed the back of her neck and she twitched her shoulders.

"If you won't leave, then I will," she said defiantly but, of the two of them, she was the more surprised when she didn't move. It was her intention to leave. Yet it seemed as if invisible hands reached out to pin her shoulders to the pillows. Excitement jangled her nerves. Eddies of danger curled like the night air about her shoulders and neck. As he leaned toward her, his broad shoulders blocking out even the starlight, anticipation warmed her cheeks and tingled her skin. In another moment he would kiss her and she would be lost.

She lifted her hand, placing the palm flat against his

shirtfront, but she had no strength to push him away. Rushing desperately into speech, she spoke the first unconsidered thought that registered in her bemused brain. "What is the scent you wear, my lord?"

To her joy and consternation, he drew back a little, and she knew she had disconcerted him. "It's called vetivert. My valet, Hugh, has found the extract useful in making my linen mothproof. Does it not please you?"

"Oh, it's quite nice."

"Countess . . . Regina," he began, directing his hand up into the fine silky hair at her nape. He bent his head in search of any part of her sweet face and touched his lips to her brow. "Don't be frightened." He brushed his lips across the pulse at her temple. "You know what I want, what I need from you."

But she didn't know! She did not know anything about the business between men and women. Her fingers curled on his shirtfront as her mind clutched at straws of erratic thought. "Is two A.M. your usual hour for seduction?"

He continued his nibbling exploration of her cheek. "Why do you ask? Do you have a preference for another?"

"As a woman of experience, you mean?" she said faintly. His lips had reached the corner of her mouth. The burning impression of his kiss was just moments away. "What does the gossip—"

"I don't listen to gossip!" he said impatiently. "Not when a man like Buckram—"

"Buckram!" Regina whispered.

Maxwell could have kicked himself for having brought up the name, but now that it was done he might as well tell her the rest. "Buckram placed the bet at White's." Adopting a worldly tone of indifference he thought she would appreciate, he added, "I suppose he's chagrined that you have left him without a word."

Regina turned her head away from the awful revelation he had made. *Buckram had placed the bet at White's!*

The memory of Percy Buckram as she had last seen him came rushing back. She saw his relentless mocking sneer, the spittle on her hand, his arrogant stance while he believed that she was at his mercy. When she had counter-threatened him, he'd been like a wolf whose cornered prey had suddenly turned and bitten him: surprised, enraged, and made ultimately all the more dangerous for the wounding. So this was his method of exacting revenge. His bet had made her the prey of every titled rake, roué, and dissipated rogue in England.

Regina turned back to Maxwell, wishing that a thousand candles lit the room so that she could see his face. He thought her an adulteress, an accomplished seductress. He believed her capable of giving herself to a man as vile as Percy Buckram . . . and still he wanted her. She took a long painful breath, determined to say the words though she could not expect to be believed. "I'm not what you think I am and I'm not what you want."

"I don't care what you are!" Maxwell muttered, frustrated by her seeming need to put fresh obstacles in their path. Was she toying with him, or was she merely afraid?

He reminded himself that he hadn't come here to make love to her then rejected the lie as too pitiful for a grown man to maintain. Making love to her was all that he had thought about for days. To avoid that truth, he had instigated a late-night card game with Leslie and Giles. For the last hour he had paced his bedroom floor, feeling himself grow in tumescence each time his gaze strayed to the hidden door that led to the secret labyrinth that riddled Blood Hall. Yet he couldn't be certain that she waited as he did, tense, taut, and aching with desire.

In the end, it was the remembrance of how she had

looked up at him after the séance that had made him hesitate. There had been a longing as great as his own in those green eyes that so perfectly reflected her feelings. It was a declaration, a shy achingly raw appeal of invitation without guilt or calculation or pride. For one delirious moment, he had read that look as one of love. She loved him! No, that was impossible! Or was it? That thought had kept him wearing out his rug until the hidden door had suddenly swung open. He didn't stop to question why it happened. The question surging through his mind had been enough to send him on his way to where it could be answered.

He ran his hands down over her shoulders and upper arms, letting his thumbs trail lightly over the outer fullness of her breasts. He felt her shiver but she didn't draw away. Stanford had said that Buckram was a rude and callous lover. Perhaps he'd shocked or even hurt her with his urgent selfish need. After all, she had only been a bride one week. Married to a man she did not love, it was easy to understand how she had become the victim of a practiced dandy's lies.

The thought of what she must have endured at Buckram's hands wrenched his gut. He didn't know Percy Buckram but he would make the man's acquaintance when next he was in London. Preferably he would like to meet him in a dark alley, without warning, and without seconds. Then he would teach the man what physical vulnerability and helplessness were like.

He lifted a hand very carefully to her nape and began to gently massage the sensitive skin. "You are what I want! If you would have proof of my feelings for you, you need only kiss me."

"That is proof of your lust, nothing else," Regina answered, refusing to acknowledge his touch.

"Then kiss me to prove that I lie, Regina, but kiss me."

His lips took her cool soft mouth in a gentle embrace. Understanding intuitively that persuasion must come in the form of tenderness, he didn't press her for a response. Instead, when she didn't push him away, he moved to first one corner and then the other of her mouth, delivering stinging sweet kisses she didn't return. After a moment he paused, pressing his cheek against the cool satin of hers. "You are so soft," he said in a hushed voice. "I remember how soft and trusting you were in my arms the night of the storm. Won't you kiss me as sweetly as you did then?"

As he rubbed his cheek on hers, the faint brush of his beard sent tiny shivers of pleasure along Regina's skin. In spite of what he thought of her, she couldn't find the courage to reject him. Perhaps she was all those lewd and ugly epithets Buckram and the dowager had hurled at her. The wantonness in her nature seeped through each and every time this man touched her, a man she scarcely knew, whom she had disliked nearly all her life. With no more effort than a few tantalizing kisses he could make her forget everything she had ever been taught about virtue, pride, and integrity. She wanted him. The wanting was like a live thing writhing within her.

Yet the struggle going on within her head seemed totally apart from the judgment ruling her body. As if abetted by a will outside her own, her hands rose to lie gently against his chest where his heart pounded hard and confidently. Was she mad? she wondered as she strained against what seemed to be an invisible force that urged her to arch her body closer to his.

Let him! Let him love you!

The unspoken words knelled in her head. With a cry half capitulation, half triumph, she turned her head to meet his kiss.

The touch of her lips was startlingly cool on his mouth,

like the kiss of marble statue. But that impression died a quick death as he was caught up in the conflagration of feeling she ignited by parting her lips and letting her warm sweet body's breath caress his lips. His arms went around her to bring her closer and the kiss deepened. He heard her faint sigh and wondered why she lamented her surrender. Didn't she realize that he would be a considerate and tender lover? Yet how could she, unless he showed her?

Regina shut her eyes and wrapped her arms about his neck as he dragged her away from the pillows and pressed her back onto the mattress. As he stretched out over her she welcomed everything about him, his vibrant warmth, the slight dampness of his skin where her nose pressed into the open collar of his shirt, the hard heavy weight of his longer, wider body concentrated in his shoulders and hips and thighs. His lips found hers again, pressing, seeking, and then more urgently demanding her response as his legs entwined with hers through the barrier of the sheet. He drove his hips against her, pressing her farther into the mattress as he grew harder and harder against her lower belly. His hands slid down over her shoulders to her narrow waist, taking the covers with them. Then they rose again in a heavy caress that molded her gown to her body's contours. Exquisite heat followed where he touched her. When his hands cupped the womanly weight of her breasts, her hands scored up through his thick mahogany hair, drawing his head down hard to hers. This time her lips parted first, her seeking tongue begging answer from his own.

Pleasure pulsed through Maxwell in urgent, ever-tightening sweeps as she initiated this kiss. She was new to the art of the erotic kiss, he could tell, but she was kissing him as if she had just invented the act. Her mouth clung to his, absorbing his taste and texture, greedy for whatever he offered. The nipples beneath his fingers stood pebble hard, the undeniable sentinels of passion so taut he knew they must ache. She did want him!

A woman's scream suddenly pierced the silence of the night, shattering the spell of voluptuous sensation that had just begun to enthrall them.

Startled, Maxwell lifted his head. "What the devil!" he muttered only to be cut off by a second, higher-pitched cry that ended abruptly.

"That's Lady Eloise's voice!" Regina jerked forward and pressed against his shoulders that pinned her to the bed.

"The devil it is!" Even as he rose from the bed, Regina reached out to set a light to the bedside candle. The tiny flame sputtered and wavered in the darkness, making lurid shadows climb the walls, then steadied and expanded its glow in a valiant effort to fill the darkness. As her gaze shifted away from it, Regina saw in amazement that she was alone. From the corner of her eye she caught movement by the fireplace and turned at the last instant to see the panel close the final inch with only a whisper of sound.

The third cry sent Regina to her feet without another thought for Lord Kingsblood or what they had done, or come so close to doing. She scooped up her wrapper and donned it. When she had tied it securely about her waist, she hurried over to her mirror and scraped back the hair from her face. For an instant she saw herself as she was, with passion-laden eyes, kiss-smeared mouth, and blushed from crown to where her wrapper covered her bosom. She stared, unable to believe the wild creature in the mirror was herself. And then she turned away, picked up the candle, and went to open her door.

The hallway was dark save for a bright glow at the very end. As she hurried along the hall, the sound of weeping reached her ears. A moment later a voice, hushed and comforting, overrode it.

"Dearest," a man's deep voice said, "It was only a bad dream."

Shocked, Regina paused just outside the door. Lord Kingsblood had arrived before her!

"Please, sweeting, don't cry. I can't bear to hear you cry."

The tender words fell like live embers upon her, each a searing sensation that registered in her heart. Dearest! Sweeting! He was comforting Eloise with words of love. He had never said anything similar to her, not even when she lay in his arms just moments before, stunned from his kisses. She began backing away, furious, ashamed, and defeated.

"Out of the way, Miss Willoby!" a voice thundered behind her, and then a hand at the small of her back thrust her past the threshold into Lady Eloise's room.

Regina stood blinking a second against the light of several candles, and then she saw Lady Eloise in the arms of the Earl of Dartmoor. Her relief was so great that her smile lighted up her whole face.

Maxwell, too, took in the scene of Eloise in Stanford's embrace. The sight stunned him. Had he not heard the screams, he would have thought he had come upon a pair of lovers, so tenderly did Stanford hold the lady in his embrace. He recalled how solicitous Stanford had been to her after the séance. For an instant he wondered if the man was in love with her. The next, he rejected it. "What's going on here?"

Eloise gasped and shoved Stanford in the chest. The sudden movement caught the earl unprepared. His hands still flexed on her shoulders and the seam of her nightgown ripped as she jerked free. As Eloise cried out in dismay, he hastily straightened his dressing gown of India silk, which had come open as she broke free—but not before both Regina and Maxwell spied a flash of naked leg.

"What's—oh my!"

"By Jove!"

The two shocked voices belonged to Cordelia and Giles, who poked their heads through the doorway at just that moment.

"Marquess! Earl!" Eloise turned to first one and then the other, her lovely face spoiled by trembling lips and bulging eyes. "You must stop the fiend! This time he mustn't get away!"

Maxwell's dark gaze shifted to Stanford. "What have you done?"

To his credit Leslie didn't shrink from the imposing figure who wore only trousers and his stockings. Lesser men might have been daunted by the powerful muscles on display in his broad chest, but the earl had right on his side. "Don't be insulting, Max," he said with an much contempt as he dared. "Lady Eloise was frightened by an intruder. I was the first to arrive after she cried out."

Maxwell's dark brows lowered. "What intruder?"

Eloise shook her head frantically when he turned his gaze her way. "T-t-that man! T-t-that Cromwellian! The ghost!"

All the fire went out of Maxwell's gaze. "Ghost?" he repeated on a whimsical note and lifted an eyebrow at Leslie, who answered with an elegant shrug of his Turkish-robed shoulders. "Ghost," he repeated. He'd been routed from a bed of sensual pleasure by the vaporish idiocy of Eloise's overactive imagination. "So, Eloise, our little parlor tricks have come back to haunt you."

He cast a dark glance at Cordelia, who had edged inside the door, her eyes as big as saucers. "I did try to warn you ladies that such deeds can have repercussions. Come here, Eloise."

Regina hid her fists in the folds of her wrapper as Maxwell opened his arms to the other woman. To her great satisfaction, Eloise backed away and held up both hands to fend him off.

"No you don't, my lord!" Eloise said angrily. "You mocked me before but I saw him this time. Positively! There!" She pointed to her bed. "He stood above me as I slept, his cold breath—"

She paused and closed her eyes so abruptly that both men surged forward in the expectation that she would faint. But her eyes flew open as they reached her, her gaze made all the more arresting because the white showed all around the magnificent blue.

"Where is Nana? Where is my Nana?" She turned her frightened gaze on Maxwell. "You find him, do you hear me? He bears a scar here and here." She pointed to her cheek and then brow. "He was wearing a metal chestplate and carried a sword. He had a grin like the devil himself. I thought I should be ravished in my bed!"

"I don't believe ghosts can rav—" Giles broke off as he realized the indelicacy of his thoughts.

"Perhaps I should look about, just in case," Leslie murmured to fill in the gap, and went to survey the bed hangings.

Thinking it time for sensible action, Regina came forward. "Poor Lady Eloise, you've had a terrible fright."

Hearing a sympathetic female voice broke the restraint Eloise had placed on her emotions, and she flung herself into Regina's embrace. "You believe me, don't you?" she wailed as tears began to stream down her cheeks. "I saw him! I did!"

"You believe you saw something," Regina answered,

thinking of her own experience a few hours earlier. She had believed it too. She patted the lady crying on her shoulder. "And that's as much as any of us may ever know of the matter." Avoiding the marquess who hovered nearby, she addressed Cordelia. "Lady, will you ring for a servant? Lady Eloise is in need of tea."

"And something stronger," Maxwell amended, and went to add coal to the fire because he couldn't think of anything useful to do. He didn't trust himself to look at Regina again. Surprise had been an effective but temporary antidote to his ardor. One look at her flushed face and lips still blurred by their kisses, and the return of passion had been so rapid that it affected his stride. So much for restraint. Would she regain her passion as easily? Knowing women, he doubted it.

At that moment a very disheveled Dorrity lurched into the room, her nightcap cocked over one eye and a frizzled iron-gray braid hanging at her shoulder. Hours earlier, after having put her mistress safely abed for the night, she had been persuaded to join the housekeeper in the pantry for "a sherry." One had led to two and so on until she could no longer say with certainty the final number. But not even a surfeit of spirits could keep her from responding to her mistress's shrieks. The length of her response time, however, had been severely hampered.

Her red-rimmed eyes widened as she saw Lord Kingsblood, his cousin, and Lord Stanford boldly striding about her mistress's room. Finally her fuzzy gaze fell on Eloise who was weeping on Miss Willoby's shoulder. "What's happened here, Lady Eloise?"

"A ghost!" Eloise cried, jumping to her feet just as Regina had gotten her to sit. "Oh, Nana, I'm been visited by a fiend!" She flew into Dorrity's arms, her momentum nearly knocking the none-too-steady woman off her feet. "He was a great grinning ghoul with flaming eyes and ravishment on his mind!"

The gentlemen exchanged glances, each thinking that for a gently reared young lady, Eloise seemed curiously preoccupied with thoughts of ravishment.

Now that her presence was no longer required, Regina moved toward the door. "If you'll excuse me, I'll return to my chamber."

Eloise whirled about at her words. "No, you mustn't! What if the fiend should choose to visit your room next?"

Regina didn't trust herself to meet anyone's eye as she answered, "I shall lock my door and take a poker to bed with me."

"Really, Miss Willoby, you sound quite bloodthirsty," Maxwell answered, unable to let the jibe pass unchallenged.

To his surprise she turned on him a cold gaze of anger. "I assure you, Marquess, if my rest is again disturbed this night, the fiend who disturbs it will get a nasty surprise!" She held his startled gaze for a moment before adding "Good night, all."

"Now see what you've done," Eloise cried petulantly. "No, please, Miss Willoby, wait a moment."

Reluctantly Regina turned around at the door.

Eloise lifted her chin and swallowed. "I wish to say something that I prefer to have witnesses for." She paused to dab a tear away before addressing her fiancé. "Blood Hall is a beastly house full of ugly furnishings and rusty swords! I refuse to stay here another day! Not one! If you care a fig for my feelings, my lord, you'll take me back to London first thing in the morning. If you refuse, I shall go on my own."

As five pairs of eyes rested on him, Maxwell felt the sudden urge to laugh. Thoughts of how to get Eloise out of his home were in the back of his mind at that very moment.

But he dared not let her know it. "We'll discuss it in the morning, when you've rested."

"My mind is made up. I shan't change it. I hate Blood Hall. I'll never come back." She stamped her foot. "Never!"

"Lord Kingsblood's right," Regina said soothingly as she took a step toward the distraught young lady. "Tomorrow is soon enough for any discussion of travel."

Admiration shone in Eloise's blue eyes. "You're not afraid, are you? Then, please, I beg you, let me sleep with you in your bed tonight."

"Oh, yes, I should like that too!" Cordelia seconded.

"Very well," Regina replied after only the most fractional of hesitations, during which she thought that for a person who had never shared her bed with any creature in all her life, she had suddenly gained a surfeit of bed partners for one night. She turned to Maxwell, her eyes resting a moment on the solemn lines of his handsome face. She thought she could smell the scent of vetivert across the room, or maybe it remained on her skin where their bodies had touched. "Good night, Marquess."

"I suggest we all retire," Maxwell said with a heavy undertone of disgust. "Stanford, Giles, we've early-morning hunting ahead."

It took Regina only minutes to regain her chamber and retire once more, this time with Eloise and Cordelia to help warm the covers. Exhausted by fright, both ladies fell asleep immediately. But Regina lay awake a long time, considering the last hours and those to come.

Though Lord Kingsblood was as yet unaware, she had just said good-bye to him rather than good night. She would leave first thing in the morning. His mention of a hunt had given her the perfect opportunity to depart without argument. Already she had risked too much by remaining as long as she had. After the events of the night, things were much clearer to her. She mustn't see him again. The aching inside her had only subsided, not abated. She was too needy to allow herself to be seduced by a little kindness and an attractive man's interest. She mustn't love where there was no hope for happiness. For, if she did, she would be destroyed.

"Please make me strong!" she whispered in prayer, for she feared her own weakness more than the marquess's passion.

"Come see what you've done!" the captain roared in ill humor as he pressed his face to the lead glass of the oriel and looked out upon the misty dawn of early morning. An hour earlier he had watched in mild amusement as the marquess and his two friends had ridden out to hunt birds. Now, below on the drive, a pony cart had been drawn up. In it were the Countess of Amesbury's trunk and portmanteau. Even as he looked down, she appeared on the steps and was handed up into the conveyance by a groom. "Look you there! You've driven the widow off!"

"I can't believe that she's simply running away," his lady answered, and joined him at the window.

"Can't you? You made her face a hard truth last night during that foolish séance. She'd have done better to have remained in doubt of her feelings. Now Maxwell's lost his game!"

"If she's been frightened off, 'twas none of my doing!" she retorted. "Who held her still until Maxwell had kissed her enough for passion to take over?"

"And who ruined a perfectly good seduction!" he roared back. "Pretending to be me, snatching away Lady Eloise's covers and leering down at her in my guise! Why didn't you frighten her to death and have done with it?"

"The female's too silly to die!"

"The widow was Maxwell's for the taking. To let her escape is dangerous. If the lad spends too much time in the chase, he will come to think himself in love!"

Her thoughts exactly! But she was not about to voice it to her opponent. She could not remember when she had had more fun. The captain, who usually did not show himself before noon, was up before dawn. Even their bickering was invigorating. After all, after nearly two hundred years, there was only so much a beautiful woman's wiles could do to rouse a man. She would regret it when their many-times great-grandson returned to London. She was just becoming accustomed to the noise and messy disruptions of human lives. In fact . . .

A sly smile turned up the corners of her bewitching mouth. "Has it not occurred to you, Captain, that no woman risks everything unless she's certain she *is* in love!"

"In my experience, a woman doesn't run from the man she loves, she gives chase!"

"That is because your experience, until you met me, was limited to whores and jades," she said repressively. "I hid my feelings for you for months, if you will recall."

"I recall that you didn't pack your bags and hie across the moors like a frightened nun the moment I made my yen for you known." He slapped her heartily on the backside. "Mistresses were made of sterner stuff in our day!"

"Perhaps," she replied, thinking of the merry chase she had led her captain. In the end, before he had recanted his loosely held beliefs for the good of the Commonwealth, he had been reduced to such a state that he stood in his breeches at every mention of her name. It took a rare man to risk his heart and his head over a woman his friends considered unsuitable. That same blood ran in Maxwell's veins. "What do you suppose Maxwell will do when he finds her gone?"

"What he should have done in the first place! Find her, swive her, and forget her!"

"I wonder," she said with a small secretive smile. The captain might grow to like the sound of children's joyous voices filling the dark empty corridors of Blood Hall: raven-haired children with green eyes and their father's smile!

As the trap rolled off down the lane, the two misty figures gazing out from the oriel of the great hall fell into a brooding silence that thoroughly chilled the maid who came to lay the morning fire in the cleaned-out grate.

Chapter Thirteen

❦

"She's what?" Maxwell demanded in astonishment as he stood in the kitchen of Blood Hall with the bounty of the morning's hunt. Leslie and Giles had gone directly up to wash and change while Maxwell had decided to visit the kitchen with specific instructions about how his kill should be prepared. The last thing he expected was trouble.

The housekeeper was twisting her apron, a familiar habit when pressed by unpleasant circumstance. "I told Miss Willoby that she should wait upon your return, my lord, but she said you knew she was going, had made certain her place was in readiness."

"Who told her the cottage was in readiness?"

"The coachman."

"Did he, indeed?" He had deliberately given the coachman enough work to do these last days that he should not have had time to see to any work on the countess's cottage, no matter how much he was being paid to do it. "Send him to me."

"He's gone with the lady, my lord, but he should be back directly."

"Very well." Realizing that he still held a brace of black cocks in his hands, Maxwell thrust the birds at her. "Remind Cook that the birds are to hang at least three days. The last came to the table too soon. I detest tough, tasteless meat." In afterthought he added, "I'm going up to change. Send a maid to ask Lady Eloise to join me for breakfast."

The housekeeper looked as if he had poked her with a rod. "The ladies have had their breakfast, my lord."

"At this hour? What else?" he prompted, for by her anxious expression there was clearly more.

"Well, my lord, the ladies are upstairs packing."

Maxwell's dark brows lifted. "Are they?" Not expecting her to answer that, he turned and thrust his fowling piece into the hands of a waiting footman. "Have a fresh horse saddled for me and standing out front in ten minutes," he directed the young man. "I'm not hungry after all."

His long legs more than equal to the task, he took the stairs two at a time. Regina had left! And without so much as a word. She was running from him, that much was clear. But that she should decamp when he was away, without so much as a by-your-leave, that was unkind of her.

As for Eloise, her decision to leave was a blessing in disguise. If she went of her own free will then he wouldn't feel guilty. Besides, her departure would provide him with time and privacy in which to reassess his feelings. He knew Eloise well enough to know that she hoped he would follow her back to London and there, in abject misery, ask to be forgiven, and then promise to marry her immediately. But, with time and luck, he would work out a method to spare her pride while he regained his freedom.

By the time he reached his room he had worked his neckcloth loose. He opened his waistcoat so quickly the buttons burst loose and scattered like tiny hailstones across the carpet, which his valet hurried to pick up. He glanced down at the man on his knees who was sweeping buttons into his palm and said, "I'm no steed to be put through society's paces! Perhaps I don't wish to marry a belle of the *ton*!"

His valet, bless him, was a quiet unobtrusive man. Some

gentlemen lived and died by their valets' advice. The marquess's man might have been a mute for all the verbal commentary he offered, and that was just to his lordship's liking.

Merely nodding, the servant returned to his work while Maxwell continued his ruminations. "Perhaps I should reconsider my position," he said as in rapid succession he stripped off his jacket, waistcoat, and shirt, and let them fall into the waiting hands of his man. He was, after all, only twenty and eight, a man in full bloom. For the last six years he'd dedicated his life to serious work and therefore hadn't had the time to enjoy many of the most pleasant distractions that city life had to offer. "Why, I've never kept a mistress! Surely a gentleman should do so before he settles into marriage!"

The thought gave him pause. *He had never kept a mistress.* Oh, there had been women, and a few affairs, but no long, durable relationship that tested his ability to sustain an understanding with a woman. There hadn't been time. But now, if he chose, he could make the time.

He stripped quickly out of his sodden wool breeches and replaced them with a pair of doeskin riding breeches handed to him by his valet. Once donned, they stretched over his thighs like a second skin. The cambric shirt his valet handed him reminded him of Regina's comment about the new scent that impregnated his clothing. "Continue to use the vetivert," he said as he pulled it over his head.

With quick efficiency he buttoned it, made a simple matter of his neckcloth, donned a suede waistcoat, and dark-blue riding coat of fine wool. By the time he had slipped on his Hessians, he was in a good mood again. All that was required to solve any problem, he congratulated himself, was a cool head, rational thought, and sensible action.

"Leslie and Giles can accompany the ladies back to London," he explained to the man who buffed a dull spot on the toe of his left boot. "I'll remain here. By the time I return to London, I'm confident that I'll have conceived a plan to free myself from Lady Eloise. Thank you. I'm off for my morning ride."

The day was warmer than it had been when he first ventured into it at dawn, but the brisk breeze made Maxwell thankful that he wore leather and wool. As he rode across the headland hills, he seemed to see it all with new eyes. The sky was a deep autumnal blue clarified by the first chill of the season. The grass had begun to fade while the other vegetation on the treeless hillsides reflected every shade of green, red, gold, and brown. The wild untamed scenery breathed new life into his resolution. He would visit Regina, ascertain her immediate needs, and then, when the moment seemed right, inform her that Lady Eloise was going back to London. Depending on her reaction, he would know how to proceed, whether to simply allow her to play out this little melodrama of widow in her cottage to his lord of the manor or invite her to come back to Blood Hall.

Desire ignited within him, suddenly, full blown, and deliciously urgent. Or would she have the courage to simply come into his arms and let him love her right then and there as they both wanted and needed?

Needed. The last word remained with unwavering clarity in his mind. He wanted her certainly. The ache that had been a subtle but integral part of him this last week had at its base, a carnal lust for a beautiful, intriguing woman. He was ready to admit it. That he found her mysterious and elusive, and unexpectedly stimulating to his intellect, were added frissons of delight to his basic desire to possess her body. She excited him, roused him, confused, and, at times, confounded him. But at the heart of the matter, he was drawn to her like iron to lodestone. There was a need: uncomplicated, unmitigated, and wholly unavoidable.

Just as her glance offered her emotions unreservedly, unequivocally, and relentlessly, her body had responded to his the night before with an honesty that had bordered on a challenge. Such vulnerability swamped him, and his feelings of protectiveness toward her redoubled. If things were different, he would have courted her with gentlemanly patience and, perhaps, won her hand as well as her heart and her passion. Did he wish things were different? Yes, dammit —he did.

If this was love, was it the wild unformed kind that adolescence is prone to, the kind that wreaks havoc for a short breathless time and then, like an autumn storm, blows itself out more quickly than the gentle spring rain? After the first time he shared her bed and body, would the feelings that now sent him pounding along the coast lessen? Or was this love the deep abiding kind he had thought to find with Eloise and now longed for with a woman the world would count as totally unsuitable?

He was amazed by how quickly he came upon the lane that curved down to the cottage, which stood in the lee of a barren hillside where an ancient line of planted oak and beech trees formed the boundary between headland and moor.

Even from a distance the new roof of thatch stood out like ripened wheat. The whitewashed walls gleamed in the sunshine. He smiled as he broke into a canter. Perhaps she'd been wise in leading him here, away from prying eyes and the constant vigilance of his staff. A trysting place. Their trysting place. He liked the sound of it. He would bring her special gifts and buy her a large bed, for he disliked the cramped narrow quarters of most beds. He would furnish her with the best sheets and a goosedown comforter for the cold nights when they would lay for hours huddled, naked, and sated between the covers. Later, when she would no longer think he was buying her favors, he would present her with a necklace of emeralds—no!

While shopping for an engagement gift for Eloise, he'd been shown a magnificent necklace of peridots set in diamonds. They had been entirely wrong for Eloise, but he'd been fascinated by the gemstones, which ranged in color from pale golden greens to a deep rich green like that of emeralds with burnished undertones. They would reflect perfectly the changeable moods that altered the color of Regina's expressive eyes. He had yet to see what color they turned when passion consumed her. He guessed . . . no, he would not guess. He would find out, perhaps this very day.

He gave not much attention to the traveling coach coming up the lane in the opposite direction until the driver suddenly reined in before the cottage. In surprise, he slowed his horse, wondering what possible reason the coach could have for stopping there. Even as the question formed, the nearside door swung upon and a man swathed in a cape and tri-corner stepped down. Maxwell brought his mount to a standstill on the road. Some innate sense of self-preservation told him that he might want to know more before he revealed himself.

The man took purposeful strides toward the door. He was only halfway up the path when the door suddenly swung open and the countess appeared. Maxwell was too far off to hear the exchange but he saw her pause as if surprised. Then with a faint cry she ran out to meet the stranger, flinging her arms about him.

Maxwell involuntarily stiffened. The action made his horse start and dance sideways. Who was this man? She had led him to believe that she didn't know anyone in the area and, further, that she didn't want anyone to know her whereabouts. As he watched, she disengaged her slender body from the stranger's embrace only to catch him by the hand and lead him toward the cottage.

Jealousy replaced surprise with a force so strong it made him shudder. She had lied to him! She must have made this assignation before leaving London. He saw again in his mind's eye how she had paused in the doorway, her white gown molded by the breeze to her slim legs, and then how she had thrown herself with unchecked joy into the man's arms. This was no random visitor, but someone for whom she held a great regard. Was this Buckram? The thought made his heart lurch unpleasantly.

"Fool!" he said roughly, and jerked the reins so brutally his horse whinnied and snorted in displeasure. Immediately he gentled his hold. He had begun to believe that she wasn't all the terrible heartless things gossip had claimed her to be. No, more than that, he had *wanted* to believe her.

Fighting the pain that was thickening his pulse, he denied the emotional snares that hovered just out of conscious thought, waiting for them to claim him. What would she do now if he suddenly rode down upon them? What excuse would she give? How would those bedeviling eyes of hers look when she met his damning gaze? Would they again lie to him and make him believe the lie?

He turned his horse and rode away, hurt and humiliation thundering through his body. If she could lie that well, he didn't want to know it.

"Once I'd given it some thought, my dear niece, I realized that there was nowhere else you might have gone," Shelby Townsend answered.

"How transparent I am, Uncle." Regina betrayed her

nervousness by a little laugh. "And I had thought no one would think to look for me here if I lived to be a hundred." She smiled brightly at him, silently blessing the coachman for his foresight in stocking her small pantry with the necessities. "Shall I pour? The tea is ready."

Now that the shock and natural pleasure of seeing a friendly face had worn off, she was alert to the unspoken matters between them. Shelby Townsend wasn't a man to travel hundreds of miles simply to check on his niece's well-being. For the nine years she had lived in a convent, he'd done no more than send money. He might have sent a hireling to discover her whereabouts. That he had made the journey himself was a momentous omen.

"Two lumps, dear," Shelby said cordially, his eyes roving once more over his niece. She was thinner than he remembered, her cheekbones standing out in stark relief, making her bold but well-featured face even more arresting. When he had first seen her in Italy, he'd wished that she were softer of cheek with a smaller mouth and a less compelling gaze. With her striking and rare blue-black hair, she'd first seemed too bold for the salons of London. But now, looking at her with a readjusted eye, he realized that she might have done better than an earl had she been given a Season. Still, he wouldn't quibble. Amesbury's estate offered him much, and he wasn't a greedy man. Perhaps, in a few years, when he had the estate fully under his control, he might encourage her to marry again. The girl deserved some happiness. After all, she was to make possible his desire to spend the rest of his life as a very wealthy man.

"I surmised the reasons why you ran away, Regina, but I must say I'm wounded that you didn't think to advise me of your plan."

Regina passed him a cup and saucer, avoiding his pale-gray gaze. "There was no plan, Uncle. The dowager countess gave me very little choice and less time to act."

"You refer to, I suppose, her threat to expose your marriage to the Earl of Amesbury as invalid." He saw her mispour and splash tea into her saucer. "You needn't be so surprised, my dear. The dowager countess wasted no time in summoning me when she found you gone." He gave her a tight little smile of satisfaction. "She was under the mistaken impression that I had engineered your flight."

Regina sipped her tea before replying. "Then you know that she seeks to annul the marriage."

He nodded and then broke into a smile that revealed the brown stubs of his teeth, the results of his fondness for a pipe. "I advised her that her claim that the marriage was never consummated was an insult to her son's, ah, virility. Besides, who would believe it, considering the manner of his death?"

Regina didn't meet his eyes. Buckram had been the one to tell her, in a jeering tone, that her husband of a week had expired while in the arms of his mistress. Until now she hadn't known whether or not to believe him. "The dowager had summoned a physician to our last interview in order to have me examined," she said softly.

"Did she, by Jove? Did you allow the examination?"

She lifted her head, her green eyes filled with righteous indignation. "Of course not!"

"Forgive me, dear niece. I forget how sheltered you've been. The dowager is of the old school. She cut her eyeteeth in the midst of the rollicking eighteenth century. Manners weren't so refined, and matters of—well—carnal interest were handled much more matter-of-factly. You might have helped our cause by submitting."

Or lost it, she thought uncomfortably. Reluctant to admit the truth or tell him of Buckram's threat to proclaim himself as her lover if she should have been found pregnant, she said, "The dowager might have bribed the doctor to lie, no matter the outcome."

He pressed his fingers into a steeple, tapping his forefingers against his nose. "I don't suppose there's any chance that you're breeding?"

Regina met his eyes again. "None."

"A pity. A child would cement our claim."

Not for the first time, Regina noticed that he kept referring to her troubles and her claim as "ours." "I appreciate your interest in my welfare, Uncle, for you did engineer my marriage," she added dryly. "At least now I'm able to live an independent life."

Shelby looked about the small cottage furnished with only the two chairs on which they sat, a small rough table from which she poured tea, and what appeared to be a very lumpy mattress in the far corner. "I'd hardly call these surroundings worthy of a countess, dear child. That is why I've sought you out." He reached into the pouch he had laid by his chair leg and withdrew several official-looking documents. "I believe that you'll find that I'm prepared to solve all our problems." He laid the papers on the tabletop and smoothed the parchment with a hand. "The first order of business is to get you beyond the clutches of the dowager." He raised a bland gaze to meet hers. "Devon isn't far enough, my dear. If I found you, it's only a matter of time before she does. I don't wish to alarm you, but there are private investigators on your trail even as we speak."

Regina's indignant gasp elicited a tiny smile from him. He tapped the papers with a blunt-tipped finger. "As the new earl, Lord Buckram retains Lynsdale Hall and the lands in Dorset, but do you realize that the bulk of the estates and the wealth are yours? I propose, for the sake of convenience and your safety, to put myself in charge of your inheritance. You must leave England immediately. I've made arrangements for you to live in Florence. I'll establish a monthly allowance, generous in the extreme, of course, so that you may have the independence of your position as a widow. The dowager can't live forever. I have it on good authority that your disappearance has caused a setback in her health."

This news amazed Regina. "In my experience, the dowager has seemed the most indomitable, unstoppable, unconquerable being alive. To think that I am the cause of her ill health makes me uneasy."

"Even so, my dear, it's a happy occurrence, for your sake."

Regina shook her head. They were enemies but not mortal foes. The news reinforced the tentative decision that had been circling in her head for days. "Thank you, Uncle, for your consideration but these documents won't be necessary. You see, I should like to return the Amesbury holdings to the dowager."

"You what?" The older man was clearly startled. For an instant, Regina thought she saw something akin to anger darken his complexion. The idea of it so surprised her that she dismissed the perception as a mistake. "Hear me out, Uncle. In fleeing London I acted hastily and ungraciously, but the dowager had provoked me beyond all reason. Now that I've had a few days to think it over, I realize that I don't want nor do I need the full inheritance. I'll make some small claim, of course, and demand the right to the title of Countess of Amesbury. The rest will be returned to the family."

The shock on the older man's face was quickly replaced by one of guile. "Dear child, recanting your right to the Amesbury estate is foolhardy. Many will continue to think that you married only for gain and that guilt forced you to give it up. You'll be considered a weak, foolish young woman."

"It doesn't matter," Regina said patiently, for she had thought of that. "You and I know I'm nothing more or less than I claim."

"But, as things stand, you are now a very wealthy young lady. You cannot appreciate what that means because you've never had the advantages of most girls of your class." He leaned forward, at his most persuasive. "Go away now, as I ask. Then come back to London, in a year. I will then introduce to you the delightful possibilities of your position and means. By Boxing Day, I assure you, you'll no longer think of releasing what is rightfully yours."

Rightfully hers. Was it rightfully hers? The marriage had not been consummated. The legality of the marriage hung on a technicality. Why didn't she simply tell him the truth? What held her back? Pride? Embarrassment? Or was it the certain though inexplicable feeling that something more than her welfare motivated his actions? "I'm sorry, Uncle, but I've made up my mind. I can't think of anything that would persuade me differently."

"Don't be a fool, girl!" He caught himself as her eyes widened at his tone. "If you hope the dowager will think more kindly of you, you are wrong! She'll hound you all the more for capitulating to her. She'll see to it that you are banned from every decent household in the land."

Regina paled. "Why, Uncle? Why does she hate me so?"

His eyes slid from her wounded expression. "She hoped her son wouldn't marry until his dotage, or that he'd select a milksop for a bride, one that she could bully and terrorize."

"He did," she answered honestly. "The dowager terrifies me."

His secretive smile came back. "Yet you have defied her.

One wouldn't have expected that of you, my dear. Certainly I never suspected the hidden wealth of stubbornness in your character. You have fooled us all, Regina."

Somehow, his words weren't comforting but vaguely unsettling. "I'm a great coward, Uncle. You should have seen me the night I arrived here. The cottage was in a terrible state and there was a storm. If not for the help of the Marquess of Ilfracombe, I might have been struck and killed by lightning."

Shelby's bland expression evaporated. "Marquess? How did you meet this marquess?"

Regina bit her lip, wishing she hadn't let her tongue run away with her thoughts. Blushing in spite of herself, she said, "We met on the road the day I arrived. His carriage had overturned and I gave him a ride to Blood Hall."

He watched her intently. "Does he know who you are?"

"No," Regina lied.

His gaze shifted to her ringless finger then he smiled. "Gad, you've the presence of mind of a man! I can see that I've underestimated you in more ways than one, little niece." Though he sounded pleased, Regina sensed that he was far from it. "In any case, that settles the matter. You can't hide in the countryside. Sooner or later you'll be discovered." He reached again into his pouch and withdrew tickets this time. "I've made arrangements for you to sail next Friday from Portsmouth. You should enjoy the voyage. Your accommodations are the finest. Once in Florence, you may reconsider your situation at your leisure." He slid the papers across the table in her direction. "You need only sign this bank draft and these papers and then put your mind at rest."

Under the power of his cool gray stare, she reached for the papers and began reading them. She perused only a few lines before lifting her head. "This gives you authority to act in my behalf."

He nodded pleasantly. "As I've done these last nine years. None will think it odd that I act on your behalf in this matter."

"It gives you full authority," Regina persisted against the voice whispering in her ear that he was her last ally.

"It is customary," he answered with a slow nod of his head.

"When will authority revert to me?"

"Whenever you feel able to manage your own affairs, my dear, though I should think that would be some time, perhaps several years. Women seldom manage their own finances. You will, of course, one day consider remarrying." By then he would have lined his own nest quite comfortably from her proceeds, he thought. "Then your husband will take charge."

Regina pushed thoughts of love out of her mind before Lord Kingsblood's image could construct itself in her mind. Concentrating on the subject at hand, she noted that her uncle was being given all but title to her inheritance. Marriage wouldn't seem to alter that. "Why did the Earl of Amesbury agree to marry me?"

The sudden question made Shelby frown. "Dear me, niece, must we cover that ground yet again?"

"Yes."

Her single syllable command had the effect of warming his complexion with a flush of anger that he didn't attempt to hid this time. "Very well. As I've told you, we were acquainted through mutual friends and I once spoke to him of my little ward. When he came to the point of marriage, he said he was looking for an unspoiled beauty with sensitivity, refinement, and modesty. He remembered my talk of you and asked if I'd put the suit to you."

"How odd, considering that I had no background or wealth to recommend me."

"You had beauty, youth, and an unspoiled nature."

"Yet he could not know that." She paused a fraction before adding, "You couldn't know it either, Uncle. You hadn't laid eyes on me in nine years until you came with your proposal, already signed by the earl."

His pale gaze grew baleful. "I considered the mother superior's letters to be sufficient. They were full of praise for you."

"Were they?" Regina smiled. "I'm amazed that Mother Superior wrote of anything other than my sad lack as a singer and seamstress, and my sullen moods."

Shelby didn't rise to the bait. "Perhaps she thought to keep you humble by pointing out only your faults."

"Yes, but to describe me as beautiful? Surely, Uncle, that was a deception of grand proportions."

"Not at all," Shelby answered shortly, growing impatient with this banter. "I'd written that I was considering a proposal of marriage for you and asked her opinion of your suitability as a wife."

"Why didn't you tell me this before?"

"Well, dear, I didn't know you as I do now. Young people often have fanciful ideas about themselves, and I didn't want to run the risk of your refusal before I had satisfied myself that this was a viable offer for you."

He was lying to her. She didn't know why or how she recognized it, but an intuitive sense of self-preservation made her dissemble this new knowledge. She managed a smile. "You didn't trust my judgment, Uncle."

He smiled back. "I stand corrected. I see now that you are a levelheaded young woman with resources that should take you far. To that end, I intend to protect your interests. You're the Countess of Amesbury. Had your husband lived, none would question the fact. We must make certain that none should question it further. Therefore, you must keep what has been given you, if not for yourself then for your future. You will wish to have children one day. For their sake, you must protect your good name."

Put like that, Regina could think of no good refutation of his argument. She gathered the papers. "Allow me time to read them."

"You will sign them?"

"I'll consider it." She glanced about her tiny cottage. "I would offer you a room here but—"

"Not to worry. I have made accommodations in Ilfracombe, in case I didn't find you today." He stood up, his hand reaching for the papers. "I would rest easier if you signed them now."

"I should rest easier if I read them first," Regina maintained, and rose to her feet.

"Very well, niece. I'll return first thing in the morning."

"No, I intend to go into Ilfracombe in the morning."

"Shall I send my carriage for you?"

"No, I've made arrangements with the coachman from Blood Hall to fetch me in the morning."

"Blood Hall again? You've become quite cozy with your neighbors. Does the marquess remain in residence?"

"Yes. He has houseguests. His fiancée is among them."

His bristling brows rose. "You've met them all?"

"The coachman talks," Regina answered lamely, and hoped he did not catch the lie. "Do you know Lord Kingsblood?"

"Never had the pleasure," Shelby answered, but his gaze sharpened when he noticed how his niece was crushing the papers in her hands. "Have a care, dear. Those documents are valuable. I'll bid you good day. I'm staying at the Dolphin Inn. Unfortunately, it smells rather like a place where

dolphins come to die." He shrugged, reached for his tri-
corner, and started for the door. "Ten A.M., shall we say?"
he asked when he stood on the threshold. She nodded in
answer.

Eloise knew she should not be in the garden accompanied only by a gentleman, certainly not this particular gentleman whom she found to be the most charming, handsome, and perfect in the entire world. Yet he was there, and
she was there, and nothing could persuade her that they
shouldn't now be together, if only this once.

She had dressed in anticipation of travel, in a high-
waisted dark-blue traveling gown with black velvet collar
and cuffs. Her bonnet was of the same dark blue but lined
in powder-blue satin with sprigs of forget-me-nots pinned
under the brim by her temples. Tender burnished curls
graced her smooth round brow and hid the pink shells of
her ears. She had hoped to look undeniably appealing to
her fiancé but now, daringly, she hoped that she was having
the same effect on the Earl of Dartmoor.

When she had received his note, slipped under her door
after breakfast, she could scarcely believe it. Looking up
shyly, since he'd said nothing yet, she asked, "Why are you
here, my lord?"

Leslie Stanford considered the most reasonable answer,
"Because you sent me a note," but rejected it as trite and
somehow insulting. Striving for a more romantic tone he
said simply, "Because you are here."

Eloise pinkened. "And now that I am?"

"My day is complete," he returned, snared by her sky-
blue gaze. "You're so lovely," he said before he could stop
himself. The widening of her eyes made him reach out a
hand to cup her elbow.

Tiny bells of alarm sounded in Eloise's ears. He

shouldn't be touching her, good sense warned. He shouldn't be so close that she could see the flecks of gold in his blue irises. She shouldn't be leaning into him as if drawn by forces beyond her control. Even as his hand tightened on her sleeve, promising the forbidden, she turned a shy blushing cheek to him and received his kiss on the delicate summit.

"You shouldn't, you mustn't," she whispered faintly, in awe of her own voice.

"You're right," he answered in a husky tone she'd never before heard him use. "You're quite right." Yet he didn't move an inch from where his lips hovered near her cheek. "I shouldn't be here, darling Eloise, but neither should you. We should be in Exeter. At my family seat. You should be wearing my engagement ring, meeting my family who would come to love you as I have!"

She had punctuated his deeply passionate rush of words with little gasps that left her too breathless to answer when he was done. Instead, she turned her face once more to his, looked up into his heartbreakingly beautiful face, at the way light glinted off the flaxen waves of his hair, at his inviting mouth hovering within reach of hers. "I love you, Eloise," he whispered. "I should have said it before now. Before all was lost."

"Yes," she answered, her tone sounding incongruously disgruntled, considering the situation. "You should have asked me to marry you months ago," she said in a stronger, more decisive tone as a frown waved her brow. "I don't know that I shall ever forgive you the slight."

"I love you," he said again because he couldn't think of anything else to say while staring down into what he thought was the most exquisite face ever wrought by God and nature.

With another little gasp of temerity, she rose up on tiptoe and pressed her cupid's bow of a mouth to his.

Maxwell burst into the garden, words flowing from him like flood water over a dam. "Lady Eloise! I would speak with you. I fear we've made a great mis—"

He had suffered a great many shocks in the last days and had come to expect that he would suffer a few more before the matter was done, but the sight of Lady Eloise in the arms of another man was a shock that not even he could bear without a start. "Good God!"

"Oh! My lord!" Eloise shrank in Lord Stanford's embrace, too stunned to do more than stare at her fiancé in horror.

Being a gentleman of the world, Leslie bore his surprise somewhat better. Without releasing Lady Eloise's waist, he half turned to his friend. "I'm sorry you had to come upon this moment, Max, but I won't apologize for its occurrence."

"I see," Maxwell answered, though he doubted he saw anything very clearly at the moment. He had turned back at the sight of the Countess of Amesbury welcoming a man. Now he found Eloise kissing another man and, from the looks of it, more eagerly than she'd ever kissed him.

"I have served you a bad turn," Leslie continued gamely, "and I'm prepared to deal with the consequences. But first, I ask you, allow Lady Eloise to return to the house."

"That speech sounds suspiciously like an invitation to a duel," Maxwell said evenly, regaining his composure as the deeper implications of the moment he had witnessed began to sort themselves out in his mind.

"A duel? Oh, no! You mustn't!" Eloise cried, breaking free of the Earl of Dartmoor's embrace and taking a step toward the Marquess of Ilfracombe. "Someone could be killed!"

"I wonder which man you hope to protect, Lady Eloise."
Maxwell folded his arms casually across his chest. "It is
your lover's or your fiancé's blood you would prevent from
flowing?"

"Why, yours, of course, my lord," she answered. Then
seeing at the edge of her vision the earl start, she added
hastily, "I would not wish either of you to shed your blood
on my behalf."

"How kind of you," Maxwell replied, beginning to enjoy
himself hugely but smart enough to know he must not show
it. "Then how do you propose to handle the situation? It is
of your making, is it not, madame?"

Perplexed and vexed and daunted beyond all recall, Lady
Eloise did the only thing she could think of. She fainted.

The Earl of Dartmoor reached her first but Maxwell was
equally agile and so, before she touched the ground, Lady
Eloise had the dubious benefit of lying in both men's embrace.

"I apologize, Maxwell, for what you witnessed," Leslie
Stanford said over her prone body. "But I have served you
worse, if you'll know the truth."

"Really, Lord Stanford?" Maxwell offered in a flat tone
as he shifted Eloise's weight into the other man's arms so
that he could loosen her bonnet strings.

"Yes," Leslie answered, tense from hearing his formal
title spoken by a man he had called friend nearly all his life.
"I came to Blood Hall under false pretenses. The matter of
the wager on the Amesbury widow was a sham." As Maxwell's dark brows lowered, he added, "Oh, the bet is real,
but my pursuit of it was only an excuse to follow Lady
Eloise, and you, to Devon."

"I'm surprised yet somehow I think I shouldn't be." It
wasn't the loss of a mistress Leslie had been pining over for
weeks. It was the loss of Eloise.

"Oh, you had no way of knowing my feelings. I hid them so well, even I didn't know my own heart until it was too late." He looked down at the sweet face pale with insensibility and marveled again at the fact that she had kissed him. "Your proposal to Lady Eloise was made in good faith. It was only after I learned that she had accepted you that I realized that it should have been my hand she accepted."

"And Lady Eloise, what are her feelings in the matter?" Maxwell asked as he briskly patted first one and then the other of her cheeks.

Leslie gathered the lady he loved more tenderly into his arms. "I can't speak for her. But I will speak for myself." He looked straight into the dark, fathomless eyes of the man kneeling beside him. "I came here with what, I swear to you, were honorable intentions. I hoped that by seeing you together that I'd convince myself that she would be happy as your wife. I want only her happiness. I thought that if she was happy, I'd leave her in peace, and go back to London to heal my pain."

"Commendable, I'm sure," Maxwell said making a considerable effort not to laugh. "Yet you didn't leave her in peace. You pursued her into my garden and made love to her before my eyes!"

"You mustn't blame her. She's innocent of wrongdoing," Leslie maintained stoutly. "I pressed my kisses on her. She was helpless to resist."

Doing it a bit brown, Stanford, Maxwell thought, but said only, "What are your intentions now toward the lady?"

Leslie looked down once more, noting that her lashes were fluttering. "If she were free, I would marry her at once."

Maxwell found himself unable to resist smiling at his

friend's sheer audacity. "You say this to my face, without pardon or excuse?"

"I love her."

In that moment, Maxwell understood something that he had been grappling with. Stanford loved Eloise. He did not. It was that simple. He didn't nor would he ever love Eloise with the simple declarative depth of feeling that Stanford held for her. And sweet, silly, beautiful Eloise deserved to be loved in such a manner, by such a man. "Tell me, Leslie. How do you plan to go on after this?"

The young man stared at his friend, his momentary elation at hearing his given name pronounced instantly dashed by the hard question. "The truth is, I don't know."

"Yet you love her."

"I do."

"And would marry her."

"I would."

"Then only I stand in your path."

Stanford shrugged. "So it seems."

Maxwell rose and allowed himself to make a small strolling circle about the rose garden before speaking again. He had returned to Blood Hall to find Stanford's carriage being readied for a journey and had decided to seek out Lady Eloise before she left. His much-put-upon housekeeper had said something about seeing the lady go into the garden. She had not added, or perhaps she didn't know, that the lady wasn't alone. If he hadn't seen it for his own eyes, he doubted he would have believed what was now so transparently obvious. Lady Eloise loved Stanford. *She* had kissed *him*, which was proof enough.

He turned to his friend, ignoring Lady Eloise's sighs as she strove to regain consciousness. "As I see it, Stanford, you have two choices. You may ask Lady Eloise to cry off from her engagement to me, or you may challenge me to a duel, hoping that you will kill me on the field of honor."

Stanford's fair brows shot up in two graceful arches even as Eloise had gasped in horror at the thought of a duel. "I would never hope to kill a man who stands in the right."

Glad that his friend wasn't lost to all reason, he smiled. "Since I've no wish to kill you either, may I suggest that you ask Lady Eloise to break her engagement."

"There is a problem with that," Leslie answered, helping Eloise rise to a sitting position. "Her father will be apoplectic when he learns that she's turned down a marquess in favor of an earl."

"You have a point, a minor one, but a point." He glanced down at Eloise who was staring dumbly up at him with shockingly bright eyes. "Then I'll beg off and she may publish abroad that I'm a cheat, a deceiver, a toyer with ladies' affections."

"I fear you would then be forced to meet her three brothers on the dueling field." Eloise nodded briskly in agreement.

"I hadn't thought of that. Yes, I should hate to kill her brothers, even for you, Leslie. Therefore, we must return to the first idea. Lady Eloise may beg off from the engagement for any reason she so chooses. I'll not deny her claims or seek retribution. As for her father, let's hope he survives the fit!"

"That's very generous of you, Maxwell," Leslie replied, feeling, at last, on firm ground. "I promise you, she'll not publish abroad anything that will dishonor you."

"Thank you, Leslie. Now, if the two of you would be considerate enough to vacate my house immediately, I'd take it as a favor." He looked at Eloise's shocked face and said with a sudden return of feeling that made his voice curt and clipped, "I think I can say that I've been a most tolerant and forgiving host."

"Of course. We are packed." Leslie gave Eloise a reassuring smile before saying "You are losing a wonderful lady."

"May Providence reward me in kind," Maxwell answered shortly. Taking Eloise's hand, so cold it felt like a fish in his, he said, "Good-bye, my dear, and God's blessing upon your new match."

Turning, he walked out of his garden, feeling both elated and depressed. He had rid himself of an eminently suitable lady whom he had no wish to wed. Yet he was farther away than ever from winning the infinitely unsuitable woman whom he ached to bed.

The last thing Maxwell noticed before falling asleep was that the brandy decanter was empty. Sprawled inelegantly in a wing chair before his bedroom fire, he didn't remember drinking a drop. Yet he must have, he decided with a vague smile as his eyes fell shut of their own will. He would rue his actions in the morning. He hadn't been this drunk since he was nineteen. Oh, well, there were so very many regrets in his life just now. No bride. No mistress. No one who cared for him in the whole wide world. What was a hangover compared to those woes?

The melancholic mood enveloped him like the heady spirits he had imbibed. Ordinarily he detested anything that smacked of self-pity or mawkishness. Ordinarily he never drank to excess, never did any number of things to excess. But just now, just this once, he felt capable of any and every sort of folly. For instance, in spite of everything—perhaps because of it—he let himself imagine that he wasn't alone but that the Countess of Amesbury stood nearby waiting his command.

He wasn't surprised to feel a cool fluttering touch on his

sweaty brow, nor, moments later, the tangling of those fingers in his hair. When a man was drunk, he mused, he was apt to accept the more extraordinary things as commonplace. He knew the moment he opened his eyes the imaginary sensations would cease. But he did not want that, not just yet. He chuckled. He was more than intoxicated, he was past "soused," beyond "illuminated," he was "woozy cockeyed pissed." But if the condition brought Regina to him as it did now, her hands sliding so nicely down his chest bared by his open shirt, then he at last understood why some men preferred inebriation over every other vice. What he wouldn't give to have her there within arm's reach!

The last thing he remembered before sleep was soft cool lips against his ear whispering, *Remember! Remember! Genna! Genna! Genna!*

It was summertime. He was nineteen, home on holiday with companions from Cambridge. They'd spent the morning fishing, but now they lay sprawled on the riverbank, having drunk more whiskey than the fish had water. Sunlight stung his cheeks and the sweet laziness that comes from imbibing too much brought forth the desire to doze. His companions were right, intoxication was a better state of mind than enlightenment.

The voices came whispering back over the years. Vague snatches of memory without any faces attached.

Are there no women in Devon, Max? What I wouldn't give for a female just now.

Willing or unwilling, huh, Crawley?

Sport, that's what we need. This fishing grows tedious.

Max? Where's the real sport? Cambridge offers better diversion than your West Country. Gad! Where are the women?

His father had labeled the young noblemen "bad company," but Max liked their reckless ways and the danger that came with their association. They'd taught him to gamble and drink and whore. He didn't like the streak of cruelty that often ran beneath the surface of their "sporting games," as they called their excesses, but most times he chose to ignore it.

There came a rustling in the underbrush. He would later remember that he expected one of his hounds who often came searching for him to bound into his lap. A sudden quickening of the young men who shared the afternoon shade on the banks of the tumbling stream made him look up.

A girl had appeared, fishing pole in hand. There was something vaguely familiar about her face framed by a tangle of loose black curls. Beneath her shabby muslin gown the shapely form of a young woman's body was barely hidden. She must be the daughter of one of Blood Hall's tenants was his first thought.

Thinking to amuse his friends by playing the gallant to a rustic maid, he rose none too steadily to his feet and made her an awkward bow. *Hallo, m'lady,* he said with exaggerated formality. *Da-da-dashed fine day, ain't it?*

His friends roared with laughter.

Never knew a lord to do the pretty for his tenants, Max. Sporting goods must come awfully proud in Devon.

More laughter.

Have you tupped her as yet?

Like a hound scenting an unseen prey, he smelled trouble thicken the warm afternoon air. The girl sensed it too, and to his amazement and chagrin, she moved toward him, an anxious look on her face. That was when he recognized her. *Genna.*

She had grown in his year's absence, become more like a

woman than her twelve years of age would seem to make her. Her gaze, too, defied her tender years. It was a clear and frank blue—no, gray—no, they were green. He had never really looked at her before.

Come, Max, share and share alike. It's only sporting.

Hoping to put his friends off the mark, he shoved her away. *You call her sport? 'Tis only a whey-faced schoolmaster's brat! Let her be!*

If she had kept her head and not bolted, they might have let her go. But she was too young to understand the necessity of showing courage in the face of a threat. And as she turned to scramble up the bank, the others suddenly took up after her.

Quick! Get her!

Don't let her get away!

Quick, she's getting away!

A scream, a feral cry of terror split the gentle sounds of the summer afternoon as they fell on her.

Shock and a surfeit of whiskey held him momentarily paralyzed. They could not mean to rape her. She was just a child! Drunken masculine laughter and obscenities buzzed round his head. Someone called his name, beckoning him to join them. Above it all, her pitiful cries for help rose through the canopy of trees.

Suddenly he was on his knees, scooping up mud from the riverbank in both hands. When he rose again, he knew would have only one chance.

Two of them held her, legs spread, as Crawley crawled between them. He tore at his breeches, which then slipped from his slim hips, cursing at the others because they couldn't hold her still enough to allow him entry.

The first handful of mud caught Crawley in the back of the neck. The second handful spattered the arms of the two young men holding the girl.

Shouts. Curses. Crawley jumped to his feet, his hands curling into fists, and the other two followed his actions. *She's just a child,* Max cried contemptuously. *What sort of sport it that for men like us? I don't tup the cradle.*

Dropping to his knees and ignoring the plea for mercy in her eyes, Max smeared both of his hands over her naked breasts, exposed by her torn gown. Then, grabbing her by the arm, he jerked her to her feet as he rose. *She's not worth our effort, a commoner's brat.*

Bending down, he grabbed another handful of mud. *Get out of here, tutor's brat!*

But this time she didn't move, too stunned to even protect herself, and so he flung the mud at her, catching her full in face. *That for my tutor's brat! I prefer a real woman!*

He shoved her, muttering under his breath, *Run, damn you!*

Not daring to wait to see if she obeyed, he turned to his companions. *Come on, then! I know of better sport, a gently bred widow in town who will gladly welcome us all!*

Suddenly mud spattered them both as his friends joined in the melee, cursing and shouting.

That for the brat. Give us a real female!

This time she ran. He knew she was frightened, abused, and humiliated, but she was alive and intact. It was as much comfort as he could offer her.

His stomach, churning with whiskey and anger, begged release but he fought the urge. He must make them follow him. Away. Away from Genna! He went to mount his horse. Miraculously he was in the saddle, the others beside him. Though conscience bade him look back once more, he turned and rode away.

The dream faded, replaced by the soft incoherent murmuring of a feminine voice. Again fingers stroked his face, pausing to cover his lips. "Please," he mumbled only to hear a lady's charming laughter.

He reached out in the darkness, the fire long faded to ash, but she was gone. Genna was gone. But no, she was not! Genna—Regina Willoby slept this very night in the cottage where she lived all those years ago.

There, my lad. A gift of knowledge to win your lady love!

Chapter Fourteen

*H*eavy low-riding clouds overlay the morning like miles of canvas sail. The captured mists clung to the ground, all but obliterating the countryside. The new windowpanes of the cottage streamed with moisture. The fire in the hearth, which sent forth waves of warmth into every corner of the small room, was the only solace against what promised to be a difficult day.

Regina turned back from the window and walked over to the table where she had left her second untouched cup of tea. Beside it was the sheaf of papers her uncle had left for her to sign. She had read them and reread them until she knew the legal phrasing by heart. What she had gleaned from the documents confirmed her suspicions. By signing those papers she would be handing over the control of her finances completely and irrevocably to her uncle. His assurances aside, she would have no recourse once the papers were signed unless he should decide to relinquish his authority.

"I won't do it."

She dreaded the impending interview with her uncle. Nonetheless she was determined to withstand every sort of pressure he might bring to bear. Her fingers played impatiently over the surface of the topmost sheet. Under no circumstances would she allow herself to become dependent upon the will of another. As for the suggestion that she leave England again, she rejected it outright. She wasn't about to leave this cottage, the only place she could call home, even if it was small and empty and seemed very lonely after her visit of nearly a week in the ever-interesting household of Lord Kingsblood.

A blaze of heat that had nothing to do with the warmth of the fire raced up her bosom and neck into her cheeks at the thought of the handsome, strong-willed lord of Blood Hall. She had told herself repeatedly that she hadn't run away from him as much as moved on into what was her rightful place. Happenstance had brought them together. Two unsuitable people, for very different reasons, had shared a mad wild moment of passion, nothing more. She had even congratulated herself being so sensible that she could view her folly for what it was, and dismiss it.

She thought she had dismissed it, and him, until she fell asleep. Then he had come stealing into her dreams, invading her defenseless drowsing hours with his seductive smile and deep, mesmerizing voice that stroked her senses as his hands had tenderly stroked her body. She had awakened with a jerk, her heart beating high and hard, her skin tingling, and her cheeks wet with tears. Chagrin, anger, and a desperate longing that made her ache with every breath had kept her awake more than half the night.

The commonsense part of her nature told her that with time she would get over her feelings of love for him, much as one did a cold. She didn't believe that one could die of a broken heart, and if she did, she had only herself to blame. In future, if they met by chance, she would treat the marquess politely but distantly. In time, she would come to feel nothing at all for him, which was exactly what should happen.

Yet she'd found to her dismay that logic doesn't speak to

the heart. Even after she eventually fell asleep, she had remained so full of misery that she had awakened with sorely agitated nerves and a nagging ache behind her temples.

"Enough of that!" She reached for the crust of bread left from her breakfast and began to crumble it. When she was done, she swept the pile of crumbs into her palm and carried them to the doorway where she scattered them on the yard. Immediately a bird from a nearby bush swooped down and began pecking at the unexpected treat.

Smiling, Regina lifted her head to the lane. The coachman had promised to be prompt. She was dressed and ready, having added two extra petticoats under her muslin gown to ward off the chill. Her bonnet was small and made of silk. She was very much afraid the small upturned brim would wilt in the damp weather. But there was no help for it. Though her late husband had provided her with an extravagant wardrobe, she had taken with her very few items. She fingered the pound notes through the velvet of her reticule, which hung from her wrist by tasseled cords. Her funds were limited and there were so many practical things she needed, like food and furniture. Clothing would have to wait until she had received more funds from her solicitor.

She heard the harness bells before she spied the vague outline of a carriage moving on the lane. Turning back to the room, she hurriedly gathered up the papers, rolled them, retied the cord, and then stuck them up the sleeve of her gown to keep them from becoming damp in the mist.

With a quick pat of her bonnet and a smoothing of her gloves, she was ready. Not waiting for the coachman to come and fetch her, she went out into the misty morning to meet him on the lane.

"You're late," she said ungraciously as he lifted his cap in greeting.

"Couldn't be avoided, ma'am," the coachman answered, then grumbled under his breath.

Regina didn't pause for him to alight but swung open the carriage door, lifted her skirt, and stepped up into the carriage unassisted.

"Now that's what I call a pleasant revelation."

Regina raised her head to find the Marquess of Ilfracombe giving her trim ankle and slim calf his full consideration. She dropped her skirt at once, dismay and foolish joy careening through her. "Whatever are you doing here, Marquess?"

He smiled at her charmingly. "'Tis my carriage, may I not be in it?"

"Yes, of course." She shifted her gaze away from his face, her pulse galloping recklessly. "I didn't realize that you would have a use for your carriage today. Forgive my intrusion."

She started to step back down but Maxwell leaned forward and caught her by the arm only to have it crackle beneath his fingers. With a startled glance he looked at her. "Why, Miss Willoby, you are as dry as parchment!"

His touch caught her totally unprepared, and silly reckless pleasure burst through her. It was as if her heart had never heard her middle-of-the-night vow to show him only indifference.

She tried to free herself but he clamped strong fingers about her wrist. "I meant no offense. I'm here at your disposal, as your escort."

Regina stared stupidly at his fingers—such lovely lean fingers—encircling her wrist. Why must he touch me? she wondered a little hysterically. Did he know that she couldn't be polite and distant to him when he brushed his thumb along the tender inside of her wrist where her pulse beat much too strongly?

"Are you reluctant to ride with me?"

She looked up into his smile.

"No? You're a coward!" he exclaimed, fairly crowing with amusement.

She was but she wasn't about to admit it. Stepping in, she settled herself opposite him then carefully arranged her skirts so that not even the hem of her gown touched his boot tips. When she had folded her arms under her bosom, she said in a neutral voice, "I fear you will be bored, Marquess."

He grinned at her, a heartbreakingly boyish grin that made her want to throw her arms about his neck and kiss it away. "I doubt that, Miss Willoby. I've never been bored in your company."

With that statement to keep her occupied for some moments, she sat in silence as the carriage set off down the lane.

Maxwell let her stew, more pleased with himself and the day than he would have imagined possible even a day ago. His engagement to Eloise had been brought to a satisfactory finish while a brandy-induced dream had left him not with a headache but the answer to the puzzle of Miss Regina Willoby. She had led him a merry chase, he thought, now it was only fair that he tease her a bit before admitting that he now knew who she was.

"Don't you find the changeable weather of Devon stimulating?"

Regina turned her head from the window where she had been watching moisture slide in slick tracks down the glass. "I beg your pardon?"

"North Devon, don't you think it's the most beautiful place in all the world?"

"I like it," Regina said noncommittally.

Maxwell smiled and stretched out his legs, deliberately

sliding one boot under the edge of her gown. "As a boy, I couldn't wait for the summer. There is a particular spot that I used to haunt, a secluded wooded stream where fishing is the best in the world. Would you like to see it?"

"No!" She had said the word too quickly for politeness's sake and, of course, he pounced on that.

"What, are you so burdened with tasks that you cannot spare a moment for a pleasant detour?"

"I have an appointment in town," she replied, evading his glance by turning once more to the window.

"So you said. With whom?"

She kept her face averted. "If you must know, it's with the bank."

"Liar."

Regina's head whipped around at his tone.

"There's no bank in Ilfracombe, or didn't you know?"

"No bank?" She was dumbfounded. It hadn't occurred to her that the village might not have a bank. How would she receive monies from her solicitor?

Realizing that her expression of dismay was genuine, he softened toward her. "If you're in need of funds, Countess, I'd be happy to make you a loan."

She read nothing but sincerity and good humor in his face, newly bronzed by his daily ride across the moors. There was a carefree brashness in his smile that she'd never before seen. "You seem quite pleased with yourself," she said without thinking.

"I am. 'Tis a rare fine morning."

Her gaze grew wary. "You've said that before when, in truth, it's quite cold and damp."

"Are you cold, Countess?" He took in her thin muslin gown with its blue satin ribbon tied under her breasts, the silk shawl that was more an ornament than protection, and her kid slippers. "But of course you are. Where is your cloak?" he demanded as a father would of a child.

"It hasn't been cleaned," she answered defensively, remembering the miserable night she had spent on the ground—yet safe within his arms. The memory exacted a shiver that the cold had not.

Seeing it, Maxwell swung his carrick coat from his shoulders and laid it on the seat beside him. He watched her gaze go involuntarily toward it, linger a moment on the thick woolen folds of dark cloth, and then dart away as a second shiver trembled on her lower lip.

"Don't you find it uncomfortable, Countess?"

"What?"

"Trembling like a leaf in a high wind?" She glanced at the coat again and he waited, hoping that she would borrow it. When she turned her head away and pulled her thin silk shawl more closely about her, he couldn't decide whether modesty or stubbornness restrained her. He decided to find out. "On the other hand, I'm quite warm. So warm, in fact, that I think I'll open a window."

That got her attention. Regina's head turned back toward him as he reached for the window latch. "You can't be too warm," she said in disbelief. Yet when her gaze skimmed his morning coat of tobacco brown, his yellow waistcoat and breeches of doeskin, she had to admit that he looked supremely fit, and warm.

"Oh, but I am," he answered, and lowered the window. The morning chill struck him wetly in the face yet he inhaled it as if it were a balmy breeze from the south. "I do love a brisk morning. You should take the air yourself, Countess." He drew back for the window and gestured toward her. "Won't you try a whiff?"

Regina recoiled from the chilling mist, her chin beginning to tremble uncontrollably. "You're mad!"

"And you're cold," he pronounced in a flat, satisfied voice. He looked down at his coat then slowly raised mocking eyes to meet hers. She knew then that he'd been teasing her.

"Oh, very well!" She snatched up the coat.

It was huge and heavy and awkward to handle. With gratitude she felt him reach out to take the greater part of the weight in his hands. He swung it about her shoulders and then drew the lapels together over her bosom, letting his hands remain pressed against her breasts. "Better?"

"Yes," she answered, refusing to look at him.

"If you'd acted more quickly, you would have had my body's heat trapped inside to warm you. Alas, I fear it's dissipated."

It hadn't but she could hardly tell him so without inviting more liberties than he was already taking. She was all too aware of his pleasant warm scent trapped in the weave, and more so, the subtle pressure his knuckles exerted as they pressed the thick cloth against her suddenly tender breasts.

She looked at him, intending to tell him to release her, but instead she found herself gazing into his intoxicating eyes.

"You're still shivering, Countess," he said huskily.

A moment later it didn't matter. He was leaning forward, reaching for her mouth with a kiss, and she was being dragged forward by the lapels to meet it. His lips covered hers in a deep and deliberately possessive kiss.

Every resolve of the last twenty-four hours flew right out of her head. There was only the pressure of his mouth on hers, the thudding of her heart under the knuckles of his right hand, and the sweet pulse of wonder that drove her blood. All she could do was raise her hands to his shoulders, curl her fingers into the material of his coat, and hold him—hold him as long and as close as her courage would allow.

When Maxwell finally dragged his mouth from hers, he couldn't bring himself to move away from her. Gently he butted her forehead against his, wishing that they were alone, in her cottage or his manor house, but completely alone. He had thought it many times during the last week. Now he was convinced of it. "There's something between us that is like madness!"

Regina's head slipped down onto his shoulder, which she let bear the burden of her head. "I don't understand. I don't even like you," she murmured in bewildered misery.

"Oh, I don't know," he replied. "I've decided that liking doesn't have much to do with loving."

Regina jerked back from him as if he had bitten her. He let her go, releasing his coat and leaning back upon the opposite seat. A moment later he reared up to close the window. When he lapsed back into a sprawl, he was strangely quiet, his gaze unfocused.

Mortified by her actions and mystified by his, Regina shrank down in the folds of his coat until the topmost collar hovered about her ears. She had kissed him, brazenly, in confusion and joy and abject misery. And then, astonishingly, he had casually interjected the word "love" into the conversation. Why had he done it? And why did she so badly want him to repeat that word while she was gazing into his face so that she could tell that he meant it? Where was all her fine resolve, her courage, her common sense? "Where is Lady Eloise?"

He didn't look at her but she saw amusement come into his face again. "Halfway back to London, unless I miss my guess."

The answer didn't amuse her. "Why aren't you with her?"

He turned to her now, his dark eyes kindling with some secret humor. "Let's just say we found we did not suit."

"Did not— Your engagement is at an end?"

His smile bordered on laughter. "Does it ease your mind to know that the man you just kissed so warmly is fair game?"

It did, it did, damn him! Regina snatched her gaze away from his, her cheeks afire in indignation. As if she had initiated the kiss! As if she cared whether he were wedded, bedded, or buried! As if she cared . . . But she did care, cared a great deal.

Maxwell let out a slow breath as she buried her chin in his coat. He had taunted and provoked her in the hope that she would betray something beside indifference toward him, and she had. Yet he had seen her with his own eyes embrace a man in the yard of her cottage the day before. And, if his suspicions were right, her appointment in Ilfracombe was not with a bank but with the same man.

His hands flexed into fists. He'd learned of the assignation from his coachman. He was determined to find out who the man was. If it was a suitor, he'd soon put the man to flight.

Her face was nestled in the collar of his coat and the upturned brim of her hat gave her face a piquancy that made him want to crush her to him and kiss the tip of her nose. A foolish thought, yet one that pleasantly occupied a corner of his mind. He knew he was not thinking rationally but the emotions pumping through him felt better than cold, flat reason. He had come wooing, and nothing and no one would be allowed to stand in his path.

He turned to her. "Tell me, Countess, who are your friends?"

The sound of his voice startled Regina, who was sunk deep in her own thoughts. "Friends? I have none."

"None?" He drummed his fingers lightly on his knee as he seemed to contemplate a very complicated phrase. "I'm your friend."

Her green gaze widened suspiciously, but she didn't reply.

"I consider myself to be your friend, a very good friend," he said dryly.

At last she thought she knew where the conversation was headed. He wanted to be much more than her friend. "I like solitude, in fact I prefer it above all else. Solitude is my desire, my sop, my aim in life!"

"Such heat! One would think you were beset on all sides by roving hordes of Mongolian tribesmen. Our little corner of Devon is unlikely to yield more than an occasional invasion by field mice. I suggest you keep your cheese wrapped against the onslaught."

Regina smiled despite herself. "Actually, I rather like mice. They have soft little ears and wiggly pink noses, and are very clean. Did you know that they wash their faces with their paws after eating?"

"I know they'd eat half my grain if I allowed it."

"One mouse doesn't eat very much," she replied.

"Ah, but unlike you, my solitary friend, every mouse has brothers and sisters and cousins and aunts and uncles, and so on. A single fertile acre would feed a veritable metropolis of mice!"

They laughed together, unrestrained and naturally, and Maxwell found that he liked the sound of their mingled voices. When they lapsed into silence again, he no longer felt compelled to draw her out.

As they drove along in silence, he looked up more than once to find her sea-green gaze resting speculatively on him. If only she would confide in him what he already knew about her, they could begin to build trust between them.

But because she had hidden the truth from the first, he was reluctant to expose her.

The narrow lanes of Ilfracombe rose dramatically from the harbor, the steep coastal cliffs having forced the fishing village to grow vertically up from the coast rather than spread out horizontally as inland villages did. From a near distance, the rows of houses, stacked upon one another like children's blocks, showed white and gray through the mists of the day. Regina leaned forward as they neared, the sight of the St. Nicholas Church steeple bringing a familiar pang to her heart. Nine years had passed since she had raced up and down the cobblestone streets with fishermen's children and played games of tag and swum in the harbor.

Maxwell watched her. Expressions of recognition and memory flirted across her face like clouds across the face of the moon. Finally, after her wonder had dissolved from poignant revelry into some unsuspected source of bitterness, he came to a different decision from the one he had planned on. "I must confess that I too have business in the village. The mine surveyor I hired is to meet me at my warehouse on the quay. I'll step down at the corner then Bassat can take you wherever you need to go. Shall I meet you, in say, an hour at the Dolphin Inn?"

"No, that won't be necessary," Regina answered. "That is, you need not go out of your way for me. I'll meet you at the quay."

"Very well. One hour," he reminded her.

By thumping his fist on the roof, he alerted the coachman of his intention to stop. As he moved to get out, Regina caught him by the sleeve. "You'll want your coat."

He smiled at her, resting his hand over hers. "You keep it."

Stepping down he turned his coachman. "You know what to do."

"Aye, my lord." Bassat touched his cap as the marquess strode away, then flicked his whip over the horses' heads. He knew what to do, all right. He was to follow the lady, find out the name of the man she met, and anything else he could without being caught doing it.

It wasn't his business to ask why. All the same, he was of the opinion that it was a hole-in-the-corner kind of business. Ever since the Willoby woman came to Devon, his lordship had been acting funny. There was something shady about her. First she was a Mrs., only now she was a Miss. Then there was the marquess. First he was marrying Lady Eloise, and now he wasn't. It didn't take much figuring to realize that one had something to do with the other. Now he'd been set to spy on her. Such goings-on were unworthy of the marquess, and the marquess's coachman.

Regina stepped out of the Dolphin Inn, clutching her shawl to her breast. The mist had become a mizzling rain. Not wanting Bassat to know where she had gone, she had deceived him by stepping down from the carriage on a street more than two blocks away. As the mist slicked her face and shoulders with fine droplets, part of her wished she had heeded Lord Kingsblood's advice that she take his carrick coat with her. But, of course, that had been impossible. The very last thing she wanted was for her uncle to know that she had come to town accompanied by the marquess. Not only was it unacceptable behavior, but she sensed that her uncle might take it upon himself to seek out the marquess for reasons of his own. Not that affairs could be much worse than they already were.

The interview with her uncle had been as horrible as she had feared. He hadn't taken well her refusal to sign the papers. He had begun by cajoling her, but quickly realized the futility of that and switched to logic, persuasion, and then long, complicated legal arguments that left her mystified but adamant about retaining her position. Finally, when his patience had reached its end, he had called her a shockingly ungrateful chit whom sheer greed was steering from a prudent and wise course. He had warned that, without his help, the dowager would find a way to defeat her.

Regina began to shiver as the cold seeped through her gown, two extra petticoats not withstanding. Picking up her pace, she hurried down the steep slope of the narrow street and into the teeth of the stiff breeze rising up from the harbor. When all was said and done, she was left with two conclusions: that her uncle was interested only in her fortune and that, as long as she held control of it, he had no power over her. Disappointment lay bitterly on her shoulders. Her fledgling hope of finding an ally in her uncle was at an end. Once more she was alone.

She saw a blur of faces as she hurried past an open doorway. The eyes of the rough men who lounged there followed her as she moved past them. Her city clothes were reason enough to draw their gazes, but the rarity of seeing a young woman unescorted on a public street was enough to whet their curiosity beyond the usual.

She didn't look up again until she reached the corner of the row of buildings. When she did, she saw that a new two-story red brick building stood on the opposite corner, its façade at odds with the faded whitewash cob of the other shops along the street. In bold letters the word BANK jumped out at her from the sign. She bit back an exclamation of annoyance and crossed the street. Lord Kingsblood had lied to her. No doubt he hoped to learn the real reason for her trip to town. Yet why hadn't he believed her?

"Because I have told so many lies, not even I can keep up with them all," she murmured under her breath, and then marched inside.

* * *

"You lost her?" Maxwell glared at his coachman from behind his desk on the second floor of the quayside counting house. "How could you lose her?"

"Don't know as how it happened, my lord. I must have been watering the horses when she came out. I took to me heels on the streets but she was nowhere to be found. I tried every tavern and alehouse 'twixt town and the quay."

Maxwell dismissed that comment. There was no doubt that the coachman had been to an alehouse. He smelled strongly of hops. "She went to the Dolphin Inn, you say?" The coachman nodded. "Did you discover the name of the man she met there?"

Bassat nodded. "That I did, my lord. She met a London banker by the name of Townsend, Mr. Shelby Townsend."

Maxwell sat forward. "A banker? You're certain there was no other?"

"Aye, my lord. The owner of the inn is a relative of mine, my wife's second cousin on her mother's side, if you will. He told me who the man was, seeing as how the Marquess of Ilfracombe was doing the asking."

Maxwell nodded. "What else? How long has the man been in the area?"

The coachman had answers this time. "Came to town evening before last, hired a room for the night, and then rode out first thing yesterday morning. Colin—my wife's cousin on her mother's side, that's his name—Colin said he was struck dumb when the man returned yesterday and asked for his room back."

"I see." Maxwell ran a hand through his hair then glanced down at the blueprints of his mines arrayed on the table before him. His business was done for the day. "You've done a good job, for the most part, but we must now find Miss Willoby."

"That won't be necessary."

Both men turned at the sound of her voice. She stood in the doorway. From the trickle running off the drooping edge of her hat brim to the pooling drip collecting on his hardwood floor from the run-off of her hem, she was the picture of soggy misery.

"You're wet," Maxwell said unnecessarily. "Bassat, get Miss Willoby a blanket from the carriage."

"Certainly, my lord." Bassat grinned at her. "Glad to see you're all right, ma'am. We were that worried about you. I'll just get you that blanket."

Maxwell's lips twitched as he studied her. He'd never seen a more thoroughly wet vision. Rain ran from the limp ebony curls pasted to her cheeks. It dripped from the fringe of her shawl and dribbled off the end of her nose. If not for the murderous look on her face, he might have laughed at her. As it was, he merely coughed politely and swallowed his amusement. "I hope your interview went well."

"You lied to me, Lord Kingsblood! There is a bank in Ilfracombe!" Regina glared at him but it was hard to maintain her dignity when she had to keep wiping rain from her eyes. Finally, in disgust, she snatched off the ruined silk that had once been her bonnet and dropped in on the floor where it lay oozing water like a dying fish.

"Bravo, Miss Willoby! I've been wanting to do that for a full thirty seconds." He reached for a beautifully carved chair with a brocade seat and pulled it before the stove. "Come and sit down by the fire. I shouldn't be surprised if you catch a chill behind this adventure."

"There wouldn't have been any adventure if you had stayed at Blood Hall," she remarked sulkily as she drew near the fire. She resisted taking the chair, for fear of ruining the seat cover, but he took her firmly by the shoulders and pressed her down upon it.

"You mean you wouldn't have had to resort to drastic measures such as walking in the rain just to keep me from learning of your assignation."

"Precisely," she answered, too miserable to pretend otherwise. "I didn't want your company, and you knew it."

Maxwell leaned against the mantel, watching her with serious eyes. "I did know it. I know a great deal, besides."

She glanced up at him with a stricken expression. "What do you mean?"

The words to tell her that he knew who she was trembled on his tongue, but her wary defiance checked him. Something had changed in the last hour. There were new shades of misery in her eyes that she couldn't hide. He felt his own heart ache a little for her though he did not know what troubled her. The first time she had looked at him with such shocking frankness he had recoiled with the natural instinct for self-preservation. Now the knowledge that he could see past her pretense to the very vulnerable but gallant spirit of this lovely young woman made him want to fold every sweet, dripping-wet inch of her in his arms. Yet she looked too close to tears to accept sympathy well.

Instead, he folded his arms across his chest. "What do I know of you? I know, for instance, that you don't weather well in a storm. But then, I learned that a week ago, didn't I? Let's see, I know you're in need of a new cloak. You're stubborn, willful, independent, and the most suspicious person I've ever met."

"Suspicious?" He thought that if she lifted her chin one more notch she'd be staring at the ceiling. "I'm not suspicious. I may be cautious."

"If you would just confide in me . . ."

She looked as if he had just suggested that she swallow poison without complaint. As always when they conversed, he felt his patience rapidly evaporating. He reminded himself that she had come to town to see a banker named Townsend, no one else. *There was no lover!*

Tired of arguing, he switched tactics. He moved quickly, reaching out to lift her from her chair by the arms. Gathering her near, he lifted her chin to better see her, but she shut her eyes tightly against his seeking gaze. He ran his finger over the feathery edge of one spiky wet set of her black eyelashes and then bent and kissed the closed eye. "For the moment I don't care that you won't confide in me." He bent to kiss her other eye. "I don't mind that you don't trust me." He paused to flick a drop of rain off the end of her nose then kiss it. Her eyes opened to stare up at him in amazement. "I don't even particularly care that you're dampening my waistcoat with your soggy bodice."

He was prepared for her to back away and tightened his arms until she was so firmly pressed against him that she was now soaking him from chest to knees while her hem trailed water across the top of his boots. "But I do care whether or not you're safe. Promise me you won't run away again."

"I didn't—"

He stopped her protest with a light, stinging-sweet kiss. "Promise me," he repeated.

"I don't—"

This time he interrupted her with a longer, more intoxicating kiss that begged her surrender. "Well?" he asked when he had lifted his lips one tantalizing inch from hers.

Regina stared at him dazedly. "If I agree will you stop kissing me?"

He grinned at her. "No, I don't think anything could persuade me to do that."

A discreet cough from the doorway broke the moment.

Regina pulled free of him embrace, her gaze one of stormy indignation as she turned to the coachman.

Bassat met her haughty gaze with a reddened expression, but he had wondered just how long he was supposed to stand at the door and keep his own counsel while the marquess made love to her. "You wanted a blanket, ma'am." He held it out.

Not in the least discomfited to have been interrupted, Maxwell reached for it. "Thank you, Bassat. You brought the coach to the door?"

"So close a drop of rain cannot come between it and you."

After draping the wool about Regina's shoulders, he pulled it close under her chin. "Miss Willoby has graciously consented to join me for dinner at Blood Hall."

"I have not!" Regina exclaimed, but he merely raised his voice a fraction to override her protest. "We'll be stopping by her cottage so that she may dress appropriately."

"Very well, my lord." The coachman saluted and left.

Furious, Regina rounded on him. "I have no intention of returning to Blood Hall for any reason."

He smiled, squeezed her shoulders, and then released her. "I know. But I'm accustomed to having my way. I'm not above kidnapping you if necessary. Have I told you that some of my ancestors were highwaymen?"

"I've never been in doubt!" she muttered as he steered her toward the entrance and waiting carriage.

Chapter Fifteen

Regina sat ramrod straight on her chair glaring at Lord Kingsblood across the sumptuous tea that had been laid for them in Blood Hall's library. It was a little past four, hours yet until dinner, but she hadn't been able to persuade him to allow her to remain at her cottage until what would have been the proper time for a guest to arrive for the evening meal. He said that he knew she would not come, and he was right. While he had waited in his carriage she had very reluctantly changed into her last fresh gown.

"Have I told you how fashionably turned out you are?" Maxwell asked as he reached for a second scone.

"You have, my lord. I thank you a third time."

He smiled blandly. "I've always admired the fact that the Empire style is all the rage, but I must confess that no other lady of my acquaintance reveals its finer points quite so spectacularly." His gaze lowered to where her breasts swelled well above the low neckline edged in silver embroidery. When he met her gaze again, his smile was full of frank admiration. "Exceptional!"

Ignoring his outrageous compliment, she concentrated on pouring tea through the tiny strainer balanced on the porcelain cup before her. Still, she was secretly pleased. The cream silk dress with its straight lines and short puff sleeves was the one gown in her wardrobe that she had chosen for herself, and without the dowager's approval. The silver-embroidered neckline accented her black hair. The blue-velvet and silver-cord bandeau fit snugly under her breasts, adding lift while flattering her curves and hinting at her narrow waist. The blue and silver Greek key design along the hem was repeated in the cashmere shawl she wore. Given so little time to dress, she had simply brushed her long masses of black curls up into a topknot and added a twist of silver braid to hold it in place. Scattered tendrils had fallen about her brow and nape, softening the severe line. She felt regal and elegant and quite a match for any peer of the realm. Though Lord Kingsblood had yet to change from his day clothes into evening wear, she was confident that she would remain his equal.

Maxwell approved of everything about her. The sheer silk skimmed her body with a tantalizing hint of the young slim lines and generous curves that lay beneath. More generously formed than Lady Eloise's coltish figure, she was firm, and slim, and desirable. The heavy black hair brushed up and away from her face revealed the elegant line of her long, slender neck, making him itch to place a kiss in the sensitive spot at her nape. Yet he had promised himself that he would not rush her. Now that he knew there was no lover lurking about in Ilfracombe, he had time to observe proper etiquette, like inconsequential conversation over tea.

"Tell me, Countess," he said as he sat forward to receive the cup she passed to him. "What do you see as your future?"

Regina poured her own cup before answering. "I think, my lord, that I should like to become a teacher."

The notion clearly surprised him. "A countess as a teacher?"

"I was not always a countess nor am I known by that title in Devon. I don't intend to hide away for the rest of my life, tending roses and passing out alms to orphans and widows." It was not lost on her that in the space of the last two months she had passed through both of those pitiable states to become a very wealthy and independent woman. "I'm possessed of a good education. I should use it."

He chuckled softly, unable to resisted teasing her. "I'm certain your needlework is charming. Your manners are flawless. You pour tea like an angel. And I must suppose that you dance like a dream. Every fisherman's child has a need to learn the waltz, don't you think?"

Regina set her teacup too hard in its saucer, making the contents splash over the side. "I'm not an idiot, my lord. A practical education is the only kind of value to the poor. I can read and write both Latin and Greek. I'm conversant in Italian and French as well. I'm not finished," she hurried on, seeing amusement twitch his lips. "I'm competent in geography, history, and mathematics. I can compute algebraic numbers!"

His handsome face sobered a trifle. "What an odd education you've had. Do all orphanages offer so thorough a curriculum?"

She looked startled. "Does rumor include even that bit of information about my life?" She felt like a piece of public property on display for any and everyone's perusal.

Sensing that he had struck a sour note, he tried to placate her. "If you are truly determined to become a teacher, I may be able to help you in your enterprise. The schoolroom on the third floor is filled with primers. After my tutor's death"—he saw her flinch but went on—"my father collected his books and slates and had them brought here."

"Whatever for?"

"My father, God bless him, was a frugal man. He said that because he had paid for the lot, he should have the use of them. I didn't know what he had in mind until he wrote

a few months later in high dudgeon to say that he had tried
and failed to hire a replacement for John Willoby as the
village instructor. He was stunned to learn that even poor
unmarried young scholars thought his stipend too small to
keep them in chalk and ink. That raised my father's opinion
of my tutor's commitment to his vocation threefold."

"Some men have loftier goals than the pursuit of money,
my lord," Regina replied.

"So true. But, if you'll allow, I must add that it was
foolish of Willoby not to demand better treatment. My father would have doubled his stipend had he but asked. But
enough of old matters," he said crisply as he saw the fire of
indignation flush her complexion. "What do you value
above all?"

"Independence."

"How promptly you answer. I couldn't have replied as
quickly. Independence? That seems an odd goal for a young
lady who wed before her eighteenth birthday."

"I'm one and twenty, my lord," she answered, unconsciously thrusting forth her bosom for his admiring gaze.

"I stand corrected. You were an ancient on the marriage
market. Yet will you not consider marriage a second time?"

Regina merely stared at him in mutinous silence. She had
finished answering his rude, impertinent, and insensitive
questions.

"Very well," he continued as if she had not shot him a
look that, had it been a bullet, would have left him writhing
in agony on the floor. "What shall we do to pass the time?"
He glanced about the library until he spied the chess board
and pieces on a table at the far end of the room. "Do you
play chess?"

Glad for any excuse to end their awkward conversation,
Regina answered, "Quite well, my lord. Shall we play?"

On his feet as quickly as she, he smiled and indicated that she should precede him to the table.

For the next hour they sat facing one another in silence, the only sound the occasional intake of her breath when he surprised her with a move or his chuckle of appreciation when she blocked his strategy. She had not lied. She played very well. So well, in fact, that when she outmaneuvered and then took his knight, he began to perceive a pattern.

"Your game bears a strong resemblance to my old tutor's. One would think you were once his pupil."

Regina kept her gaze fastened on the game board so that he missed her quick blush. She had forgotten that he might recognize her father's game! "Thank you, my lord."

Cursing inwardly, Maxwell wondered why they were playing this game—not chess—but this hide-and-seek deception that put them at cross-purposes. Why didn't she want him to know who she really was? What did it matter? Now that he had put the pieces together, he was only amazed that he had not done so sooner.

Aware of his scrutiny, Regina immediately changed her game. She knew she couldn't continue to play as her father had taught her or the marquess would become even more suspicious. Yet old habits die hard. Deliberately avoiding the best plays went against everything in her nature.

Maxwell sat back in his chair and leisurely crossed his legs, content for the time being simply to watch her. She sat with elbows on the table, her chin resting in her upturned palms, unconsciously gnawing her inner lip as she worked out her next four moves. He knew she was anticipating four plays because that is what her father had taught all his pupils to do, think ahead. So intense was her scrutiny of the board, she didn't even seem to notice the room darkening as the sun set. She scarcely looked up when a pair of servants came silently into the room, one to remove their half-eaten tea, the other to light candles.

As the new-lighted flames flickered light over her face, he scarcely paid attention to the game at all. He was more interested in the way her lashes swept spiky patterns over her cheeks, how a tendril of inky hair strayed across her cheek each time she leaned forward to make a move, and the way shadows slid in and out of the cleft between her breasts. When her little finger crept into the corner of her mouth and she began unconsciously to suck the tip, the response of his nervous system was direct and abrupt. He shifted uncomfortably in his seat. Propriety be damned! Let her win the game, and quickly!

Each move had stretched Regina's nerves tighter, making her ponder every strategy until, finally, perspiration trickled down her back and beaded up in the cleft between her breasts though the room was far from warm. Added to her annoyance was the fact that she was now losing when she had been winning before. To her overworked mind, it seemed that he was playing with her, advancing then retreating when another advance would have brought victory. When the second hour gave way to the third, her brow had become permanently furrowed and her fingers trembled whenever she reached out to move a piece.

At last, he moved his queen to checkmate her and her relief was so great that she sagged back against her chair in exhaustion and closed her eyes.

"Well played, Countess," Maxwell congratulated in his deep voice. "You would have won, had you not purposely and repeatedly given the advantage to me." Her eyes opened, her consternation so clearly unmasked that he couldn't keep from laughing.

Regina sat upright and delicately smoothed the moisture

from her upper lip with a fingertip. "I was being a good guest, my lord. One does not trounce one's host."

"Nor a lady a gentleman?" he suggested out of devilment.

"Of course," she answered, and turned her head so that he would not see the flash of anger that lighted her green eyes.

Maxwell didn't need to see the anger. If her head was a kettle, he thought in amusement, steam would be rising from her ears.

"I'd like to test your board skills again, Countess, at another time. Now I should like to do something else."

The tone of his voice made her lift her head. He stood up and, out of courtesy, she rose also.

He held out a hand to her. "Come here."

Perversely Regina laced her fingers behind her back. "What do you want?"

He knew she was still smarting from the defeat that she had brought upon her own head. His hand drifted back to his side. "I had thought that we might discuss the matter that is uppermost in both our minds." He paused to make certain she was looking directly at him. "I want to make love to you. And you, my dear, very badly want to make love to me."

She took an involuntary step back. "You're quite wrong, my lord. I don't wish anything of the sort!"

His face formed lines of disapproval. "Oh, Regina! I expected better of you after your spirited if misguided duel over the chess board. Will you protest again that you don't like my kisses, that you are indifferent to my caresses? Why make a Drury Lane drama of your virtue? After all, you are a widow."

Phrased like that, she could think of no good way to

contradict him without sounding like a fool. "It's not my virtue that concerns me, my lord. I simply don't love you."

"Were we speaking of love?" He took a step toward her and she took a corresponding step back. "We speak of *amore,* of passion, of bliss, of the carnal expression of desire."

All that? Regina felt the push of nervous laughter at the back of her throat. She glanced around and frowned. When had the day darkened into night? Who had lighted the half-dozen tapers that kept the large room from darkness but did not destroy the intimacy of shadowed corners and veiled seclusion? When she looked back at him it seemed he had grown a full half foot. His dark hair caught the candlelight, reflecting back deep shades of red and gold. His handsome face was more provocative for the sharp silhouette given it by the tapers' glow. The sheer masculine power of his presence seemed to shrink everything to the breadth and height of his stature.

"Come here, Regina." He held out his hand once more. "I dare you to kiss me and say I lie."

A dozen protests came to her lips. She heard them clamoring in her head. *But this is foolish, absurd! My lord, you insult me! Cad! Roué! How dare you! Kiss you? I'd sooner die!*

Each sounded more ridiculous than the last. "I don't want to kiss you," she said finally, lamely.

He knew he had won when she resorted to a lie. "We speak of desire. And you do desire me."

He was moving toward her, his hand still outstretched. She thrust her hand into his as much to halt him as to grasp the reality of the moment that seemed to have no substance beyond the hammering of her heart. She desired him but she desired more than his body, she wanted his love. And that, of course, was impossible.

Maxwell almost felt sorry for her as she clutched his hand in a viselike grip. This was no act of false modesty. Meeting her own desire face-on was the hardest thing she had ever done. He saw that expressed in her pale face when he reached out with his free hand and brought her chin up. He wanted to give her courage, to give her pleasure, and then more pleasure, but he couldn't succeed if she didn't let him. "You know what I want of you."

She refused to meet his eye.

"And you aren't indifferent to me."

His hand tightened on her chin, forcing a response. "No, my lord," she said softly.

"I'm no tyrant, nor brutal seducer. You needn't worry that I shall take selfishly what I desire from you. I'm considered an accomplished lover by the women who have shared my bed." She sucked in a quick breath, anger a sudden sharp green glint in her eyes. "Why do you balk? I'm simply being frank. You wish me to be frank, don't you?"

Reluctant though it was, he took her slight nod as consent. "Very well. I realize that your—experience is somewhat limited, but the act cannot dismay you. So we speak simply of a matter of skill," he continued though her lack of response was beginning to trouble him. "You may rest assured that you won't be disappointed in me."

Her eyes narrowed. "Is this how you talk to your other women? It isn't very romantic."

He smiled at her aspersion because it was proof that she had not entirely lost her confidence. "Would you have romance?"

"Yes." She gave it a moment's thought. "Definitely."

"You have only to tell me what you prefer." He pulled her gently into his arms, smoothing a hand down her back so that she was forced to step in closer to him. "Now, my dear, would you like words of love, tender expressions of sentiment of the most delicate kind? Or do you prefer the more direct approach?" He looked down to where her bosom was pressed lightly to his shirtfront. "Would you have me tell you that your breasts are exquisite and that your soft mouth makes me ache to feel it upon my skin?"

Regina reacted as if she had been stung. "Too much too soon?" he mused aloud.

"I've changed my mind. Let me go!"

"Not if Saint Peter were doing the asking!"

Several important admissions forced their way into Regina's consciousness during those first moments of his kiss. First: she did, desperately, want him to make love to her. Second: she knew nearly nothing about the "act" of lovemaking. And third: he would soon be in possession of that knowledge himself, for his fingers were already working the lacings at the back of her gown.

"Please, Marquess," she whispered between the kisses he was pressing on her.

"Please what?" he murmured against her lips

"You mustn't . . . we couldn't—not here."

Maxwell lifted his head to look about and made a calculation. The library wasn't the most romantic place for an assignation. The horsehair settees were beautiful but narrow and hard, and not very accommodating for the use to which he wished to put them. For his need, the carpet would do or the top of one of the long hardwood tables. But, he supposed ruefully, for a first encounter, they needed the privacy and ease of a bed. He would have to take her upstairs—but not until he had convinced her beyond all doubt that they were going to finish what they began here.

He caught her chin lightly in his fingers and lifted it so that he would see her reaction to his words. "Tell me that you desire me, Regina."

To escape his dark vivid gaze, Regina lowered her lashes. Somehow she had to protect herself. If she gave too much away, if she let escape the words of love that hovered on her lips, she would be lost. "I don't wish to injure your pride, my lord, but my interest in you is one of, well, pure curiosity."

"Look at me!" he demanded. Unable to refuse, she did. "Now, what sort of curiosity moves you?"

"You are a handsomely made man, my lord," she said, keeping her eyes on his face though her cheeks stung with embarrassment. Better he should think her a wanton than a fool. "Surely other women have cast their eyes covetously upon you."

Maxwell blinked. "Are you telling me that your curiosity is that of a woman who seeks a skilled lover, no more?"

"Yes," she lied. "Precisely." Daringly, she traced a finger down his shirtfront. "That's often how it is with men, isn't it? A man sees a pretty face, a neat figure, a generous bosom, and he wants what he sees. Yet a woman may not be so blatant in her desire, no matter her wants."

Maxwell studied her face but, for a change, it gave surprisingly little away. She had shocked him, oh, yes, she had! It was the last thing he expected after her cavil of the last days. But there is was, plainly said. She was in heat for him —his body, he amended. Well, it was a beginning, and he wasn't about to back down from the challenge. "Very well, my dear. My body is at your disposal. Satisfy your curiosity, and me."

His own challenge was translated into action as he drew her back into his arms. His mouth fastened urgently on hers, no longer pleading but demanding a response. His hands went to her hair, pulling out the silver braiding and freeing the thick fall to tumble down her back. Then his hands moved lower to the lacings at her back, plucking them free.

"Please, my lord—no!"

"Don't lose courage now, Regina," he said against her mouth, and slipped her bodice from her shoulders. "I wouldn't for the world leave you in doubt of my capacity to please a lady." He slid his hands down her arms, baring them as he dragged her gown down and off the ends of her fingers. Stepping back, he looked his fill.

"My God!" He had expected—well, this was more, much more. The perfectly formed globes could have been fashioned by an artist's touch. Blush-pink areolas, lush and velvety as tea-rose petals, crested each lifted peak. "Yo-you're—" He caught himself at the beginning of a stutter and chuckled at his own lack of aplomb. He had promised better. "You're superb!"

The admiration on his face was more daunting than his lust had been but when he began to laugh, Regina's courage crumbled. Even as his belated words of praise reached her mortified ears, a whimper of despair escaped her and she crossed her arms to shield her nakedness.

Realizing he had handled his reaction ineptly, Maxwell put his arms about her and drew her resisting body against his chest. She jerked, trying to free her arms, which he had trapped between their bodies, but he was afraid to let her go just yet. "My love," he whispered against her hair, "you're so lovely that the customary phrases a man offers a woman at such moments failed me. Forgive me."

She looked at him, her parrot-green gaze as alert as a cornered bird's. "You are beautiful," he repeated slowly. "You're more than beautiful. You're magnificent!"

Regina searched his dark eyes for any sign of mockery but found none. She wanted to believe him, yet doubted so many things, most of all her adequacy as a woman. No one had ever before called her beautiful. Yet she let him hold her, for as long as his arms were about her he couldn't look at her body.

He bent toward her but she dropped her head so that silky black hair swept forward like a protective veil between them. Very gently he brushed the hair aside and anchored it behind her ear. Then he found her mouth with his, his tongue sweeping over her lips with a deliberate slowness. His embrace gentled as his hands slid down over her back.

The resistance gradually went out of her as he stroked her. His warm hands glided slowly up and down her spine until the hypnotic rhythm soothed the fraying edges of her courage. She did want him, wanted his kisses, wanted to know what it would be like to be loved by him. He said he wanted to make love to her. It was what she wanted too.

One hand moved from her back to slip between them. His fingers wedged under hers, which spanned her breast, and when he cupped the glorious flesh she gasped softly. "Does this please you, my lady?" he murmured into her hair.

"Yes!" She said it without thinking of the consequence. She felt his smile stretch his lips as he kissed her ear, her cheek, and then her bare shoulder. All the while, his fingers continued to lightly squeeze her breast. When he bent his head lower she had no idea what he would do until she felt the warm moist heat of his mouth on the sensitive peak. He lathed it with his tongue then nipped the taut nipple, teasing it to life.

She felt herself being lifted out of her body, being drawn into his. She had told him she wanted his body but the reverse was happening. Her body was becoming his. Everywhere he touched her, he claimed another part. Her breasts ached with the need to be touched, to be stroked and kneaded, to be—wonder of wonders!—suckled by his lips

and tongue. The powerful action made her cry out in strangled surprise, her need so keen it bordered on pain. But
there was no hurt in the aching, only the sharpened sense
that there was more, so much more just beyond her understanding.

Yet her body understood what her befuddled mind could
not. Her hips arched intuitively to meet his, pressing and
retreating and pressing again, the deep hard rubbing a relief
and provocation at one and the same time. She heard him
groan as he caught her by the hips to drive himself harder
against her, forcing her lower belly repeatedly against the
strangely rigid part of himself.

She was overwhelmed by him: his scent, his taste, his
heat. When he lifted her skirts, bunching them about her
waist so that he could knead the bare skin of her buttocks
with his hot hands, she thought she would swoon with the
intimacy of the act. But he had only begun to assail her
senses. He thrust a knee between hers and lifted her up so
that she straddled his thigh. As he began the same push-
pull rhythm of his hips, the rough weave of his pants leg
stroked her in a place where she had never known such
sensation was possible, let alone this startling pleasure that
made her gasp and moan wickedly. Embarrassed, she tightened her thighs about his leg to hold herself away from the
touch.

"Don't resist me," he whispered against her ear, and
stilled his movement. "This pleasure is for you. Take it.
Enjoy it. And I will give you more." He squeezed her buttocks gently then slid his hands lower to press outward
against her constricted muscles. "You are a woman and are
meant to be touched here. Did you think it only a man's
place of pleasure?"

"I—I don't know." Regina gasped, confusion and desire
holding her reason equal parts hostage.

The thought struck him that her husband had not taken the time to please her. Perhaps, like many aristocratic husbands, he hadn't wanted his wife to enjoy coupling. She was to be the pristine brood mare upon which he sired children. He had mistresses for pleasure. What a stupid waste of a young woman's sensuality!

He crooned into her ear, "Let me show you the capacity for pleasure you possess." He licked her earlobe then plunged his tongue hot and moist into the orifice. As she shivered he murmured, "It's for you, this pleasure, only for you. Let me pleasure you."

Regina began to tremble, wanting and ashamed of the wanting. She licked her lips, striving for the courage to give him the permission he sought, yet remaining mired in natural modesty and the nagging fear that what they did was wrong.

Maxwell lifted his head to look at her, felt the tremors coursing up and down her spine, and knew that she was fighting herself. He saw her tongue dart out to smooth her trembling lips, and his body answered in a shudder that shook them both. Her eyes opened, and he saw that those changeable green eyes beheld him as they would a wizard: stunned, daunted, and in awe of a greater incalculable force.

The sight disturbed him. He didn't want to seem a mystical or mythical being to her. He wanted to be a man, wholly and totally male to her female.

He loosened his embrace, letting her slide ever so slowly down his muscular thigh until her toes once more touched the floor. With one hand his smoothed a tendril from her face and then brushed his thumb over her lower lip. In response, she licked the spot he had just touched. The pulsing knot tightened inside of him. He bent toward her, his lips less than an inch from hers. "Kiss me, Regina, with your little kitten tongue."

And Regina did, because the kissing was easier to bear than his gaze. Rising on tiptoe, she placed her mouth on his. He tasted good and warm and spicy sweet. Slightly parting her lips, she licked the smooth expanse of his lower lip. His sigh of pleasure thrilled her, for it meant she wasn't alone in being affected by their touching. She repeated her action with her eyes closed, concentrating on the sensate pleasure of his satin-smooth, mobile lips. His mouth firmed under hers then softened again, varying the pressure and depth of their kisses. The slow beating heat building within her set off tiny sparks of dizzying sensation.

Reassured by her response, he gathered her to him once more. His fingers cupped her hips tenderly and lifted her with great care until she once more sat astride his thigh. This time he moved with a slow, easy rocking rhythm that rubbed the aching and assuaged the gnawing hunger in this most intimate of places.

Everywhere they touched a new sensation registered. Her breasts grew swollen from repeated contact with the fabric of his jacket. Her lower belly quivered each time the buttons of his breeches raked it. And, strangely to Regina's mind, the more he rocked her, the more she ached. The feeling sank beneath the surface ache of her skin, deep down into tissues and blood vessels that clamored to be stroked as he did her skin.

Only with this man, she thought, no longer afraid of him or her own body. He had protected her, just as he'd promised, he had kept her secrets and defended her even against his friends. She had lied to him but she hadn't known how completely until now. She wanted him to love her as badly and as completely as she loved him.

Somewhere deep inside her a place was opening. The gulf

widened as their kisses continued to feed the hunger between them, as his hands strummed her spine. She wanted this, welcomed the slow, sweet, wild yearnings of her body turned stranger in his embrace. Her hands shyly clasped him, her arms going about his neck as she strained of her own free will to deepen the contact between them.

Maxwell quickened the pace, driving her harder against him so that her thigh touched his rigid manhood with every stroke. He knew he couldn't keep up the friction for long. Every muscle in his body was already locked in a struggle to keep his passion under control. When at last she turned her head away from his, gasping for breath, he was trembling with tension. He hadn't meant to take her here, but suddenly he knew he couldn't wait for the comfort of a bed or the seclusion of a bedroom. He must have her now.

Firmly but reluctantly he released her, steadying her as he set her on her feet. He saw the surprise in her face and immediately bent to lay his cheek against hers, as if only by touching he could reassure her. "Let me but lock the doors, my love."

Regina watched his retreating figure with new eyes. He was broad of shoulder and narrow of hip. As he shrugged his coat off and tossed it on a chair, she saw how well his stride revealed the graceful masculine power of his muscular body. There was a supple movement in his walk that made him a natural horseman and, she suspected with her new, if incomplete, knowledge of the way between men and women, a wonderful lover.

In that moment when he released her and turned his back, she realized she might have done several things, such as slip back into her gown, rush over and ring the servants' bell, or scream for help. But she didn't give those thoughts a moment's consideration. All that was on her mind was that she loved this man, that she might never again have the chance to be with him, and that, if she didn't, she might die from the feelings that had grown so strong that they seemed to stretch the limits of her skin. Delight and dread chased themselves along her spine as she waited for him.

Maxwell turned the key in the lock and pocketed it with a grin. Never before he had been more glad to be lord of the manor. No one would disturb them, no one would dare. Before turning back to her, he untied his stock and unbuttoned his shirt to give himself a moment to master his desire. He took three long breaths and then turned.

She stood half naked in the center of the room, looking like an ancient Greek statue come to life. The silken folds of her gown draped her hips, entwined about her legs, and then pooled at her feet. The candlelight bathed the impossibly soft and generous curves of her breasts in golden shades, highlighting her taut nipples. It sharpened the marked indentations of her slender waist, revealed the slight vulnerable curve of her belly buttoned by her navel, and polished the womanly flare of her hips.

As a grown man, he thought he had experienced the finite depths of his desire. But as his gaze wandered over her beauty, he was shocked by the intensity of his need. It threatened to bring him to his knees. The complex intertwining of aching tenderness and full-throbbing passion racking him had beneath it still other emotional currents. They ran quick and treacherously just below the surface of his consciousness, feelings of affection, of generosity, of astonishment, of love.

He came forward slowly, smiling gently when she belatedly remembered her modesty and lifted her hands to cover her breasts. He paused a few feet from her, wrested his shirttail from his breeches, and pulled it over his head.

As his magnificent torso emerged from the material, Regina stared in admiration. She hadn't been wrong to compare him to an ancient Greek figure. The broad planes of his chest might have been carved by an artist's chisel. Yet there were differences. He was not white marble but flesh-and-blood colors with dark-brown nipples and a light furring of hair that began at his collarbone and marched down his flat belly in a narrow line that disappeared into his waistband. She felt her whole body warm with desire and her heart began to ache. How was she ever going to walk away from him after this?

"What do you think? Are you pleased?"

She lifted honest eyes to his face. "You are perfect."

Maxwell found himself blushing. Her remark was not that of a connoisseur of men, but the startled admission of a naive girl. "And you, Regina, are exquisitely formed for love."

He reached out and drew her hands away from her breasts, placing them instead at the placket of his breeches.

As he pulled her gown from her hips, she followed his lead to try to finish undressing him. But her fingers were clumsy, made so by nervousness and inexperience. When her gown fell in a silken rustle about her ankles, she suddenly pulled away from him and bent to snatch it up.

Maxwell caught her even as she moved. "Don't. You must know how much your beauty pleases me. I will undress myself."

He did so with amazing ease. First his boots, which he sat on a chair to pull off. Then he stood and worked the buttons of his beeches. Finally he looked at her, absorbing the look of anticipation of her face, and then quickly shucked his last bit of clothing.

The first thing that Regina saw—all that held her attention—was his arousal. She couldn't look away from it.

The incredulous expression on her face astonished him. If he hadn't known differently, he would have suspected that she'd never seen a naked man before. Then he remembered that if Lynsdale had not wanted his wife to be stirred by passion, he might not have shown himself to her. He might have taken her under the covers, in the dark, with her nightgown lifted only to her waist. "You've not seen a man before."

She stared at his groin, moved beyond the ability to lie. "No."

He smiled ruefully. "I beg your pardon. I would have been less precipitous had I known. Do I frighten you?"

She looked at last at his face. "No."

He held his hand out to her, drawing her close, then sat on the chair he had used to remove his boots and pulled her down into his lap. The satin smooth feel of her naked hips upon his thighs was a tormenting pleasure. He encircled her waist with an arm and raised his other hand to touch her face in a gesture so kind and comforting that she leaned her cheek into his palm. For several moments he merely stroked her face, learning her features through his warm and gentle fingertips. Finally she turned her face to his and, to his joy, kissed him.

He knew something of the struggle that had been going on in her. Her every breath had been a shudder of conflicting emotion. But when her lips parted on his and her tongue touched his first, he knew that she had won her own battle and that pleasure lay ahead for them both.

He touched her shoulders and then her breasts and belly, which quivered with every breath. His hand at her waist rose to cover a breast as he trailed his other hand down over her hip and then brushed the tops of her thighs with his fingertips.

Lost in ardor, Regina turned to him, pressing her flushed and aching breasts to his hard chest in the hope of finding release. She didn't even realize that his hand had slipped between her slightly parted thighs until he touched her intimately.

Maxwell smiled. She wanted him, her body wept for him. His fingers gentled on her as he held her even tighter and kissed her so deeply their teeth touched. His tongue found hers, curled about it, and drew it back into his own mouth where he sucked it long and hard. She whimpered against him as her hips began to move against his hand, though he doubted she was conscious of her act.

His only regret was that she didn't touch him back. Her fingers were laced through his hair when they were not clutching his back, and he resented again the twisted sense of morality of her former husband. He wanted her to touch him—his chest, his stomach, his manhood—but he would wait until another time.

He was careful to lift her slowly, to slide her off his knees as he rose, keeping his body as much in contact with hers as possible. When they were standing, he insinuated a knee between hers, and then drew her down again as he sat. She slid naturally forward and astride him.

Regina felt the hard hot length of him against her lower belly but his hands were on her hips, holding her so beautifully, and his mouth was on hers, offering wet, warm kisses that melted so deliciously through her skin that she no longer cared what he did to her.

Maxwell eased himself forward on the chair until his hips were braced on the edge of the seat for better leverage. Then he began to rock against her, each movement driving his hard body upward to stroke hers. She gasped and her head nodded forward onto his shoulder, her long hair veiling them as her slender thighs dangled over the tops of his. It was a perfect position for him to control their lovemaking. He lifted her by the waist and held her a little away from him so that her breasts rose proudly into the waiting vacuum of his mouth.

Sighing her pleasure, Regina arched naturally into him, balancing on the balls of her feet on either side of the chair. She was past modesty, past shame, past all feeling except those he was providing with his hands and mouth and body. As he released one swollen nipple, she gave a deep groaning sigh and sagged down upon him.

He felt the hot moist center of her body press his lower belly, leaving a warm slick trail of desire on his skin. He caught the other peak with his lips and flicked it with his tongue. She bounced against him, her arms jerking forward to catch him by the shoulders for balance. He felt that he could play with her forever and then realized as suddenly that he could not. The deep pressure building in him at the base of his groin tightened a notch.

He opened his eyes, focusing on her face as he lowered her back onto the apex of his hips and thighs. She was flushed and the outline of her full lips was blurred by his kisses. Her eyes were dreamy, not really seeing him any longer. Beneath his hands she was velvet and cream, so lush and smooth and sweet that he could scarcely believe he held a real woman in his arms. Very carefully he reached down between them, found her wet and swollen, so ready for him that the mere touch of his fingers sent a shudder through her.

He moved a hand and lifted himself into position between her softly pouted flesh. This was the moment he had waited for, the moment that was an accumulation of only a week by normal reckoning, yet it seemed the sum of his lifetime.

With his free hand he guided her down on him, sighing in satisfaction as she opened a little to admit him.

Regina felt his hot rigid flesh enter her, and her own

body's instinctive response to resist. "Please," she heard him whisper as from afar. "Please open to me, love."

She tossed her head restlessly, not knowing how to accomplish what he asked of her. Her hands tightened on his shoulders as he bucked under her but again her body resisted the intrusion. Her eyes flew open. "I don't know—"

"Sh!" He grasped her about the waist with both hands. "Brace your feet upon the floor," he directed, and leaned forward to kiss away the harshness of his command. She did as he asked. "Now breathe in," he whispered. "Again. Relax. Open to me, love. Yes, that's it. Don't struggle. It's so easy. You are so ready."

Regina closed her eyes and listened only to his words, followed the direction of his hands on her waist, the thumbs stroking low on her abdomen. When she was all but mesmerized by his husky murmurings and roaming hands, his fingers suddenly clutched her waist tight and his body arched up under hers, the thrust taking her relaxed body by surprise.

A sharp cry of pain broke from her at the same moment Maxwell realized that he had met and broken through a barrier that should not have been there.

Regina's nails tug painfully into his shoulder muscles. White-hot burning replaced her pleasure. The thick hot length of him was wedged too tightly within her. Automatically she tried to rise, but the pull was as traumatic as the pushing had been, and she moaned. For one awful moment she thought that her body would split open, and then he was cradling her to him, pulling her head onto his shoulder as his arms folded her tightly to him.

"You're a virgin!" he whispered, his stunned voice next to her ear.

She shook her head in denial and didn't even know why. When he lifted her head from his shoulder, she tried to turn away but he captured her face between his hands and held her still. "Look at me, Regina." Ashamed and hurting, she met his troubled dark gaze with great wariness. "Am I right?" She nodded miserably.

His face seemed to reflect every nuance of the misery she felt, and she wondered why. Had she not given him what all men sought? Why did he look as if he wanted to take back every second of the last minutes? Had she failed somehow to please him?

Damnation!

Maxwell wasn't certain that he had said the word aloud, but it reverberated throughout the library and, to his amazement, the echo blew out every candle in the room.

Regina welcomed the veiling darkness. Even as she retreated behind a jumble of confused feelings that included, but was not limited to, mortification, humiliation, and a sickening plummet of thwarted ecstasy, his hands drew her face to his and he kissed her, softly, tenderly, with a butterfly's delicacy and infinite care, as if he thought she might shatter. And she thought she might at that.

The nibbling quest of his lips made her tremble. She felt an answering shiver in him and then in the throbbing core of his flesh deep inside her. Deep down her own body quivered in answer and then his body repeated the quaking sensations. To her surprise, he chuckled against her mouth. "Oh, love, thank you!"

He began moving under her again, his mouth moving more insistently on hers, and when his hips began plying hers, gently at first, a series of slow rolling upthrusts that elicited tiny gasps from her. After a few moments, she began answering his thrusts with a little dancing movement of her own. He smiled. She liked it. He hadn't driven her away from her pleasure. If only he could keep his promise to make her pleasure complete.

She was so narrow and, thank Providence, so wet that sensations quaked through him with every movement. She didn't realize it but her muscles were constricted about him, tighter than any hand, smoother than any glove, better than any mouth that had ever encompassed him. Oh, lord! He must not think of her mouth now.

Regina tried but she couldn't stay still over him. When his thrusting deepened, she found herself rising naturally on her tiptoes and then plunging down upon him, riding his hips as one rode a horse. But, oh, the pleasure! The sweet sensations that set off fireworks behind her eyes. The push-pull rhythm that made her blood rush hotly along her veins. The absolute throb of pleasure-pain where their bodies were joined!

Maxwell heard her gasps grow quicker and more harsh as his body heaved under her. Though her rhythm was a little ragged, he knew she was following the primitive stirrings of nature, and it led them both where he ached to take her.

Finally she was bucking wildly against him. He held her firmly, allowing her to set the pace. When she suddenly arched against him, her breath caught back in a sob, he knew that she had reached the summit. Volcanic tremors coursed through her. Her legs gripped his hips and her hands flexed repeatedly on his shoulders.

As naturally as breathing, his body followed the dictates of hers, hurling him over the abyss, mouth open, body arched as tautly as a bow beneath hers. And then came the release, his eruption deep within her in so strong stream of passion that it hurt.

He cried out, unashamed and unheeding of any who might hear. In that moment, there were only the two of them in the world. And it was enough.

Chapter Sixteen
❧

She lay draped upon him in the darkness. Her breasts heaved upon his chest, the curve of her belly moved slickly along the flat surface of his, her arms dangled over his back, and her thighs still trembled. Her head was buried in his neck, her quiet sobs the only sound in the room beyond his own deep breathing. Though he was far removed from tears, Maxwell was as shaken as she by what they had done.

Surprisingly, he smelled sandalwood in the air. The fragrance teased his nostrils and mingled with the effusions of their bodies that scented the room in primitive desire. He held her as he had never held another human being, protectively, all-consumingly, possessively; against her feelings and fears, against his hopes and desires, and because he couldn't imagine in this instant ever again letting her go.

She had more than satisfied him. She had made a new being of him. In her gentle arms he had been all heat and muscle, a magnificent male creature capable of any and all desire. Yet he had not forgotten for a moment that she was the cause and the medium through which he reached this new understanding of himself.

She had been a virgin.

The gossip, the outright lies about her, together with his expectations because he had thought her Amesbury's bride —nearly everything he thought he knew about her was a

fabrication. After a little thought he had come to the only
reasonable answer to all the contradictions and confusion
of the last days. *She was not the Countess of Amesbury.*

He couldn't begin to guess the reasons behind her elaborate charade, nor did he even want to in this moment. One
thing was stunningly clear amid the confusion. She had
offered her body to him, knowing what he believed about
her. Now he knew there had been more courage in that act
than he suspected. What else could it mean but that she felt
more than desire for him? Her feelings must be deeper,
stronger. Was she, like him, in love?

He felt her stir against him, her face turning into the lee
of his neck where she pushed soft lips against his skin. The
little nibbling caress, so small a thing yet so poignant in its
act of trust, shut down every rational, reasonable, deliberate, and sage thought in Maxwell's mind. He remembered
only the last moments, and the woman he held so tenderly.
Things would sort themselves out in time. Now he must get
her upstairs and into his bed where they could begin again
to learn one another with the intimacy that these moments
deserved.

He lifted a hand to her hair, feeling the heavy silk and
the heat of her skin beneath. Everything about her was
precious to him, even the curve of her skull beneath his
fingers.

Regina opened her eyes in the darkness, her lashes
sweeping the tender skin of his neck. She couldn't see a
thing but it didn't matter. She was acutely sensate in every
other faculty. She inhaled the tangy aroma of his warm
skin, learning its complex bouquet as one does a rare perfume. She recorded the minute shift of muscle and bone
under her hands braced about his shoulders, measured the
thud of his heart along her breastbone, rode the corded
muscles as his thighs flexed under hers, and deep down,

exulted in the whisk of his groin hair on the skin of her inner thighs. With her ear pressed to his shoulder, she heard his breathing, rumbling like distant thunder inside him. And, underneath it, the *shirr-shirr* sound of blood moved rhythmically in his veins. Her lips parted on his skin and her tongue darted out, hungry for the taste of him.

She had never before been this close to another human being to really understand that they were exactly like her, solid and finite, made of blood and bone and sinew. The realization shocked yet pleased her, for it made him very real in a new and astonishing sense, and human. He was no finer being, no glorious special wonder of the earth, but like her, vulnerable, prone to ills and aches and feelings . . . like love. Yet that didn't diminish him in her eyes. It made him all the more wondrous and special. For, in spite of the ordinary functions of mortal existence they shared in common with all mankind, he was the one, the only man she loved.

She felt his hands reach for and lift her head, each strong hand framing a side of her face. And then he was kissing her. He kissed her cheeks, her forehead, her chin, and her eyes. She kissed him back wherever her lips found skin, his chin, his temple, the place just below his little finger where it joined his palm. She shuddered, and shuddered again with delight and awe and joy.

"Come," he said, holding her back when she would have made him kiss her full on the mouth. "We can't remain here like this."

The stricken look he couldn't see on her face communicated itself to him through the suddenly tense lines of her body. He kissed her then, full and hard, wet and clinging, on the mouth. When at last he broke their contact, she moved urgently against him. He smiled. "We'll go upstairs."

She lifted her face from his. "But the servants!"

He butted his forehead gently against her chin. "There are ways of thwarting their curiosity."

He lifted her off him, holding her about the waist until she was steady on her feet. Then he stood up and went to a nearby table. Familiar with the room, he found by touch the tinderbox and struck a light to a single candle. The flame spread its halo of light a few yards.

As Regina watched him light the candle, doubts began crowding in on her astonished senses to replace the glory of the last moments. She had wanted him to love her, but now she was afraid of that desire. Those moments in his arms had been as fragile and brief, if as bright and glorious, as a falling star. What if these feelings, this love for him, died as quickly and irrevocably?

As he picked up the candlestick and turned toward her, Regina reached down and grabbed the first article of clothing she could find. It was his shirt. Too new to intimacy not to be daunted by the novelty of nakedness, she held the shirt before her, yet its meager covering revealed more than enough to tempt the man before her.

Maxwell saw her eyes move down his body to where once again his erection arched full and proudly. When her gaze rose again to his face, he was moved by the look of uncomplicated desire and shy anticipation he saw there. She lowered the shirt and there was no embarrassment in her face as she stood naked before him.

Maxwell sighed and gave his head a quick shake, his body thumping with desire. To break the too-tempting tension of the moment, he bent and picked up the article of clothing nearest him. It was one of her sheer petticoats. On impulse, he slung it onto one hip but it slipped off the hard angle and draped itself over his erection.

He heard her startled laughter, nervous and high, and

answered it with his own amused chuckle. Bending quickly, he grabbed up another piece, this time one of her silk stockings, and flung it mufflerlike about his neck. She laughed again and, following his lead, scooped up her shawl and wrapped and knotted it about her hips. Like mischievous children, they giggled and laughed as they hurriedly snatched up pieces of one another's clothing and invented new uses for them as covering.

Finally, when the last item had been retrieved, they stood face-to-face, looking like a pair of Bedlamites with articles of silk and wool and leather and muslin put to wrong use. He smiled at her, thinking that his breeches had never been better used than as a shawl tied, legs together, about her lovely breasts. She wore his Hessians, several sizes too large, on her feet and had made a turban of his shirt for her head. He, in turn, looked like a Barbary pirate. He wore his waistcoat open over his bare chest and, having used her two sheer petticoats as leggings, had girded his groin with his neck cloth. He had thrown her gown over his left shoulder where it fell togalike, revealing its hem of Greek design. They looked and laughed softly until the looks became stares and passion urged them to move together.

Maxwell put a hand to her cheek, wanting to kiss her but not daring to initiate what he knew he very likely wouldn't be able to control. "Come, love, let's go up."

He picked up her satin slippers and candle and, with a hand at her back, guided her to the far end of the library where a bookcase, a little narrower than the others, swung forward when he touched a hidden latch.

The captain watched them disappear into the passage, one gauntleted fist on each hip. "A virgin!" he pronounced when the panel closed on them, leaving the room in darkness.

"I told you she was meant for Maxwell," his lady answered in elation, opening her hand on the silver flame that rose from the center of her palm. The fairy light revealed her exquisite face wreathed in smiles. "A virgin! I knew I was right to send those notes to Lady Eloise and the earl. Now Maxwell is free to take the bride of his passion." She cast a sidelong glance of triumph at the captain. "Surely you agree?"

"I agree that it's a damned coil, madame! No more."

"Who blew out the candles to give them privacy?"

"It seemed the least I could do. The girl was untried!"

"You blushed for them!"

He turned a sour face to her. "You forget, madame. I cannot blush!"

"All the same, I felt it. Your gallantry touched me deeply."

"Hrumph!" He strode confidently across the library floor as if the noonday sun shown upon it, stopping to retrieve the reticule Regina had left behind. "What's this?"

"You're going through her things! That's snooping."

"I would learn why she had lied to the lad about being wed. There must be some clue somewh—" He pulled out a wad of papers and unfolded them. "Come here," he ordered, and she brought her flame closer. "Aha! Legal papers." He scanned them and, expelling an vulgar oath, headed for the secret door.

"Where are you going?"

"Follow, madame, if you will. There's something here that Maxwell should see!"

"But they're going upstairs to make love again," she protested, following him. "You mustn't disturb them."

He paused near the door. "I was never a man to stint another's pleasure." A wicked gleam lighted his eyes. "I never tried coupling on a chair. Perhaps Maxwell knows other tricks."

"Men!" she murmured in exasperation, and hurried after him.

The passage was narrow, the stones closing in to a shoulder's breadth at times. Regina clung with both hands to one Maxwell trailed behind him. Her footsteps sounded like those of a clumsy army as she climbed the cold flagstones in his Hessians, boot heels ringing noisily up the stairwell. Before and behind them the darkness closed in. Regina felt it almost nipping at her heels and shut her eyes, wondering how on earth he had found the to courage to traverse this dank stillness without aid of a candle the night he had come to her room.

Finally, after what seemed like an eternity of climbing and descending, Maxwell paused abruptly. Regina, so close behind him her shoulder bumped his arm with each step, trod on his bare heel. He caught her behind him with an arm and then pushed her back up against the wall. In a voice as hushed as a sigh he said, "Stay here."

He felt along the stones until, suddenly, a door in the wall swung open onto a dimly lighted room. She saw him step back into the shadows with her, then, after a moment, he moved forward and entered. For the space of a dozen heartbeats she stood alone in the dark, listening to his bare feet smack the floor. Then he again loomed up in the doorway of the secret passage, a smile on his handsome face. "We're alone. Come in."

She knew whose bedroom it was even before she entered and looked curiously about as he moved to light another candle and then stoke the fire for their comfort. It was of imposing size, more rightly called a chamber than a room. The walls were of plain whitewash and mottle-brick. The fireplace boasted a four-centered arch. Above it lances of medieval design hung in a fan-shape pattern. The window embrasures were as large as small oratories. The ceiling was high and timbered, the wooden floor so old the slats were worn and rounded and polished to a fine glossy finish by centuries of footsteps and wax. Heavy wooden tables and chairs fashioned with the Elizabethan love for leather and brass studs furnished the room. Without being told she knew it was the master chamber, now Maxwell's, the very one where the Cromwellian captain and his Royalist mistress had made love that defied the laws of the country and, to the thinking of many men, God.

Against the far wall, amid shadows and gold and violet brocade swags, stood a bed larger than any she'd ever seen. Laid out on the counterpane of rich violet were the marquess's evening clothes. The claret frock coat was double-breasted with genuine gold buttons, the white evening breeches made to be close-fitting. The sleeves of his shirt were folded neatly across the front, and a waistcoat of piqué lay beside it. The starched unwrinkled white linen that was to be his cravat lay smooth and seamless across the bed's foot. It seemed too pretty and immaculate a tableau to disturb by dressing.

She was astonished when he suddenly moved past her and swept the expensive finery aside with impatient hands. As the pristine garments slid off in a heap beside the bed, she stared in amazement. She would have hung up each and every item with care. But then, he had never been poor, nor had he ever washed and ironed a single item of clothing. His careless arrogance reminded her of the gulf between them.

As she watched, he quickly shed nearly all of the clothing that had made him look at once silly and endearing and vulnerable. There remained only his loincloth. Unaccustomed yet to the sight of him, she pretended to survey the rest of the room. "This is your room," she said inconsequentially.

Maxwell rested his hands on his hips. "Do you like it?"

The sound of his voice brought her gaze back to him. "Yes."

The room was cold, though he had stirred the fire, and she wondered why he didn't shiver as she did. There wasn't the slightest ripple or twitch of cold muscle beneath the sleek smooth expanse of his naked torso. The broad contours and washboard ripple of ribs moved only to the rhythm of his breath. A shiver that had its origins not in chills but in fever rippled through her from head to toe.

Embarrassed by her fascination with him, she slanted her gaze away. He said nothing. Why was he silent? What was required of her answer that she had not given him?

From out of nowhere a radiant warmth touched her nape. As reassuring as a friendly hand, it slipped over her shoulder and down her back. The invisible stroke seemed to settle something within her, or perhaps it only dulled the prickly edges of the doubts assailing her. Suddenly she needed to talk to him, to share her feelings. "Have you not found, my lord, that some places seem to absorb whatever human emotions they've housed? I believe this room is one that has known great love and harmony, if not peace." Her gaze sought his for reassurance. "It's strange but I feel welcome here."

"That's because you are welcome. I welcome you." He came forward and gently enfolded her in his arms, sighing contentedly when she lay her head against his chest without prompting.

"What will you tell your staff?"

He had known that question would come. "That you became faint and that I brought you up to my room to make passionate love to you while you were too weak to defend yourself." She lifted her head from his shoulder with a quick motion and he laughed at her expression. "Would you rather I tell them that I ravished you first in the library?"

He saw her begin to laugh, but the laugh caught in her throat and she made a helpless little gesture with her hands. "What will they think of us?"

He smiled warmly. "The world may mind its own business! What we do here is private. My staff is loyal. They don't gossip."

"No. They protect you. How fortunate you are." Regina turned her head away, remembering all the gossiping of the last weeks and how hurtful those malicious whispers had been.

"I'll protect you," Maxwell replied. "Nothing, no one, will ever hurt you again."

She needed to think, to make clear decisions, but he was holding her, sliding his hands up and down her back. Each pass carried them a little lower, each caress a little stronger, until it seemed that there was nothing between his warm hands and her skin. Then she realized that it was true. He had removed her things and now there was only the cashmere shawl wrapped about her hips and the span of their warm skins separating them.

Tentatively she raised her hands and, palms-flat, skimmed them over each shoulder blade. His skin was dense and plush, unlike the thinner skin that covered her flesh, and she luxuriated in the feel of it.

"Touch me, love. Oh, yes, Regina, touch me. Anywhere. Everywhere. Hold me in your small hands and love me."

They went onto the bed together naturally, as if they had done it a dozen times before. Yet he didn't hurry her or himself. He had lighted only two candles, not wanting to intimidate her with the brilliance, but even as he stretched out over her she stopped him, both hands levered against his chest. "The light," she whispered, looking up at him with pleading eyes. He rose quickly, snuffing the candles, and then came back to her.

For a moment Regina lay looking up at him through deep indigo shadows as he paused by the bed. She knew it wouldn't be like before, when sensation and feelings so long denied had catapulted her into desire's dizzying embrace. This time she fully realized what they were about to do. Perhaps, in his own way, he was trying to be certain that she wanted this as much as he did.

He stood erect and proud in the near dark, his strong body bathed only in the red-gold glow of the fire. He was comfortable with his nudity as she thought she might never be with hers. Yet that powerful confidence made her want him all the more. He had said he would protect her, that she needn't fear as long as she was with him, and if that was not love, at least it was a bond between them.

Doubt flashed cautionary images across her mist-shrouded memory. There'd been pain, yes, but something more, something that dulled the discomfort and made the low-down sensation of being filled impossibly sweet. This man whose very look made her tingle with yearning had, for too short a time, been part of her. Yet the immeasurable pleasure of being joined to him eluded her like a half-remembered dream.

In the end, it was this impossible calculation that made her lift her arms to him. She couldn't yet believe, had to judge again for herself, to make real, to re-record those wild, inexplicable sensations that only he could make possible. He had sent her spiraling over the edge of sanity and reason. She wanted him to take her there again.

Maxwell released his pent-up breath as she reached out

to him. He came down upon the bed with the sweet inevitability of a man who had found something precious, something he hadn't even known he was without, but had stumbled upon, blind, groping, and grateful.

Regina sighed as their bodies surged together on the coverlet, her hands reaching a little awkwardly to encompass him as he confidently did her. She wanted him more than she had an hour ago when he had taken her clothes from her and pressed her to admit her need of him beyond her capacity to withstand that temptation. She rediscovered the feel of his hair-crisped skin on hers, the weighted strength of his larger body laid over hers, the gentle urgent fire in his hands, the power of the mystery that was now a little clearer but still shrouded in the sheer overwhelming onslaught of so many new sensations.

When he entered her she gasped in pleasure, her hands going automatically to his hips to help and hold him deep within her. She heard him moan, the inarticulate sound a compliment better than words, and then he was moving on her. Different from the first time, he directed their rhythm, and his pace was harder, deeper, more urgent than her maidenly movements had been. Each grinding thrust of his hips sent her a little higher on the bed, eliciting a gasp of pleasant surprise. It was a dance as old as time, the dance of love, for all ages, for all lovers who have found in their love the expression of physical joy.

Not wanting her to catch her breath, he varied the pace from swift, deep, and hard, punctuated by his own choppy grunts, to tantalizing slowness where he nearly pulled out of her before plunging long and smooth and even deeper within her narrow wet warmth.

Trying to meet his need, she arched up under him, intuitively giving him better access to her. Smiling, he scooped a hand under her hips to brace her while he reached for a pillow and tucked it up under the place where he held her. Her thighs fell open even wider and her breasts thrust forth as she arched her spine. He bent his head and kissed each, lathing the deeply tinted nipples until they stood proudly under his tongue.

Her hands tightened in his hair, tugging at his scalp as he tugged at her breast. When her hips surged against his, her soft stomach arching up to rub his hard belly, he grinned. He had nearly stopped the motion of his hips and she was impatient with his preoccupation with other parts of her body.

"You are so ready for me!" he murmured as his mouth wetly rode her breastbone up to the hollow of her throat. He rocked his pelvis sinuously on hers. "Tell me, Genna! Tell me you want this, you want me!"

Lost in a sensuous fog of desire, she heard him use her childhood name but it seemed right, so comforting in this dark velvet sea of charged emotion that she didn't register the fact that he shouldn't have known it. "Yes!" she whispered as his lips found her chin in a sucking kiss.

"Yes!" Her hands fell from his hair to lay palm-up on the bed beside her head. He was rocking her, working her, using her so sweetly and so well that she wanted only to float, to be within the sensations that he created for her.

"Are you so eager, mistress?" he whispered as his hands moved to her waist to lift her higher and tighter against him.

She looked up at him, her heart beating high and hard and proudly in her chest. "I love you."

She saw his eyes flicker, the lashes in a quick downward stroke that lasted less than a second. Then he smiled. "Marry me."

He didn't wait for a reply but took them quickly over the edge of the cliff until they were both falling and keening out their pleasure of the blissful flight from the peak of voluptuous tension into rapturous abyss of release.

As their cries echoed in the vaulted ceiling of the room, other fainter cries of lovers centuries past resounded in answer.

Maxwell knew the exact moment she began to think rationally again. It was a good while after their hearts had ceased racing against one another. He had rolled off her and pulled her up on his chest so that they lay belly to belly. Her head was tucked under his chin, her fingers rhythmically squeezing his biceps . . . until she began to think. Her hands moved away from him onto the bedding. He felt her start to rise but he splayed his fingers over the small of her back and then lower down, over her buttocks, to hold her to him.

He had asked her to marry him! Was she thinking of that? He certainly was. He had asked her to marry him without first responding to her words of love. How stupid, how clumsy. That was not the moment, not when she was too fresh and raw with emotions to comprehend what he was saying to her. But now that he had said it, he was glad. He would tell her in concrete terms everything he knew so that there needn't be any more secrets between them.

He brushed her face with the heel of his palm. "Regina, Genna Willoby, I know who you are."

She stiffened, arching her spine against an invisible pain as if he had driven a sharp object into her back. The action brought her head up and he saw that her eyes were very very wide. "You know?"

He smoothed the unexpectedly rigid muscles of her back. "I know and I think I understand." His voice was soothing, quiet, nonjudgmental, as he meant it to be. "There's no need to dissemble. For whatever reasons, I know that you've only been pretending to be the Countess of Amesbury."

When she started to pull away, he captured her shoulders and held her still. "I admit that I believed you for a time, especially after you produced that crested mirror." He lifted his head and planted a kiss on the tip of her nose so that she would know that he wasn't angry with her. "That was a splendid touch. No doubt you found it in a pawnbroker's where some thieving servant had sold it. Did the mirror give you the idea of the masquerade? No, don't answer. I don't think you deliberately meant for me to believe you were a countess. It was a joke—wasn't it?—that went too far."

He didn't wait for a reply, because he wanted to explain himself clearly before she responded. "I remember how strangely you looked when you begged me not to tell anyone you were the countess. Why didn't you simply tell me the truth, or were you too embarrassed by then to reveal your little deception? You must have known that I would figure it out sooner or later. I suppose Stanford gave you a turn with his announcement of the bet in London. No wonder you nearly fainted. You must have thought they would find you out. I don't care why you did what you did, because the deception brought you to me." His gaze turned thoughtful. "Was that reason for it, to bring you to my attention?"

Regina had listened to him, stunned by the avalanche of conflicting emotions rushing on and over her. First was surprise, followed closely by shock and acute embarrassment. Then, somewhere in the midst of his torrent of words, she had begun to feel the need to plead her case and beg for understanding. But that swept past her too, borne on his tide of self-congratulation and condescending indulgence. Lastly, and so most strongly for having usurped the momentous power of the feelings that had gone before it, anger raged up within her just as he gave her an entry into the conversation.

She rolled off and away from him. Her black hair swirled about her shoulders and back as she came to her feet on the opposite side of the bed. He turned toward her, half rising up on an elbow, and then his gaze strayed lazily down her naked body and his expression turned whimsical as his eyes lit up.

Feeling wretched in her vulnerability, Regina grabbed the first thing she could find on the floor, his discarded dress shirt, and clasped it tightly over her breasts. "You think I came to Devon with a scheme to gain your attention? You couldn't be more wrong, my lord. I had no idea you would be here. If I had, I'd have stayed away because, the truth is, I've hated you nearly half my life!"

"Hated me?" Mild confusion entered Maxwell's expression. "Why should you hate me?"

Anguish made her close her eyes. "Have you forgotten, my lord, an afternoon nine summers ago?"

So she had not forgotten the incident between them years ago. He had known the subject was bound to come up between them. He was only sorry that the moment was now. "I have not forgotten," he said softly, "but I hoped you had."

Regina trembled at his gentle reply. He had said that day so long ago that she was only a tutor's brat, not good enough for a marquess's son to soil. It had remained at the back of her thoughts all these years . . . yet now she had lain in his bed.

She opened her eyes to the glorious sight of his masculine body stretched on the bed as he watched her. "When did you realize who I am?"

"Yesterday."

All her love and joy and sweet longings of the last hour collapsed into a sickly pile of thwarted hopes. He had decided she was only a commoner, not a countess, before he made love to her. The lord of the manor had sported with a common cottage maid. To her bruised and chastened heart, it seemed the final humiliation. Somewhere in the back of her mind she knew she wasn't thinking clearly, but all she could remember was foolishly blurting out her love to him the instant before she ceased to think as he had taken her over the edge of desire to fulfillment.

He reached out to her but she flinched, and he stopped the gesture in midair. His handsome face lost its good humor and his eyes were suddenly shadowed. "What's wrong, darling?"

"Once you weren't so eager to touch me, my lord," she answered, grasping at straws of memory as though they were a lifeline.

"Genna," he whispered chidingly.

"Don't call me that!" She lifted her head to look at him, her eyes as charged with emotion as his own. "When I was little Genna, you scorned me. But then I wasn't yet a woman, a fact you so graphically pointed out to your friends." She caught her breath to keep back a sob. "You and your friends made me wish I was dead!"

The concern in his face was quickly replaced by a deep flush. He had never forgotten the look of sick humiliation that had been on her young face when he had turned away from her that day. How to tell her that he understood, and that he still carried the burden of his own guilt?

He sat up and swung his legs over the side of the bed but he didn't try to touch her. "You have every right to your hatred. There's no excuse for what happened."

"You should have stopped them!" she cried out, drawn back nine years to the most vulnerable moment in her life.

"I didn't expect them to act so—" But he broke off. What had he expected of companions known for their cruelty and excesses? Not Sunday manners. He was as guilty as they because he had chosen them as his friends. "I told you some days past that I was ashamed of many things I had done in my early life." He lifted his gaze to look into her stricken face, and the knife blade of guilt twisted within him. "I am most ashamed of that day."

"At least you stopped them before it was too late." Regina tried to hold on to her anger but it had been eroding for days, ever since the first moment she had seen him again. She had learned so much about him since then. He had grown up, become a good man whom others respected and praised. He had protected her when he didn't know who she was or why she needed his protection. But the old pain was too deep to dismiss outright.

She took a deep breath. "This must seem very foolish of me, my lord, to still be weeping over so long ago. I was not, after all, permanently damaged. I never told anyone what occurred. But it is the kind of thing a woman never forgets, it hurts more than anything else in the world, and it seems it remains even after . . ."

She didn't need to finish the sentence. The emotion in her voice moved him more strongly than anything he'd ever known. He knew what she meant. Even after they had made love, the vulnerability was still there.

"I am so damnably sorry. Tell me how to make it up to you, if it can be made up, and I swear I will do anything you ask."

But she merely turned away from him and began searching in the fire's glow for her belongings. As if offered by a magic hand, the pieces seemed to come into her grasp even as she reached for them but she was too overwrought to realize it. She dressed, trying desperately not to cry, not to show any emotion beyond the occasional rip or tear caused by her hurried movements.

Maxwell said nothing, only watched her and resisted the temptation to stop her. He should have suspected that she would not have forgotten the trauma of that day. Perhaps their lovemaking had brought it all back. After all, she had been a virgin in his arms.

Have patience, he counseled himself. She needed time to reconsider her feelings. He, too, had feelings of his own to deal with. He was appalled to realize that now that the truth was in the open between them that his feelings were still as raw and fresh as hers. Their loving one another was a new bond, one that was delicate and might easily be snapped by an incautious act.

He watched with loving eyes as she dressed, unable to move or speak or comfort her as he wanted to do. But though she wouldn't even glance at him, he knew that she no longer hated him. By her own admission, she loved him. When, he wondered, would it would dawn on her that he had asked her to marry him . . . and that she had yet to answer him?

When she had snatched up her shawl, Regina turned on him like a cornered animal: her head down, her feet firmly planted, and her shoulders hunched against an onslaught. "I want to go home. Now, my lord!"

Her gown was only half fastened, her hair was a witch's tangle of blue-black waves. One stocking had already fallen about her ankle. And yet he had never seen a more charming or fetching sight. But then, he surmised, they had always been at their best when one or both of them were a mess. He glanced at the darkened windows then said with a smile, "I don't want you to leave. We haven't even had dinner yet."

Regina was too outraged to see the smile as anything

other than a red flag of smug male arrogance. "If you don't let me go I'll scream these walls down upon your noble head! I will!"

He sat up gracefully. "Don't you care what people may think?"

"No!"

"Very well," he said calmly, and reached for the bell cord beside the bed. "I'll send a servant to have the horses harnessed."

He sat down on the edge of the bed, wondering how to spare her the inevitable looks and whispers that would follow if she appeared before his servants looking as she did now. "Wouldn't you like to straighten your hair?" He pointed to the folding screen set in the far corner, which hid his copper tub when it was not in use. "There's a mirror behind there."

Regina glanced over her shoulder as she heard footsteps in the hall. She had the presence of mind to realize that she shouldn't be found in the marquess's bedroom while he sat on the foot of his bed in nothing more than the finely made body with which Providence had graced him.

She slipped quickly and quietly behind the blind as Maxwell bent to retrieve his evening breeches.

He fastened the first button just as a knock sounded on his door. Several long, rapid strides brought him to the door and he turned the lock and opened it exactly six inches. "Good, it's you, Hugh." But he didn't let the valet in. "Miss Willoby isn't feeling well so I need the carriage to take her home. See to the preparations."

As usual, Hugh merely nodded and retreated down the hall, no questions asked.

When he had secured the lock, Maxwell returned to the bed where he retrieved the rest of his clothing. He scarcely paid attention to the fact that his cravat was hopelessly wrinkled or that one of his silk stockings had a rip in it. He was preoccupied by thoughts of the lady who remained hidden behind the screen.

Later, perhaps not until tomorrow, he would talk to her and they would work through this morass of conflicting purposes. For, as surely as his body felt the luxurious satisfaction of the last hours, and his mind was calmed for the first time in weeks, there must be a reasonable, rational, sensible solution to their misunderstandings. After all, he thought with a returning smile, she had said she loved him, and he had asked her to marry him. What could stand before that?

When Regina had dried her eyes and rearranged her clothes, she picked up the marquess's tortoiseshell comb and raked it through her hair until most of the tangles were tamed. The mechanical action seemed to calm her. She had always loved to have her hair combed by the other girls in the convent school, and familiarity was what she most desperately needed in this moment.

When, at last, she found the courage to peep out from behind the screen, she saw the marquess standing behind the heavy oak table in the center of the room, his head bent over a pile of papers. He was fully dressed in the claret-and-white evening wear he had earlier swept from the bed. To find him dressed was comforting. She stepped out from behind the screen and came silently forward.

Maxwell knew the instant she appeared but didn't look up until she nearly reached the table and paused just outside the fan of light given off by the table lantern. "Are you feeling better?"

Regina nodded, aware the moment his dark eyes rested on her that the familiarity and comfort she had felt moments before were treacherously transient sensations.

He straightened from the survey drawings before him. "I was just rechecking the mine excavations I picked up in Ilfracombe this morning. The signs are good. If all goes well we will be open by Christmas and that, I can tell you, would be the best gift the area could receive." He smiled encouragingly. "Do you know anything of mining, Regina?"

"I'm afraid not, my lord." Regina caught the inside of her lower lip in her teeth as it began to tremble. He was being so courteous, so well mannered, when she had expected anger. She wondered fleetingly if this was how he behaved with his London mistress. She didn't doubt he had one. According to the dowager countess, every gentleman kept at least one. But she wasn't as hard or sophisticated as an experienced courtesan. She felt very shy, and sick, and afraid. "I want—I want to go home now, my lord."

Maxwell's dark eyes widened a trifle and his hand reached out to her, but she stepped back beyond his reach. "Are you certain?"

"I am."

"Then I must regretfully accede to your wishes. We will meet again tomorrow. We've much to talk about." He let her see the full power of his desire in his gaze as he added, "In case you've forgotten, I asked you to marry me."

The casual assurance with which he spoke those momentous words struck Regina with the full force of a cannon's blast. Reeling from shock, she backed quickly away from him. "Don't be insulting, Lord Kingsblood. You know that that is impossible."

Maxwell nearly smiled but her tone was too cutting for him not to feel the sharp edge of it across his pride. "I know nothing of the sort. I *will* see you. Tomorrow. Before luncheon. At your cottage."

She looked back at him, her chin trembling. "It will do you no good."

He did smile this time. "That's a risk I'm willing to take."

Chapter Seventeen

Something was terribly wrong. She realized it the moment she entered the garden at dawn, as was her habit.

A pledge had been made the night before, a pledge made in love and belief and faith. And it had gone unanswered.

A rare cold wind shivered through the garden. Where it touched, the full-bloom colors of the garden faded a bit in its passage.

Making little mewling sounds of distress in her throat, she bent down to cup the full blossom of the nearest rose. It lay limply upon her palm, not frail and faded by the passage of its brief natural life, but as if it had been plucked in full bloom and left for a day without water. The petals were shriveled on the edges, the central portions bruised by ruptured veins that shone darkly beneath the velvety surfaces. It had been unnaturally sapped of its vivid beauty at the peak of its glory.

She looked up in anticipation of the captain's appearance but as the ill wind of misfortune gathered in about her, she sensed he wouldn't be coming to her this day.

She smoothed a delicate finger over the withered remains as a ripple of dismay washed softly through her. It was a bad omen, a frightening one. She hadn't felt the ominous presence of impending disaster since the morning before Cromwell's army had come to Blood Hall to arrest her and her captain. That sixth sense had made her smuggle their son, Gower, out of the house and into the safekeeping of loyal peasants. The action had saved his life, and the Kingsblood line, even as she and her lover had given their own lives rather than recant their love. She had gone to her death secure in the knowledge that love, though it might not conquer all, could withstand the harshest assaults of man and nature—if the lovers believed in it above all.

Your first mistake!

She swirled about with a gasp of joy but it died in her throat. The rear of the garden was empty. "Captain? Captain!"

You should have left it. His voice was dark, censorious, distant, resigned.

"Look!" She offered up the wounded flower in the direction of his disembodied voice. "The garden is dying, Captain."

Whose fault?

She drew herself up, three hundred years of Kingsblood nobility riding high and hard in her veins. "She loves him."

Love! What is love?

"Everything!"

Then, Mistress, get thee hence and uncompromise this love!

"I have tried! 'Tis you who disbelieve! You threaten them, not I!"

Your interference has put the mark of eternity on them. Their fate has become ours. If they remain apart, then so must we! Think, Mistress, of what you have done!

Suddenly the most incredibly loud sounds came rushing upon her. They swooped in on flapping wings and low thunder, squawking and hissing, rising in volume until the frenzied calliope grew deafening as it ricocheted off the stone walls enclosing the garden. Wind whipped her golden hair into ragged banners and sent her farthingale swinging at crazy angles from her hips. Caught amid the wheeling dust and smothering whirlwind of leaves and petals stripped from trees and bushes, she felt the furious tug of a hundred different currents. Overwhelmed by the onslaught, she fell to her knees and bowed her head.

The fury left as quickly as it came. Suddenly the noise and the wind were gone, the scratch of a dry leaf and whisper of a tender petal the coda to the mad symphony's end.

The pandemonium left her exhausted, sick at heart, and very much afraid for the pair of lovers whom she had nursed as carefully as a mother hen with her first brood of chicks. Yet she wasn't a Kingsblood for naught. She wasn't to be cowed by adversity.

She rose gracefully and regally to her feet, her chin tilted at an angle the gods of old might envy. "They must love! They must! It is their destiny!"

Only the chill silence answered her.

Regina awoke in her own cottage, feeling as if she were emerging from a long, dark corridor. Her eyes itched even before she opened them and found that sunlight lay full across her face. She winced at the brilliance, wondering how she could have slept with the fullness of it burning down upon her. But as soon as she tried to lift a hand to shield her eyes, a great dumb misery pressed so hard upon her she gave up the effort.

As the sun warmed her cheeks, two large salty tears rolled out from under her sooty lashes, having absorbed as much of their mistress's difficulties, disappointments, and doubts as they could bear.

They were not the first, but the last of the battalions that had flowed down her cheeks during the night. When she first returned to her cottage, she had cried long and hard, with racking sobs that soaked her bodice. When the stormy congestion had clogged her nose and her throat, she had been reduced to quick, horrid little knotty gasps that made her chest ache and her head pound. Finally the tears had run out of her like rivulets from a leaky faucet: silently, continuously, unchecked. Yet in the end, nothing had drowned or filled the misery, and she had fallen asleep from defeat rather than release. But now it was morning. And things must be faced.

In the dim recesses of her mind, she remembered her own fateful words, "I love you," and then the marquess's reply, "Marry me."

It should have been a beautiful moment of joy and pleasure and shared love. Yet before it could be fulfilled, more worldly concerns had ruined it. Lying perfectly still in the morning light, the only emotion left her was a profound sense of loss.

Regina rose, washed, and dressed without once allowing her mind to rove back over the night before. She made tea and drank a cup without again recalling the marquess's face or words. When she had tidied up, she went and lifted her mud-spattered cape from its peg and went into the bright sunshine of the autumn morning.

Lord Kingsblood had vowed to visit her. Before he came, she needed time to think, time to decide what she must do. The moors offered solitude for her brooding.

Maxwell regarded his unexpected guest with interest as he entered the library. When he had returned from his morning ride and the housekeeper had informed him that a guest waited, he had hoped Regina had come to see him. Mention of the visitor's name dashed that hope. Yet it had

kindled immediate interest, for this was the man whom
Regina had so mysteriously visited in Ilfracombe.

Maxwell's piercing gaze took in Shelby Townsend at a
glance. Townsend wore a full-skirted hunting coat of good
plain brown cloth and boots of worn but polished leather.
His cravat was simply tied and his waistcoat was service-
able. He was past the middle years of his life. His graying
hair had retreated to the back half of his head where it
bristled outward like a false beard turned the wrong way
around. His complexion was sallow and the skin had begun
to sag away from the bones to hang in slight pouches beneath his eyes, cheeks, and chin. Whatever the man's relationship to Regina, he was certainly no competition as a
lover.

Even as the thought crossed his mind, Maxwell rejected
it as unworthy—if understandable. Any man who knew
Regina better than he did possessed all the makings of an
adversary in his jealous mind.

"Mr. Townsend," he greeted when the man turned his
head suddenly and noticed he was being watched.

"Lord Kingsblood." Shelby stepped quickly away from
the bookshelves he'd been perusing and toward his host.
"Forgive my intrusion, my lord. I wouldn't have come had
the matter not been urgent. I've come about Miss Willoby."

Maxwell's bland expression changed to one of intensity.
"Is something wrong?"

The man's deep voice rolled over Shelby like distant
thunder. "No, my lord. That is, well . . ." He flushed. "I
don't quite know how to put this."

"Let's have it, man!" What sort of trouble could Regina
have gotten into since he had deposited her at her cottage
door the evening before?

Shelby squared his shoulders at this imperious tone. "My
name, my lord, is Shelby Thornton Townsend. I'm a Lon-

don banker by trade, and the guardian of Miss Regina Willoby, my dead sister's child." He puffed out his chest a bit
more before adding "I understand that she's here at Blood
Hall. I'd like to see her."

At the word "guardian," Maxwell felt a further easing of
his jealousy. "Miss Willoby isn't here."

The man appeared to be severely provoked by that reply.
"I've just ridden out from London to see her. I stopped by
her cottage a short while ago and found she wasn't there.
Shortly after my arrival, two laborers knocked. They said
they'd been hired by you, my lord, to see to the upkeep of
the cottage grounds. I asked them where the lady of house
was and they said that she was likely to be found here, as
she had been your guest this last week!"

Maxwell let the man's indignation flow over him. "It's
true that I extended my hospitality to Miss Willoby, but
your effrontery is misplaced. During the time that she visited Blood Hall, I was also host to two young ladies, one of
them my cousin, and two gentleman, the Earl of Dartmoor
and my cousin, Sir Giles Kingsblood. Your niece was more
than adequately chaperoned."

Refusing to be mollified by the mention of a few noble
names, Shelby demanded, "Why was Regina here?"

Irked by his tone, Maxwell nonetheless strove for patience. After all, he was Regina's blood kin. "Your niece
arrived to find her cottage in a state of disrepair. In short,
there was no roof. She needed shelter and, having done me
a courtesy on the road by stopping when my carriage overturned, I felt that the least I could do was open my house to
her for her comfort."

Maxwell noticed how the man's eyes widened fraction by
fraction as the points of the story were revealed to him.
Evidently Regina had told him nothing of her situation or
his part in it.

"I see. Thank you, my lord, for looking after my niece. Since she isn't here, I'll trouble you no more."

But now Maxwell's curiosity was piqued, for the man was clearly pretending that he hadn't spoken to Regina when he knew the man had, on at least two occasions. If Regina hadn't told Townsend of their acquaintance, there must be a reason. "If it would be useful to you, Mr. Townsend, I'll have one of my servants search for your niece. She has a fondness for walking the moors, and today is an especially fine day for it. No, I insist," he hurried on to cut off the man's protests.

He went and opened the library door and spoke to the footman who hovered nearby, then came back into the room. "Have a seat, Mr. Townsend. Coffee will be brought in shortly." He took a seat himself, forcing the man to do likewise. "Now then, I'm surprised that we've never met. John Willoby was my tutor, a fine man. You were his brother-in-law?"

"I was," Shelby answered, most uncomfortable to be hostage to the marquess's presence but at a loss as to how to regain his freedom. "Sarah, my sister, was some years younger than I. We were never close. I hadn't set eyes on Regina until she was orphaned. Naturally, as the only living relative, I took her into my guardianship."

"Naturally," Maxwell murmured. "My father was most distressed to discover that the child had disappeared. He'd thought to see to her livelihood himself," he invented, hoping to draw the man out.

"Indeed, my lord?" He seemed genuinely amazed. "I wasn't aware. In any case, I was in the foreign service at that time, in Florence. When I'd collected the child, I took her with me back to Italy. Naturally, as a bachelor, I couldn't provide the sort of home she needed. Therefore I sent her to a convent school where she could be properly cared for."

"Yet you recently brought her back to England?"

Shelby considered his options and quickly decided that Lord Kingsblood might prove an ally in his plans for Regina. "She returned to England to be married, my lord, to the Earl of Amesbury."

This time it was Maxwell's eyes that widened perceptibly. Regina *was* the Countess of Amesbury! She had told him the truth.

"I see by your expression, my lord, that you've heard the rumors. I can only say that Regina has been most unfairly treated by both the earl's family and the *ton*. That is why I'm here, to convince her that she should return to Italy at once, until the turbulence of recent days has died down."

"Do you think it will?"

Shelby spread ten fingers wide. "Who's to say how long gossip may linger? But a year, surely, is but a little time to one of Regina's tender years. I know, it seems impossible that rumor could be so wrong. But consider, my lord, the slim resources of a young woman, without friends and connections in London, who has married above her position in society. When rumor turned dark against her, there was little I could do to prevent it."

"One wonders why you sanctioned such a marriage, feeling as you do about the excesses of privilege."

"I meant no offense, my lord. At the time, the earl's offer of marriage seemed an answered prayer to one of Regina's slender means." His gaze no longer met Maxwell's. "The earl's reputation was known to me, of course, but his offer was honorable."

Maxwell did understand the temptation. Was Lady Eloise not concerned about her father's reaction to the news that she desired to wed an earl rather than a more noble marquess? For an orphan, a commoner, and a girl of little social acumen, Lynsdale's offer must have seemed a gift straight from heaven.

"You've met my niece, been in her company, and dined with her, my lord. Do you believe that she's the woman that rumor would paint her?"

"No, Mr. Townsend. In my estimation, she's been thoroughly misused on all sides." Maxwell dodged the accusing finger that his own conscience pointed at himself.

"Then, perhaps, you'll encourage her to accept my advice to leave England for a time. I firmly believe that the very next scandal to rock London will erase from memory the black marks against her."

Maxwell knew enough of the sometimes vicious nature of the *ton* to doubt that. Regina was an outsider, with no family to protect her, no social position to ingratiate her, no power with which others might wish to align themselves. Her reputation would remain in ruins unless and until an active campaign by powerful allies was waged in the best salons and gentlemen's clubs to right the wrong. But why distress her uncle with that news? "What do you suggest she do in Italy for a year?"

Shelby smiled. "I've arranged for her to purchase a house. She may do anything she likes. Who knows, she may not wish to come back to England. She may find that the clime suits her. One day she might even wish to remarry."

The footman arrived just then with coffee and cakes. Feeling the need for action, Maxwell rose to his feet. While the servant went about the business of serving both men, Maxwell walked to the far end of the library and gazed out at the window. He would rather not make the decision without first talking with Regina, but it seemed perhaps the appropriate time to tell Townsend that he had asked Regina to marry him.

As he turned back from the window, an errant breeze lifted papers from a nearby table and sent them skimming toward him. Almost absently, Maxwell snagged them from the air and glanced down at them. Immediately he was riveted. By the time the footman had done his job and departed, Maxwell had come to several decisions.

He came back and took his place across from Townsend, his dark eyes gleaming with mischief. "Tell me, as a banker, how do you suggest your niece deal with her newfound wealth?"

Shelby heard the ominous undertone in the marquess's voice but couldn't fathom a reason for it. "Why, I've suggested that she put the estates in the hands of an experienced administrator."

"Like yourself."

Feeling well within his rights, Shelby answered, "That's exactly my suggestion to her."

"Until such time as she remarries, of course."

"Of course," Shelby murmured, and sipped his coffee, hoping that would break the conversation.

"I've another suggestion. Let me manage her finances."

Shelby's sudden jerk of surprise spilled hot coffee into his lap. He yelped and rose to his feet, clattering the cup in the saucer as he quickly set it aside to withdraw a handkerchief from his pocket and sponge himself off.

Maxwell smiled, not moving a muscle to offer aid. "I've surprised you, but don't mistake my intentions, Mr. Townsend. I wish to marry your niece."

Shelby's head shot up. "But, my lord, you—can't!"

"She's a widow, and I'm a bachelor. I believe, Mr. Townsend, that I can." He studied the nails of his right hand before lifting his eyes to the man who stood before him in a coffee-stained suit. "There's only one matter left. How much?"

"I beg your pardon?"

"How much will it cost me to buy you off?" As the man began to sputter indignantly Maxwell waved a disclaiming hand. "There's no need for protestations." He held up the papers that had flown into his hand, the papers that Townsend had left with Regina. "You hoped to cheat Regina of her inheritance."

"She showed them to you?" The incredulity in the man's face was proof enough that he had been caught unprepared.

"You may take them back with you," Maxwell said, not answering the question. "I'm willing to sign a betrothal agreement that will settle monies on you, only because you are Regina's uncle. Don't tempt me to change my mind."

Shelby swallowed twice before finding his voice. "She has agreed?"

Maxwell's brows lowered ominously. "She's considering my suit."

The banker's mouth fell slightly ajar. "She hesitates? I shall speak to her at—"

"You'll do no such thing. Your niece has a fine head on her shoulders. If she doesn't wish to be hurried into a second marriage, I can well understand it. In fact, if you were to press my suit with her I'm certain I should be refused. Your lack of judgment in marriage partners speaks for itself."

Too rattled to keep his thoughts to himself, Shelby spoke them aloud. "You can't have fallen in love with her upon so short an acquaintance. It's *you* who are after her money!"

"You begin to annoy me, Townsend. I intend to encourage her to return the inheritance to the Amesburys. I use the word 'encourage' because, unlike you, I don't assume that she needs my direction in the matter."

Effectively caught, frustrated, and angered by the marquess's high-handed manner, Townsend struck out in the only way left him. "I wish you joy of the union, my lord, but I wonder what Parliament will make of a marquess's wife who was the talk of the *ton* upon her previous husband's passing. I wonder how many of the ladies will receive her with open arms. Indeed, it will surprise me if they greet her with anything other than shudders and snubs."

With more restraint than he had shown in weeks, Maxwell replied, "See that you don't contribute to the gossip, Townsend. I'll make my engagement known at the appropriate time. Until then, I expect you to begin the repairs on her character. In fact, I expect to hear when I return to London that you've come to the public defense of your niece on several occasions."

"What about the Dowager Countess of Amesbury?"

"The dowager isn't expected to like Regina's remarriage but as Regina is trading an earl's coronet for that of a marquess, I don't think the dowager's wrath will signify with the masses."

"I'd not be so certain, my lord. Regina isn't of the nobility. She's viewed as an interloper. A second advantageous marriage will make her seem, well . . ." He was practically sneering now, feeling that he'd found a way to get even for all the insults he'd just suffered. "Marriage to such a woman could jeopardize your social position, perhaps cripple your political career."

"You surprise me. You arrived demanding that I hand over your niece, as if *I* posed a threat to *her*. Now, in a quarter of an hour's time, you have reversed yourself to warn *me* away from *her*."

Maxwell came to his feet, which made him tower over the other man. "Get out, Townsend. Get out now before I change my mind and decide to give you what you really deserve, a fist in the face!"

* * *

Regina saw the horse on the lane before her cottage, and though she didn't recognize it, its patrician lineage was apparent in every graceful line. It was a nobleman's horse. The Marquess of Ilfracombe had come to see her.

She quickened her pace even as she pushed a hand through her untidy wind-tossed hair. Her navy-blue gown was spattered with sand. The hem was edged in a saltwater crust because she hadn't been able to resist going down to the beach and wading barefoot in the stinging cold tide. Yet she didn't care.

The marquess was waiting for her. The only thought in her head was that he had come to see her. The only emotion in her heart was joy. Her fears and worries had been for naught. He had come to see her!

On the moors she had had a chance to think, and remember the night before. And the love and joy she had experienced in his arms had come back to overshadow every other consideration. After his revelation that he knew who she was, her old feelings of humiliation and anger had momentarily eclipsed her new stronger feelings for him. Now those feelings had triumphed, and the barriers before them seemed no more than the figments of her imagination. He *had* acted to protect her. To a child, his method had seemed as harsh as the rape from which he'd saved her. To the woman she had become, his actions were more understandable, if no less distressing.

But that was the past, and the future was theirs to determine. If he could be as real to her as he had been last night, then so could their feelings. He had asked her to marry him. He had done so knowing who she was, what she was.

She rushed through her door with a smile that reached from her heart to her lips.

"Well, at last, the Countess of Amesbury!"

Standing in the center of her cottage was the handsome,

elegant, and cruel Lord Percy Buckram, the new Earl of Amesbury.

She had forgotten how handsome he was. She had forgotten how the waves of his hair were as golden as filtered honey when held up to the sun. She had forgotten how the clean cut of his jaw and the bold thrust of his nose gave his face a masculinity that saved it from weak beauty. But she had not forgotten the thin sensual slash of his mouth nor the razor's edge cut of his crystal-blue eyes hooded by the jut of his brows.

He came forth with both hands outstretched. "Countess —Regina, how glad I am to see you! I'd begun to think that my directions were in error."

"How did you find me?" Regina said through numb lips as she glanced around for signs of additional visitors.

"Your uncle told me, of course," When she didn't extend a hand to him, he gently grasped her by the upper arms. "God, but you look wonderful! You can't know what tortures you put me through since you disappeared from London. Why did you do it? No, it doesn't matter. All that matters is that I've found you!"

He bent forward from the waist as though he would kiss her, but Regina dodged the gesture and his lips grazed the slope of her cheekbone. "Let me go, Lord Buckram," she said coolly.

She saw anger flash in his sharp blue eyes but it disappeared. "Of course. I'm rushing you," he said, uncurling his fingers but letting his hands remain. "It's just that I've thought of nothing else but finding you these last days."

Recovering quickly from her surprise, Regina shrugged free of his hands. She wasn't about to reveal to him that she knew the reason for his search until she heard his excuse. For, since he had made the journey himself, he must be determined to win the bet he had laid at White's. She suppressed a shudder at the thought.

"After our last meeting, Lord Buckram, I'm amazed that you'd ever care to see me again."

He smiled his most charming smile but it was brittle at the edges. "I suppose I deserve that. I admit it, I behaved badly. But then so did you." When she didn't respond to the appeal in his gaze, he went on. "There was my aunt to encourage my misconduct. She had charged me with a distasteful duty, which family loyalty forced me to accept. Surely you understand and, because of your generous nature, can forgive?"

"The fact that you would stoop to cruel and vicious lies in order to do what you call 'your duty' to the dowager doesn't impress me. You threatened to publish abroad that I was an adulteress, your mistress!"

The accusation, oddly enough, made his eyes burn brighter, as if the memory gave him pleasure. "That is because I wished it were so!"

Again he reached for her and Regina sidestepped him, saying hotly "Don't touch me!"

He lowered his hand. "I don't mean to press you, but all that is in the past. Now is the moment for us to be honest with one another." He gave her his beautiful smile. "Do you not remember that I was with Harry the morning you stepped off the ship in Greenwich? You had not yet met the man you had wed by proxy. When we stepped forward to greet you, your gaze went first to me. Don't deny it, for I watched you. You hoped it was I whom you had wed!"

To her profound shame Regina couldn't deny it. When the two men had approached her, with her uncle by her side, she had looked hopefully at the taller, more appealing man with hair like spun gold. It was a natural if fallible human hope that her husband would be the more handsome man.

"I understand," Buckram went on when she didn't dispute his assertion. "From the moment I saw you, even though you were wed to my cousin, I wanted you too. How can you blame me for my feelings, madame, when you so plainly shared my interest?"

"It was a mistake," she said, backing away from him for he seemed to be crowding her as he did every time they met. "I saw the error of my thinking at once." She met his mocking gaze squarely. "You quickly showed yourself to be a cad, and a liar."

"That was my damnable temper." He shrugged. "I was jealous of what my cousin had and didn't appreciate. And you, after you'd looked at me once with desire in your glorious green eyes, you spurned me. Of course I was angry, perhaps treated you badly. But that was because you tried to pretend the look between us had never occurred."

Regina felt caught. His words made all that had happened between them her fault, and there was just enough truth in his accusation to make her guilt work against her. "If I did—"

"You did!" he cut in. "You encouraged me and then turned me away as not good enough. Was it because I wasn't titled? Well, now I am. And I'm still hopelessly snared by your green gaze just as I was that first day."

Regina reeled away from his reaching hands, but this time he wouldn't allow her escape. He caught her by the shoulders and pulled her against him, his fingers digging cruelly into her flesh. She didn't struggle, for it seemed unwise to let him think that she was afraid of him. "Unhand me!" she demanded, feeling she'd suddenly become part of a bad play where actors mouthed words that real people wouldn't say to one another.

"No! I won't let you go until you listen to me." He drew her even closer, until her bosom pressed against his coat front and his face was only inches from hers. "What would you have me do, Regina? Play the gallant? Languish at your feet? I am no lovesick pup. Shall I give you real proof of my feelings toward you?" He looked as if he were about to say more but a spasm of pain crossed his attractive features. "No."

He suddenly pushed her away and shook his head as if trying to dislodge an unpleasant thought. "We mustn't even speak of that."

Despite her desire to get as far away from him as possible, she couldn't let his words go unchallenged. "Speak of what?"

His head turned toward her, a hand going to his temples to massage his brow. "I didn't come here to speak of it. But perhaps we must." There came a look of such sweet misery into his handsome face that, had he been a stranger, she would have believed that he was laboring under an arduous and difficult task. "Let me say this much." He paused then hurled the words at her. "I love you. And, if need be, I'm prepared to protect you even into my grave!"

"Protect me?" Her tone was openly skeptical. "From what?"

"Must we speak the ugly truth aloud?" He came quickly toward her and raised a hand to touch her cheek. "I fear for you, for your lovely neck." His hand slipped down to encircle her throat. "I don't want to see this sweet skin bruised and torn by the hangman's rope!"

He released her, but not before Regina had felt the life-threatening pressure of his fingers constrict cruelly for an instant about her throat. She fell back a step, her own hand rising protectively to her abused throat. "I don't know what you mean. I've done nothing wrong, committed no crime."

"Regina." The anguish in his expression was poignant. "I know!" His voice dropped to a husky whisper. "I know you murdered your husband!"

Regina was shocked beyond mere denial. There was something so compelling about his emotional intensity that she didn't doubt that he believed what he said. "Murder?" She, too, whispered the word. "Who says Lord Lynsdale was murdered?"

He bit his lip, his gaze lowering before hers. "I beg you not to press the matter. It's enough that I know the truth and can live with it, have lived with it for weeks."

"Well, I don't know the truth," Regina answered, her voice rising. "And I won't live with another lie!" She moved forward and touched him on the shoulder to turn him fully to her. "Who's spreading lies that my husband was murdered?"

He lifted abashed eyes to hers. "No lie, Regina. I've the evidence in my possession. 'Twas I who removed the poisoned wine from his mistress's boudoir before anyone else noticed."

Regina heard the words but they didn't make sense. "What wine?"

Buckram seemed to grapple with painful memory, his even features distorting with the effort. "Earline, your husband's mistress, sent for me at my club after—after Harry collapsed at her home. She didn't know what else to do. She couldn't very well go to you with the news that your husband had died in her bed. When I got there, she was hysterical. She said Harry had been complaining of not feeling well all evening, and that he'd brought with him a bottle of port you had given him as a wedding gift because he thought it would soothe what he assumed was indigestion."

"I never gave Lord Lynsdale a bottle of port."

His gaze shifted from hers again, and Regina felt as if he couldn't bear what he thought were her lies. "You did. Your name was still on the tag."

Regina tried to think, to remember. Between her uncle's gifts and the dowager countess's demands, she couldn't remember whether or not one of them had bought a bottle of wine for her to present to her husband during the first days of their marriage. "I don't remember. There were tags on so many presents, someone might have switched them."

"That's what I thought," Buckram quietly agreed. "That it was a mistake, that someone else must have given him the bottle."

"In any case, a gift of wine doesn't label me a murderess," Regina protested.

"True enough. You might have gotten away with it if he'd drunk the entire contents before he collapsed. But I spied, quite by accident, the unusual amount of sediment in the bottom of the bottle the next day." He looked at her as if expecting her to comment on his claim, but her question surprised him.

"Why did you have the bottle in the first place?"

His expression grew tender. "I'd gone back to remove all evidence of my cousin's presence in Earline's house in order to spare the family's feelings. Only later I realized how much more I had spared you."

"You spared me nothing," she answered, grateful to feel the first stirring of anger beneath her numbness. "If you thought I'd committed murder, why didn't you report me to the authorities, or at least tell your aunt?"

"Because, my darling, from the moment I saw Harry lying there, all I could think of was that you were free. I know, it's a despicable thing to say, but it reveals how much I want and love you. The authorities accepted the assertion of a heart attack because Harry ate and drank far too much for his own good. A few days later I took a little of the sediment to an apothecary. He told me it was powdered foxglove." He looked at her, his eyes almost kind. "Given in enough quantity it can overstimulate the heart. Because I would do anything to protect you, I went ahead and played the part that my aunt expected of me. To do else would have made her suspicious."

"There was nothing to suspect."

His light eyes sliced through the air between them. "Wasn't there?"

Regina turned away and sank into a nearby chair. She couldn't think, couldn't imagine that what he was telling her was true. And yet, intuitively, she accepted his word that her husband had been murdered. From the moment she'd entered it, the Amesbury household reeked of intrigue and mystery and sordid ugliness. She'd known she was a pawn, but for what purpose? Had someone planned murder? If only she could remember the bottle of port. She lowered her head into her hands. "I can't think. I can't remember!"

Buckram came and knelt before her and because she was too wretched to care, Regina let him take one of her hands between his. "Don't cry, darling. I swore to myself I'd never mention the matter to you but, well, you forced me to prove how much I love you. And I do love you, Regina. I know you were married against your will, just as I know Harry didn't even pretend to be a husband to you . . . did he?"

The last two words held more than polite inquiry. Regina lifted her head to look at him. It was there again in his expression, unconcealed lust. She shivered. "Lord Amesbury was no more or less than I desired."

He smiled at her. "I'm now Lord Amesbury, my dear.

And I would gladly be no less and no more than you desire."

Regina shook her head. "I don't feel anything for you, my lord. I'm sorry. You mistook my error to mean more than it did."

"Regina," he said reproachfully. "I'm not asking that you love me yet. But let me help you. If you married me, then I could protect you always."

"There's nothing to protect," Regina said wearily. "I didn't kill my husband. And whoever did is going to go free."

The fact that he didn't answer, didn't rush to reassure her, made Regina's hair lift on her neck. Suddenly she understood what she had not, that his offer of protection contained in it an implied threat. She withdrew her hand from his. "Will you tell the authorities of your suspicions if I don't agree to marry you?"

"Regina," he chided, his hand falling possessively on her knee. "Regina, dearest, think of my position. A well-loved cousin slain, the apprehension of the murderer within my grasp, and yet I have hesitated. Doesn't that prove my love?"

"They won't believe you," she said softly, straining not to bolt from him. "You've waited too long. You will only implicate yourself."

He shrugged. "What can I say in my defense but that I was in love, unwilling to believe the worst about you, that you had enthralled me, as you had my cousin. I was a victim of my own ungovernable desire."

Somehow it was all the more horrible because he said it in a wistful sad voice without a single undertone of threat. Either she must agree to marry him or he would destroy her. But why was the marriage necessary? Could he really love her? She couldn't credit that. Then why?

She thought of Lord Kingsblood but at once discarded the idea of seeking his help. From the moment she had arrived in England, she had been a dupe to the sort of scandal that broke careers, sundered families, and ruined lives. The marquess mustn't come anywhere near her again unless and until she had freed herself from the Amesburys and all that they stood for. As for her uncle, he had shown himself to be more interested in her inheritance than her well-being. Why, if she stood trial for murder and was found guilty, he would inherit all that she had. As she had been for so long, she was once more completely alone.

She rose slowly to her feet. "What must we do?"

Buckram was on his feet at once. "Come back to London with me. Or, if you'd rather, we'll go directly to Gretna Green to be married. There's bound to be scandal either way, but we'll weather it more easily if we are wed."

"No." She almost said "I wonder if the dowager countess might know who would have wanted her son dead?" but caution prevented her from doing so. There was a trap in this for her, and she couldn't be certain who had baited it for her. Until she was, she'd have no confidants to her thoughts. "How is the dowager?"

"Ailing," he answered disinterestedly. "The physicians bleed her almost daily. There's little hope for recovery."

"Then we must go to London first."

He looked suspicious. "Why?"

She turned to him, facing once more, without protection or aid, an enemy. "Because she's dying in my house."

The wicked grin that spread across his handsome face was as unholy as it was beautiful.

Chapter Eighteen

LONDON

Regina stared up at the bed hangings in the early-morning light. The gold-and-white Empire draperies and swags that decorated the opulent bedroom of the Amesbury town house still bore the initials J T L above the Amesbury crest. To all outward appearances, nothing had changed. She didn't know what she had expected. Perhaps, because her own life had changed so radically since she had left London, she thought there should be changes of every sort in the rest of the world. After all, she had entered this room a new bride and had left it less than a month later as a widow.

Regina shut her eyes to the finery. *She* had changed in many ways since she had left this room. She had learned to be self-sufficient. She had found new sources of will and strength of purpose in dealing with adversity. She had learned how to hold her own in the world of earls and marquesses. And most important of all, she had learned how to love a man.

Maxwell Kingsblood had been in her last thoughts each night and in her first each morning since the day they had met. Now the memory of their parting lay anxiously upon her conscience. She hadn't wanted it to happen like that but there had been no way to prevent it. The look in his eyes, the accusing, disbelieving gaze of a betrayed lover, had haunted her every mile of the long journey back to London.

He had come to her cottage as she was packing. She had thought it was Buckram, returning with the traveling coach he had rented and left waiting on the fork of the main highway in the expectation that she could be persuaded to leave with him.

"I'm ready," she had said, turning about as she heard a man's boot steps enter the cottage. And then she had turned to find Maxwell standing there, a smile of joy on his beloved face.

"That's wonderful, darling. I—"

Her look of unpleasant surprise must have stopped him because he never finished what he was about to say. "What is it, Regina?"

"I—I didn't expect you, my lord."

"I said I'd come." He smiled ruefully. "I'm sorry I'm late but I was detained by an unexpected visitor. But I see that I needn't have worried." His gaze swept approvingly over her half-packed trunk, and the expression on his face when he looked again at her was full of triumphant love and joy. "I have my answer. You were coming to me!"

Before she could reply other footsteps sounded in the yard. They both turned to the doorway as Buckram strode in without bothering to knock. Each man was clearly startled by the presence of the other, while Regina knew a frustration and anger so great she nearly screamed her displeasure.

"Who's this?" both men asked her at the same time.

Calling upon every ounce of dignity, she resorted to parlor manners. "Marquess, may I present my cousin by marriage Percy Buckram, the new Earl of Amesbury." Noting that Maxwell didn't seem in the least disconcerted by the introduction, she continued. "Lord Buckram, this is Lord Maxwell Kingsblood, Marquess of Ilfracombe."

"Marquess?" Buckram put out his hand but it was ignored by the other man. A look of indignation glazed his eyes but he merely moved to Regina's side as if he had the right to stand so near her. "I don't know that we've met, Marquess. How do you know Regina?"

Regina winced as she saw Maxwell's reaction to the use of her Christian name. But he only said, "We are neighbors, and old friends."

"Is that so?" Buckram murmured, turning his keen gaze on her.

A guilty blush stung her cheeks. "We knew one another as children. My father was Lord Kingsblood's tutor. This cottage was our home."

Buckram's fair brows shot up. "Your father was a penny-poor scholar? How droll, Countess."

Buckram's presence was annoyance enough but his provocative speech made her want to grind her teeth. "I was very happy here."

"In this hovel?" He sneered. Then, as if realizing a new thought, he looked at Maxwell. "Ah, but forgive me, Marquess, for you must be her landlord."

"No," he said slowly. "The countess is an independent lady, free to come and go as she pleases. Isn't that so, my lady?"

Regina heard the deference in his tone and realized that he had used her title. Had Buckram's presence convinced him that it was not a ruse? There were a dozen questions she wished to ask him, and a dozen more explanations she wished to make, but Buckram's presence prevented her.

Maxwell glanced out the window as a coach lumbered to a stop before the cottage path. When his gaze swept back to her, his dark eyes held an angry challenge so vivid it made them appear black. "You are packing, Countess. Where are you going?"

She held his troubled gaze with a beseeching look. "It's not what you think."

But she knew Maxwell had heard too many conflicting things in the last ten days to give her yet again an assurance of his open-mindedness. "What am I thinking?" he said in a expressionless voice.

"That Regina is coming back to London with me," Buckram inserted smugly.

Maxwell's gaze never left Regina's face. "Is that true?"

"I must. You see—"

"Regina!" Buckram cut in warningly, and laid a hand on her arm.

Maxwell clenched his fists, looking as if he wanted to strangle the man, but he didn't move. "Are you returning of your own free will, or are you being forced?"

"Of my own free will," Regina answered, sending him a silent plea not to question her further . . . to no avail.

"Why?" The question was curt and uncompromising.

Standing there looking at the determined expression on his face and the deeper, more vulnerable question that only his dark eyes dared speak, Regina felt as if she were drowning in agony. How could she explain to him that Buckram professed to love her, that he thought he was protecting her from a charge of murder, and that she was going to London to exonerate herself?

She didn't doubt for one minute that Maxwell would stand beside her if she asked it of him. He had done so long before he had asked her to marry him. But there were reasons he mustn't attempt to aid her in this difficulty. She couldn't say a word to him without drawing him into the tangled web that threatened to snare her. Every other evil that someone had dared speak about her had been believed.

What if she couldn't prove herself innocent and she was brought to judgment? If the marquess stood beside her, his reputation would be ruined as well. No, he mustn't be allowed to interfere, whatever the cost to her. And, at the moment, it felt as if her heart were being pulled out by the roots.

"I must leave, for a short time," she said finally, and an echo of the pain that crossed Maxwell's face was reflected in hers. "But I plan to return." She hesitated, thinking more rapidly than she had ever done in her life as she searched for words that would assuage her guilt and subtly reveal her thoughts to the one person in the world she loved. "This is my home."

"So I thought." He seemed to be struggling with some inner demon but said nothing more.

"Will you be returning to London shortly?" She couldn't resist asking though she risked a great deal by doing so.

"No," he answered, a flicker of an eyelid the only sketch of emotion in his face. "I find the solitude of the country more suited to my needs just now."

"Then you shall be the first to hear our news," Buckram said, injecting himself once more into the conversation. He put a proprietary arm about Regina's shoulders. "I've persuaded Lady Regina to become my wife."

Even as she shrank from Buckram's embrace Regina knew the damage had been done. "That's not true, my lord!"

Buckram's look was reproachful. "But only an hour ago, Regina, you made me believe that I should entertain hopes in that direction." He looked back at the marquess. "Women are such delightfully contrary creatures, prone to fits of whim and temper. And yet, in spite of all, we can't help but love them. Isn't that so, my lord?"

Maxwell didn't answer and the travesty of lies in which

she was trapped made Regina want to retch. She laced her fingers together so tightly the knuckles ached, but that was nothing compared to the pain that seared her from the look on Maxwell's face. "I will come back," she mouthed soundlessly.

His stunned expression gave way to one that was more awful than any anger or rage she could have imagined. It was a mixture of fury and torment, misery and confusion. And it was directed at her, because she couldn't explain even one part of her actions to him.

"I'm certain she will give you an answer in time, Lord Buckram," he said in a terrible voice devoid of all its natural depth and timbre. "I, too, am waiting for a reply from the lady I would marry."

Regina didn't realize that she was crying again until a tear slipped down her cheek and ran hotly into her ear. Maxwell had left her then. When she had taken a step toward him, Buckram had grasped her by the arm to stay her, and she had let him go because she didn't know what else to do.

She closed her eyes in shame for the pain she had inflicted upon the man she loved. She had been over every moment of their last conversation a hundred times, wanting to change the words, and order, and outcome. If only she had been more quick-witted, if she had been prepared to face him, if she could have told him that she loved him before Buckram found her . . .

But no, it was better this way. Under no circumstances must she allow Lord Kingsblood to become embroiled in the treachery and lies that enveloped the Amesburys. The scandal that had plagued her for weeks could ruin his reputation. If she'd said "I love you" a second time, she knew he wouldn't have allowed her to leave him. Yet leaving him was the most painful thing she'd ever done.

She and Buckram had exchanged few words on their journey back to London; both agreed that the strain and discomfort of an unbroken dash for the city was worth the price of returning as quickly as possible. Except for frequent expensive pauses to exchange horses and gulp quick meals, they had spent three miserable days in one another's company while Buckram brooded and she steeped in the full misery of her situation.

A charge of murder had been laid at her door. Buckram said he had proof. He also insisted that he wanted to marry her, yet he had been a strangely reticent suitor. During their travels he hadn't once attempted to take any liberty with her. His manner had been courteous but detached, as if he had other concerns on his mind. She was grateful for his distance, but found his cool manner disturbing. Did he suspect that she had no intention of marrying him, or was he certain she would? At first she was afraid that she had betrayed her love for Lord Kingsblood or that the Marquess's own unusual behavior had alerted Buckram to the fact that there was more between them than a neighborly relationship. But Buckram had asked only one question about the marquess, and that was about how well she knew him. She had truthfully answered that she hadn't even recognized him when they met after nine years. That seemed to satisfy Buckram. Still, she was uneasy.

They had reached London the night before. The footmen had collected their baggage while the housekeeper had gone up to light the fire in the bedrooms. In that moment they had been alone in the foyer of the Amesbury town house, and, for the first time in three days, Buckram had smiled at her in that salacious way that made her feel she needed a bath.

He had touched her cheek with the back of his hand and said, "After you have rested the night, we'll make plans for our future." Leaning near, he had added, "Don't worry, dearest, we'll celebrate our wedding night by destroying all evidence of our little secret."

Something was wrong. The thought ran as deep as the marrow of her bones. There was the ring of conviction in Buckram's assertion that her husband had been poisoned, but by whom, and why? Buckram had inherited the earldom with Lynsdale's death. Yet if he'd committed the murder, what reason could there now be to try to implicate her? With every mile that had brought her closer to London, she had become more convinced that the answers to those questions could be found only beneath this roof.

Buckram didn't love her. Of that she was certain. He wanted to possess her, own her. After one night in Maxwell Kingsblood's arms, she couldn't imagine allowing another man to so much as kiss her.

"Oh, Maxwell," she whispered, "please be patient, and trust me a little until I can be with you again."

She had no other choice but to brave out the next few days, to discover if murder had been done, and if so, to exonerate herself. If she rebuffed Buckram too soon, she was afraid that he would turn his "evidence" over to the authorities. The key to the mystery was, she was certain, the dowager.

She reached for the servants' bell and rang it. By the time a maid came in answer, Regina had risen and washed and donned a wrapper. "Good morning," she greeted the pale young maid in white who entered bearing a breakfast tray. "I wish to see the dowager countess as soon as she awakens. Please see that she's informed of my desire at the first opportunity."

"Oh, my lady, didn't they tell you?"

Foreboding snaked up Regina's spine. "Tell me what?"

"Why, my lady, that the dowager took a turn for the

worse two days past. The physician says she won't live out the week."

"Is she conscious?"

"I wouldn't know that, my lady. There's a nurse been hired to look after her, and she won't have any of the staff inside the door. The dowager's companion, Miss Williams, has been turned out. No one comes and goes but the doctor and Lord Buckram."

"I see." Regina pretended to fiddle with her brush while the girl poured her cocoa. "Who determines who the dowager's visitors are?"

"The nurse, my lady. And a great old Tartar she is!"

Remembering belatedly to whom she spoke, the girl flung a hand over her mouth. "Beggin' your pardon, my lady."

"That will do," Regina said kindly, and was glad that the girl left at once.

Because she was still tired and ached in every joint from the bruising ride from Devon, Regina took her time with breakfast, forcing herself to eat two pieces of toast and even a bit of the ham with her cocoa. Once fortified, she dressed quickly and braced herself for a visit to the dowager's room.

The hall on the main floor was without candlelight, and the draperies had been drawn over the window at the far end. Already the house seemed to be in mourning.

As she neared the great double doors that led to the dowager's suite, she heard voices beyond the door. She drew herself up and gave one door a brisk knock.

The voices stopped. Several moments later one of the doors was opened a crack and Regina saw half of a thin sallow face and one piercing gray eye. "What is it?"

The haughty tone was all Regina needed to set her resolve. "I'm the Countess of Amesbury. I've come to visit with my mother-in-law."

To her surprise the woman didn't budge an inch. Instead Regina saw the single eye narrow as half a mouth said, "You cannot see her today!"

Regina put her foot in the breech as she saw that the woman was about to close the door. "I repeat, I am the Countess of Amesbury. This is *my* house. If you cannot be civil, I can see to it that you're out on the pavement in five minutes."

The threat gave the woman a moment's pause, but only that. "I was hired by the earl. Only he can sack me."

"I wouldn't count on that," Regina snapped, but removed her foot. "I'll be back after luncheon, and I expect to be allowed in." Because she didn't wish the door to be slammed in her face, she turned quickly away and marched down the hall, her head high.

She rang for a servant when she reached the drawing room. A footman came immediately. "Have the carriage brought round, I'm going out."

"I'm sorry, my lady, but Lord Buckram gave strict instructions that no one is to leave the house in his absence."

"Nonsense," Regina replied. Having borne the incivility of one servant, she wasn't about to be bullied by another. "This house and everything in it belongs to me. That means you work for me. Do as I say at once."

The footman's features remained impassive but Regina had the vague impression that he was amused. "Beggin' your pardon, my lady, but Lord Buckram hired me just last week."

Regina realized that she hadn't recognized the maid who had come into her room that morning, nor had she seen any familiar faces among the staff she'd passed in the hallways. Yet she had lived here only a short time and there were so many servants that she couldn't be sure that her own memory was not at fault. "Has the entire staff been changed?"

"No, my lady, only the butler and the footmen."

Only the men, Regina mused, men who could easily overpower a woman. The thought truly frightened her but she wasn't about to show it. "Never mind. I shall send a note declining the invitation I was to accept this morning." It was a small lie but the footman wouldn't know that. "I suppose that I'm allowed to post a note."

"Yes, my lady."

When she had withdrawn paper from the nearby writing table, she sat and wrote a note to her banker, asking him to come to see her at once. She folded and sealed it with hot wax then presented it to the man. "The address is on the note. Have it delivered at once. I have asked for a reply. See that it is sent up to me at once."

"Very well, my lady." The man took the note but something about the way he didn't even glance at it made Regina doubt it would reach its destination.

When he had withdrawn she went to the window and looked out at the busy street beyond the iron gateway. She was virtually a prisoner because Buckram didn't trust her not to run away again. He believed her to be a murderess. Her hands began to tremble and her heart pounded thickly in her ears. Had she already stepped into the trap?

The day was raw and misty but Maxwell scarcely noticed. He had just risen from the depths of a tin mine, but the satisfaction on his face didn't reach the dull depths of his eyes.

"As you've seen for yourself, my lord, there's a broad vein of ore to be worked with little excavation required," the surveyor said, sounding well pleased with his findings.

"O' course, you'll need to replace them beams before it's safe to commence working. But that's easily done."

"How much?" Maxwell said, looking up toward the gray expanse of sky.

"Oh, one hundred and fifty quid should see a beginning."

"Then make your beginning, Mr. Fowler." Maxwell walked away without even a glance at the man.

It was the morning of the fourth day since he had let Regina ride away with Percy Buckram, and he was beginning to think that he'd made a mistake. Perhaps he had misread the look in her eyes, the look that had made him turn and walk away from that cottage when every instinct urged him to turn back and take her away, by force if necessary, from Buckram.

But he had seen that look and the silent words she'd mouthed to him, and he couldn't shake the memory of them, whether in his dreams or in the black bowels of the earth. In her glance he had discovered the source of the fear that he'd seen lurking in her gaze from the first day. She felt she was alone in the world, totally and completely alone, and there was no one she could or *dared* trust.

There was no one to see the savage look that came into Maxwell's face as he trod the wild moors, quickly putting a good deal of distance between himself and the surveyor. If only there had been more time for him to prove his love for her, she would have turned to him to protect her, to fight for her and best her enemies. But she hadn't.

He took the note from his pocket that had arrived at Blood Hall the morning after Regina left. She had given it to a man at an inn, where she and Buckram had paused for their evening meal, and asked him to deliver it. It was terse and unemotional yet he cherished every word written in her hand.

My Lord,
I have gone to confront my past. Please do
not follow me. You asked how you might
make up for past wrongs. This is how.
Trust me.

                        R.

Maxwell swore viciously and came to a standstill at the
crest of the headland. Below the sea surged and foamed and
ebbed. Pride had sent him striding out of her cottage when
every male instinct had urged him not to leave her with
Buckram. Yet she had stood so silently when he had
wanted her to answer the question uppermost in his mind.

He stared at the moody coastline, feeling the tug of opposite emotions as strongly as the shifting waters beat upon
the shore beneath him. But farther out, where the swells
flattened into a glossy surface, the sea became a serene
green expanse. Watching the sea, he recalled how Regina's
expression had altered at the last moment, and how her
love had shone clearly and unstintingly in her green gaze.
The memory teased a smile to his lips. All his questions
were still unanswered, and all his doubts about Buckram
still festered hotly. But for all that, he did trust her. He
believed that she loved him.

The rest—the doubts, the obstacles, the problems and
confusions and misunderstandings—could all be worked
out. And that was why he was trying to prove his trust in
her. Yet his patience was being hard-won by each daily
struggle. He wasn't eating properly or sleeping well. Letting
her go was the hardest thing he had ever done. And he
wondered how long his resolve would hold.

He needed simply to be near her to be content. That is
why he had moved into her cottage. It was as close as he

could get to her. He felt that she would go there first when she returned. And he would be there waiting.

"Two weeks!" he muttered. "Dammit, Regina, I give you two weeks to return to Devon, and then God help the man who stands between you and me when I come to London to claim you!"

Regina entered the dowager's bedroom with trepidation. She had waited until she saw the hired nurse slip out of the room before she went to the door. For three days she had been barred from entering the sickroom, on one pretext or another. Even the doctor couldn't be persuaded to brook the earl's assertion that the sight of her hated daughter-in-law would inflame the dowager to unhealthy flights of passion. But tonight Buckram was out for the evening and no one would stop her.

To her relief the door opened easily and she saw that no other servant stood guard inside. The room was hung in red-and-gold brocade. Portraits covered the walls. Porcelains and bric-a-brac lined the mantel and covered the tops of gilded furnishings from half a century earlier.

Though by far the most elegant bedroom she had ever seen, it held that peculiar odor common to all sickrooms, the faint stench of decay, the feverish breath of illness, and smothering overheated air. On the opposite wall on a two-tiered dais stood the dowager's bed.

Regina approached the bed almost on tiptoe, uncertain that it was occupied until she reached the foot. There on a pillow, her head shrouded in a great nightmop, lay the dowager countess. Without her face powder and rouge, her complexion appeared drawn and nearly as white as the linen that flanked it. Her eyes were closed and she lay so still that for a moment, Regina thought she might have died. But then her eyes opened, the lids drawing back so slowly they did not seem human.

"You!" the dowager said. "You came back! Stand closer to the light, damn you!"

Regina obeyed the command and came forward into the light by the bedside, not because the dowager's voice still terrified her but because illness had weakened it to a pathetic croak. As the dowager's pale gaze moved over her, she could almost feel its baleful weight on her skin. "You've changed, gel! There's a new look in your eye. Who put it there?" The dowager laughed, a dry little crackle that sounded like it came from another source. "You've been with a man, haven't you?"

Regina met the woman's malevolent stare with an impassive look. "I've been living in a cottage in Devon, but you know that, don't you?"

"I know everything about you!" the dowager replied. Her gaze shifted away from Regina as a small absent smile appeared on her sunken mouth. "I once knew everything! I knew even the number of mice that dwelt within the walls of this house. I had my sources, my spies, my methods. Nothing ever escaped my attention. No one ever escaped my will until . . ."

Her hand suddenly reached out and gripped Regina's wrist, surprising her by its unexpected strength. "You! It's my low-born daughter-in-law, is it not?"

"Yes," Regina replied, flinching under the pain of the sharp nails digging into her wrist.

"Why are you here? Have you come to gloat?" The harsh words were spoken in dreadful gaspings.

"I haven't come back out of fear, or anger, or to do you harm, Countess," Regina said calmly

"Lies! Lies! Always lies!"

As suddenly as it was grasped, Regina's wrist was released. The dowager's head fell back against the pillow. The lace edge of her nightmop slid back from her forehead to reveal sparse white hair that didn't succeed in covering her blue-veined skull. Her gaze wandered to the ceiling and held, as if she saw something or someone Regina could not. "She thinks because she is young and beautiful, with eyes like those of a wild creature, that she can take him from me. But she's wrong! I told him she's a peasant. No family! No breeding! No refinement! Even the meanest weed can produce a beautiful blossom! That's what she is, a splendid blossom borne of the muck! But he defied me! He'd already married her!"

The dowager's speech unnerved her but Regina stood perfectly still as the woman continued.

"Harry says he chose her because he doesn't want a society wife whom he will have to squire about to boring parties and dinners and dances. A convent foundling will be pliable. She'll give him sons whom she'll rear in the country while he lives in the city and continues his life unencumbered. She's to be mine, a quiet biddable companion to wait on me, see to my every need, someone docile, meek, and tractable."

The dowager began picking fretfully at the coverlet with her yellowed nails, completely unaware that anyone stood beside her bed. "But she tricked Harry. She's no biddable chit! She has the eyes of a witch! They scored me to the bone the first time she set them upon me. She watches us, learns our secrets. Hate her! Hate her! Must dissolve the marriage before it's too late!"

The dowager drew the covers up under her chin as if a chill had wafted through the sweltering heat of the room. And then, once again, she was lost in her own thoughts. "I should murder her!"

"Murder?" Regina repeated faintly. "What of murder?"

"I see the look in Harry's eyes," the old woman continued, lost in her own thoughts. "There's a new secretiveness
about him. Even Buckram has mentioned it. I suspect Harry's playing some deep game of his own in which the girl is
only a pawn, but he won't confide in me."

She smiled, the uneven stretching of her pinched lips a
travesty of good humor. "Still, he comes to me for advice
about his bride. She is afraid of him, he tells me, she shies
from his kisses. I tell him that he must give her time to
become accustomed to him and her surroundings before he
claims his husbandly rights. With luck I may be able to
convince him to be rid her."

Suddenly her face crumpled into a crisscross network of
lines and creases that made her seem a hundred years old.
"How could I guess that he would burst his heart within
the week?"

Regina bent low over the woman. "Are you certain the
earl's heart burst? Was there nothing more?"

Her pale eyes seemed to cloud. "Of course there was
more. He betrayed me, his mother! He changed his will!
Gave his fortune to a foundling. That was the final blow.
Harry—dead! The witch loose in my house. My house! And
the bulk of the monies in her greedy peasant hands. Too
late! Harry is dead! Too late! Oo-oh no—oo!"

The howling shook Regina to the soles of her feet but as
she reached out in instinctive need to comfort another in
pain, the dowager suddenly turned her head to meet Regina
eye to lucid eye. "You! You murdered him!"

Regina shrank back. Had Buckram told her what he suspected? But even as the question hovered on her lips, she
saw that the dowager's concentration had drifted again. She
was looking at the ceiling, her gaze unfocused.

As the dowager's eyes fell shut, Regina realized the full
extent of the toll that illness had taken on her. She saw the

dowager for what she had become, an enfeebled, ailing old woman whose influence and malevolence had been usurped for all time by her waning mortality. This was no enemy to fear or to exult over, but a sad lonely old woman to pity.

Regina was turning to leave when the dowager's eyes opened again. "Who's there?"

Regina moved back to the bed and bent low so that the candle flame on the bedside fully lighted her face. "I'm here, my lady."

The dowager's milky gaze darted back and forth, taking in every contour of Regina's face. "Who are you? Do I know you? No, I think not. But—yes!" Her thin lids half-shuttered her eyes. "You are my son's widow come to gloat. Then look your fill, and be damned for it!"

"Not to gloat," Regina said softly, "to compromise."

"Compromise?" she said scornfully. "Why should I compromise? I hate you, fully and completely. There'll be no compromise!" A malicious smile lifted the corners of her sunken mouth. "You would shame me with your magnanimity, but I won't be treated like a lackey, chastised and then forgiven! Not by you! To humble myself with compromise would kill me. When I am better I will show you. Those eyes, those strange unearthly eyes that see my mortality. I would pluck them out!"

Regina recoiled from the venom spilling from the woman's lips. Neither her illness nor infirmity made the words any the less hateful or easier to accept. One thing was clear, the woman's hatred of her was deep, impenetrable, and unalterable. She would go to her grave with that twisted enmity her only companion.

"Tell me about Lord Percy," Regina said suddenly. "Shouldn't he have a say in whether or not the inheritance is to be returned?"

"My nephew all but shat in his breeches when the will

was read." She cackled with laughter. "Serves him right, the rutting little bastard. Harry said he wasn't fit to be an earl of Amesbury. Changed his will to punish Buckram. Well, now Percy has a golden coronet but no shillings to fill his coffers."

The news electrified Regina and she bent closer to the aged face. "What do you mean? Did Lord Buckram not inherit a great deal besides the earldom?"

Suddenly great tears formed in her rheumy eyes and leaked down her withered cheeks. "My . . . son! Buckram thinks I don't know! But I know," she said, becoming more and more agitated.

"What is it you know, Countess?" Regina whispered by her ear.

She shook her head as if to dislodge a disagreeable thought. "Mustn't tell. He mustn't guess. I'm sick. Old. But I'll best him yet!"

Her body arched up from the bed, her great pale eyes starting forth from their sockets. Her mouth opened on a soft moan of pain that sounded as if all the life was being breathed out of her. Even as Regina reached for the servants' bell, the dowager went limp against the bedding and lay absolutely still, her eyes still staring fixedly.

A moment later, the bedroom door was thrust open by Buckram with the nurse at his heels. "What is going on?" he cried.

Regina turned fearlessly to face him. "The dowager countess has fainted."

The nurse rushed to the bed, pushing roughly past Regina. She threw back the covers and pressed an ear to the dowager's thin breast. "She's breathing," the nurse announced. "But only just. Better send for the physician."

"Then do it," Buckram said, and beckoned to Regina.

With a last reluctant look over her shoulder at the dowager's emaciated body, Regina followed him into the hallway.

A little mocking smile played about his mouth when he had drawn her aside. "Did the dowager talk to you? Yes, I can see by your look that she did. What did she tell you?" He caught her arm in a cruel grip. "What did she say?"

Regina met his gaze steadily. "Release me at once."

His smile hardened at the edges, but he complied. "Of course, dear cousin. You greatly upset her, didn't you? You may have done me a great favor after all. Come downstairs. Dinner is ready."

"I'm not hungry." Her gaze took in his evening finery. "I thought you were dining out."

A cynical smirk drew down the corners of his smile. "Is that why you came up here against my wishes? I was out. I came back because I missed being with you." He touched her arm again; this time the slight movement of his fingers on her bare arm was a caress. "Come down and join me. We haven't been together in days, and I grow restless for your company."

His passionate wording left her cold, but Regina went with him because anything else would have made him suspicious, and she needed time to think.

Dinner was eaten in near silence for Buckram seemed reluctant to say much before the footman who hovered about. For her part, Regina couldn't swallow a thing. Only the wine seemed to help steady her nerves. When the final course was removed he sat nursing a glass of port while she toyed with a glass of sherry. At last he spoke. "We must set a date, Regina."

Regina gazed down the length of the table. "What date?"

"The date for our marriage." He grinned at her and she realized that he had drunk a good deal of wine.

"Marriage is out of the question." She hesitated long

enough to see the good humor die in his expression, then continued. "The dowager hovers near death. In any case, I'm a widow in mourning. It will be at least a year before I can wed again without society snubbing us both."

To her amazement, he simply said, "Perhaps you are right, my dear. Perhaps we should wait a bit for the formal ceremony, but you must know how I feel about you." The lust that she had been relieved not to have to confront until now kindled his gaze. "I can't wait a year to bed you."

Regina dropped her gaze, hoping that he would think she was being modest, but she nearly choked on the words she said. "If you please, my lord. I must have time, to know you better."

That meek answer seemed to please him, for he chuckled. "But not too long, Regina. I would teach you much so that you will be the most skillful bride in all of England come our wedding day."

Regina said nothing. She didn't dare speak the thoughts that occupied her mind. The dowager had given her the pieces and during dinner she had put the puzzle together. Buckram had murdered his cousin in order to inherit the earldom. She had been amazed by the extent of the wealth her uncle had outlined in the papers he'd given her to sign. Now she understood. Everything that was not entailed by the earldom must have come to her. Buckram got a title but little wealth. By marrying her, he could have it all . . . and then, she had no doubt, he would murder her too.

Regina rose to her feet. "I am tired, my lord. If you will excuse—"

The dining-room doors were suddenly thrust open by the dowager's nurse. "She's dead! The dowager's dead!"

Chapter Nineteen

❧

$\mathcal{R}$egina lay fully clothed upon her bed. The dowager's funeral had taken place in the afternoon, in the rain. The tiny church, which had received the patronage of the earls of Amesbury for more than two hundred years, had been filled to overflowing. Rumors of Regina's return to London had prompted many who never attended such events to brave a drenching in the hope of glimpsing her face. But she hadn't given them a chance. She'd worn a heavy black veil over her mourning gown, the cloth so dense that none but those who stood next to her could penetrate its depths. She had felt the avid gazes of strangers on her, their palpable annoyance because they couldn't see her, and their envious, insatiable need to strip her of her privacy.

She couldn't mourn the dowager. The woman's hatred of her had been too virulent for her to summon anything like sympathy for the woman. But she was her husband's mother and was owed the respect due that position.

Yet Regina hadn't remained downstairs beyond the moment Buckram had released her from the obligation of standing in the receiving line while the *ton* paid its respects to the family. He'd been angry that she refused even then to lift her veil. But, short of snatching it from her, he could do nothing.

They were still downstairs eating and drinking. The volume of voices penetrated up to the floor and through the thickness of her closed door. Buckram had already sent for her once to demand that she sit by his side at dinner. But she had pleaded a headache and sent the maid for a draught, which she had then poured out.

She glanced at the clock on the mantel. It was early, not yet eight. Sooner or later most of the guests would leave. Those who remained would gradually succumb to inebriation. That was what she was waiting for, and while she waited, she gathered her strength.

She had already stolen a master key from the butler's pantry while on a supposed errand to find bootblack for her shoes. She would take no more than what she carried on her back. She had less than ten pounds in cash. There wouldn't be a hired coach this time to take her back to Devon. But she wouldn't allow herself to think of how that arduous task would be accomplished. First, she must escape. She was a prisoner, and she knew it, but she had to pretend otherwise to keep from going mad or succumbing to paralyzing fear.

The only thing that had kept her going since that nightmarish visit to the dowager's room was the knowledge that the Marquess of Ilfracombe waited for her. She didn't care what he said when she saw him again. She wouldn't care if he was angry or spurned her. She knew now that she loved him completely, totally, without reserve, and that if he would take her back, she would accept him on any terms he chose.

She didn't expect him to repeat his offer of marriage. He was a proud man, not out of self-deluding arrogance, as she had once imagined, but from a strong sense of high principles and self-respect. Any woman whom he loved could consider herself the most fortunate of women. If he would love her again, she would ask for nothing else. Just to be kissed by him again, just that much, she was certain would heal her pain.

Occupied with pleasant thoughts of Lord Kingsblood, Regina lay drifting among dark shadows and lavender scents of mourning until, faintly at first, and then ever more clearly, she heard the sounds of horses' hooves and the lumberings of a heavy coach drawing near. The horses seemed to be riding in tandem, as if in a parade, and when they halted she knew the coach was before the Amesbury house. She rose quickly and flung open the drape to her bedroom window that overlooked the street.

In the faint torchlight burning by the iron gate she saw four horsemen and a carriage. They wore military uniforms and carried muskets. The carriage door opened and a man exited, wearing the badge of his office as the king's magistrate. Even before any action would justify the notion, Regina knew they had come for her.

She knew who had laid the charges against her, the only person who could have, Buckram. Had he known that the dowager suspected him? Was that why he had not brought to light the fact of murder while she lived? Instead, he had sought to regain the Amesbury fortune through marriage. But now that the dowager was dead, and there was no one else to suspect him of the crime, he had dispensed with the idea of wedding his cousin's widow. There would only be her word against his, and he would make certain by innuendo and rumor that no one in London would believe her innocent of the crime. She swung away from the window, driven by the instinct of self-preservation, and grabbed her cloak and reticule. She had already locked her door from the outside, and after slipping through the dressing room and out the adjoining bedroom door, she hurried into the hall. Pausing briefly, she turned the key in the lock to the second bedroom and pocketed it. The tactic would gain her only a small delay, but every second counted.

Yet when she heard the trampling of boots into the foyer of the house, perverse curiosity drew her to the shadows by the banister. Below, she saw the magistrate and two of his soldiers had been allowed in. Buckram, resplendent in mourning black, appeared from the salon, a crowd of funeral guests at his back.

"What is the meaning of this? Don't you know that this is a house in mourning?"

The magistrate had removed his hat but he wasn't cowed by Buckram's haughty tone. "Sorry I am to intrude, my lord, but this matter cannot wait. I've been charged with the duty of arresting a member of your household."

"Arrest?" Buckram's voice rang out so that anyone who had missed the commotion thus far would be instantly drawn in. "Who?"

Reading from the paper he had unfurled, the magistrate declared, "A charge of murder has been laid against Lady Regina Willoby Lynsdale, Countess of the late Earl of Amesbury, Lord Harry Lynsdale."

Above the roar of shock that swept the gawking throng, Regina heard Buckram say clearly, "But this is preposterous! Whose murder? Who laid the charge?"

"I'm not at liberty to disclose the details, my lord," the magistrate replied formally. "But the charge is murder, murder of her late husband, Lord Lynsdale!"

As the words rang out, Regina turned and fled. The servants' stairwell was empty—she was certain that the arrival of the magistrate had drawn the attention of everyone in the house. Even now as she descended the back stairs she could hear dozens of footsteps on the main stairway as one and all rushed to watch what they hoped would be the singular sight of a countess being arrested. When she reached the first floor, she took the purloined key from her pocket, unlocked the back door, and slipped out through the servants' gate into the side street and began to run.

She had thought to simply elude Buckram this night; now she knew that she was fleeing for her life.

"Who's your customer, Jed?" the innkeeper's son asked.

"Don't know her name," the coachman replied, the capes of his coat flapping in the stiff wind that blew through the yard of the coaching inn. He looked up at the lone figure huddled in a great cape who sat atop his coach. "Don't talk or won't talk. Picked her up in Simonsbath yesterday. Rode across the moors with nary a peep."

"A considerate man would offer her a pint to come in out of the wind and rain."

The coachman snorted. "A soldier tried yesterday but she gave him such a look that he later said he felt she'd put a spell on him. Maybe she's mad."

The innkeeper's son stared up at the young woman hunched against the mizzling rain, but all that he could see was the tips of her shoes. "She's not the looks of a witch, Jeb. With those fine leather shoes, she could be quality. Is she pretty as paint, into the bargain?"

"For whatever good it does a man to see it," the coachman groused, and stamped his feet against the cold. "I've a need for a rum to set me up for the run over to Ilfracombe."

"Come in, then, but . . ." The young man let the matter drop, but not before he had given the girl another look. "Pretty as paint, did ye say?" he called as he followed the coachman into the inn.

Once the men were gone, Regina pulled back her hood a fraction and saw that she was alone in the yard. She refused to look at the windows of the inn where lights shone warm

and inviting, but she couldn't shut out the aromas of stew
and fresh bread that twisted the knot in her stomach. She
hadn't eaten in nearly two days, at least she thought it was
two days. Perhaps it had been longer. She couldn't remember. She had been on the road for a week, hiding and retrac-
ing her steps in the hope of eluding the military as she made
her way back to north Devon. Her plan had been simple.
She'd first gone east, thinking her would-be captors would
be watching the roads to the west. Then, after a few days,
she had turned back west, taking many an out-of-the-way
leg in her journeying.

Two days ago, her money had run out and she'd been
forced to ride all day atop the coach exposed to the wind
and rain and chill. By nightfall she'd been thoroughly wet
and cold and miserable.

At the inn where they stopped the night before, she'd
traded her services to fetch buckets of coal for shelter instead of a meal, feeling that rest was more important than
nourishment. She'd spent the night in a common bed with
four other women: a farmer's wife and her adolescent
daughter, a minister's widow, and a housekeeper from an
estate near Okehampton. The bed had been lumpy and the
linens suspicious. She had awakened in the middle of the
night to furious itching and decided that either the bed or
the farmer's wife had fleas. Rising, she had gone to finish
out the night by the fire in the tavern's main room. She had
awakened with a tight rough feeling in her throat and a
slight cough. While the others ate sausages and eggs, she
had barely been able to swallow her tea.

Now, after another day of crossing the moors in wet
weather, her fingers and feet seemed to have turned to ice
while her cheeks burned from within. She longed desperately for something warm to drink, but she didn't even have
tuppence for tea. The only thing that kept her going was

the thought of returning to the safety of Maxwell Kingsblood's arms. His face was always before her mind's eye.
When her shivering became nearly intolerable or her cough
made her chest spasm with pain, she had only to close her
eyes and view his strong magnificent face to feel renewed
strength. Once she returned to him, she would be safe. He
would believe her innocent of murder. He would fight her
enemies. And then he would take her in his arms and hold
her, and kiss her, and make her forget the pain and anguish
and fear and misery of the past. And she would love him—
she did love him. She would tell him so and never, ever
leave him again.

"Miss?"

Regina turned her head toward the voice and looked
down to find the young man who'd been conversing with
the coachman standing with a hand upstretched toward
her. He held a steaming tin cup. "It's tea," he offered.
"There's milk and honey in it. It's free. My gift to a lady."

His manner was unexpectedly kind, his voice low-pitched
so as not to frighten her. Even so, Regina shook her head.

"Oh, then, won't you be accepting an honest man's trib-
ute?" he encouraged, and reached into his apron pocket.
"I've got bread as well." He glanced back over his shoulder
toward the warmth and light of the inn and then smiled up
at her, the wind ruffling his fair hair. "Take it before the
others come. Else you'll wish in a hour you'd not been so
stubborn."

Regina waited three heartbeats before reaching down for
the food. As she bent over the edge, her hood slid forward
over her eyes. With an impatient hand she pushed it back
and then took the cup. She also snatched up the bread he
thrust at her. Righting herself, she turned away and pulled
her hood forward again as she took a great gulp of tea. The
liquid burned her raw throat but after the fire came the

blessed relief of numbness. Then, remembering her manners, she turned to the young man and said huskily, "Thank you."

"No thanks needed, miss," he answered. "When you're done just toss the cup in the yard. I'll fetch it later."

He turned reluctantly back to the inn, knowing that his father would notice his absence with a tavern full of passengers to feed. No doubt he'd receive a cuff to his ear, but it would be worth it. She was as beautiful as a painter's palette: black hair, green eyes, and a blushed complexion that rivaled roses. And she wasn't dumb. She had spoken to him, which was more than the coachman had received. Feeling quite pleased with himself, he entered the inn with a big grin on his face that not even his father's knotty fist could knock loose.

Regina finished the tea but tucked half the thick slice of bread he'd given her away for later. It was afternoon but the day was darkening more quickly than she had remembered it doing a scant two weeks earlier. It would be nightfall before they reached Ilfracombe. And then she would have to go another two miles on foot to reach Blood Hall. But she refused to think about that. As the coach lumbered out of the yard, its other passengers fed and warm, she closed her eyes to the bleak moorlands over which they traveled. She shut out the whistle of the wind, and ignored the mists and rain that made her clothes cling cold and sodden against her chilled skin. For, behind her closed lids, the face of Maxwell Kingsblood kept her company, and she slept.

The coach stopped half a dozen times, as passengers climbed down from the top or exited the relative comfort of the coach's interior, but Regina scarcely noticed. Fatigue and the effort of breathing were taxing more and more of her strength. The journey over miles of rough ground un-

broken by the appearance of a village had become an agonizing test of endurance. Occasionally a cottage dotted the
barren landscape, its meager light the only protection
against the foreboding day. But because none of them were
her destination, the sightings only made her ache with the
need to reach home. As the edge of darkness crept into the
sky, the rain increased while the groans and creaks of the
coach mingled with the keening wind to form a calliope of
malevolent sound.

Finally, at dusk, the coachman stopped the coach at a
fork in the road. "Here's the last stop afore Ilfracombe!" he
called over his shoulder.

His harsh voice woke her. Regina roused herself to find
that she was the only remaining passenger riding outside.
Her head went up and she scanned the horizon until she
saw in the distance to the west, where the sun had just
disappeared, the looming shape of the great old house. "Is
that Blood Hall?" she cried out.

She regretted at once her indiscretion but the coachman,
too astonished to hear her voice, didn't think anything of
it. "Aye, miss. That's the home of the Marquess of
Kingsblood. You going there?"

Regina gathered her cloak about her. "Set me down."

The coachman did as she asked, lifting her easily from
her perch, but he was frowning when he had down so.
" 'Tis a rough night for a girl to be about on the moors
alone. You'd do better to ride into town and stay the night,
then take to the road in the morning."

"I'm not going far," Regina assured him. "Only just over
there." She pointed in the opposite direction of her path.
Suddenly a coughing fit doubled her in pain. When it was
over, she was leaning weakly against a coach wheel, the
coachman standing over her.

"You're in no shape to go it on foot," he said roughly. "Stop the night in Ilfracombe."

Regina shook her head, too weak to do more. After a moment, she pushed herself upright and turned and walked away.

"Hey, didn't ye have a bag?"

She didn't stop because the answer was no, she didn't have a bag or a sack or even a bundle. She had only her cloak with a half-eaten slice of bread in one soggy pocket.

"Mad lass!" the coachman called after her. Then, shaking his head, he climbed back onto his perch and whipped up his team.

Regina lost track of time as she traveled westward, her head lifting now and then to the rapidly disappearing rim of reddish light that marked the place where the sun had settled on the horizon. The wild rough country that just a few weeks ago had seemed friendly turned alien and hostile with the coming darkness. The barren moorland, inky purple under the evening sky, was crisscrossed by treacherous snares. More than once she floundered knee deep in brackish water then plodded over fern-strewn wet ground that dragged at her cloak hem with greedy fronds that seemed to want to hold her back.

After a mile the pain in her chest deepened, every breath an effort restricted by pressure upon her lungs. Rain ran down her face and down her back beneath the wet wool gown she wore, but she no longer felt it. With every step her shoes swished with damp. Her head pounded with her heartbeat. Her cheeks burned with what seemed to be the only heat in her body.

It was fully night before she found a bridle path. The rain had stopped. Stars even appeared in the breaks in the clouds, lighting up the track as a trace of white on the dark wild tumble of moorland before her. Following it she knew not where, she stumbled along for perhaps another hour until, like a miracle, she saw a golden glow in the distance and then the dark shape of Blood Hall looming darker than night against the autumn sky.

Safety lay a short distance away yet her shoes seemed filled with lead and her muscles felt as soft as lard. She fell more than once as she flung herself headlong toward the light. Rough stones dug into her knees and serrated her palms. She was crying and laughing and then crying again, each sob a painful reminder that her lungs were sickening. Finally the night sky was eclipsed by the high walls of the house as she neared it. Pausing by the gate, she pressed herself into the yew bushes that grew nearby and waited.

The house was unusually quiet. There were no lights burning on the main floor. The oriels of the great hall were dark. In fact, except for the steady burning of a light in the main hall, she might have thought the house shut up.

Hard shivers rocked her as she hid in the shelter of the shrubs. It had not occurred to her that the marquess might leave Blood Hall. Buckram would have informed the military that he expected her to return to Devon as, of course, she had because there was no place else to go. Surely the marquess believed her when she said she would return.

Yet she stood and waited in the darkness, suppressing her painful cough, until gradually she became aware of light issuing from the walled garden. It poured through the gap in the gate, and so did music. She was certain she heard a minuet being played on a lute. Someone at Blood Hall was entertaining.

The gay music drew her even against her will. The rhythm was so persuasive, the melody at once so joyous and yearning, that she shed her fear in the fervent hope that Kingsblood was among the group. The thought of him made her quicken her steps across the distance. Peering inside, she sought the broad-shouldered silhouette and arrogant dark head of the Marquess of Ilfracombe.

She saw instead a pair of dancers skimming along in unfamiliar steps. The woman wore a gown of pale-gold silk, deeply decolletaged and with wide panniers of another age. the man wore doublet and breeches, boots and gauntleted gloves. The woman was petite, blonde, and beautiful. The man was tall and broad, with sun-darkened features and dark hair cropped like a soldier's.

She knew at once who they were. Their portraits hung in Blood Hall's entry. Moreover, the lady was the spirit who had come to her at the séance. Regina knew no surprise, no fear, no hesitation. She burst through the gate, her arms outstretched. "Help me, please, help me!"

She didn't feel the stone that caught her shoe, but suddenly she was flying toward them. As she fell, petals rained down upon her in the softest shades of pink, red, lavender, and yellow. And then she was on the ground, amid the scented splendor of a garden in full bloom. She pressed her cheek to the cool stones of the walkway, closed her eyes, and saw Maxwell's smiling face.

"Is she dead?" the lady inquired.

"The dead don't bleed," he answered impatiently. He had lifted Regina from the slate paving stones and wiped the blood from the scrape on her cheek. "Stand aside, madame, you block the light!"

The lady backed out of the glare of the garden's Chinese lanterns. "You knew she was coming back! That's why you came to the garden tonight after staying away nearly a fortnight, isn't it? Why didn't you tell me?"

He glanced up at her in exasperation. "As I recall, madame, you didn't give me the chance." His eyes raked her voluptuous body in appreciation. "Appetites sharpen with abstinence, and, being a gentleman, I didn't want to interrupt your very gratifying demonstration of welcome. In short, madame, I clean forgot. Besides, I didn't know she would come back tonight, precisely. Nor," he added grimly, looking down at the semiconscious young woman in his lap, "so dramatically. She's all but killed herself."

The lady touched Regina's cheek and recoiled. "Mercy, she's burning up with fever. What can have happened to her?"

The captain snorted. "Do you no longer listen at keyholes? Where were you when the militia came yesterday? The girl's wanted for the murder of her husband."

"Oh, that." She shrugged her elegant shoulders in dismissal. "Maxwell will soon set things to right."

The captain's dark brow furrowed. "Come to think of it, where is he?"

At that moment Regina began to cough. The wretched sound of it was painful even to the pair who had long since shed their flesh. Together they held her upright as she fought for breath. Finally the seizure passed and she lay exhausted and insensible against the captain's chest.

"We must wake the house!" the lady said. "I shall contrive to make a footman enter the garden so that he may find her."

The captain shook his head. "Do that and she will be arrested. No, we must wait until Maxwell returns. Where the devil do you suppose the lad took himself off to?"

The lady couldn't answer, for, in her depression over the captain's desertion, she'd taken to walking in the garden for hours at a time, uninterested in the comings and goings within the house. "We must save her for Maxwell. We are together again and the garden has resumed blooming. Surely these are good signs."

He stared at her grimly. "Hasn't it occurred to you, madame, that I was only able to return to you moments before she arrived? I tell you again, your sentimental interference has hitched our future to the fickleness of mortals. We're ghosts, madame, no more substantial than our wills make us. 'Tis better to leave living and loving to mortals. But you defied me."

"And whose idea was it to make her Maxwell's mistress?" she rejoined. As he glared at her hard enough to daunt the most courageous mortal, she smiled. "She must live to love Maxwell so that we may remain together. Or are you afraid of a little croup, Roundhead?"

"We tax ourselves greatly in aiding her," he warned her. "If she dies, we may well dissolve into nothing."

"Then she must live," she returned sweetly. "Make her live, Captain!"

He swore an oath at her that made her blush, then ended with "Upon my soul, you try me too hard!"

"Nay, Captain, you are never too hard for my liking. But"—she put out a hand to stop him when he would have put aside the ailing girl to reach for her—"first we must save Maxwell's bride."

"Trust a woman to add a condition to a man's lust!" he grumbled. "Very well, what do you know of the physician's art?"

"Little enough." She frowned slightly. It had been more than a century and a half since she'd been called upon to remember cures and remedies. "Aha, I remember a cure for a fever. A head of garlic, peeled and bruised, then blended with a quarter pound of butter and boiled will make a poultice. When it cools, it is spread on flannel and applied to the soles of the feet."

"It sounds more like a cure for blisters," the captain remarked. "What else, madame?"

"There's a fever tonic to be made of fennel, parsley, suc-

cory, and yellow dock roots. They must be steeped in a
gallon of water to which violet leaves, young mallows, and
endive have been added. When the gallon is boiled down to
one-quarter, a pint of white wine vinegar and one of honey
must be added to make a syrup."

" 'Twould take a week to gather that lot. We'll use a
soldier's cure. We'll need roasted chestnuts beaten into a
powder and mixed with honey. See what you can find in the
kitchen. And be quick about it, madame!"

As the lady moved away to do his bidding, the captain
gathered Regina into his arms and followed her toward the
rear wall of the house, only to be confounded when Regina's body refused to pass through the four-foot-thick stone
wall as his would.

"Plague me for a fool!" he muttered, and turned to use
the gate as mortals must.

Breathe, damn you! Breathe!

Regina opened her eyes and stared up into the face of a
stranger. It was a hard face, an impressive and angry face.
She was afraid. "Am I dead like you?" she whispered past
the pain in her throat.

He didn't answer and she soon realized that her words
had not been said aloud. Her throat was so constricted she
could scarcely pass air through it. Her head ached worse
than before and her chest felt as if he had piled stones upon
it.

She remembered fleetingly stories of how peasants had
once tortured supposed witches by crushing them slowly to
death beneath the weight of stones. If she was dead she
must have been sent to Hell, she thought remorsefully, and
then the agonizing cough began again, stealing her breath
and setting her throat afire.

The world behind her lids turned blood-red, her head

growing lighter and lighter with each spasm until she seemed to float free of her body and cease to exist.

There were voices in the air about her, strange voices with unfamiliar cadences, but it was impossible to see if they belonged to real people or were only imagined.

Are we going to lose her, Captain?

What you ask is, am I going to lose her? Bloody Hell, and no! Maxwell took the devil's own time deciding on the lass. Now that he's made his choice, I'll not put myself through the trouble of finding him another. He'll take this one and be glad of it!

But she's so sick!

Damnation, madame! Take your mourner's face away from me! She'll live, I say! A pox on disbelievers!

Someone was lifting her, forcing warm liquid into her, sometimes cajoling her like a child, and at others swearing great frightening curses at her, as if she were a recalcitrant soldier requiring the fear of God to force her into battle.

She fought the hands that pressed hot plasters to her naked chest, but she was too weak to best her opponents' efforts.

Hours came and went, short spans of semiconsciousness followed by deep troubling dreams.

She was in court, sentenced to be hanged. Maxwell was there, his face reflecting all the anguish she felt. She didn't want him to witness her shame. She shouted for him to stay away but he remained.

The gibbet loomed before her, the hangman's knot swinging free in the breeze. But she knew it was meant for her. Once more Maxwell was beside her, urging her to be strong, to fight the panic and heart-stopping fear of what lay ahead.

The noose was tightening about her throat. She couldn't breathe for the fiery circle that bit into her flesh, shutting off her breath. And then his face was before her, soothing her, promising her release from the pain and the sorrow and the loneliness.

She screamed and struggled but there was no air, nothing but the free float of space and the choking that ended with a plunge into the black void where even the dreams could not penetrate.

More than once Regina gave up the effort to breathe, but the suffocating was worse. She felt as if the sea were closing over her head, and that she would drown just as her parents had.

A silent scream rose in her throat. And then arms caught her from behind and enfolded her to hold her still. "I don't want to die!" she whispered brokenly to the unseen person who held her. "Where is Maxwell? I must tell him! Before I die!"

He came to her then, his handsome face bending over her, his dark eyes shining more warmly than any mere candle. And she felt so cold in every part of her body but in her heart. Her heart was full to bursting with love and tenderness for this man. "Maxwell!" she whispered, ignoring the pain the word caused her.

You must live, Regina. I need you to live, so that we may be together forever.

"Forever," Regina repeated, feeling tears on her cheeks and not knowing whether they were hers or his. "Forever," she repeated. "Kiss me. Please."

His lips were cool and smooth, like satin-covered marble, but his mouth deepened the breath in her body, as if she inhaled in his breath what she could not draw from the air. She felt herself relaxing, the knotted pain easing, and the darkness was no longer so frightening. With Maxwell beside her, holding her, she would survive.

"I love you," she murmured when the kiss ended.

Aye, lass, and the lad loves you too. Now rest, sweet lass. Your Maxwell will want you strong and pretty.

A little later a spoon was pushed gently against her lips, and Regina obeyed the unspoken command to open her mouth. Hot soup was poured into her dry mouth, thin but wonderfully aromatic.

Now again.

She obeyed though she had not thought she could swallow. Yet she found she could do anything he asked, as long as Maxwell knelt beside her. For him, she would not die.

'Tis almost midnight that marks the beginning of All Hallows' Eve. You've not forgotten what it means?

No, madame, I haven't. Drunken revelry, infernal fiddling and blowing of horns, bonfires, carousing, all manner of pagan doings will be abroad tonight.

It is also, my captain, the only night of the year in which we may manifest ourselves as real flesh.

No need for that reminder, madame. With the next nightfall a strange mischief that we cannot control will run hand in hand with Fate.

You fear for the girl. What can we do?

We've done all we can. We must away, madame. It grows close to the hour that marks the beginning of All Hallows' Eve. We must leave our young mortals to Chance.

Regina had heard the voices often during her illness and, too sick to care, had long since ceased to wonder to whom they belonged. Now there was an urgency in their tone that made her want to see as well as converse with them. But when she opened her eyes, there was no one there, only a candle burning in the wall sconce above her head.

Her heart began to beat in slow heavy strokes that reverberated through her chest. There were ghosts at Blood Hall! Were theirs the voices she'd heard?

It began as a whisper of a breeze upon her cheek. A moment later the candle flame dipped, nearly extinguished by the inexplicable wind that swooped suddenly down the passageway. The smell of sandalwood and sea air rode the currents, pricking up goose bumps on Regina's bare arms and legs. Fear melted her last reserves of composure and tears flowed from her eyes even as the scent of roses filled her nostrils.

She heard the words so softly she couldn't be certain they didn't simply form in her mind.

Nil desperandum!

Like vapors in the dark, a gentle comforting silence stole in to replace the thrilling cold.

Never despair.

She didn't know if she was awake or dreaming, if she was alive or dying. But relief wafted through her and she fell almost at once into a deep, dreamless sleep untroubled by coughing fits or nightmares.

Chapter Twenty

Regina nibbled hungrily on the piece of bread she had taken from the pantry in Blood Hall's kitchen just after dawn. She was as wobbly as a newborn foal on spindly legs, but hunger had driven her to the kitchen to seek food. Soon the servants would be up, but now there was only the darkness held at bay by the dim light of the candle she had brought with her from her hiding place.

The fiery pain in her throat had subsided into a raw ache at the very back, permitting her to swallow the chewed bread. It was the first solid food she had had in . . . Regina shook her head in wonder. She did not know how long she had lain sick and senseless in Blood Hall's secret passage. It seemed a miracle that she was alive.

She still couldn't remember entering the house, or how she had managed to carry out the arduous task of caring for herself inside the cold walls of the passage while illness claimed her. Yet she knew she must have done so, because she now knew that there had been no one else to aid her. She had gone to Lord Kingsblood's bedroom before coming to the kitchen and had discovered that he wasn't there. In fact, there hadn't even been ashes in the hearth, which meant he had not only not spent the night there but that he hadn't been expected. A quick check of his closet revealed that many of his clothes were missing, as were his razor, comb, and boots. With a sinking heart she realized that he must have left Blood Hall, perhaps had returned to London even as she traveled here. She had only imagined his presence in the passageway because she had needed so badly to believe in something that would prompt her to fight her illness and live. As for the real source of the voices she'd heard and the comfort she'd experienced, she'd come to a startling conclusion.

Common sense told her that the "ghosts" must be figments of her feverish delirium. Yet, like pieces of a shattered glass, her memories of them were fragmented but sharp. She had seen them clearly, been touched by their cool hands, heard their voices as whispers in her mind. They had collected water and blankets when she had been too weak to even lift her head. They had bathed her when she was in a fevered sweat, and then changed her filthy black gown for a pair of the marquess's breeches and one of his shirts. The beautiful lady and her Cromwellian soldier had been as real to her as any living soul. Blood Hall's ghosts were real!

When she finished the bread, Regina picked up her candle to let it shine on the shelf where several covered dishes stood in a row. She lifted the cloth of the first and found a risen loaf of bread. Beneath the second was another loaf, and so on. She turned away and went into the main kitchen. On the table were two other dishes. The first, to her delight, held the remains of a roasted fowl. Quickly setting down her candle, she delved into the dish with her hands and broke off bits of meat, which she tucked into her mouth. Nothing had ever tasted better than those cold, congealed scraps, she thought, savoring every morsel. Yet, after several bites, she made herself eat more slowly. After all, she hadn't eaten in days and her body might not welcome being fed too quickly.

"Who's there?" cried a woman's voice from the servants' dining room. "Who's there, I say?"

Swiftly as a frightened deer Regina scooped up her candle, blew out the flame, and fled into the shadows at the far end of the long room.

A moment later she spied the flickering light of a different candle. Shortly, Cook stepped cautiously into the kitchen, her candle held high to make the most of its halo of light. "Is there anybody there, I'm asking?"

"What do you see?" a young girl's voice inquired from behind the woman.

As Regina pressed herself flatter into the shallow alcove between the cupboards and the wall, Cook beckoned to her unseen companion. "Come along, Jenny."

Peeping out, Regina saw a thin young girl of perhaps twelve. Like Cook, she wore a plain rough gown and heavy shawl. The girl looked about timorously, as if she expected every shadow to jump out at her from its corner, and then she spied the disturbed dish of roast fowl and forgot her fear.

"Look!" she cried, and hurried over to the table. "Someone *was* here." She pointed to the tiny bits of chicken that littered the table. " 'Tis All Hallows' Eve," she whispered in awe. "There be spirits abroad!"

" 'Tis no danger of being accosted by spirits before dusk," Cook answered brusquely. "And if there were, they'd not be interest in a bit of cold fowl when there's tender warm virgins the likes of ye about."

As the girl squealed, Cook laughed and reached to light the first of the lanterns that gave the basement kitchen its light. "More like that new footman Holford's been thieving again. He's too thick about the middle for my liking. If I ever catch him at it, I'll be carving a little of that lard off of him." The maid squealed again, this time in amusement.

"Now stir up them coals in the oven. Got bread to bake before the rest of the house stirs."

"Will Lord Kingsblood be returning today?"

"Will he will or will he won't, 'tis no concern of yours."

Jenny tucked her shawl more tightly about her thin shoulders. "I was just asking 'cause there'll be a basket of food to be fetched to the Willoby cottage."

"Till you hear different, a basket's to be sent to the cottage as usual. And don't forget to add a jar of plum jam this time. His lordship is particularly fond of it."

As the girl came toward the cupboard with a candle in hand, Regina began feeling frantically behind her. Somewhere along that wall was a latch that would open the door through which she had entered the kitchen. Finally, when the girl was so close Regina could hear her anxious breath, a stone moved beneath the pressure of her fingers and then darkness yawned open behind her with a burst of cool air. Regina stepped back into the abyss just as the girl's candlelight fell upon her face. For an instant their eyes met, and then the secret door swung shut as Jenny's scream pierced the silence.

Once on the other side of the wall, Regina paused to press her cheek to the cool stone of the stairwell and gather her strength. Her heart was galloping and her weakened muscles had turned liquid with fright. Faintly through the stones, she heard voices.

"Foolish girl!" Cook scolded. "There's nothing here but solid stone. Devils, indeed! You woke spooked and you'll stay spooked till All Hallows' Eve is done."

"But I saw her! I did! Honestly! Frightful it was! A witch! Black hair and wild eyes in a face so white there weren't no blood in it! A Banshee, that's what she were. Me ma seen one once!"

"Then your ma is as daft as you! Now get on with your

work or you'll be abroad at dusk not to dance around the
bonfires but because you've been turned out!"

Regina closed her eyes in relief as the voices faded. She
knew she should hurry away. There were things to be done.
She had learned where to find Lord Kingsblood. He was
living, amazingly enough, in her cottage. Sweet pleasure
moved through her at the thought of him being there, sitting by her fire and sleeping in her bed. He must care for
her, must be missing her and waiting for her return.

And now she also knew today's date. It was All Hallows'
Eve, just as the disembodied voices had whispered. She had
been ill three days.

"My guardian angels," Regina murmured, wishing that
they would come now to help her climb the long way back
to her secret lair. But her feet would not move, and her
body grew heavier with every moment. Even as she strained
against the inevitable, she sagged down weakly onto the
steps. Just a moment, she thought, she would rest there for
just a moment. Laying her head on the cool stones, she fell
instantly asleep.

Much later, Regina awoke. For a moment the darkness
and dank rancid smell of a long-enclosed area brought back
the natural fear of abandonment. But gradually she realized
that there was a faint light shining high above her. She rose
slowly, astonished and pleased to realize that she felt much
stronger than before. The dizzying sense of exhaustion that
had plagued her earlier was gone. Taking her time, she
mounted the stairs toward the light, gaining confidence
from the endurance of her strength.

Finally she reached the source of the light and discovered
that it came from a grillwork screen set in the stone wall
that looked down from the minstrel's gallery onto the great
hall. Beyond the room, the windows showed a low-riding

sun flanked by lead-gray clouds. It was late afternoon. In an hour it would be dark.

The maze of secret passages was much more complex than she had at first realized. She had to backtrack several times before she found the passage that led to the master bedroom. There she found and took a clean shirt and frock coat. Working her way back through the maze, she finally located the Chinese Bedroom, and slipped inside. It was prepared as always, with fresh flowers, clean towels, and a pitcher of water for bathing, as if at any minute an expected guest would arrive to occupy it. After turning the lock in the door to the hall, she quickly stripped off the shirt she wore and poured water to wash herself.

A quarter of an hour later, she stood before the mirror in the clean shirt, rebelted breeches, and frock coat. It wasn't much of disguise but it would do. This was a night when folk went about in costumes and cork-blackened faces. No one would think it strange that she wore a man's clothing. She pulled an ivory comb through her hair one last time and then tied it back at the nape with a silk ribbon she found. She didn't know what she would say when she reached Lord Kingsblood, but she had come a hundred and fifty miles to read the answer in his face to her one question: Did he still want her?

"Please, please let him be there!" she whispered to the image in the mirror. The reflection was silent but the clear green eyes of the too-pale, solemn-faced young woman held a world of love and hope.

Dusk was eroding rapidly into night as Regina ventured forth from Blood Hall. She wore a servant's rough wool cape as protection against the fresh sea wind. The moors were usually quiet after dark, the austere stretches of grass and bog lying still and silent under a starlit sky. But this night, everything seemed touched with strangeness. The sky seemed to carry specters of restless spirits. Dark shadows of iron-gray clouds, like highwaymen's cloaks, dragged their tattered remnants across the night. The wind stung her cheeks until they felt as if they had been pinched by many unseen fingers. Nor was the land itself peaceful.

She paused on the lane as an eerie glow began in the northern sky. Turning her head, she saw that off in the distance half a dozen bonfires were being lighted on the crest of the headlands that overlooked the sea. The wind carried the excited cries of those who had turned out to celebrate the pagan holiday. The golden-orange briars of flame, set at sunset, would be kept blazing constantly on this, the most perilous night of the year. The purifying flame and smoke were said to destroy all malevolent forces that would be unleashed at nightfall.

When she was small, her mother had never allowed her to go out, even into the garden, once darkness closed in on All Hallows' Eve. It was said to be the most dangerous night of the year, a night when mischief and the supernatural reigned. The door was bolted, the curtains were pulled, and the fire was kept burning in the grate all night long. Made uneasy by her thoughts, Regina turned and walked on, her step more brisk than before.

Not long after she spied, coming up the road toward her, a farmer's wagon loaded down with people. Others walked along beside it carrying lanterns against the night. One and all, they were singing a cheerful country tune that a fiddler set the pace for. As they drew closer, she saw they wore toothy grins in their cork-blackened faces, and knew they were on their way to the bonfires to participate in the Witch's Sabbat.

As she paused by the side of the road as they passed, they hailed her and motioned for her to join them. Regina smiled and shook her head. She didn't want to be waylaid, however well intentioned their invitation. They would only grow rowdier and more drunk as the night wore on, perhaps wreaking as much havoc to the countryside as any spirit might. Sometimes the younger men would pick fights or attack a rival fire in hopes of carrying off the fuel. Then, before dawn, the bonfire dancers would play the hazardous game of leaping the flames or running through live embers.

Regina put her head down as she saw yet another group of people approaching. Walking purposefully and quickly, she soon passed them and, later, still others. The country lane was soon thronged with people so no one questioned the fact that she, a woman, was out alone. Yet she was the only one who wasn't headed for the headlands and the spectacle of the Hallowtide bonfires.

Nearly an hour later, the wooded combe near her cottage came into view, and Regina began to run. The effort made her still-sore throat ache, but it didn't matter. There was light coming from the cottage, and that meant Lord Kingsblood must be there. Once before the door, she paused to catch her breath, suddenly shy. What would he say when he saw her? What should she say? Lifting a trembling hand, she knocked. The rap sounded hollow as it echoed inside the cottage. Regina held her breath but there was no answer. She knocked a second time, more patiently, then reached for the latch when it went unanswered.

She saw at once that no one was inside. The fire in the grate had been banked. Yet, to her delight, signs of the marquess's presence were everywhere. A frock coat hung over the back of a chair. Someone had replaced her wooden hearth stool with a leather wing-back chair. She moved about lovingly touching his things, a razor, his silver-backed brush, even his soap. By her bed she found and picked up a worn shirt and buried her face in the folds. It smelled of vetivert and its owner's own unique male scent. Sweet longing enveloped her. He was so close. She imagined him standing beside her, stripped to the waist. She rubbed the fabric against her cheek, pretending that he held her. Desire fluttered in her stomach. Dear lord! She loved him so!

All at once she imagined him walking in and finding her like this. She laughed and placed the shirt on the bed, embarrassed by her strong reaction to so simple a thing as an article of his clothing.

She turned and began pacing the floor. Why had he chosen this night, of all nights, to be absent? Had he gone to watch the bonfires? Or had he returned to Blood Hall, thinking that it would be safer to spend this night behind stout stone walls? Had they passed on the road when her head was down? Because she was dressed in men's clothing, he'd never have thought to look twice at her even if they'd passed within arm's reach.

With a cry of relief she heard the scrape of footsteps on the new flagstones that led to the cottage, and ran to fling open the door. "At last, you're back!" But it wasn't the marquess on her doorstep. It was Percy Buckram.

She tried to slam the door but he put a hand out to halt it and stuck his foot in the breech. "What sort of welcome is this?" he asked, his handsome face registering annoyance.

Regina gazed past his shoulder into the dark. "Have you brought the magistrate with you?"

"Regina," he said reproachfully, and stepped inside, passing so close to her that Regina moved back. "Did I not promise I would protect you?"

"You have publicly accused me of the late Lord Lynsdale's murder. Don't bother to deny it. No one else knew about it."

"Alas, I was wrong about that. Your late husband's mistress was suspicious. She too had noticed the unusual amount of dregs in the open bottle." He looked like a disappointed parent. "You were careless, my dear. Very careless."

She couldn't imagine why he was continuing the masquerade of pretending that she had committed murder, unless he didn't yet suspect that she knew who had done it. "I've committed no crime."

His fair brows rose. "Your word against hers. Of course, I should think a jury's sympathy would be with the widow rather than the mistress, don't you?" He again moved toward her, intimidating her by his presence. "I offered you my protection but you ran away. Why did you run away?"

Regina moved a little away from him, trying to keep her voice steady. "I went to London with one purpose, to offer my inheritance to the dowager. She refused it."

"Did she?" He seemed truly astonished by the news. "Then she was more mad than I realized. But do go on."

It took a great deal of will for Regina not to glance at the open doorway. "I don't wish to marry you, Lord Buckram." The news didn't seem to surprise him in the least. "But, if you recant the charge of murder against me, I will give the inheritance to you."

Skepticism lent his handsome face a sinister cast. "Give? Just like that? Why?"

"I no longer want it."

"I don't believe you. Only a fool would give up such wealth. You have no other means of support." He folded his arms before his chest, smiling now. "How do I know you can be trusted?"

"Do as I ask and you'll find that I'm not an Amesbury. I stand by my word."

"Little cousin! To think I needed only to ask you for the fortune and you'd have given it to me." His smile was mocking and indulgent. "But, tell me, who shall we now accuse of the crime?"

"I don't know," Regina answered, fear a sharp painful jab just below her heart. She clung to the feeble hope that he didn't know she suspected him, and that his ignorance of her thoughts was her protection. "Perhaps there was no murder."

"Oh, there was a murder all right." His voice was dry and matter-of-fact. "The magistrate has the evidence in his possession. We must have a culprit."

Buying a moment to think, she went to poke the fire. She knew he was watching her. She felt his intense gaze on the shape of her hips outlined provocatively in Lord Kingsblood's breeches, and wished she hadn't removed her cloak. The nerve-wrecking silence grew so long that she glanced back over her shoulder. He had now noticed the marquess's belongings. Yet when his mocking gaze rose to meet her defiant one, he said nothing. Hands shaking, she turned to replace the poker.

Suddenly his hands, hard and unyielding, were on her shoulders, turning her toward him. There was a predatory look in his eye that even the most inexperienced woman would have recognized. In another moment it would come to a struggle between them, and she knew she was too weak to win.

Clenching her hands at her sides, she refused to look away. "The dowager told me that her son changed his will after we wed in order to punish you. What did she mean?"

Anger leaped in his eyes. "That bastard! I hope he's burning in Hell!" He let her go with a little shove that made her stumble backward. He smiled evilly. "He was jealous, of you and me."

Regina reached behind herself for the poker she had used moments before but she was too far away from it.

Buckram noticed the movement but merely smiled. "Harry too noticed the way you had looked at me on the dock that first day. He was stupid but not without guile. He knew that you'd piqued my interest and that, sooner or later, I'd try to seduce you. He offered me a bargain to keep me away from you. We both knew that if he produced an heir, I'd lose not only the earldom but the fortune as well. He said, if I behaved myself, he'd see to it that I'd receive at his death half of the Amesbury inheritance not entailed by the title. But he didn't tell me, the bastard, that in the meantime he was removing me from his will entirely!"

Regina shrank back, sensing that their conversation had veered onto very dangerous ground. "I didn't know anything until the will was read. I expected nothing."

"That's what you deserved. But your very existence drew the murderer's mind to the deed."

"I don't understand," Regina said, trying to keep the fear quaking through her from rattling her words.

"Yes, you do," he answered softly. Then more roughly: "You've shown yourself to be resourceful in so many ways, dear cousin. I'm neither a selfish man nor an especially impatient one. I was willing to wait my turn. Harry was ten years my senior. I had resolved to give him six more years to drink himself to death. But someone put the mad scheme into his head that he should marry. Was it you?"

Regina shook her head, not to deny his words but because she didn't want him to admit another single bit of his treachery to her. For then she would have to admit to herself that he hadn't come to take her back, but to kill her.

He smiled most tenderly at her as he approached. This time he framed her face with his hands. "I admit I wanted you. But I also wanted to break your neck. There you were on the quay, looking at me like I was a sun king, and then at your husband with that sweet awful face of resignation.

God! Innocence should not come packaged in your like, Regina.

"That's what decided me. The plan was working in me like yeast for days while I played a cat-and-mouse game with Harry. You'll never know the lengths I went to to keep him out of your bed. All the while I ached to breach your maidenhood myself and so discredit you in your husband's eyes. But you were so meek, so pious. You hid your passion as if it were stolen goods. Show it to me now, Regina, and we'll leave this place together. Kiss me!"

Regina twisted away from his seeking mouth, his kiss falling on her cheek. Releasing her, he threw back his head and laughed. "That's it. That's why Harry is dead. Because you wouldn't be seduced."

Regina turned back to him, all the loathing she felt revealed in her expression. "How can you talk to me like this?" she burst out, more angry than frightened in this moment. "I'm not wood or stone. You've just told me you murdered a man, my husband. It makes me sick to think of it."

"But I did you a great favor. Look me in the eye and say that you aren't glad to be free of an unwanted husband."

Regina shook her head. "Don't twist my thinking to suit your conscience. I didn't love him and I am glad that I am rid of him, but I didn't wish him dead."

"A convenient shading of the truth to shield your guilt," he responded in amusement. "Unlike you, I'd grown desperate. It was only a matter of time before he came to you and made you with child. I couldn't have that, now could I?"

Regina didn't answer.

"It was to seem a natural death, but I needed a dupe if my handiwork was discovered. Then the will was read and *you* inherited the bulk of the estate. Before I could act you ran away, and unwittingly into my trap. I followed your uncle to Devon. I thought I could frighten you into marriage. But on our return journey to London, I realized that sooner or later you'd begin to turn matters over in your witty mind. When you did, you would realize—as you already have, my dear—that I committed the murder."

They stared at one another. The dreaded words were spoken. Regina wondered how he could be so calm when she was wild with the desire to flee into the night and be lost.

"To kill a second time seemed redundant," he said simply. "That's why I went to the magistrate."

"But if I were hanged, you wouldn't inherit a thing," Regina answered, thinking her way though his hideous plot in spite of herself. "My estate would go to my uncle."

"Not if your marriage was declared invalid because you married with the sole intent to do murder, and so become a rich widow. You are the stranger in our midst. Your reputation is the talk of London. Do you think the *ton* would have doubted your motive? And so your ill-gotten goods would revert back to the Earl of Amesbury, me. And so shall they still."

"I'll stand up for myself and speak the truth," she replied, sidestepping the hands that reached out for her and drawing closer to the fireplace.

His hands found her shoulders as she touched the mantel, his fingers curving possessively about her. "And that is why, sweet difficult Regina, you must find your death. All Hallows' Eve is the night of the spirits when anything can happen. Perhaps folk will say the rising of your husband's ghost drove you to commit suicide. But first, kiss me goodbye."

Regina didn't resist the mouth engulfing hers. Reaching back, she found and fastened her hand about the poker handle, and swung it up from behind in an arc. He must have sensed something but she was quicker. Even as he tore his mouth from hers, the poker connected with a sickening *whack* against the side of his head. She saw his eyes widen and heard his cry, no more than a little grunt of surprise, and then she jerked free of his hands.

She gained the doorway, looking back, but she heard him roar a curse and knew that she hadn't seriously hurt him. Perhaps, she thought wildly, she should have struck him again. But she wasn't a cold-blooded killer or an experienced fighter and the thought made her sick.

She stumbled out of the doorway and ran, eschewing the lane where it would be easier for him to follow her. Instead, she took to the moors, into the heather and granite that bore no man friendship after dark. Glad for the freedom of breeches, she took long-legged strides that skirts wouldn't have permitted. Even so, the coarse grasses, gnarled by the wind, made passage treacherous. Though she knew the area, she was grateful to the bonfires burning on the coast, for they gave her flight a focus and purpose.

Buckram was a city man, unaccustomed to rough ground, and she prayed that it would slow him down more than it did her. Yet though her heart beat a military tattoo in her ears, she soon heard him coming after her, thrashing and cursing and falling when he misjudged his footing. How did he know where to follow? she wondered in near panic, and then she realized that, moving ahead of him, she was silhouetted by the bright glow of the fires toward which she ran. She wouldn't be able to throw him off her trail. The best she could hope to do was to reach the crowd first.

The wind suddenly picked up and, as if touched by a inhuman hand, Regina shivered. She heard them faintly at first, and then she was certain. There were other footsteps in the night, coming up behind her, footsteps that moved more quickly than hers, more assuredly, and with an urgent sense of purpose. Frightened, she whipped her head about to see who else chased her. But she saw nothing. The next moment the ground beneath her foot gave way and she sank up to the ankle in bog water.

With a cry, she extracted her foot and scrambled backward, realizing she had stumbled into a marsh. A wet fetid smell hung in the air and long reeds rustled softly in the night, their quivering restlessness a reminder of the black water that lay just beneath them and could swallow a man or an animal almost silently. She began to shake. If she hadn't slowed down to see who was following her, she might have plunged in too deeply before she realized where she was. She glanced quickly about, recognizing the nearby granite tors as those that ringed a deep and dangerous bog. There was a path through it, but now it was lost in the impenetrable blanket of night. The other sounds had vanished but she heard Buckram coming up behind her. He was yelling and swearing, uncaring who heard him. Was he so mad, she wondered a little desperately, that he intended to murder her before whatever witnesses who cared to look on?

Heart agallop, she hurried to make a circle around the fen. Shivering, she began to lose courage. Tears stung her eyes. She didn't want to die on the moors, whether murdered by Buckram or drowned in a bog. But as she moved on, it seemed the night intensified, as if the very air vibrated with unseen and unknown currents. Something seemed to be at her back, pushing her along like a blustery wind when she would have stopped to catch her breath. When she looked up again, the bonfires were much closer.

The dancers were black silhouettes cavorting before the pumpkin-gold brilliance of the huge fires strung out for miles now along the coast. She ran toward them, screaming until her throat flamed with pain, her lungs ached, and her breath was nearly gone. But the countryside rang with laughter and shrieks, and her cries were lost in the merry-making.

She was among the revelers before they knew of her existence. She tried to grab one of them, to stop them, and tell them what was wrong. But no one would listen. The fiddler was playing a tune, and there was a man with a drum, and another with a whistle. Everyone else was dancing and smiling and clapping his hands. Instead of pausing for her need, they pulled her in among them, grabbed her by the wrists, and swung her about in time to the wild dancing beat.

The fire stung Regina's cheeks as she was swung dangerously near it. And then the moors were before her again. She saw crouching in the vast darkness humped shapes that seemed to watch the proceedings with stony eyes. Then once more she was swung back into the midst of the dancing and urged to lift her feet in time to the music. Feeling giddy and momentarily safe, Regina gave in to the moment until, across the line of dancers, she saw Lord Buckram appear out of the night. He came straight toward her, ignoring the others as if they didn't exist.

She paused like a stricken rabbit caught in the glare of a lantern. The dancers swirled about her, but she couldn't move. The music drummed in her ears. The fire was behind her, the blaze a solid sheet of flame ten feet across and as many high. It licked at her back and calves, and made her itch to move away.

And then she was caught up again by the ring of dancers. She saw Buckram pause, then begin to stalk her as she was pulled willy-nilly around the bonfire's girth. Frightened nearly witless, she watched him. He was smiling now, watching, seemingly unconcerned that they were surrounded by people. All about her the world moved to gaiety and life. Yet it was as if there were only the two of them. The look of murder was in his eyes, and no one saw it but her.

All at once she knew what he intended. She made a tiny sound of protest and tried to pull away, but her partners wouldn't release her. Her feet kept moving. One false step, one graceless stumble, and she would be shoved into the flames before help reached her.

From the corner of her eye she saw another shape emerge from the dark moor, but her gaze never left the man who stalked her. When he suddenly sprang forward, she was ready. She jerked her hand from that of the man on her left and hurled herself into the arms of the man on her right.

For one heart-stopping moment, she was staring up into the dark eyes of the Marquess of Ilfracombe, the next she was torn from his grasp and swung about.

Buckram had her by the shoulders. "Dance with me!" he cried. Regina swung her head toward the marquess but he had disappeared. It happened so quickly that there was no time to think. Buckram's arms went about her, one hand fastening on the loop at the back of her breeches, the other latching on to her hand. She struggled but he was amazingly strong, jerking her toward him and into a quick turn that made her lose her footing. Once, twice, three times he forced her into quick turns that swept her off her feet, each one bringing them closer and closer to the flames.

All at once he freed her waist, spun her about, and jerked her arm up behind her back as he made her face the fire.

Regina screamed, feeling the heat so hot upon her skin that she thought she would be singed. Then, to her disbelieving eyes, she saw a figure moving amid the flames. Against her ear she heard Buckram's curse of surprise, and she knew he was staring into the fire as well.

"Do you see it?" she whispered, hoping to distract him so that his grip would slacken.

The figure came toward them. Buckram took an instinctive step back, dragging Regina with him. "What is it?" he whispered, his voice sounding as frightened as she felt.

The figure moved more quickly, emerging from the flames as through fog. And still no one else took notice. The music played and the dancers swept past them.

The apparition became a black silhouette before the fire and, suddenly, Regina knew who it was. On this pagan night, when the wretched of spirit, the restless, and lost souls of the world were permitted once again to tread for a few hours upon the earth, an avenging specter had come to face his murderer. "It's Lord Lynsdale!" she whispered in awe.

"No!" Buckram cried out and shoved her away.

Regina fell hard to her knees, the granite beneath the soil sharp and unforgiving on her skin, but she scarcely noticed. Her head came up at once as her gaze was drawn to the phantom from the fire. He didn't move or speak, simply stared at Buckram.

Buckram raised his hands before his face to shield his eyes. "Go away! I do not believe in you! You are dead! Go away!"

His terrified cries broke the spell of merriment, and the noise and music came to an abrupt halt as the revelers gathered in on them, muttering among themselves.

Suddenly hands were lifting and enfolding her from behind. Regina began to struggle until a voice said softly by her ear, "Regina, darling!" She knew then it was Maxwell Kingsblood who held her, but even so she couldn't look away from the specter of her dead husband, or the man who had killed him and wanted her dead as well.

Buckram had begun backing away, the specter following.

He waved his hands and cried, "Keep back! Keep back! You aren't real! You can't be real! You're dead!"

Like a grotesque game of blind man's buff, Buckram continued to try to elude the specter until he came up against the solid wall of onlookers. His path blocked, he began to move in a slow arc within the circle, all the while crying "Keep back! Go back to Hell where you belong. I am the earl now. Go away!"

Murderer! The raspy moan that issued from the phantom drew goose bumps on Regina's skin.

Buckram screamed, high and keening like a woman, and launched himself at the image. Before Regina's horrified eyes, the specter shimmered, the image shifted through the spectrum of colors like a distorted rainbow, and Buckram's solid bulk passed through it as through smoke. He saw too late his mistake. The bonfire was before him and momentum carried him into its fiery center as men cried out and women screamed.

He stood for an instant like a toy figure inside a lantern, and then he began thrashing about as his hair and clothing were engulfed. Flapping his arms, he ran toward the back of the fire and out the other side, only to plunge off the cliff and down into the surging surf below.

Even as Regina shrieked in horror, hands reached out to shield her eyes and turn her away.

"Good God!" Maxwell said roughly, his deep voice shaking with the power of his surprise. "What drove the man to that mad act?"

Only then did Regina realize that none but she and Buckram had seen the shimmering image of her husband. But she was too stunned and sick of heart to try to explain what had happened.

As cries and shouts and the roar of pandemonium raged about them, she felt herself being lifted up and carried

away. She knew where he was taking her. There were so
many things she wanted to say to him, to tell him, simply to
be with him and look at him, but she was too shaken and
sickened and confused to do any of those things just now.
As the dark closed in about them, she rested her head on
Maxwell's shoulder and shut her eyes.

When they came to her cottage and entered it, she
reached up and put her hand to his cheek. "I came back to
you," she said in a weak husky voice.

"Don't say anything," Maxwell answered as he tenderly
lay her on her bed. "Tomorrow. There will be time enough
for talk tomorrow, and the rest of our lives." He bent and
placed his lips carefully over hers, and then pulled the covers over her.

Closing her eyes, Regina gave up to exhaustion and relief
from trembling fear.

She slept for hours but, just before dawn, something
awakened her. Her eyes flew open to find pale silver-blue
light flooding the tiny cottage. Beside her on the narrow
bed, she felt Maxwell stir, his warm solid arm tucked protectively around her. And then she saw them, the images
who had disturbed her dreaming. A man and woman, the
dancers in Blood Hall's garden, came to stand over her. She
felt no fear because smiles lighted their familiar faces. She
knew then that they were the ghosts of Blood Hall, and that
she had not been delirious when she thought they'd saved
her life.

Rest well in peace and love.

You have found your heart's desire.

Regina felt hot tears on her face. "Thank you," she whispered.

They left then, the soft eerie light dying out as if eclipsed
by the closing of a door.

"What is it, Regina?" Maxwell murmured near her ear,

his voice sounding sleepy yet content. "Who are you talking to?"

Regina turned to him, her green eyes wide with the awe of the phantom world still reflected in their depths. "Ghosts," she said softly. "Only ghosts."

Chapter Twenty-one

❧

LONDON
NOVEMBER

"Countess Lynsdale, I'm pleased to inform you that all charges have been dropped against you," the magistrate said warmly from behind his desk. "You have the apology of this office and the eternal gratitude of the Amesbury family."

Regina doubted that. She had met the new earl, a distant relation from Scotland. While he had neither the dowager's indomitable will nor Buckram's handsomeness, she had seen a family resemblance in his faint sneer. The Amesbury reputation wouldn't be improved upon in the near future.

"Thank you, magistrate," she replied, rising from her chair. "Now if you'll excuse me, I have much to do before I leave London."

"Certainly, my lady." The man rose and hurried around his desk to open his office door for the lovely young widow.

When she'd first entered, he'd noted with some surprise that she wore bright blue instead of mourning black, but the cut of her high-waisted traveling gown spoke of discriminating taste from the high neck to the hem. Her bonnet was demure and heavily veiled. She was, without a doubt, a lady.

During the weeks of his inquiry, first into the murder of her late husband and later into the circumstances of Lord Buckram's harrowing death, he'd come to hear all the ru-

mors that had ever circulated through London about the
countess and her marriage. Now, having met her, he didn't
believe any of the first and doubted half of the second. By
far the wildest tale making the current round of the gossip
mills had begun in Devon and worked its way back to the
city. Folks in Devonshire claimed that there had been
ghosts abroad the night Lord Buckram died, and that one
of them was the ghost of Harry Lynsdale, who had come
forth from the grave on All Hallows' Eve to accuse his own
murderer. That preposterous assertion flew in the face of
the truth, which was that Buckram had fallen by accident
into the flames. Or perhaps he had realized that his plot
was about to be foiled and a guilty conscience had driven
him to take his life. After all, everyone knew that there
were no such things as ghosts. Still . . .

He cleared his throat discreetly as she offered him her
hand in salutation and said, "Forgive me, Countess, but
there is one question that I would ask now that matters are
officially settled. What do you *really* think happened the
night Lord Buckram died?"

Regina turned to him with a secret, sad smile. "Why, the
wages of sin caught up with a guilty man, sir." Before he
could detain her any longer, she swept past him through his
door.

It was a short carriage ride to her temporary residence in
High Street, but it gave Regina more time than she wanted
to think. The last two weeks had been a continual round of
questions and answers, and still more questions as the magistrate's office tried to re-create the events surrounding
Lord Lynsdale's murder and Lord Buckram's death. It was
her word against that of a dead man, and the events surrounding his death were too fantastic to be revealed. If her
late husband's mistress, Earline, had not been apprehended
at Plymouth a few days earlier, where she'd gone in hopes

of boarding a ship bound for America, Regina knew she would now be sitting in prison with, perhaps, no possibility of exoneration.

But the woman had been found and, having been threatened with being an accessory in the death of Lord Lynsdale, she had confessed that she had known nothing of murder until Lord Buckram had offered her a great deal of money to help him place the blame for Lynsdale's death on his innocent wife. He had told her about the poisoned wine. He had told her what to say to the police, but only if and when he gave her permission. Fearing him, she had agreed.

Once Earline's statement was taken, further investigation turned up the extent of Buckram's debts and financial straits. Traces of the poison and a tampered bottle of wine were then found in a search of his rooms. The authorities, now convinced of Regina's innocence, had released her.

Regina's smile was bitter. After two harrowing weeks in which her very life had hung in the balance, she was once more acknowledged as the rightful claimant to the title of Lady Lynsdale and the Amesbury fortune. No one demurred to call her countess. She seemed to hear her title being used every minute of the day. Her stock had never been higher within the *ton*. The accusations of fortune hunter had vanished overnight. Now that Buckram had been exposed as his cousin's murderer, Regina was a celebrity, and that made her a very sought-after guest. In particular, since she was a young, beautiful, and wealthy widow, she was considered a top prize on the marriage market for widowers and aging jades.

Regina sighed and drummed her fingers impatiently on the leather seat. She hadn't answered a single invitation, nor did she mean to. As soon as she could, she'd leave London for good. She was going far away. Just how far away would depend upon the answer to the letter she'd sent

Lord Kingsblood, and to which she had yet to receive a reply.

At last, and as always, her thoughts turned to the Marquess of Ilfracombe. She'd seen him last at Blood Hall when she'd begged him not to come with her or even follow her to London. She hadn't known then what lay ahead for her, whether prison or exoneration, and she didn't want her scandalous life to touch his respectable reputation. Oh, he'd been angry, defiant, shocked, and hurt that she didn't want his support, but in the end he'd acquiesced to her wishes, though his last kiss had had more anger in it than passion.

"None of that, my girl!" Regina said briskly, and sat forward to look out. She mustn't think of Maxwell or his kisses when she didn't know when, or if, she'd ever see him again.

When the carriage stopped before her house she swept up the steps and in through her door without even a glance at the gawker who stood outside her gate. Each and every day someone was skulking about, seeking a glimpse of her.

"Send the butler out to clear the street," she said to the footman who'd open the door. "I won't be a spectacle in my own home!" Without pausing, she marched through the hall and into the salon, removing her bonnet as she went.

He was standing there, his back to the windows, in a black frock coat and white buff trousers, his hands in his pockets. He looked tall and grand and handsome, and wonderfully real.

Regina stumbled to a halt. "Marquess!"

He smiled at her and the world disappeared. There was only his beloved face, the warmth in his dark eyes, and the beating of her heart, which, she was certain, was in synchronization with his.

"Forgive me for staring, Countess, but you are a spectacle of delight for this sad and solitary man."

His deep rich orator's voice swelled round her. He had overheard her remark to the footman, and she blushed for the ungraciousness of it. But it also reminded her of her situation and how she must behave. She might no longer be a social pariah but she was still the source of gossip and conjecture, and he mustn't be drawn into it. All the exquisite longing and love that threatened to buckle her knees must be tamped down, at least for the present.

She came forward and extended her gloved hand. "It is so good to see you again, Lord Kingsblood. I trust your journey in from Devon was a pleasant one."

He frowned at her tone but took the hand she offered then covered it possessively with his second. "It was damned uncomfortable! But, forgive me for swearing, my lady."

"Have you returned to take up your post in the House of Lords?" she inquired, trying not to think of the fact that his thumb was brushing a caress across the back of her hand as it once had the peak of her breast.

"I have come to see *you*!" he bit out. "What is this, that you treat me like a long-forgotten acquaintance?"

Regina snatched her hand back and began to stroll about the room. "I can't think what you mean."

"Regina!" He deep voice was full of gentle reproach. "What has changed? Your letter was damned unfriendly, cool one might call it, stingy, almost insulting."

She turned quickly back to him. "I didn't mean to insult you. I only thought it best that I speak plainly and to the point."

"Then do so now, to my face," he said in challenge, and moved to block her path.

Regina noticed that he was taller than she remembered, and his hair thicker, and his face leaner. "Have you been ill, my lord?"

"I've been worried sick about you," he answered, and made it sound like an accusation. "I nearly came to London before this. I've had couriers daily on the West Road since you left me behind. Ah, madame, you didn't think I'd have let you leave me a second time, without taking precautions to make certain that you were safely provided for?"

He smiled, the charm of it not lost on the workings of her heart. "You've been in my care since the moment you left your cottage. *My* driver brought you here. *My* solicitor labored in your behalf. The man lurking about by your door just now is one of several men I hired to watch and protect you." He looked about the salon in satisfaction. "*My* roof has kept you warm and dry."

"Your roof?"

"Whose house did you think it was?"

"I didn't know." Regina glanced nervously about, half hoping that some object in the room would refute his claim. "My solicitor said that a nobleman wished to lease his town house for the Season because he was remaining in the country . . ."

"Precisely, Countess." His grin was triumphant. "*My* house. *My* staff. *My* butler. I had the house stripped of all personal effects before you arrived but I couldn't be certain that one of the staff wouldn't slip and tip my hand. I see by your face that they deserve a bonus for their conduct."

"Oh, yes," Regina said faintly, and turned away. "Your servants are amazingly loyal to you. I don't doubt that you could bury any number of bodies beneath the basement floor and that not one of your household would think to call a magistrate." She moved to a settee and sat down because her legs wouldn't carry her another foot. He still cared about her! That made things so much harder.

As he came to sit beside her she turned her head away, wishing fervently that he were a hundred, no, a thousand miles away, anywhere but within arm's reach. The urge to touch him was like a fever in her blood. Yet if she did touch him, she knew she would go on touching him, make love with him, and then her resolve that they must spend a year apart would collapse. "Thank you for your good care, Marquess, but it wasn't necessary. I've been exonerated of all charges and suspicion."

"I know." Maxwell caught her gently by the chin and turned her face to his so that he could look into the eyes of the woman he loved and try to understand what motivated her strange behavior.

Her letter had asked him what his plans were for the next year. He had thought at first that she was making plans of her own, marriage plans. But then her second paragraph had made him more angry than he could remember being since the day he'd encountered her on the road. She had informed him that it was her intention to return to her cottage and take up a teaching post in Ilfracombe, but only if he promised to stay away from Blood Hall for at least a year. If he couldn't give her this assurance, then she would make other plans. In other words, she didn't want to see him. That could mean only one thing, that she was again trying to protect him through some sweet but misguided sense of right. That was why he'd come to London to face her, to prove that nothing mattered but that she loved him. And he was going to prove it to both of them.

He stood up abruptly. "I've decided, Countess, that this interview must needs wait, after all. I'm road weary, travel stained, and very hungry." He made an elaborate gesture of his fatigue, stretching out his arms and yawning broadly. "If you'll excuse me, I shall go upstairs to bathe and change."

"But you can't do that!" Regina protested, appalled at

the very idea of his stripping and bathing practically in her presence.

"It *is* my house," he reminded her. "And you know how loyal my staff is to me. They won't talk, if that's what worries you."

"Oh, you're quite impossible!" she cried, with a flash of her old spirit. Then, realizing that her protest had amused him, she said stiffly, "Very well, but you cannot spend the night beneath this roof."

"I wouldn't be too sure," he muttered too low for her to hear.

As he turned to leave the room, she turned away from his retreating back sputtering "Arrogant, presumptuous, high-handed!"

She had worked it out so well in her mind. Her reasoning was flawless, her rationale square on the mark. Maxwell was a man with a brilliant political future. Those in the service of the Crown were held to higher standards than even the *ton*. Though she was proved innocent of evil intent, the scandal surrounding her marriage and subsequent widowhood marked her as a liability for such a man. Those lords and ladies of the Royal Court who held Maxwell's future in their hands must be convinced that she would make an acceptable Marchioness of Ilfracombe. Therefore, it was imperative that she observe every propriety, beginning with a year of strict mourning for her dead husband.

She was after marriage, nothing less. Because she didn't trust herself to be in the marquess's company without succumbing to the temptation to become his mistress, she had decided that they mustn't see one another for the next year. Now, blast him, he had shown up unexpectedly, and all she could see in her mind's eye was a vision of the marquess in the copper tub upstairs, his chest hair full of soap suds, and his glorious naked body flushed with heat from his bath.

She felt flushed herself. "Damn!"

For the next half hour, Regina sat in her bedroom, staring at the same page of a book without ever reading it. Through her open door she saw the procession of footmen carrying buckets of hot water to the room across the hall, and then the maid who was taking his traveling clothes to be brushed and cleaned. She spied the marquess's valet with his master's Hessians and then caught sight of the maid who carried fresh towels. On and on, the procession never seemed to end. There was the housekeeper with a luncheon tray and then the butler again with a bottle of wine. Back came the valet with a tobacco humidor and then a maid with the most enormous bouquet of roses. The silver candelabra was the last straw.

"He makes a great deal of a bath!" she muttered to herself and, in disgust with the elaborate arrangements, laid her book aside. She'd had enough. She rose to her feet and went to her door. She had no true purpose in mind beyond telling him, in no uncertain terms, that he had made his point about this being his house. She would be out of it before nightfall. She felt very confident when she knocked on his door and felt only mildly timorous when his deep voice called imperially "Come in." She put her hand on the latch and lifted it, thinking in annoyance that he expected yet another servant.

A highly polished copper tub stood in the center of the room, and from its steamy surface came the most fragrant scents of sandalwood and roses. Beside the tub a table had been set with the finest of linens and silver and crystal. The huge bouquet of roses stood in the center beside the silver candelabra.

"Countess, I was about to send for you."

Regina tore her gaze away from the formal setting to find

the Marquess emerging from his dressing room in a silk Turkish robe. "Do you like my arrangements?"

Regina's brows lifted. "It seems trifle overdone, my lord. Will the steam not wilt the roses?"

He smiled. "Does it matter?"

Regina suddenly frowned. "What do you mean, you were about to send for me. Have you finished your bath?"

As he padded barefoot across the floor toward her, she refused to look directly at him. And so her gaze was drawn gaze to inconsequential things, like the high arches of his large but well-formed feet.

"What I mean," he said when he stood before her, "is that I had hoped that curiosity would get the better of you but, if it hadn't, I was prepared to send for you." He reached out and undid the first button of her gown, which lay against her throat. "There is a grievance between us which I have yet to redress." He slipped another free while she merely gazed unblinkingly at him.

"Once I treated you abominably. In my defense, I was young and drunk, yet it was scarcely an act to do a man proud. I thought at the time I was saving a young girl's virtue, and that it was better for her to be a little dirty than to be raped."

"It was abominable," Regina said breathlessly, for his fingers had worked their way down to the buttons that kept her gown closed over her breasts.

"It was clumsy, thoughtless, and rude," he answered. "I was only a boy, and boys are sometimes impulsive." He paused in his work to slip a hand through the gap in her gown and take the weight of a breast in his hand. He saw pleasure dilate her eyes as he caressed her. "I am sorry, Regina. I went back later to look for you but you'd disappeared. The next day I went to see your father to explain to him but . . ."

Regina's eyes misted. "I know."

"Don't cry, love. It's an old hurt. It'll never be forgotten but it can be laid to rest, as I intend to cleanse away the old pain between us."

He carefully withdrew his hand and continued unbuttoning her gown until he could slide it off her shoulders. Only then did she react. "Don't." She stepped back from him. "We mustn't."

He didn't argue but went and turned the key in the door. "Now," he said, turning back to her. "I owe you an ablution and you shall have it."

Regina backed away as he neared but she found herself smiling in spite of her determination to elude him. "You're mad if you think I'm going to allow you to touch me, much less bathe me."

He merely continued to smile, throwing his arms wide to herd her in the direction he wanted her to go.

"Stay away! Stay away or I shall scream! I swear it!"

"Embarrass us both if you must, Genna," he replied, "but won't you feel more comfortable if no one else knows exactly what's going on?"

She felt the edge of the tub against the back of her thighs at the same moment he reached her. His hands went to the bodice she was clutching closed. "Won't you save your gown by stepping out of it, or must I dunk you clothes and all?"

"You wouldn't!" He caught her up so quickly she could only squeal as he lifted her off her feet and swung her high in his arms. "All right, all right!" she cried as he held her menacingly over the steamy water.

"All right, what, Regina? Are you finished with excuses and denials? Are you finished with concerns for my good name and your supposed inferior position in life?"

She looked at him in alarm, her face only inches from his. "How did you know?"

"I'm accounted as something of a scholar, a wise and thoughtful man. Didn't you think I wouldn't consider the same concerns as you? Well, I have, and what I've decided is I don't give a damn about conventions and rules when they keep apart two people who want and need very much to be together. Do I make my position clear?"

"Very clear," she answered contritely.

"Well then, madame, off with your clothes."

He set her back on her feet, and quickly finished the job he had begun. When she stood in only her knee-length chemisette and silk stockings, he stepped back to view his work.

"I haven't seen nearly enough of you often enough," he said warmly, and bent a knee to the floor. Reaching up under her chemisette, he skimmed his fingers along her thigh until he encountered her garter. He felt her tremble and looked up to see that she stared down at him, her eyes wider than ever. Using a crooked forefinger, he slowly drew the silk down her leg. His eyes never left her face so that he saw her lips part and her cheeks flush when he paused to massage the back of her knee.

"Turn around, Genna," he said, and she obeyed. This time when he reached up for the second garter, he lifted her hem. As he began pulling it slowly down her leg, he leaned forward to lick the indentation in her skin where the garter had been. He heard her gasp and chuckled. She was more responsive than any woman he'd ever known. He bent lower to kiss the soft damp skin at the back of each knee. "Sweet," he murmured, and then rose to his feet.

He embraced her from behind, his hands cupping her breasts through the fabric. For a moment he drew her back against him and held her there, feeling her quickened heartbeat and the desire beating in his own blood. Then he gently prodded her with his hips and said, "Step in, Genna."

As Regina lifted her leg to step into the tub, she felt him lifting her chemisette. It flew past her hips as she set one foot into the warm water, and then it was past her shoulders as she put the second foot in. Lifting her arms, she allowed it to skim past her head. Quickly she crouched in the scented water, the oily liquid her only cover.

Maxwell stood back for a moment to enjoy the sight of her, skin flushed pink, the curves and valleys of her body provocatively displayed beneath the rippling water. Then he knelt beside the tub and scooped up a handful of scented water and trickled it over her shoulders. "This for the wrong I did you, darling." He scooped up another and then another, letting it run freely over her.

Regina lifted her face to the fragrant stream, enjoying the warmth of it on her heated skin. When she would have reached for handfuls of her own, he caught her by the wrists and said, "No. Lie back and allow me to be your handmaiden." He pressed her gently against the high back of the tub, scooping up a towel to make a pillow for her head. Afterward, he lifted each of her arms arranged them so that they rested along either edge of the rim.

"Better," he said, smiling, and bent forward to kiss her.

It was the first kiss they'd shared in weeks, and their lips clung moistly together for far longer than he intended, but not nearly long enough to satisfy either of them.

He reached for her hair, pulling out the pins that held it in a coil on top of her head. And then he ran his fingers through the heavy silk, spreading it over her shoulders and trailing the ends over the sides of the tub. As he toyed with the ends, adjusting each curl to his satisfaction, Regina watched him through eyes of love. If she'd ever doubted the extent of his love for her, she no longer did.

When he was satisfied, he reached up to the bouquet on the table and withdrew several flowers. With a quick stroke of his hand, he stripped the rose petals off and then sprinkled them over her head. The petals of pink and rose settled in the inky waves of her hair and floated in the water near her breasts. As the floral scent filled the air, and Regina thought that it must be impossible to be more happy than she was. But she was wrong.

When he was done with that, he reached for a slender crystal-blue vial on the table and opened it. He poured the contents into his palm and then rubbed his hands lightly together. Bending close, he began by anointing her forehead and cheeks with the most expensive scent in the world: attar of roses.

"I bought this as a wedding gift," he said huskily, "but it is now for atonement." He brushed his hands lightly over her exposed shoulders and then bent to kiss her again. But his kiss was only a tease, and Regina leaned forward to stop his retreating lips as he drew away. The action made her shoulders come away from the tub and her breasts rose from the water.

Maxwell reached down and made a slow hypnotic massage of her breasts, working the sweet oil into her skin. Each brush of his hands over her nipples made her gasp with pleasure. "You are so lovely," he said into her ear. "So sweet and responsive, such a joy to stroke. You make a man feel he was born to give you pleasure."

When she leaned back, weak with desire, his hands delved into the water and gently parted her thighs, which he then plied with the remaining oil. "Such nice thighs," he murmured. "Such soft places." His fingers found and teased her, working her so sweetly that her eyes fell shut and her mouth trembled with every breath.

Maxwell watched her face intently to gauge the intensity of each and every stroke until he knew that she was ready to reach her peak of pleasure. But he had more in mind than that. Withdrawing his hand, he rose to his feet. As her eyes fluttered open, he untied the belt of his robe and let the garment slide from his body. "Ah, Genna, you make me burn for you."

He saw the dreamlike quality of her gaze turn with startling clarity to desire as she looked at him. He saw her shiver, felt it answer in his own body with a tightening of desire. And then she was rising like Aphrodite from the tub, her sleek, gloriously flushed body sluiced with scented water. She lifted her hand and touched his face. Then her water-heated skin was against his, dampening him from chest to thighs. He caught her fiercely to him in a kiss that soldered them together once and for all.

The heavy scent of roses filled the air as he carried her to his bed. He wondered fleetingly what would happen if he couldn't rid himself of the odor, if for the rest of his life people would turn when he passed in the streets, surprised and amused that a man of his form and stature chose rose as his fragrance. He decided that he wouldn't mind because the perfume would forever remind him of this day, this hour, and most of all, the woman in his arms.

They made love slowly, luxuriating in every touch, every kiss, every impression and texture of skin on skin. And then they were joined in love's caress, each holding the other with their bodies and their hearts and their souls. They were one rhythm, one life force, one sensuous tangle of arms and legs and sweet hot desire that triumphed in the mutual fulfillment of being loved for love's sake only.

Much later, when they sat together wrapped in towels,

sipping champagne and licking plum juice from one another's chin, Maxwell suddenly said, "Marry me, Genna."

"I would ruin your political career," she answered, and heard him grumble, "Not that again!"

"I intend to keep my inheritance," she added. "That should doubtless reinforce the opinion of some that I am an adventuress. Now they call me countess but in a year, after I've been known as Miss Willoby, schoolteacher, and can in all decency wed again, I shall be considered far inferior in station to you."

He bent a hard look on her. "Do you love me?"

"Your friends will consider it a quite ineligible match that should be reconsidered."

"I asked if you still love me, Regina."

"Oh, what am I but an wealthy widowed commoner with the title of countess and dreams of glory?"

"And do you dream of the glory of being in my arms?"

She tossed her head, refusing to look him in the eye. "I'm a foolish weak woman. Who would count such a woman's dreams as worthy of consideration?"

"You've a woman's confounded fondness for equivocation, madame!" he thundered, sounding amazingly like his long-dead ancestor. He caught her chin and dragged her face around to meet his. "For the final time I will ask you, do you love me?"

"For the final time?" She looked into his dark eyes, seeing in them the full extent of her world, and then she took his face between her hands. "I do love you, Maxwell. And I will marry you in a year, though heaven knows what the world will make of it."

She decided that the answering smile on his face was the most precious gift he had yet given her. "I believe you. Do you know why? Because it's the first time you've said my name. There'll be no more 'my lord' and 'my lady,' just Genna and Maxwell."

When he had kissed her to his satisfaction he said, "We need only show the *ton* a good marriage to put their long noses out of joint. Do you think we can do that?"

"I'm most certain that it's possible, Maxwell."

"I see that I must visit Blood Hall often these next months," he mused, "so that I may keep my eye on a certain schoolteacher. But after we're decently wed, will you come to London and be a spectacle once in a while, so that I might admire my wife in public?"

The joy in her green eyes dimmed a fraction. "Must we?"

"Not if you detest the idea. But you do have friends here. Eloise and Leslie expect you to come to their wedding in December. Giles and Delia are already touting you as a close friend who is the most sensible and clever lady they know. You'll be a pillar of respectability in no time."

Her smile was the more beautiful for being poignant. "Then I shall, because I enjoy being a spectacle for you."

"If you'd drop that towel, Genna, you may be a spectacle for me this very moment."

Regina rose from his lap and whisked away the offending cloth. "What of you?" she challenged when she stood naked before him.

With a rakish grin, he stood and whipped off his towel, and the sight was, by Regina's accounting, truly a spectacle.

Then she forgot about spectacles and gossips and all the pain that had gone before, because it had brought her to this moment, and this man, and this most precious of loves.

Epilogue

BLOOD HALL
CHRISTMAS 1801

*I*n the distance, a whispering shower of crystal flakes fell, mantling the moors with a rare white beauty. Within the great house, the light from a hundreds of tapers filled the windows and spilled into the darkness beyond, so that every passerby knew that the Marquess and Marchioness of Ilfracombe were in residence for the holidays.

Only within the sheltering walls of the garden was the winter held at bay. Here, Michaelmas daisies flirted with white tufts of ramsons, ornamental jasmine snuggled with sturdy English ivy, while full-blooming roses ran riotously over trellis work and stone walls alike. From the window that overlooked the garden, faint light illuminated the two figures who danced to the tune of a tinkling music box.

"Well, Captain, what do you think of the new dance fashion of the waltz?" the lady asked her partner.

"I think that it will lead to a great many hastily arranged marriages followed by short confinements," he answered with a lusty laugh. "God's body! It makes a man stand in his breeches to hold a woman—"

A man's cry of delight broke in upon his speech, causing the captain to lift his eyes to the window above them. "Now what the devil do you suppose that was about?"

"Maxwell's response to his Christmas gift," his lady responded with a mischievous smile. "I suspect that Lady

Regina has just told him that they are going to have a
child."

A rare surprised look stole into the captain's forbidding
gaze as he looked down at her. "A child? Why was I not
informed?"

"But, Captain, I've just told you."

"Women! You will have your secrets!"

"But naturally, Captain." She had received a premoni-
tion the morning before Maxwell and his wife had arrived
from London two weeks before, but had decided not to
announce the news before the lady herself knew. "Is it not
the most magnificent Christmas present Maxwell could receive?"

"A child." The grin lifting the captain's battle-scarred
features was almost comical. Then he caught himself. "So
much for peace!" he said gruffly. "Within the year there
will be nursemaids and nannies, and then governesses and
piano teachers and dancing masters cluttering up the hall.
There will be no end of disruption, consternation, and
noise, always noise!"

"But you love children."

He looked askance. "I? Never!"

She reached up and touched her fingers to the scar above
his left brow. "You always wanted more children. If we had
lived, I would have given them to you."

His cold gray stare suddenly warmed and, in a rare display of simple affection, he hugged her to him and kissed
the curl that hung in the middle of her brow. "I had you.
That was enough."

She hugged him back, her slender arms barely meeting
around the expanse of his leather jerkin. She had never
cared for those who lived and died within these walls since
her death, but now things were different. She and her captain had had a part in this love match and, because of it,

were now newly tied to Blood Hall in a rare and wonderful way. "Of all our descendants, don't you think Maxwell and Regina are most like us in temperament and spirit?"

The captain raised a single brow. "Then Maxwell will produce a son."

"Oh, I shouldn't think so, not at first," she answered with a secret smile. The vision had come to her of a tiny girl with dark curls and her father's gentle eyes. "Wouldn't it be delightful if the first child was a girl?"

"Maxwell needs a son!"

"A daughter, certainly."

The captain released her, ever ready for a battle of words. "A son, I say, madame! If the lad is at all like me, he will produce an heir first."

"Since you have naught to do with it," she replied saucily, "I expect your wishes will be deferred to the birth of the next child."

The idea of more than one child struck the captain like a bolt of lightning. "Next child? Will there be others?"

She smiled. "Most certainly, Captain. Lady Regina is young and strong and fertile, and our Maxwell is so much in love with her. He shall keep her with child for some years, I should think."

"Boys!" the captain pronounced. "He will rear warriors!"

"Confound you for a soldier! He shall rear diplomats, not cannon fodder. Within two generations, the name Kingsblood will be synonymous with the governing of the empire."

"I don't think we possess the pedigree to reach as high as the throne," he inserted in an unexpectedly mild tone. "But, madame, if your will can be exerted, no doubt the future will bend to your desires."

She turned on him an innocent expression. "Oh, no, Captain. I've learned my lesson. Never again will I meddle in the affairs of mortals."

He bent a flat stare on her. "I might be tempted to believe you if you weren't crossing your fingers behind your back."

Blushing, she pulled her hand from behind her back. "Wretch!"

She glanced toward the house and the lighted windows. Inside, she knew that Maxwell and Regina were embracing before the fire in the great hall, the warmth and strength of their love about to be given physical expression.

Unexpectedly, the ghostly shadow of tears came into her eyes as she found herself wishing that, just once more, she could experience the heat of another human body next to hers and the simple pleasure of a fire's warm glow.

Conscience-struck, she turned back to her captain. Their time was past, had passed long ago. They were no more substantial than their wills made them, and there was a price in even that. Caught halfway between heaven and earth, they had delayed their departure into the hereafter by sheer force of will, in order to remain ghosts of themselves in the place where they had lived and loved.

But now her purpose wavered, the impetus to remain was less compelling since true and binding love had come once again to Blood Hall. "Perhaps we should leave them in peace," she said wistfully. "We are redundant in their lives."

The uncertainty in her voice, something he'd never before heard, scored the captain to the quick. Shaken, he bent his sternest look her on. "Rubbish! The lad would never have won the lass without our help. Who would watch over the new babe, and then the ones after that? Who's to say some one of them won't again make a muddle of things? No, madame! We must remain. We are needed!"

"Oh, do you really think so?"

The tears became stars in her eyes and the captain wondered how he, mere ether in the wind, could feel so full of love and pride. "Have I ever told you how much I love you?" he whispered.

"Not lately, Captain," she answered huskily.

"Then we must find a remedy for that," he answered, and took her by the hand. "Maxwell and his lady wife seem content to share the carpet in the great hall. Shall we usurp the master's chamber for an hour?"

"Make that two, Captain."

He smiled down at her. As always, the deep stirring of desire and the miracle of love that transcended mere mortality deepened their resolve to remain as substantial as their wills could make them.

Dear Reader,

Something rare and wonderful has happened! One of the joys of writing is in creating characters who truly seem to take on a life of their own. The captain and his lady of *For Love's Sake Only* were two such characters for me. They hovered about my word processor and whispered in my ear. Two such headstrong individuals had very definite opinions, let me tell you!

When writing comes that naturally, I hate to end the book. Luckily for me, the captain's prediction on the final page has come true. My next novel is under way, and my ghostly matchmakers are enmeshed in the lives of another generation of Kingsbloods. Only this time, they're about to discover that they're not the only ones haunting the corridors of Blood Hall—and that Maxwell and Regina's headstrong granddaughter, Lady Julianna Kingsblood, is more than a match for them! Look for them all in my next book in the spring of '92.

Let me take this all-too-rare opportunity to say thank you to you, my readers, for your loyal support. I always enjoy hearing from you and what you have to say. Though I may never meet each and every one of you individually, please know that you are the reason I write and that sharing my stories with you is truly one of the great delights in my life. Thank you!

LAURA PARKER